A World Ful

Also by Keith McCarthy

A Feast of Carrion
The Silent Sleep of the Dying
The Final Analysis

A WORLD FULL OF WEEPING

Keith McCarthy

Constable • London

Constable & Robinson Ltd
3 The Lanchesters
162 Fulham Palace Road
London W6 9ER
www.constablerobinson.com

First published in the UK by Constable,
an imprint of Constable & Robinson Ltd 2006

A copy of the British Library Cataloguing in Publication
Data is available from the British Library.

ISBN 13: 978-1-84529-217-1
ISBN 10: 1-84529-217-0

Printed and bound in the EU

Part One

There is no good way to die, but to burn to death is perhaps the worst.

John Eisenmenger had twice seen such a death. He had held a six-year-old in his arms and watched the awfulness, felt the agony deep within his own flesh, an agony that he would carry with him until he, too, died. He had also witnessed the tortured suicide of Marie, his ex-girlfriend, in a petrol-driven fire; a pointless expression of something that perhaps frightened him as much as the pain she must have felt.

Twice; two times too many.

He did not wish to encounter a third.

Part Two

'You're lost.' Helena's voice carried amusement on tiredness. 'You should have listened to me.'

Eisenmenger said nothing.

'I told you to turn left a mile or so back.'

Eisenmenger drove, keeping alert for a road that would take the car towards the imposing house that was just visible above the skeletal treeline of beeches and oaks on their left. From what he remembered of the map, there should be another road soon that would lead them to their destination. Silence reigned more or less benignly between them for another couple of kilometres.

'Typical, pig-headed male.'

At last stung into entering the dangerous realms of multitasking, Eisenmenger said tersely, 'I seem to remember you told me about the turning *after* we had gone past it.'

'You could have turned around.'

'And you weren't exactly overfilled with confidence that you were right.'

She said nothing for a while. He glanced across to see the profile of her head back against the headrest, eyes closed in her perpetual lassitude. Her gauntness still caused him surprise, even though seven months had passed since the diagnosis of her breast cancer. Surprise and guilt.

It's made you even more beautiful.

This thought repeatedly recurred, spurring emotions and hormonal reactions that he found pleasurable and therefore culpable. How could something as ravenous, as despicable, as destructive as cancer mould something of pulchritude? It had no right to be a creator, a sculptor. Cancer was ugly, yet it had made of Helena a thing of the most fragile beauty.

She pointed out, 'I haven't been here for eight years.'

6

It was then that he spotted a turning some hundred metres ahead. 'Here we are.'

The smoke awoke him but only slowly. He began to cough but he was still in sleep and it was to him part of a dream.

Even when the fire took hold, and the smoke became thick and black and corrosive, when the heat increased, and the flames became white and reached towards the ceiling, even then he came to only slowly.

And then, as the fire started to breathe, as it crackled and drew in deep, hushing breaths like a ravenous god come for its sacrifice, he felt at once the intense heat and the terror.

Overwhelming terror.

'Somebody's got a bonfire or something.'

Eisenmenger gestured with his head to the right as Helena opened her eyes. A dense column of smoke rose from the metachromatic evening sky to their west. It rose perhaps five hundred metres in the air before it was dissipated by swirling winds unseen and unfelt by the ground, all the more visible because the car was breasting a hill that gave views of dense woodland and a small lake to the north.

'Yeah,' she said, uninterest fighting with disinterest.

The heat and the smoke had filled the car within seconds. He was bound at the wrists by a thin white plastic strip through and around the rim of the steering wheel; he was also gagged by adhesive tape that stretched his skin and compressed his lips. The plastic strip was sharp and had already abraded the flesh of his wrists. His legs were free but only to thrash about uselessly; all he could do was jump and rock, banging into the door, trying to open it, but the door handle was missing and it was locked.

His coughing was continuous but because of the gag he was retching, and he knew that he was about to vomit and that would be disastrous, but he did so anyway.

'Where on earth is this castle?' asked Eisenmenger, but

Helena was in the light sleep that was her ever-present companion these days.

The first burn – the first time that flame actually *licked* flesh and charred it – and he screamed. He was gagging and near mindless with squirming terror. The burns that followed, that ate with increasing voracity and increasing, blanketing agony, turned him into a thing of thrashing, mindless pain.

But then the car exploded.

'Bloody hell,' remarked Eisenmenger as the sound boomed dimly across the twilit winter woodland. He looked instinctively across the landscape, failing to catch the flash of the blast at the base of the column of smoke.

Helena did not awake.

'Helena! It's so wonderful to see you again!'

Theresa Hickman was clearly delighted to embrace her visitor and Eisenmenger could see this reciprocated in Helena's face. He decided that they had made the right decision to come to Westerham Castle to celebrate the New Year.

Helena said, 'I'm so pleased to be back, Theresa.' She turned to Eisenmenger. 'This is John.'

Eisenmenger stepped forward with smile and hand thrust to the fore. 'Hello, Mrs Hickman. It was very kind of you to invite us.'

'Theresa, please.'

He nodded and broadened the smile. She was, he thought, gracious in a state of burden and he wondered what that burden was. He said, 'This is magnificent. It must be a fantastic place to live.' He was indicating the house that rose to three storeys around them, the rounded and crenellated turrets that stood guard at its corners.

She smiled and shrugged dismissively and he might almost have believed that she was genuine when she murmured, 'A horrible eighteenth-century piece of kitsch, nothing more.'

But you like it, he found himself thinking while she went on, 'It's terrible to keep clean.'

'I'm sure it must be,' he said.

He was at the time wondering how she would know and he swore afterwards that he had not meant his words to sound sarcastic, but he had the feeling that he failed for she cast him a sharp glance. He thought it wisest to get the luggage from the car.

She had led them through the magnificent if somewhat cluttered entrance hall that was replete with suits of armour, grand piano, minor oils and marble busts. It was high-ceilinged and overlooked by a balcony that ran along all four walls, above which on one side was a series of ancient stained-glass windows illuminated only dimly by the evening light. Two staircases were situated in the far corners of the hall and she had led them up the right-hand one to a long but tortuous and narrow corridor. Left along this, up a short flight of stairs at the end and they found themselves on a wider landing. Their bedroom was situated directly ahead.

After Eisenmenger had put their bags on the bedcover and she had pointed out the en suite, Theresa said, 'I'll leave you to freshen up. We'll have some tea in half an hour.' To Helena she said, 'In the family sitting room. You remember?'

Helena smiled. 'I think so.'

'Of course you do.'

She left them and Eisenmenger smiled at Helena. 'Good to be back?'

Helena glanced around the room, then moved to the window. 'Look at that. How couldn't it be?'

Their view was to the south and was one of striking beauty. Immediately to the fore was the south wing of the castle with, at its far extremity, an ancient-looking clock-tower over a small courtyard. Beyond this and to their right was undulating woodland sloping down to a flat plain. As well as minor roads, a small cricket ground, the hamlet of Westerham and, in the distance, the town of Melbury broke the woodland into irregular pieces.

'I see what you mean.'

'It's even better out to the north and west; the northern terrace on a late summer's night is a magical place.'

He heard something in her voice that he hadn't detected

for a long, long time and momentarily he was at a loss to place it. Only when he glanced at her pale profile did he recognize this alien quality.

Of course. Relaxation.

He found himself unaccountably happy.

She turned away. 'We'd better unpack.'

He remained staring out of the window, straining to look as far to the right as he could. His view was blocked by the bulk of the castle including one of the fairy-tale turrets, and try as he might he couldn't see any sign of the sombre plume of smoke that had accompanied their arrival.

The shower felt good but these days Beverley Wharton always thought that, no matter how hot the water, how much her skin complained and her breath was taken from her, it wasn't hot enough. Perhaps, she reflected bitterly, only the heat of hell was hot enough for her now.

She turned off the water and stepped out on to the mat, feeling cold dampness because it had been used not twenty minutes before. It was a sensation that she hated. It was a sign of alien intervention in her closeted world, a sign, too, of selfishness. Why couldn't he have stepped on to a towel and allowed her the feel of warm softness?

She began to towel herself dry, looking as she always did, in the full-length mirror on the far wall. Through the condensation she could see enough of her body to like, even to arouse, herself; the frosted effect worked to smooth edges, hide the imperfections that she knew in the back of her mind were there, allowed her to believe that age was leaving her untouched.

Perhaps she was cursed, doomed to eternal youth.

Doomed also to eternal guilt, of course.

'Fuck that,' she murmured, a tired smile on her face that was lost into caricature in the condensation on the mirror. She was too exhausted to be angry, too self-aware to be really happy.

Dried and dressed in a towelling gown she went out to the kitchen where, as she knew she would, she found unwashed wine glasses and coffee cups. Was that the difference between a fucker and a lover – the latter cared enough to wash up? Cared enough to return, as well, even when he didn't want sex.

Peter, she had thought, had been her lover and perhaps he might have grown into the role of permanent partner. Certainly she had not used him for anything other than love and he had not, she thought, wanted anything more from her than companionship and affection. Only circumstance had intervened to corrupt that conception and she felt a familiar bitterness that once again her chance of contentment had been stolen.

She sniffed as she put the glassware and crockery into the dishwasher. She was getting a cold, too. She never got colds, though. She must have been working too hard.

Doing something too hard, anyway.

The job done, she wiped the surfaces, poured a glass of filtered, chilled water and went to the window that looked out over the darkening cityscape, her favourite place to think.

She knew that she was deceiving herself. She had been saved by circumstance, not thwarted by it. Perhaps Peter really had loved her – she liked still to believe that it had been more than the usual biological ritual – but it had been a weak emotion, one that had broken too easily when placed under strain.

She drank some water. A nearly full moon was rising in the east, its lustrousness badly abraded by the dying light of the sun and the dirty orange glow of man-made light just beginning to rise from below.

Where were all the decent men?

She almost laughed, even before the thought had reached its death, knowing that she was far from the first woman to ask such a question. The laughter didn't make it any easier to answer, though. Some women seemed to find their perfect partner with sickening ease – so were they lucky or just self-deceiving? Others, like her, seemed condemned to search in vain – misfortune or perceptiveness or once again (God help her!) self-deception? Maybe that was it; maybe she chose the wrong men, happy to be unhappy, delighted to be disappointed and therefore ultimately proved right.

And over the past few years not even work had been a compensation for this yawning black hole in her life. A series of mishaps and blunders (many she admitted of her own making – she had always made a point of honesty with herself even when dishonesty with others had proved extremely useful) had blighted her previously accelerating upwards flight through the police force. Not even sexual favours had enabled her to continue her steady success in the promotion game, serving only to prevent a fatal fall to earth. Only now was she beginning to stabilize, to see the possibility of a resumption of her career. The current operation would help. In a few days she would lead the raids on three premises housing, she knew, a large quantity of equipment for cloning credit cards. It would be like the old days, when she was seen as not only a fantastic fuck but also a bloody good copper.

She finished the water and the moon drifted behind some light cloud, hiding behind its own curtain of condensation.

Maybe John Eisenmenger would have been different.

This came from nowhere, but it was not the first time that the name had entered unbidden her ruminations. She snorted quietly. *Oh, yeah?*

John Eisenmenger would have proved to be like all the rest. He would have been interested only in the things that interested all men; he would have been impressible only by the superficial, untouched by the deep. All men were the same, and all women were the opposite, and it was why she would never find anyone – including John Eisenmenger – who would suit her. She would only ever attract men through her beauty, and her intellect would be ignored. Eventually her attractiveness would fade and there would be nothing; she could not allow that to happen for it would be a betrayal too great. Ugly women were safe because they had nothing to fear from ageing, because the fools who forged relationships with them did so unblinded by beauty.

She turned from the window, refilled the glass of water, then went to squat down in front of the television. It was a large, plasma-screen model and beneath it were stored numerous DVDs, many of them confiscated stolen or pirate copies she had acquired in the course of work. She had the evening free and she would watch one, she decided. When she settled down on the sofa, flicking through the on-screen menu, her uncertainties resurged.

You never know. Maybe he would have been different.

12

John Eisenmenger had been interested – she had sensed that as easily as she heard a bell sound or saw a lightning flash – and yet he had not followed the usual, weak-willed, prick-led fashion.

He stayed faithful to Helena and, let's face it, she's not that attractive . . .

The film began.

As the initial credits ended, she put him to the back of her mind.

She would probably never meet him again anyway.

They were now in a cosy sitting room that they had reached by climbing a staircase that led off the farther end of their landing, then turning left along a long narrow corridor. There was a feeling of the vertiginous about its position, as if they were perched on the edge of a precip-itous drop. The windows looked out on a sky that was by now nearly completely dark. There were Christmas dec-orations around the walls and a small, decorated tree sat in the corner, multi-coloured lights flashing gently in a nostalgic, fairyland memory of childhood. Some of the decorations were clearly very old, almost heirlooms.

'Tea? Coffee?' Theresa adopted the mantle of a perfect hostess with admirable insouciance. Eisenmenger guessed that he was in the presence of a seasoned performer in the arts of social etiquette and therefore in the arts of selective perception and total deception. He had met many such performers before and never failed to be both impressed and depressed by the experience.

'Tea, please,' said Helena while Eisenmenger murmured his agreement with that proposal.

The chairs were old and worn and no longer quite comfortable. The room was small and cluttered and a log fire burned obediently in the gate, while from the lamp fittings on the walls came light that seemed to be from some sepia-tinted world of the past where the war had just been won and England were still doing well in the cricket.

The tea was Earl Grey and, although they were not small and crustless and filled with cucumber, the sand-wiches were homely and caused Eisenmenger to think of his childhood. Egg and cress, ham and mustard, strong cheddar cheese.

'How have you been, Helena?' The victuals dispensed, Theresa was sitting in the chair opposite their deep, sagging sofa, her elbows on her knees, a look of what appeared to be genuine concern on her fine features.

'Oh, not too bad.'

'It must have been awful. It was such a shock when we heard your news. I'm so sorry we couldn't come and see you in hospital – Tristan was made Visiting Professor at Baltimore . . . Baltimore's such a dreadful place but it was a great honour and we couldn't refuse . . . Have you ever been to Baltimore? Ever since Tristan was made President of the College we've hardly had time to think . . . In fact, I think this Christmas was the first time all year that we've had the whole family with us . . . even Hugo. He's due to arrive tomorrow.'

It poured forth, with Helena making occasional contributions, a balm of flowing conversation, almost soporific in its effects, almost hypnotic. Eisenmenger found himself lulled into this world, where the father was distinguished in his field of plastic surgery and lately become the President of the Royal College of Surgeons, where the wife was doyenne of local charitable works, a matriarchal grandmother lurked unseen as yet, the son was following the father's chosen path and they all lived together in a castle . . .

'Sounds like a fairy tale.'

Helena considered. 'I suppose it is a bit like that,' she admitted. She used the tone of one looking at things from a novel angle. 'I spent so much time there as a child, I suppose I take it for granted.'

Helena's surgery and subsequent chemo-radiotherapy had been hard for her and hard, too, for Eisenmenger. Even now, three months after the last course, she had the pallor of one only half in this world, one faded slightly from sight. When he looked at her he saw someone who had retained her life but lost her vitality, and that worried him greatly. This invitation to spend the New Year at Westerham Castle would, he hoped, help to rectify the situation and the initial signs were good. Helena's delight when she had opened the letter from Theresa Hickman had been resplendent and genuine.

'So how, precisely, do you know the Hickmans?'

He knew because she had told him before, but he wanted her to immerse herself in happy memory. That had been the whole point. A subterfuge that had come about because of an article in a Sunday supplement that extolled the wonders of Westerham. Even once he had learned that she knew the place it had taken diligent and persistent investigation to piece together the skeletal structure of the story.

'Daddy and Tristan Hickman were at college together. Theresa was there, too. They both fell in love with her – took her out, that kind of thing – but it was Tristan who won her.'

Another fairy tale, then . . .

'Daddy, though, took it in good part. They remained friends; he was best man at the wedding, and Tristan reciprocated when Daddy married Mummy. We used to spend most summers at the castle when we were children.'

'And they've got two children?'

She nodded. 'Hugo – he must be about twenty-seven now – he's training to be a surgeon like Tristan. He's at Nottingham, I think.'

'And the daughter. Eleanor, isn't it?'

'Nell, yes. She's still at home . . .'

Her tone had changed and Eisenmenger heard faint warning bells. History, he suspected; perhaps best to leave it alone.

'So when was the last time you went to the castle?'

'Oh, gosh. It's years. Theresa used to write, of course – she was a great letter-writer – but not for years and I haven't been to stay for a long time . . .'

She lapsed into memory and he sensed that she was swimming through deep waters. He said, 'So how come they own a castle?'

It took a moment for his question to bring her back to safer bathing. 'Oh. It's been in Tristan's family for years.' Then, as if this mattered, she added, 'It's not a real castle, you know. More of a conceit, really. An eighteenth-century house built in the style of a castle. It never defended anything and nobody has ever attacked it or laid siege to it . . .' She drifted back into the past. 'We used to play-act

15

though. When we were children, it was the perfect place to pretend that we were princes and princesses, knights and their ladies. Jeremy used to be Sir Lancelot and Hugo was King Arthur. I was Guinevere.'

'And Nell?'

She frowned. 'You know, I can't recall. She was that bit younger, of course.'

He had never been allowed so much access to her history and he found it both fascinating and touching. Helena before had always seemed to him to be firmly resolved to remain free of the past, the place where resided so much hurt and pain, yet it now seemed to have been a fairly idyllic one, at least until the terrible events of eight years before. He let her enjoy some good memories as he got up from the sofa saying, 'I'd better think about starting some supper.'

In the small kitchen, as he sorted through the vegetables at the bottom of the fridge he allowed himself some relief. The idea of engineering an invitation to Westerham Castle had come to him some weeks before, an act of desperation born of fear that Helena was irretrievably lost in a rut of depression. His covert phone calls to Theresa Hickman had eventually resulted in the letter that Helena had opened that morning, but it had not been easy. He had had the distinct impression that their hostess would really rather not have put up houseguests and it was only the obvious affection that she held for Helena that had persuaded her otherwise.

He supposed that he couldn't blame her, but all the same he wondered.

Eisenmenger didn't believe in fairy tales.

'And you're a pathologist.'

He only took a moment to come back to Theresa Hickman and her polished small talk but it felt like an aeon. 'That's right,' he smiled and to cover his embarrassment that he should be thought rude he went on, 'Itinerant, anyway.'

'I beg your pardon?'

He had taken a bite of a ham sandwich and had to chew and swallow while she looked at him and waited patiently. 'Itinerant. I don't have a permanent job.'

16

'Really? Why?'

Which was a good question and therefore hard to answer. It was Helena who came to his rescue. 'John prefers it that way.'

He elaborated. 'I decided that I didn't want to be too tied.'

Their hostess looked slightly disapproving, as if she suspected him to be a shirker. Clearly Helena had not told her much of his past and he was uncertain whether he was pleased or otherwise. He felt compelled to say, 'I do the odd consulting job, looking at suspicious deaths, old murders, that kind of thing.'

'We act as a kind of team,' explained Helena. 'If someone comes to me, John's a sort of in-house pathology opinion.'

He had never thought of it quite like that; it had seemed to him to be a more informal arrangement, one brought about by circumstance, but now she mentioned it, he saw benefit in the idea. Perhaps here was another way to bring her out of her depression, once she was fit enough to return to work.

Yet if they hoped to boost his image in Theresa's eyes they appeared to fail for if anything she became even more distant. She managed a polite but slightly below-temperature, 'Well, I'm sure you won't need to employ your skills over the next fortnight . . .' before suggesting, 'Now, who wants more tea?'

They both did, but mainly because that was the proper thing to do and, this ritual over, Theresa gave them both a piece of Christmas cake.

'Where's Nell? Is she well?'

Theresa Hickman had a long face with features that tapered; when she frowned the tip of her nose moved quite appreciably in a southerly direction and the furrows on her forehead seemed deep enough to hide secrets. 'Much the same, Helena, much the same.' Her eyes darted towards Eisenmenger then quickly back again as she went on, 'You will be *sensitive*, won't you?'

And Eisenmenger was relieved that he had not bothered to bring his hobnailed boots or his donkey jacket.

'So what's the secret with Nell?'

They had just set off, a light, night-time's sprinkling of snow turned to daylight slush, the wind cold and wet and sharp as they had packed the car.

Helena stared at him. 'Who said there's a secret?'

'No one.' He drove on for a while and had just passed some traffic lights as they turned to amber when he said, 'But there is, isn't there?'

Helena sighed, her eyes as usual closed in the sleep that seemed incapable of refreshing her. 'I told you about Tom, remember?'

'Her son.'

'Well, he's eight.'

'And?'

'And Nell's only just turned twenty-three.'

'Ah.'

A man in a hat was driving a burly woman in another hat and doing it very, very slowly. It was some time before Eisenmenger could safely overtake him.

He guessed, 'An underage pregnancy. A scandal in the family.'

'A big one.'

'Who was the father?'

'One of the summertime casuals. They employ a lot of people when they open the castle to the public, most of them aged from fourteen to seventeen or so. Nell fell for one of them. Richard something, I think.'

'But no shotgun was produced, I assume.'

Helena shook her head. 'I don't think marriage was ever an option. He was told in no uncertain terms not to bother coming back. As far as I know, he just kept his head down and never turned up at the castle again.'

As scandals went, Eisenmenger felt that it wouldn't play well in Bohemia but he could see that it might create waves amongst the respectable and rich landed gentry. Helena hadn't finished. 'And then, when the baby was born, Nell had a complete nervous breakdown from which she's never really recovered. I don't know the details, I had troubles of my own at the time.'

Eight years . . . I should have realized.

The call to Superintendent Tanner about a burning car on the edge of the Westerham estate interrupted his preparations for a speech he was due to give the following week to the Trefoil Guild on 'The Challenge of Rural Policing'.

He asked rather tetchily why he was being bothered with such trivia; the reply changed his attitude. 'It looks as if there's a body in it, sir.'

Tanner fired off more questions, most of which were met with negatives or ignorance, while he wondered what was his best course of action. Eventually he said, 'Right. Notify Inspector Sauerwine. Tell him to report back to me when he's had a preliminary look around.'

He put down the receiver. Sauerwine wasn't the most experienced officer in the station, but it was likely that there was nothing of great significance about the fire. It certainly wasn't worth calling Chief Inspector Syme in from home, not at this stage anyway.

No. Sauerwine could handle it for now.

He returned to his speech.

'Tom's fine, though. He's a lovely little boy. Getting on fine at school and obsessed by sport. He spends hours watching football and cricket on the television.'

Helena asked, 'How is Aunt Eleanor?'

'She hasn't been too well of late. In the late summer she had a bout of pneumonia. Wouldn't go to hospital, of course. Dr Wilson got quite cross with her – and so did Tristan – but she wouldn't budge. Still, you know Eleanor.'

Eisenmenger, who didn't, twitched a smile and jerked a small nod. Helena had mentioned this formidable lady in tones that suggested that she was more akin to one of the Three Fates than a human being.

'She's better now, though. Tristan says that she'll outlive us all.'

'She must be over eighty now.'

'Eighty-two next April. She's getting a bit forgetful, but apart from that . . . well, touch wood.'

They all smiled and nodded, even Eisenmenger. To fill a pause he said, 'Are you having forestry work done on the estate?'

'There's always something to be done. It's a constant job, managing the estate.' She sipped her tea. 'Why do you ask?'

'We saw a large fire on the way here. Actually, I thought that there was an explosion too.'

She frowned. 'An explosion? Surely not. It's quite likely that they were burning refuse or something, but I can't think why you might have heard an explosion.'

He shrugged. 'Perhaps I was mistaken.' He didn't think so, though.

Helena said, 'I didn't hear anything.'

He smiled. 'You were asleep.'

There followed a pause, a chance for silence to reign and the occasional crackle of the wood in the grate to add its note to the ambience, but such lapses were not allowed by the rules and Theresa said at once, 'Tristan should be home by seven. We'll eat at eight thirty. Pheasant, I thought. We had a shoot last week so we're slightly overrun with them at the moment.'

'You still have shoots?'

'Only four a year. They don't bring in much income but Malcolm enjoys organizing them. He says that they're good for the estate – helps with estate management, or something. I don't see it, myself, but it gives Tristan a chance to play the Lord of the Manor, so he's happy.'

'And you still open the house and grounds?'

'That's essential. It's the only way we can afford to run the place. Only on Sundays and only from Easter to the end of September, though. It's fairly awful having the hoi-polloi traipsing around the place and leaving litter in the vases, but what can one do?'

What, indeed?

The consequent call to Inspector Sauerwine found him running through expenses claim forms with a less than diligent eye. His strategy for undertaking such management tasks was to take the broad picture, allowing the details to lie unmolested unless they insisted on shrieking for his attention. One such had just come to his eye and he lifted his head and bellowed, 'Felty!' as the phone began to ring. He picked it up and listened. At first the information he received failed to alleviate his boredom but then the voice of the officer in the control room said, 'It looks as if there's a body in it, sir.'

Sauerwine's body language shifted; he straightened up

20

slightly and his chin came off his chest, while his gaze came from the desk to rest on the open doorway in the far wall where Detective Constable Felty now appeared. His eyes flicked on to her small, slightly rotund frame but he wasn't paying much attention.

'Where, precisely, is this car?'

'Just north of Westerham village, on a private road leading on to the estate, about a hundred metres from the B4194.'

'A single body?'

'Apparently, sir.'

'Any identity?'

'I think the fire damage is pretty extreme . . .'

'Okay.'

He put down the phone then looked directly at Felty. 'Come on, Felty. You can drive.'

The bath was a splendidly imposing thing of cracked white enamel gilding heavy cast iron, and ornate brass taps that had been old when the Boer War raged. It sat in the centre of their en suite bathroom, fully aware that it was the star of the show. The hand basin was a mere handmaiden in this display, and the toilet and bidet cowering serfs; that they wore the same robes as the bath merely emphasized their servitude. The full-length mirror on the far wall was simply there to reflect the bath's splendour.

Helena's head was only just visible above the bath's edge as she lay in the scaldingly hot water, and the lazy curls of water vapour were thick enough to make even this small profile hard to see when Eisenmenger glanced in from the bedroom.

'Tell me, is a dinner jacket okay or should I go for the full top hat and tails?'

He heard water splash and there was the bathroom echo that was almost a part of childhood. Through the misty warmth he saw the cuprous shimmering hair move as she tilted her head back and called to the ceiling. 'In my book, sarcasm doesn't even rate as a form of wit.'

'I'm being serious. I mean, if the US ambassador's coming, or I'm sitting next to a minor royal, I don't want to let the side down by wearing jeans or forgetting the cummerbund.'

Her laugh was short but genuine and he felt an irrationally strong surge of joy at the unfamiliar sound; it had been a while since he had dared to hope that she was happy. She said, 'It'll be like any other informal dinner party. No need for a bow tie, no requirement even for a tie. If you want to wear jeans, then as long as they're clean and stay up, I'm sure that will be acceptable.'

'No builder's crack, then. Can't have the artisans round to dinner.'

This last was enough to provoke her to sit up with a splashing swirl of bath water and twist round to look at him from bright, wide eyes set in a wet, shiny face. 'Tell me, Dr Eisenmenger, are all the chips on your shoulders perfectly balanced, or do they sometimes cause you to topple over and take a prat-fall?'

He smiled at her. 'Every so often, one falls off and then I stumble, but on the whole I cope.'

She returned the smile, then twisted back round to her former position with yet more turbulence. He advanced into the room quietly and stood at the end of the bath, looking down on the top of her head, her shoulders. The rest of her body was half hidden by the soapy water, contours and surfaces appearing and disappearing as the water moved. Unaware that he was so close she called out, 'You're a bitter and twisted shit, Dr Eisenmenger. Why can't you accept that the Hickmans are just like you and me? They haven't got any more airs and graces than we have.'

He waited two seconds before leaning down to whisper in her ear, 'I'd quite like to lick you all over.'

She jumped, a swirl of lucky water lapping on her thighs and around her midriff. From where he was standing he couldn't see the healing scar on her breast or its sister under her arm, but he could see how beautiful she was, how he had missed making love to her.

'You sod!' she hissed as she twisted round.

He straightened up, laughing. 'That's a "no", then.' He walked out of the bathroom and said over his shoulder, 'I'm sure that as I get to know them and they get to know me, Theresa and Tristan will gradually appear more and more like your everyday folks, but you must see it from my point of view. They live in a castle, they hold shoots, they open the house to the public and they have suits of armour dotted around the place – what else do you expect me to think?'

She was still looking at him as she assured him, 'Believe me, deep down they're as normal as any other family.'

Sauerwine chose to leave it until they were nearly at their destination before he said to Felty, 'Tell me, Constable, how do you justify claiming black stockings as an expense?'

Felty's eyes were looking for the left turn that would take them on to the road towards the Westerham estate. Her left hand was fiddling with the heater that was refusing to work and she had a tight feeling in her chest that portended a cold on the way. She murmured in reply, 'The Snyder case, sir.'

'What about it?'

'I was the prostitute.'

Sauerwine remembered. Felty had only been in CID for a little over six weeks and this had been her first undercover job. He hadn't liked the idea of Felty playing a hooker but her nearest rival for the role had been the wrong side of forty in the matter of age and the wrong end of the bus in the matter of looks. 'So?'

'My tights got ripped to shreds in the little fracas at the end of the operation.'

He had guessed as much. She found the turning, abandoned the heater to its uncooperativeness and then accelerated, trying and failing to ignore the cold, reminded of it constantly by the sight of her breath pluming out before her eyes. He said, 'Nice try, Sally, but no banana.'

'Do you know how much those tights cost, sir?'

Sauerwine didn't have the foggiest. Along with the price of eggs, the value of gratitude and the purpose of God's creation this was one of many imponderables that he had long ago found that he was happiest ignoring. 'Three weeks ago, that drunken little shite – what was his name? – the one we pulled in for burglary. He brought up his kebab all over my best pinstripe, remember? *I* didn't get reimbursed for that. The Super was quite explicit.'

In fact, Superintendent Tanner had explicitly used

some very explicit words when Sauerwine had put in *his* claim form.

Felty, who hadn't actually expected to get anything out of it, was philosophical. 'Well, I don't think it's fair, sir. I think I should get money for my tights and you should get money for having your suit cleaned.'

They had gone to bed only once, but it had been good for both of them, the summit of an attraction that had been growing ever since she arrived at Newford station. First coffee, then a rushed sandwich lunch whilst they looked into an abattoir's illegal meat sales, lastly dinner on three occasions. They had had to overcome not only her shyness and wariness but also the barriers of rank.

It did not do for inspectors to become attached to their subordinates; the sporadic bout of fornication was ignored but he was acutely aware that prolonged liaison was not tolerated. They had said nothing to anyone and Sauerwine was refusing to think of such things as future consequences, content to enjoy the present.

The road was narrow but straight and they could already see the flare of arc lamps and the dim ghosts of blue flashing lights some three hundred metres ahead. There was deep wood either side of the tarmac. Sauerwine said wearily, 'You're in the police force, Sally. Law and order, justice and control – they're what we're about. Nothing at all to do with fairness.'

Which left Felty decidedly uncomfortable but her thoughts on the subject were left unsaid as they reached the source of the lights and parked behind a dark red Fire Brigade car. No sooner was Sauerwine out of the car than a uniformed constable came up to him. 'It's out, sir. The Fire boys say that it's safe to approach.'

Holt looked half dead with cold and Felty was already becoming aware of a creeping, dread iciness that was seeping through the soles of her shoes and that sought to suck her into the frozen earth. They were taken down a lane that led off into the woods on their right. It was tarmacked but badly needed attention. About fifty metres down was a fire tender with hoses leading from it and with the side-lockers and driver's door open. Behind this was an ambulance, its back doors gaping wide. The paramedics were talking to some of the firemen between the two vehicles, while various uniformed police stood looking at a smoking black fire sculpture, a mockery of a car's chassis, a symbol of destruction.

One of the firemen was writing on a clipboard but when he saw Sauerwine he put the pen in his pocket and the clipboard under his arm. He and Sauerwine knew each other well from innumerable fires. 'Single occupant. We're waiting for the doctor, but I can't see he'll argue that the poor bugger's not dead.'

His tone was blinded by the darkness of the cynicism. Sauerwine asked, 'Who reported it?'

The fireman shrugged. *Not my problem.* From behind Sauerwine came Holt's voice, replete with cold-induced tremor. 'Passing motorist. Chap by the name of Killip. Oram's got him in the car, taking a statement.'

Sauerwine said to Felty, 'Go and see him.'

He turned back to the fireman. 'So how did it start?'

'The usual. Crisp packets on the front passenger seat.'

This was the standard way to fire a car; the grease was readily flammable and caused a flame hot enough and long-lasting enough to ignite the seat fabric. Sauerwine grunted. 'Except that there isn't usually some poor sod sitting alongside.'

Even the cynicism of the fireman was cracked by that. He dropped his gaze and muttered, 'No.'

'Any chance of forensics?'

It was a hope, and a forlorn one at that, but Sauerwine tended towards optimism. The fire officer's response was to laugh and shake his head and say, 'No way. If you don't believe me, you're welcome to form your own opinion.'

Sauerwine took a deep breath. He didn't want to go and look inside the thing that was pretending, but pretending badly, to be a car, but he knew that he would be negligent if he didn't take at least one close inspection, no matter how ghastly the sight, how gruesome the death might have been in his imagination. It was a rule he had picked up early in his CID career and one that he believed helped him ultimately to solve cases. He walked resolutely forward, aware that he was entering an arena around which was an audience made suddenly attentive by the entrance of a new player.

The car was still smoking, or perhaps it was steaming. It was surrounded by pools of water cooling rapidly to icy, muddy slush; the remnants of the firemen's work. A red saloon car, perhaps a Toyota, and apparently old; the fire had done a good job in hiding the rust but the rear number plate lay on the ground, the plastic lugs that had attached it now a thing of the molten past, and it showed the car to be sixteen years old.

Old enough to marry.

He made a note of the number on a scrap of paper from his breast pocket.

The driver's door was on its far side and it had been opened. He skirted around the boot of the car, noting in passing that it, too, was open and that it was empty. Then his gaze fell upon the driver's seat and what was in it.

Shit.

He had seen burnt bodies before and this should have been no worse, but it was.

Oh, it was.

He knew at once that this victim had been alive while the fire had come to feast, while it had remorselessly gorged itself and ignored – perhaps even enjoyed – the agonies it was creating. The body was bent into the usual heat-induced flexion contractures and it was so badly cremated that it wasn't even possible to tell at first glance whether it was male or female, but Sauerwine *knew* that there was in the posture of the figure a dreadful pain and the hell-sent knowledge that he or she was going to burn to death.

The woodland night was cold and crisp and smelled elsewhere of damp and vegetable mould but here the odour was the sickly one of charcoal and burnt fat and as he leaned closer into the metal charnel house it became nauseatingly overpowering. The last thing he wanted to do was get too close to this thing that had once been a human but he had a job to do. As he moved his head and upper body to look around the interior of the car he was aware that all around him people were watching him, presumably glad not to be in his shoes.

The passenger seat had been completely consumed by the fire, a black hole of ash its only memorial. All of the inside was burnt down to metal skeleton, only a few globular shapes of melted grey plastic remaining of the dashboard. The normally unseen wiring that ran behind the dashboard had been almost completely destroyed so that there was just a void at the back of which the rear wall of the engine compartment lurked. Streaks of soot flared across the inner surface of the roof from an epicentre directly above the passenger seat, as if a pyre had been built or a bolt of lightning had struck it there.

Inevitably, though, his eyes were drawn back to the figure in the driver's seat, over which he was now surveying the fire damage. Drawn back and then repelled, a dreadful oscillation that he could not stop.

The sickly-sweet whiff – a hideous caricature of burning meat on a Sunday lunchtime, of the barbecue left untended while the burgers are incinerated – came to him stronger than ever and a moment later brought rising sickness. He pulled rapidly back, twisting his head away and then up to the clear frost-filled skies above his head, deep breaths bringing pluming mist that was quickly lost in the night. He remained like this for several seconds before taking a deep breath and looking again inside the car.

The victim of the fire – recognizably human but not convincingly so, as if a second-rate artist had attempted to persuade the world that a concoction of bonfire debris had once lived and breathed and talked – sat bolt upright, what remained of its hands by its sides. Because the heat of the fire had bent the elbows, knees and, to a lesser extent, the hips, Sauerwine had the impression that this corpse had tried to avoid contact with the flames around it as, indeed, perhaps it had. Even the head was thrown slightly back and to the right, away from the burning passenger seat.

Sauerwine was so engrossed in his thoughts and fancies he didn't hear the tread of the fire officer behind him and consequently he jumped when he heard the words, 'Funny thing, though.'

'Shit!' He jerked his body out of the fire wreck, swinging round as he did so. 'Don't do that!'

'Sorry.' The tone belied the word.

Sauerwine looked back at the car and, of course, at the body. 'What's a funny thing?'

The fireman leaned in front of him, indicating the inside of the opened door. 'The handle's missing. Would have made it bloody inconvenient to get out in the event of a fire.'

*   *   *

27

Eisenmenger was eventually forced to concede to himself that he was nervous and this in turn made him perplexed and annoyed. What the hell was wrong with him? He wasn't meeting the US President or a band of Mafia hitmen, and he wasn't normally someone to be overawed by the prospect of meeting strangers. In fact his usual custom was to treat such occasions as an opportunity to observe – not infrequently also to smile at – the strange rituals of human interaction. It didn't necessarily make him the most popular of guests at such gatherings – Eisenmenger had found that some people unaccountably found the discovery that they were being treated as objects of study somewhat irksome – but unpopularity had never been a badge of dishonour for him.

So why was this particular event proving so daunting? Theresa had been a type – uppermost middle class, moneyed and cocooned, but not wanting to be so vulgar as to actually *crow* about it – yet not one with which he was unfamiliar; in his medical career he had come across hundreds of similar patricianly types. He could not believe that the slightly awkward tea with her had induced in him this feeling of anxiety. Perhaps, then, it was what he had been told by Helena of the other members of the family. Certainly they sounded a strange, almost exotic mix. The husband and father who just happened to be one of the country's most distinguished surgeons and, to boot, newly elected President of the Royal College of Surgeons; the grandmother, Eleanor, who to judge from Helena's description would have cowed Lady Bracknell; a son who was apparently God's gift to British medicine; a daughter who was, according to Helena, strangely beautiful yet strangely disturbed.

There was little doubt that this was an intimidating company in which to find himself, yet Eisenmenger could not believe that they were solely responsible for his diffidence. He had come across luminaries such as Tristan Hickman before and found them either approachable and pleasant, or worthy of his contempt; never had he found them a cause of concern. Similarly, elderly ladies who ruled all that they beheld tended to be either reasonable and therefore companionable, or unreasonable and therefore irrelevant.

No, he decided. The answer lay elsewhere.

'Are you ready?'

Helena's query interrupted his analysis. She had emerged from the bathroom dressed only in bra and panties and was now standing just inside the bedroom, hands on hips. 'More or less,' he replied. 'Are you?'

Her lips formed a smirk. 'None of your sexist crap about women taking a long time to get ready in the evening.' She went to the cupboard and brought out a dark green low-cut dress.

'I thought you said they didn't dress for dinner.'

She looked over her shoulder as she was stepping into it. 'Smart casual.' She appraised him as he sat on the bed. 'You look all right.'

'Thanks.' He failed to keep sarcasm from his voice, but she ignored him. A short period of wriggling and gyration that he found quite erotic to watch then followed. He said, 'Will all the family be there?'

'Apart from Hugo.'

She reached over her shoulder with a degree of flexibility he found amazing; the position formed contours of smooth flesh that only added to his vague feelings of arousal. Successfully zipped into the dress she sat at the dressing table from where they could look at each other in the mirror. 'I can't wait to see Nell again.'

'Not Hugo?'

This seemed to catch her by surprise, as if she had not considered asking herself the question. She said, 'Well, I suppose I was closest to Nell. Hugo used to be absolutely rotten to his sister and I used to take her side. Protect her.'

'A delicate soul, was she?'

She had begun brushing her hair, although for the life of him Eisenmenger couldn't see that it needed any further attention, but she stopped to consider. 'Well, I suppose there was always something other-worldly about her. She was so fragile and so beautiful she seemed almost to be fairy-like.'

It struck him as an interesting word to use and it was spoken in an interesting tone. 'Fairy-like.' He considered this. 'Titania or Tinkerbell?'

She laughed. 'Oh, definitely Tinkerbell. There's nothing frightening about Nell.'

'And Hugo was mean to her?'

'Sometimes. Especially in the early days. Later on, I think he grew quite fond of her.'

He stretched and stood up, looked at his watch. It was seven twenty-seven. She had finished her hair and was now applying some dark red lipstick. 'Anyway, you'll soon settle in. You'll find Tristan to your liking, I'm sure. He's just as irritatingly know-all as you are.'

Eisenmenger wasn't sure if he wanted to dine with a 'know-all' clone of himself but refrained from comment. Helena carried on, 'You might find Malcolm slightly off, though. At least until you get to know him.'

'Malcolm?'

'Malcolm Groshong. He's the estate manager.'

All this was news to him. 'He's eating with us?'

She laughed into the mirror as she hooked a silver pendant earring into her left ear then picked up its partner. 'Is that so shocking? I didn't realize what a snob you are. Why shouldn't Malcolm eat with us? He's looked after the estate for over forty years and he's practically a member of the family. He's devoted to Eleanor.'

'I didn't mean that I thought that he shouldn't dine with us. It's just that nobody told me he would be there.'

She stood up. 'He doesn't normally dine with the family – he's got his own annexe to the castle – but Theresa thought it would be nice. It's a compliment, really. A special occasion with me returning for the first time in eight years.' She hunted for a small clutch bag that was hidden on the bed under a cardigan. 'Don't worry. Apart from the New Year celebrations, all the other meals will be decidedly informal.'

She went to the door. 'Coming?'

He stood up and went to her. As he gave her a light kiss he saw not only that she was smiling but that there was a vague look of anxiety in her eyes; he suddenly realized why he was so nervous. He was meeting her family – the only family that she had left – and he was to be judged.

Felty was thoroughly frozen but even though it felt as though her feet and legs were numb it didn't mean that they weren't painful, and her face and hands were being licked by the rasping icy wind. She was caught in the dilemma of wanting to move her feet to relieve the bone-deep ache she felt and knowing that such an action would only result in pain of a different kind, no less unpleasant. She was standing beside Sauerwine who seemed less affected by the conditions, at least to judge from the concentration that was displayed on his face. He was watching Debbie Addison, the forensic pathologist, directing the Scenes of Crime Officer in which photographs she wanted taken of the body.

'She looks bloody young,' she heard him murmur and was unsure if he had addressed the remark to her or to no one. He was right, though. Debbie Addison gave the impression that she was out of place, here at the scene of a body burned to death; she looked more like a slightly anorexic, extremely pale debutante, a young girl who had probably been called from a cocktail party in Whitehall. She was newly appointed as consultant, although she had spent two years as a specialist registrar in the locality learning from her more senior colleagues.

Not that Felty could criticize. She had been a detective constable for only four months and she thought that she was a long way from losing the feeling of inadequacy. Had Dr Addison been a more approachable personality she might have risked some form of commiseration.

She shivered and even that involuntary action hurt her. Sauerwine glanced at her. 'Not too warm, is it?' he asked.

'No, sir.'

He smiled grimly. 'A while to go, I'm afraid.'

She returned the smile, grateful that he was there. Her career in the police was relatively short but she had already learned that few senior officers had consideration for the tribulations of their juniors.

He suggested, 'Tomorrow I want you to check Killip's story. When he left Swansea, when he arrived with his "friend", how long he was with her. That kind of stuff.'

'Yes, sir.'

Sauerwine checked his watch. It was nine o'clock.

Debbie Addison had finished making notes and directing the photography and she now came towards them. She wore a white all-in-one suit that successfully hid her slight, almost skeletal figure and made her look curiously rotund. The lights made her look even paler than normal.

To Sauerwine she always came across as being arrogant and aggressive, and he wondered if this was a defence against underlying diffidence.

'Well, I can't see any signs of trauma on an initial examination, but until we get the body out and I've had a chance to do a proper examination, I obviously can't be sure.'

Felty made a face. 'Will you be able to tell, even then? I mean, won't the fire have destroyed any evidence?'

Addison didn't even to bother accompanying her patronizing tone with a smile. 'It's very hard to destroy a body completely, Constable. Fire does a haphazard, sloppy job, unless you employ a proper furnace or crematorium; in this case some areas are burned to bone, true, but significant areas show only superficial fire damage, no deeper than the subcutis. I'm fairly confident of being able to assess the presence or otherwise of any pre-existing injuries.'

Felty's face was too cold to redden but she flashed a look of dislike at the pathologist before dropping her eyes and muttering, 'Thanks for the information.'

Addison turned to Sauerwine. 'If you can get the body moved to the mortuary, I'll do the post-mortem first thing in the morning.'

'I'd rather you did it straight away.'

Addison was surprised. She clearly considered this to be unnecessary. 'Why? There's no hurry.'

Sauerwine said simply, 'Yes, there is.' He stared at her and she stared back for a moment before shrugging.

'Very well. As you wish.'

She walked away to her new and clearly expensive Mercedes coupé, Sauerwine's eyes on her. He said softly, 'I don't like that young lady.'

Again Felty wasn't sure if he were talking to her and she decided that it was safest to say, 'You think it's suspicious, sir?'

Sauerwine was still looking at Addison's car, now driving away down the lane back to the road. He said, 'Well, it's not accidental, that's for sure. That means intent on someone's part – possibly the victim's, possibly not.'

'But surely you don't think he was murdered . . . not like that.'

He said, 'We don't know yet that he was alive when he

burned, or he may have been alive but drugged – that's why we need the post-mortem.'

'It must have been suicide,' she insisted.

Sauerwine, though, was more willing to face the depravity of humankind; he was less convinced that no one would deliberately burn a man alive in a car. He was also kind, though. 'It wouldn't be the first time someone's done themselves in like that,' he admitted. Then, 'Come on, no use speculating. Let's wait and see what the autopsy shows.'

'Helena! How fantastic to see you again!'

The man who uttered these enthusiastic words was tall and blessed with a leonine mane, a slightly protuberant nose and a wide smile that boasted perfectly formed teeth in large number. He moved forward from his position in front of the imposing marble fire surround, arms opened in greeting. Helena returned the smile. 'Tristan.'

They hugged and Eisenmenger could see that it was a genuine and affectionate gesture. They parted and Tristan stood and looked her, his arms outstretched, his hands grasping the tops of her arms. The smile, impossibly, widened. 'You need feeding up,' was the verdict, followed by a guffaw and a kiss on both cheeks. Only then did he take Eisenmenger into his consciousness. 'And you must be John.'

Eisenmenger smiled and took the proffered hand. The handshake was nondescript. 'And you must be Tristan.'

Another guffaw. 'Quite right. Quite right.' He turned so that he was standing between them facing the room, an arm around each of them. 'You must come and meet my mother and I must serve some drinks to celebrate.'

If the room in which they had taken tea was cosy and regressed by five decades, then this was a different thing, far grander and regressed by centuries. Eisenmenger could imagine soirées in this place attended by Mr Rochester or perhaps Squire Trelawney. The ceiling was high and the wallpaper a deep, almost hungry red; an aged but clearly expensive chandelier threw shattered light about the room, while the fire surround that Tristan had claimed for himself seemed to Eisenmenger to be someone's attempt at outdoing the Elgin Marbles. Had it

33

not had a raging inferno in its maw, he estimated that he could have put a full-sized pool table in there. Above this was a landscape that he assumed was genuine and valuable but that he didn't recognize; it was the big brother of various other oils dotted around the room, most portraying eighteenth-century nobility, almost certainly with varying degrees of fidelity.

Arrayed around the room were six chairs and two couches, all matching, all antique. Their legs were so thin and ornate that Eisenmenger seriously doubted they would take his weight. In the centre of the room was a low, octagonal table made of a dark, highly polished wood that supported a beautiful and delicate coffee set. The carpets on the wooden flooring were old and worn but no less impressive for that; there were a few magazines in a rather quaint wicker basket in the corner, Eisenmenger noted, and it struck him as both incongruous and touching.

All this was impressive, yet it was subsumed into insignificance by the frail yet erect and hawklike presence that occupied one of the chairs. She was sipping sherry from cut glass and – whether through insensibility or inscrutability, Eisenmenger wasn't sure – was ignoring everyone else in the room. She was wearing a purple dress with a brightly coloured dragonfly brooch on her left shoulder. She had grey-white hair that was gossamer-thin and stretched back over her scalp into a bun so tightly that it was suffused with a pink underglow from her skin. Her eyes were widened and brought into preternatural prominence by narrow-frame glasses while her mouth was linear and rimmed by pale, severe lips. Her skin was so thin that Eisenmenger fancied that he was looking directly into her subcutis, that he really could see the skull beneath it, the underlying mechanicals of life: it seemed that only the sun blemishes so abundant on her face and spidery hands acted as a screen by which she could hide. Her arms and legs were impossibly fragile yet the grip in which she held the sherry glass – only her fingertips making a contact that Eisenmenger could see through the glass was forcing the blood from her skin – appeared perfectly capable of crushing it.

A formidable woman.

Tristan stepped forward. 'Mother?'

She turned to his voice but it was not the action of one who is surprised or even interested in surprise. Behind the glasses her eyes moved first to her son as if he were insignificant, then to Eisenmenger as if he were absent, then to Helena. It was only then that her expression changed from hauteur to something more amenable.

She frowned first, then said hesitantly, 'Yes?' Her eyes did not leave Helena, nor did the expression of vague yet unfulfilled recollection.

Tristan came forward. 'You remember Helena, don't you, Mother? Claude Flemming's child?'

Eisenmenger noted a smile on his face that suggested nervousness. He noted also a look of incomprehension on the old woman's that suggested another state of mind entirely.

Helena came forward, bent down. 'It's Helena, Aunt Eleanor. Helena Flemming.'

It was this, apparently, that changed matters. Her eyes widened and her face moulded itself into a welcoming smile, something of genuine pleasure; yet impossibly before any visible change occurred a light, a life, came into her features that was almost luminescent. 'Helena! Why, of course! How wonderful! It's been so long . . .'

She reached out desiccated, arachnid fingers and Helena took them and bent down to kiss the dried parchment of her face. 'It's wonderful to see you again, Aunt Eleanor.'

As if the stream were now undammed there came forth a torrent of recollection.

'We used to have such fun, didn't we? You and Hugo and Nell . . . There was someone else, wasn't there? And your mother and father, they used to be such lovely company! I've often said to Tristan that we should have them to stay again . . . It's been so long since you last came. How long is it? A year? Eighteen months?'

Tristan said quickly, perhaps too quickly, 'It's been a bit longer than that, Mother.' The smile on his face was partly a bright beacon of amusement, partly a stuttering flame. 'Eight years, actually.'

Eleanor said at once, 'Has it? Has it really?' She turned to Helena. 'My goodness, how time has flown!' She moved easily on, her hands still held by Helena who was also smiling, also eager to help. 'You must forgive an old lady, Helena. My memory isn't what it used to be.'

'Of course, Aunt, of course. Are you well?'

'Oh, yes. Never been better. Tristan is amazed because I'm never ill, am I, Tristan?'

He shook his head. 'You'll outlive us all, Mother.'

She laughed, an old woman's laugh; one that was as cruel and dry as her skin. 'I will, won't I?' Then she turned to Helena. 'I will, I will!'

They all laughed but it was nothing more than a noise, a covering over a wound. Helena said, 'You haven't changed at all.' At which Eisenmenger found himself wondering if she could possibly be as genuine as she sounded.

'Neither have you! Neither have you!'

Repetition and exclamation. These polysyllables wandered into Eisenmenger's head as he looked at the old woman but before he could develop his analysis the magnified eyes swept to him accompanied by a deepening frown. 'And who is this, Tristan? Do I know him?'

It wasn't quite Lady Bracknell but it was a fair, if clearly unconscious, attempt at it.

Helena said, 'This is John, John Eisenmenger. He's . . . He's here with me.' Her hesitation and her brief glance first at Eisenmenger, then at the floor, threw into sudden relief certain aspects of their relationship of which until then he had been oblivious. Thankfully Eleanor Hickman was not interested in the subtleties of what, precisely, he was to her and vice versa. She said loudly, 'Are you really? Come here, then. Let me have a look at you.'

He stepped closer towards her, his hand held out. She examined first his face, then the hand, then his face again, as if she were suspicious that they might not be connected and almost as if she were trying to work out what he wanted from her. When she took his hand he felt papery skin sliding over honeycombed bones, yet the grip was anything but delicate. He felt commiseration for the sherry glass in her left hand.

'It's a pleasure to meet you, Mrs Hickman.'

She smiled and nodded and he could see that she was happy in this minor track of meaningless formalities. 'Mutual, I'm sure, Mr . . .?'

'Eisenmenger.'

36

She tried this out for size under her breath, then evidently took against it. 'What a peculiar name, Mr Eisenmenger. Where on earth did you get it?'

'Mother.' Tristan's tone was one of affectionate warning.

Eisenmenger smiled. 'Having been given it, I was too polite to discard it.'

For a second he wondered if he had gone too far, if she would consider him too familiar, but there was then a cackle and she exclaimed, 'I like you, Mr Eisenmenger!'

They all broke into laughter at this, a welcome relief of tension. 'It's John, Mother. You must call him John.'

He turned to Eisenmenger and Helena. 'Champagne?'

Helena nodded. 'Oh, yes, please.' Eisenmenger also assented. Tristan turned away to go to an ice bucket on a small marble-topped table by one of the two large bay windows on the far side of the room. They followed him, standing around the table while Tristan poured champagne into flutes that matched Eleanor Hickman's sherry glass. 'I thought we should have something special to celebrate Helena's return.'

'Thank you.' Once more Eisenmenger heard happiness, almost excitement, in her words.

As they turned back to face the room, Theresa came in, looking flustered. She was dressed in a black satin trouser suit with a red silk cravat and was pulling the cuffs down with impatient tugs. 'Malcolm's going to be late,' she announced, more than a hint of asperity in her tone. The movement with which she took the glass that her husband held out for her was almost violent enough to spill its contents.

'Problem?' he asked. In contrast his was an easy, almost flippant tone.

'Isn't there always? Some absolute disaster, apparently.' She took a long drink, the charms of the champagne failing to soothe her, probably failing even to make mucosal contact so that the liquid hit her stomach with nothing breaking its fall.

Tristan explained to his guests, 'Running the estate is a twenty-four-hour-a-day job. I don't know how Malcolm has managed it for so long. He's a real godsend.'

Eisenmenger couldn't help noticing that his wife snorted at this eulogy. From her chair Eleanor called, 'Am I going to sit here alone all night?'

At once Tristan responded. 'No, no, Mother.' He turned to his guests. 'Shall we sit down?'

As they went to the chairs around the octagonal table Eisenmenger saw out of the corner of his eye that while Theresa was refilling her glass she was staring at her husband. The glance that Tristan directed towards his wife was oddly threatening.

Once they were settled – Eisenmenger and Helena together on one of the sofas, Tristan beside his mother, Theresa in a chair next to Helena – Tristan asked, 'How are you, Helena? Recovered, I hope?'

Helena, far from recovered in Eisenmenger's opinion, said at once, 'Oh, yes.'

'Who did the op?'

'Mr Dupont.'

He frowned. 'At St Benjamin's?'

'That's right.'

He nodded. 'Good man, I understand.' Although there was something about the way that he said this that was ambiguous; was he entirely unsure of the accuracy of this recommendation or entirely sure of its inaccuracy? He went on, 'What did he do? Sentinel node biopsy?'

Helena looked lost and it was Eisenmenger who said, 'I believe so.'

'Fantastic advance, so they tell me. Not my field, of course, but one has to keep up.'

'Helena tells me you're in plastics.'

More champagne, perhaps to whet the lips for a defence of his chosen speciality. 'That's right. We're not all money-grubbing parasites, though. I find the most rewarding work to be the reconstruction work. Following cancer surgery, that kind of thing.'

Since neither Helena nor Eisenmenger had suggested a prior contrary opinion, this seemed superfluous, although Eisenmenger noted that he had not actually denied doing private – by definition, *cosmetic* – work.

'What are you talking about?' Eleanor's voice was strident and querulous.

Tristan leaned towards her. 'Poor Helena's had to have a breast lump removed.'

She looked at Helena, her face concentrating. 'Have you?' she demanded loudly, but it was the voice of someone shouting in the dark. Then confusion lifted and she repeated, 'Have you?' Her tone was altogether softer, entirely more compassionate. 'Oh, my poor dear Helena. How dreadful for you. Was it . . . was it . . .?'

She didn't want to use the dreaded 'C' word and this reluctance infected them all like scabies mite. It was Theresa who dared to drop words into this well of awkwardness. 'You should have told us earlier, Helena.' This scold was issued in a gentle tone to obviate the words.

Helena smiled but dropped her head. 'Well . . .'

Eleanor said, 'Cancer's a dreadful thing,' She turned to her son. 'Your Uncle Rufus died of a brain cancer, Tristan.'

Whatever Tristan was about to say in response to this was lost in his wife's strident correction. 'Uncle Rufus went bonkers, Mother. He thought that he was Captain Bligh and that his neighbour was Fletcher Christian bent on his destruction. It was Uncle Angus who had the brain tumour.'

Eleanor looked at her, her eyes wide, her mouth open but no words forthcoming for a while. Then, 'Are you sure?'

'Yes.' This with a mix of force and boredom and a good smattering of exasperation.

Eleanor subsided but the look on her face suggested dissatisfaction.

Helena asked, 'Where's Nell? I'm looking forward to seeing her again.'

'She won't be long. She takes an age to get ready.'

'And Tom? I'm surprised we haven't seen him already. I can hardly wait to meet him.'

It was Tristan who said, 'I expect he's with Dominique. She'll be getting him ready for bed.' A pause. 'We thought it best to wait until tomorrow. He's quite excitable.'

Which no one could deny was entirely reasonable in a strangely disconnected way.

Eleanor had finished her sherry and she held it towards Tristan without saying anything; indeed she did not even look at him. His expression appeared to be entirely relaxed and good-natured as he took it, rose and went to the sherry decanter, while she said, 'Tom's wonderful. He's the best thing in this family.'

From the decanter, Tristan called, 'He's an excellent chap. Going to be a surgeon, too. Just like his grandpa and his uncle.'

Helena said, 'I can't imagine Hugo as an uncle.'

As Tristan returned with the recharged sherry glass in one hand and the ice bucket in the other he joked, 'I don't think Hugo can either.' He gave Eleanor her glass, put the ice bucket on the carpet by his chair, then refilled their glasses. 'He goes quite puce when he's reminded of it.'

'Is he doing well? He's at Nottingham, isn't he?'

'First-year specialist registrar in surgery. Got his MRCS first go.'

And already Theresa had finished her champagne. As she put the glass on a coaster on the table she said with a smile, 'He's quite the *wunderkind*.'

Yet abruptly the smile didn't seem quite so smiley but Tristan was already saying, 'Well, I'm not sure how else to describe someone who wins the Anatomy Prize in his first year at medical school, then tops it off with the Gold Medal in his final year exams.'

Eisenmenger was interested in Theresa's smile. It struck him as a contradictory con. She looked at her watch as he scrutinized her and said irritably, 'Where is Nell? The cook will have dinner ready soon.'

'I'm sure she won't be much longer.'

'Is there any more champagne?'

Tristan didn't break his easy, relaxed attitude in either voice or expression as he said, 'I'll get some. Nell will want a little anyway.'

He left the room to some silence. Eleanor was staring at her daughter-in-law but her next words were addressed to Helena as she jerked her head round. 'It's wonderful to see you, dear. How have you been? Have you been well? It's been such a long time . . . how long is it? A year?'

Helena expressed surprise at this moment of forgetfulness but Theresa supplanted her mother-in-law's reply. 'It's been eight, Mother.'

'Eight? Eight?' This with loud incredulity, almost as a pirate's parrot might have said. 'Are you sure?'

Helena smiled. 'That's right. We lost touch . . . after my parents died.'

Which might have been intended as a way of sketching in some context but which had unintended consequences. 'Died? Penelope and Claude dead?' She looked distressed and turned at once to Theresa. 'Did you know this?'

More of the smile, Eisenmenger noted. 'Of course I did. And so did you, Mother.'

'I didn't!'

'Yes, you did. You've forgotten, that's all. It was a long time ago.'

Eleanor looked worried, her magnified but somehow still weak and watery eyes moving from Theresa to Helena and back again. 'How did they die?' she demanded, as if this trick question would expose the lies being told to her.

More sticky seconds were suddenly congealed around them. Helena suddenly found that she didn't have the words and Theresa glanced quickly at her before saying quietly in a voice that was stretched to rigidity, 'They were murdered, remember?'

Eleanor didn't move. She might not have heard, for she looked puzzled for a long time before sighing, 'Oh, yes. Oh, my Lord, yes.'

The door opened and Tristan came in, fresh champagne in hand. 'Here we are. Not only more champagne but the prodigal daughter as well.'

He stood to one side of the doorway and emerging slowly from the relative gloom of the hallway beyond there came a small, slight figure that Eisenmenger found at once to be almost ethereal.

A Faerie Princess.

He stood, partly out of politeness, partly better to look at her, aware that a curious dislocation was occurring in his thoughts. Objectively, he was looking at what he saw, noting details in his customary manner, yet a subjective commentary had unconsciously started and every observation was immediately translated into curiously whimsical terms.

Put clinically, he saw that she was about a metre sixty in height, that she had skin that appeared to be frozen into blue whiteness, hair that was dark and straight and fine and long enough to reach her small hips, eyes that were large and sapphire blue; yet somewhere else in his head there were simultaneous thoughts of unearthly children, creatures not of this world, impossibly beautiful yet impossibly unattainable and uncontactable creatures from other dimensions.

She's beautiful, he decided, *quite, quite beautiful.*

'Who's this?'

It was the man, not Oram, who answered. He was tall and powerfully built, with wiry, close-cropped, grey hair. He looked unhappy but, Sauerwine judged, he probably always did. He was wearing a tatty jacket that looked as if it might once have been waxed and a flat cap that was pushed back, while his feet sported heavy, scarred, steel-capped boots. 'Groshong. I'm the estate manager.'

'Are you? And how did you get to hear about this?'

'I was passing. Saw the assembly.' He used short sentences and clearly begrudged the irresponsible use of the comma.

'Passing? Coming from and going to where?'

Impatience shone through the reply. 'From a meeting. To my house.'

'A meeting with whom and where?' In asking this, Sauerwine employed exactly the same tone and rhythm as before, as if he and Groshong were engaged in courtly ritual.

The estate manager clearly also felt compelled to dance for he, too, repeated his scansion. 'Peter Prinzmetal. A fencing contractor with offices in Melbury. He asked me over for a drink'

'This started when?'

Groshong breathed heavily before his reply. 'About six o'clock.'

'And finished?'

Groshong forsook the heaving respirations for a moment and took to glowering as he said, 'About fifteen minutes ago.'

Sauerwine considered. 'A long meeting,' he commented.

Groshong decided the best effect was to combine the glowering and deep breathing. 'What the hell is going on? Are you accusing me of something?' He moved a pace towards Sauerwine. It wasn't exactly aggressive but Groshong was a big and clearly easily roused man. 'Do you think I set fire to the car? Why on earth would I do that? This is the work of hooligans. You would spend your time more profitably if you questioned the scum who hang about the streets of Melbury at night.'

42

'Nobody's been accused of anything, Mr Groshong. A crime has been committed, however, which means that we have a duty to ask questions.'

'Pah!' Sauerwine had never heard this delightful syllable actually spoken before but from Groshong it was somehow right. It certainly eloquently demonstrated scorn and derision. 'If anything, I'm one of the wronged! I have responsibility for the care of the estate and if yobbos set fire to abandoned cars on Mr Hickman's property, it's my responsibility to clear up the mess.' He was now prodding with his finger towards Sauerwine, no contact being made.

'Maybe, Mr Groshong, but I can't but feel that you're not the most wronged party in all this. Not by a long chalk.'

Groshong's face assumed a suspicious expression. 'What do you mean?'

Sauerwine watched him carefully as he said neutrally, 'The poor bastard who was in the car has a right to feel more aggrieved than you, wouldn't you say?'

Sauerwine saw Groshong transmute from outraged official to horror-struck bystander. *Not bad*, he decided. *Quite possibly genuine.*

Then Groshong stepped back. He glanced at Oram who had born mute witness to this exchange, as if to check that it wasn't a joke, that Sauerwine and Oram would not suddenly break down into uncontrollable laughter and claim to have 'Got Him'.

Satisfied on that score he returned to Sauerwine. 'What?' he demanded.

Right tone, Sauerwine judged. There was something about the eyes, though. He said, 'There was somebody in that car, Mr Groshong. I don't know whether he was there because he wanted to be or not. Which means I want to know all about everybody, at least until we have established all of the facts.'

Groshong's face spoke of embarrassment and acquiescence. He said with considerably less aggression, 'Of course.'

'Now. Perhaps you could furnish Constable Oram with the address of Mr Prinzmetal, and I'm sure that you won't object if we contact him to verify your story.'

Groshong didn't look delighted at the idea, but he

nodded. Sauerwine then said, 'We haven't got any ID on the victim yet, but the car is an old Toyota. Red. Do you know of anyone around here who drives a car like that?'

Groshong considered for a moment, then said slowly, 'I might have seen a car like that about, but as to whose it is, I couldn't say.' Sauerwine was listening as much to the tone as to the words.

'And although you might have seen the car about, you never spoke to its owner?'

'No.'

Sauerwine had long ago discovered that the hardest words for a liar were the shortest; too little cover and too much time to think about inflexion and nuance. Groshong hurried on to say, 'It might not even be the same car that I saw.'

Sauerwine looked at him for a long time before replying softly, 'No. It might not.'

Groshong dropped his gaze and Sauerwine let the noise of death's aftermath intrude upon them for a while before saying, 'Where do you live, Mr Groshong?'

Groshong's face carried hope with it as he replied, 'I live at the castle. In an annexe.'

Sauerwine splayed a smile across his face. 'Thank you, Mr Groshong. That wasn't too bad, was it? We'll be in touch.'

'I can go?'

Sauerwine nodded, his eyebrows raised. 'Of course. Unless there's something else you want to tell me.'

Groshong dropped his gaze for a second. 'No,' he said. 'Nothing.'

Sauerwine left him then, turning over in his mind whether or not the estate manager had been telling him all of the truth, some of the truth or none of it. Felty came up to him. 'The driver, Killip, is a regional rep for a stationery firm. He was on his way home from Swansea where he's been visiting his mother. She's severely demented and lives in a nursing home. He lives in London.'

'No connection with the area?'

'Just happened to be passing through.'

'Bit off the beaten track, isn't he?'

She grinned. 'Ah. That's what I thought. After a bit of persuasion he admitted to having dropped in on an old "friend".'

He sighed. 'I see. Do we have a name and address for this person?'

'He didn't want to give them to me, but he eventually saw the sense in doing so, as long as we don't tell Mrs Killip.'

'Good.' Then he added, 'Well done, Felty.'

He saw her straighten slightly and a brief, satisfied smile pass across her face. 'There's more, sir.'

He raised his eyebrows.

'The car is registered to one William Moynihan. Last known address in Leicester.'

'Leicester? Far from home, then.'

'Shall I arrange for the local force to make enquiries at the address, sir?'

A more experienced detective wouldn't have asked, but he was very much aware that she was still feeling her tentative way. He nodded.

'And then the next thing you do is check Killip's story with his girlfriend. Discreetly, unless she plays silly buggers. There's no need to stir up muddy waters unless we have to. Okay?'

She turned back to the car's charred skeleton.

'Poor bastard,' she whispered.

'Nell!'

The eyes turned towards Helena and her expression of uncertainty was swept aside by joy. 'Helena!'

She held out her arms, a huge smile somehow managing to make her even more stunningly beautiful. Helena went to her and they embraced, gyrating slightly. Then they exchanged kisses and hugged again.

'How have you been, Nell? I've missed you so much.'

Eisenmenger was interested to see that as Nell said, 'Oh, so have I,' there were tears in her eyes. He began to appreciate how close Helena had been to this family.

Helena said, 'You're looking well.'

And curiously the tears began to fall down Nell's cheeks. She embraced Helena again, sniffling, holding her as if here were sanctuary long sought. Over Helena's shoulder she said, 'So are you. So are you.' Then, releasing her, Nell began to giggle through her weeping and said, 'Oh, I'm sorry, Helena. I'm being silly . . .'

'No, you're not.'

Eisenmenger might not have used the word 'silly', but he certainly thought it an extreme reaction. He glanced at his hosts and saw only happy smiles. Nell said with a tear-wettened smile, 'It's so wonderful to see you again. To be reminded of all that we did together.'

Helena, too, had been affected and, whilst not quite crying, was fighting something as she said, 'I often think about the wonderful times we had together. The picnics, the games, the trips to the pantomime. Do you remember the pantomimes we went to, Nell? Remember Aladdin, when Wishy-Washy's trousers fell down?'

And Nell laughed and said, 'Yes! Yes, I do!'

Eisenmenger at that moment looked across at Theresa and saw a reciprocal light in her face, one that he found both enlightening and puzzling, but then he caught her glance towards Tristan and his perplexity deepened for it had broadcast something that resembled fear.

Nell, however, distracted him, for her tone and face suddenly fell. 'It's all gone now. All destroyed. There's nothing left of the past. Aladdin, Wishy-Washy, Widow Twanky – they're all dead.'

The change was shocking. Now there was something of the graveyard about this sprite, something that seemed locked in a coffin. Helena took her hands, almost coercing Nell to look her in the face. 'Rubbish! Things like that don't die. They're still alive, still laughing and still running with the joy of it all. You mustn't talk like this, Nell; really, you mustn't. The memories live on, as alive as ever the moment was, still giving us pleasure, still a place to lie and breathe a little more easily.'

For a second it looked as if Nell would not be persuaded, then she looked up Helena with a hopeful expression; Eisenmenger found himself almost holding his breath – he even fancied that everyone in the room was doing likewise – waiting to see which way things would go. When the smile returned – a beautiful radiance that he thought almost supernatural – there might conceivably have been fireworks in the skies overhead so great was the relief.

'Yes,' she said. 'They do, don't they?'

Tristan had walked over to the champagne in the ice bucket and now returned with a glass. 'Here you are, Nell.

Champagne to celebrate Helena's return. Long overdue, wouldn't you say?'

She took the glass, held it up to Helena and silently toasted her. Tristan ushered them back to the circle around the low table where Eleanor, seeming to notice her arrival for the first time, exclaimed, 'Nell! Come and sit next to me. Where's Tom?'

Nell's smile was slightly strained as she explained, 'He's in bed.'

'In bed?' Eleanor seemed to find this odd. 'Who's looking after him?'

There was a moment of quiet before Tristan said, 'Dominique.'

It struck Eisenmenger as a curiously painful and embarrassing moment and he was lost as to why; he looked at Helena just as she was looking at him, faint consternation on her face. He raised his eyebrows and she shrugged slightly. *I don't know either*, she was saying.

'If I were you, Jack, I'd torch that tree. Put it out of its misery.'

The speaker, a tall ruddy-faced man with short curly hair and bright blue eyes, was gesturing at the Christmas tree, which had not lasted the Christmas holiday well and was beginning to look sorry and sticklike.

Jack Dowden, the landlord of the Dancing Pig, ignored this advice as he counted the mixers and noted the results down on a clipboard.

'I'd do the same for all the decorations, if it comes to that,' continued the ruddy-faced man. 'They look as if they were first used by Mary and Joseph. I mean, take that fairy . . .' A large and painfully callused finger was pointed at a small plastic doll partially dressed in a white miniskirt and crooked white short-sleeved blouse on which tattered wings were attached. 'It looks to me as if she's no better than she ought to be. That's not a fit object to have looking over the birth of our Lord Jesus.'

When the clipboard came down on the ring-stained wood of the bar, it did so with a loud thwack. 'Look, Michael. I'm sorry if it's a bit quiet in here for you, but can't you just shut up for a moment? I'm trying to count the stock.'

47

Michael looked hurt. 'Only trying to help.'

'Well, don't.'

'I mean, you might get a few more customers in if the Christmas decs didn't look so crappy.'

Jack had resumed his stocktaking but was forced once again to abandon this. 'It's always quiet at this time of year.'

'Never used to be. Not when Barney was in charge.'

Jack, who had been landlord of the Pig for coming up to three years and who had been told at least twice a day during that time that he didn't match up to his predecessor, contented himself with an indistinct, 'Fuck Barney.'

Michael finished his pint. ''Nother please, landlord.'

Forced yet again to abandon his task, Jack sighed, put the clipboard, this time gently, down on the bar and picked up the glass in front of his only customer. Michael returned to his theme. 'I mean, it's a small pub so it hardly needs a football crowd to fill it up, but you need more than one.'

It was indeed an extremely small pub, with only one bar and that no bigger than a large domestic sitting room.

'It's early.'

'Not that early.'

Jack put the full glass down on the counter, then held his hand out, palm upwards. He didn't bother asking for money because Michael knew the prices better than he did. Coins were produced and as his fingers curled around them Jack said, 'Sometimes I like it quiet. Gives me a chance to relax.'

Michael said nothing while he took a deep sip, then, 'Fire on the estate, then.'

'So I heard.'

'Car on fire, or something.'

'Apparently.'

'Ambulance and all was there.'

Jack, who hadn't heard that particular nugget, said, 'Oh, really?'

Michael nodded. 'Neville saw it. Lots of police, too.'

'No need to ask what Neville was doing on the estate.'

They both grinned. Neville and his wife, Jenny, owned and ran a stable, but Neville possessed not only a lot of saddles but also a lot of guns, and Neville liked a bit of game for his tea.

'Did he see anything else?'

'Naw. He couldn't get too close. Groshong was there, though.'

'He would be.'

'Lording it, no doubt.'

'No doubt.'

Michael took another sip. 'I wonder why the ambulance was there,' he said ruminatively.

'One of the firemen was hurt, perhaps.'

'Perhaps.'

This idle speculation was interrupted by the far door being opened. Both preceded and accompanied by a severely cold flurry of air, there entered a figure who was dressed in a dirty and torn waxed jacket, thick woollen scarf and flat cap. This apparel served to obscure the figure beneath – the scarf was so high that the face was all but lost in nothingness – but, despite this, Michael's face changed at once; as the figure advanced towards the bar, his expression darkened rapidly. Jack put his hand on his sleeve. 'Please, Michael.'

He didn't react to what Jack said and kept his attention fixed on the figure, but at least he didn't move. The figure came to the bar, standing at the opposite end to Michael. Eyes only for Jack, there emerged a voice that was trembling, feeble and croaking. His breathing was loud and laboured, the tongue protruding slightly. It was clear even to the fairy on the Christmas tree that he was well aware of the reaction he was having on the assembled company. 'Pint, please.'

Jack was nervous, even though many might have considered this a fairly simple request for a publican. He drew in some breath before moving off, somewhat slowly, towards the pumps. Michael continued to stare.

The pint pulled and presented, the figure proffered a wavering fiver which was taken. As Jack put this into the till and fished out the change, the beer was brought to cracked lips. Jack handed over the change. Michael continued to stare.

The figure then began to move away from the counter but hesitated. There was a suggestion of a brave decision made, as it turned to face Michael. The figure straightened as if about to speak, but then Michael gave a syllable's worth of advice – 'Don't.' The figure turned at once and went to a table at the back of the room, near the door; its back was towards the pumps and optics.

Michael stirred. 'Fucking bastard,' he growled.

'Please, Michael. Not in the pub.'

Michael didn't appear to hear. He took a long drink of his beer, then began to straighten his back, as if about to get off the barstool.

'Michael.' Jack had again put his hand on Michael's sleeve although this time with more force. His tone, too, was more coercive. 'I told you. Whatever gripes you've got – and I don't deny you've got good cause – I don't want any trouble in the pub.'

For a few seconds it looked as if he was going to get it anyway, but then Michael subsided back on the stool. He picked up his glass, upended it and removed all trace of beer from its interior. The glass came down on the wood of the bartop with a bang that illustrated perfectly violence repressed.

'Another one?'

Michael gave him a look that could be translated into words only with the liberal use of profanity. 'I don't want another one. I don't want to drink in here at all. Not if you're going to serve any piece of scum that comes in.'

'Now, then . . .'

Michael was already on his feet. 'Don't worry. I'm not going to start anything.' He walked to the door, looking at the back of the figure hunched over in the corner. At the door he stopped and turned and said loudly, 'Not in here, at any rate.'

He walked out of the pub, slamming the door loudly behind him.

The figure didn't move at all; not when Michael shouted, not when the cold wind swirled in as the door was opened, not when the door slammed shut with enough force to shake the room.

Felty had not experienced nerves this bad since she had sat her A-levels. As she walked through the large, brightly red door at the back of the mortuary, she felt ready to faint or fly, certain that either way she was not going to remain attached to the ground by her feet for very much longer. The man who had held the door open for her was well built and powerful, his hair grey and thick, a similar moustache partly hiding a broad smile. He was dressed in theatre blues with bright white clogs on his feet; she vaguely noticed that he had kind eyes.

'You must be Constable Felty,' he said brightly.

She nodded.

'Your boss is in the office with Dr Addison. She's having a cup of tea. Want one?'

This time she shook her head, somewhat more vigorously. He asked judiciously, 'I haven't seen you before, have I?'

'No.'

'First time?'

'That's right.' She tried a touch of defiance about this response, but a hint of querulousness negated the effect.

'Well, if I were you, I'd stay at the back of the crowd and near the door. If you come over funny, don't be a hero, just turn and run for it.'

This was not said unkindly and she smiled and said, 'Thank you. I will.'

'Don't get me wrong. It's not you I'm worried about, it's me. If you're sick on the floor, I have to clean it up; if you fall over and bang your head, I'm the poor schmuck who has to fill out the forms.'

He led her into the small office, where there were two desks and a filing cabinet. At the desk by the window sat Dr Addison, a mug of tea held in pale, thin hands, while Sauerwine sat in a low easy chair to her right, also replete with tea. To add to the crowding a tall, grizzled man whom she recognized as a Coroner's Officer leaned against the edge of the second desk and in the doorway the Scenes of Crime photographer was laughing uproariously at something that Sauerwine had just said. That this stopped suddenly, and that there followed an interval of apparent embarrassment, convinced her that the joke had been at her expense. Sauerwine said, 'Ah, Felty. Any news?'

She pushed past the photographer, ignoring his gaze. He had a reputation for wandering hands despite, or maybe because of, his marriage and parentage of four children. He smelled of whisky.

51

'I'm afraid not, sir. The car's been impounded and we should have a preliminary report on it tomorrow or maybe the day after. Apart from that . . .'

Sauerwine nodded. 'Ah, well. Early days, Constable. Early days.' He drained his tea and looked across at the pathologist. 'When you're ready, Doctor.'

She sipped her tea. There was a distinct air of the star about to make her entrance in the way that she said nonchalantly, 'When I've finished my tea, Inspector.'

Sauerwine grimaced, saw from his watch that it was now getting late and turned his head with raised eyebrows and thinned lips to the other inhabitants of the small room. They also wanted to get this over with, they also thought that she was being a cow, though no one thought it appropriate to speak. Only after another six minutes had passed did the good Dr Addison find that she was able to take in the rest of the beverage, whereupon she stood up and said, 'If you'll excuse me, I'll go and change.'

She left the room, walking past her small and unenthusiastic posse. Only when they had heard the door to the changing room shut behind her did Sauerwine observe, 'She's one snotty bitch.'

'Still, wouldn't crawl over her to get to you,' was the picturesque contribution of Scenes of Crime.

The Coroner's Officer agreed, adding the rider, 'As long as she was gagged.'

Sauerwine laughed. 'I bet she'd have something to say about your technique afterwards. Point out how you should have done it.'

'You mean there's more than one way?' enquired Scenes of Crime seriously.

'Yeah, didn't you know?' asked the Coroner's representative. 'You can do it without resort to date-rape drugs.'

More laughter.

Felty was torn between enjoyment and disapproval of this exchange and said nothing. They didn't even seem to realize that she was in the room and she was unsure whether this was because she was too unimportant to be considered or because she was a police officer and therefore an honorary man.

Sauerwine stood and walked out of the office, the others following to take their place in the sociological pecking order, Felty to the rear. They went into the corridor, thence to the body store where a bank of fridges occupied one wall. In there they put on disposable gowns and over-shoes. Sauerwine pulled Felty to one side. 'You don't have to come in if you don't want.'

Surprised she replied, 'Oh . . .'

'I don't suppose you've seen many autopsies and cases like this are the worst.'

'Well, I admit I've never seen a burned body before . . .'

'It's up to you.'

So many people looking after her welfare; Felty might have been quite emotional had the circumstances been different. She had been in the force long enough to know that consideration for the feelings of others was a rare orchid indeed. She said, 'Thanks, sir, but I think it's important to get used to things like this.' She hadn't meant to sound stand-offish but was suddenly afraid that he would be offended. She smiled and added, 'I promise not to let you down.'

And he smiled back, something that she could not recall having occurred at work before. 'Good.'

The man who had let her in opened the door between the body store and dissection room. 'We're ready, ladies and gentlemen.'

He held the door open for them. As Sauerwine walked through he said, 'Thanks, Stephan.'

Felty took a deep breath as she followed. For a moment the scene was hidden by Sauerwine's back and just before he moved aside she heard whispered in her ear, 'If you thought *Silent Witness* was a star performance, wait till you see "Lady Quincy" do her turn.'

It caused her to turn and give Stephan a brief smile but then she saw what was to be the subject of 'Lady Quincy's' attentions and her expression turned to horror even as she bent her head down and turned her face away.

She had hoped that the glimpses she had already caught of this grotesque – from a distance, distorted by shadows and quickly snatched – would prepare her for this moment. She had hoped that like all the best horror films the real terror was in the imagining, that the monster when revealed was never *that* scary.

She had hoped wrong.

53

Taken from its shadows and placed into the sterile, bright and shadowless world of the mortuary dissection room, this particular monstrous thing was in no way, shape or form a disappointment. Indeed, it rejoiced in this revelation, basked in the solo spot that it had been given. The humanity – and therefore the agony – of what this had once been was the worst. The flexed posture and bared, lipless mouth (almost screaming silently) were eloquent to the point of deafness on the subject of pain. The few visible areas of unburned flesh spoke loudly of the humanity of this hideous thing, a soliloquy on the awfulness of fate.

Yet that was not the worst, for Felty became also aware of the smell. The odour of burned fat, charred and brittle meat was inescapable; instantaneously the associated memories of lazy summer barbecues when her father inevitably overcooked the sausages were wiped to be replaced by far more nauseous associations.

Dr Addison was less affected. She cast an eye that was clinical to the point of cryogenic and said to Scenes of Crime, 'The usual to start with, please.' She was dressed in blues similar to Stephan except that on her they were curiously unfilled; to Felty they reinforced the strong impression of an eager student, lecturer's pet, out to make an impression. Nervous but defiant, she exuded trumped-up but indefatigable pseudoconfidence, a child determined to step up to the adult world.

Whilst the photographer spasmodically bathed the room in even brighter but even less loving light she looked on, until he had finished and with a nod was dismissed. It was at this point that attention inevitably turned to her. Felty, nervous and unhappy as she was, saw some panic as the good Dr Addison in turn looked to someone else to do something. Stephan stepped forward. 'Would you like me to fix those contractures?'

Felty didn't know what he meant and, there was a suspicion, neither did the pathologist. She nodded reluctantly, however. He stepped forward with a short-bladed but wicked-looking knife in his hand, then grasped the right, charcoaled hand with rubber-gloved hand. With a small expression of surprise he looked closely at what he was holding, then looked up. 'Did you see this?'

Addison came over. 'What?'

He was rubbing the black carbonized skin of the fingers.
'A ring.'

She didn't bend to look too closely, said merely,
'Oh, yes.'

There was a moment when she might just have been
about to claim that she had known all about it but then
she looked across at Sauerwine. 'There's a signet ring on
the right little finger.'

Stephan slipped it off and put it into an opened evidence bag proffered by the Scenes of Crime Officer. Stephan
then took the corpse by the hand again. What he did next
caused Felty to gag, for he took the knife then sliced
deeply across the inside of the elbow. Felty gasped,
shocked by this desecration, but worse soon followed as
the mortuary technician then straightened the arm, having
to exert a great deal of force, and exposing as he did so a
lividly pink mouth of flesh as the lips of his cut were
widened. She felt herself losing control, the nausea rising
in a crescendo of muscular contraction.

She turned and ran back through the doors of the
mortuary, hardly aware of the commotion she made, that
Dr Addison was looking on with a mocking smile and
that Sauerwine was offering her a commiserating hand.

'So you're a pathologist, John.'

'So to speak.'

Eisenmenger had decided that he had just tasted the
epitome of pâtés and did not particularly want to spoil the
experience by unnecessary use of his mouth. Tristan,
though, was clearly more accustomed to the palatal
delights on offer.

'I'm so glad that the speciality has been recognized for
its importance. For too long pathology has been relegated
to the backroom, its significance in patient management
ignored.'

Eisenmenger thought that he could have closed his eyes
and imagined that he was in the audience of a presidential
address. 'Well,' he murmured, 'it's about time.'

Tristan nodded enthusiastically. To Helena he said,
'We're desperately short of pathologists, Helena, and we
can't function without them.'

Helena said easily, 'So John keeps telling me.'

'Even quite educated people still think that all they do is cut people up; no matter how many times I tell them otherwise, they insist on picturing a pathologist as some sort of corpse-butcher.'

Eisenmenger graciously accepted the smile of commiseration that accompanied this lament while harbouring the suspicion that he was being patronized. Tristan continued, 'Mind you, that awful business at Alder Hey didn't do much for your image.'

Despite feeling that this was a bit undiplomatic Eisenmenger managed to hide his irritation and said merely, 'I think that most people can see that Alder Hey was a despicable aberration.'

'Oh, absolutely.'

Eisenmenger might have said more but for the fact that he happened to glance at Nell who was sitting diagonally opposite him. Until then she had been talking animatedly to Helena, their reminiscences causing frequent giggles and squeals and producing an atmosphere of easy relaxation. Now, however, he saw that she was staring at him and he found that the effect was quite hypnotic; perhaps it was the light but her face seemed pallid with large, almost drowned eyes. She radiated dislocation.

The entry of the cook, followed by the maid, from the kitchen next door with a large warming trolley between them broke into his trance. From the trolley they proceeded to distribute large covered vegetable dishes before placing a pile of plates beside Tristan. Last out was an enormous rib roast that was placed by the plates. He picked up a carving knife and fork. From the other end of the long table Theresa said, 'With a pathologist and a surgeon at the table we're certainly well off for potential carvers.'

'Pathologist?' asked Eleanor. 'Who's a pathologist?'

'John.'

'John who?'

Theresa's reply was issued with a thin lacquer of asperity. 'Helena's partner.' She indicated the object of their conversation with a slight nod of the head. Eleanor peered at him as if he had just appeared at the table like an uninvited apparition. Tristan who had begun to carve said loudly, 'John's a forensic pathologist, Mother. Corpses and mutilations, that kind of thing.'

Having put several pieces of meat on to the top plate he now handed it to Helena to pass down the line but when she in turn proffered it to Nell, the girl ignored her. Her eyes were again fixed on Eisenmenger but they were even wider, even more expressive, though this time it was of horror.

Helena said gently, 'Nell?'

The violence with which this small, slight thing stood up was surprising enough but during her upwards trajectory she hit the plate that Helena was holding and it flipped out of her grasp and fell to the floor. China pieces and moist beef slices splayed out on to the Wilton carpet as Nell ran from the room, her faint but frantic gasping lost in the crash of the crockery and the sounds of assorted exclamation.

For a second that might have been years there was stasis, and it was the entry of the maid – timid and querulous – that fractured this moment and converted it from shock to life, that forced them all to stop hiding behind the instant and crawl into embarrassment.

It was Theresa who was brave enough to speak first. She called to the maid, 'Can you come and clean this up, Sarah?' Then she turned to the company around the table. 'I must apologize for Nell.'

The maid disappeared. Helena asked, 'Is Nell all right? Would you like me to . . .?'

'Oh, no.' Theresa's voice was quite confidently reassuring but there was something about her eyes that was less happy. 'She's very tired. Tom hasn't been sleeping well.'

'And she's not very fond of beef,' put in Tristan – perhaps overenthusiastically – as the maid reappeared with a dustpan and brush, kneeling down to remove the pieces of gold-rimmed china crockery and slivers of red-rare meat. 'Always been tending towards vegetarianism.'

Eleanor said as if nothing had just been said, 'What's got into Nell?'

She was ignored by Theresa who said to Helena, 'I'll go and see her after the meal. She'll have calmed down by then.'

There was a degree of inevitability about Tristan's second contribution. 'She'll be contrite and apologetic; ashamed, I expect. She's been so looking forward to seeing you again, Helena.'

Has she? Eisenmenger tried to find evidential support for this in Nell's behaviour since they had first met her but found it oddly variable.

Felty knew that if she didn't return soon she would never go back in, and she knew also that she would then be unable to face Dr Addison without seeing a mocking look in her eye. She forced the wave of nausea down and then took three very deep breaths. *Come on, then.*

She pushed the door open as quietly as she could. Only Stephan, standing at the head of the corpse and therefore facing her directly, noticed. He gave her a smile and wink and she felt at once better. In front of her were the backs of Sauerwine and the Coroner's Officer, while next to them were Oram and a uniformed sergeant she didn't know too well but who was close to retirement and so shot through with cynicism it seemed to her that he was nothing *but* cynicism, that it had snatched his body and the paunched being she now stood behind had lost all claim to humanity.

She moved to one side so that they no longer obscured the view.

'Can you take a picture of this, please?' The good Dr Addison indicated the groin of the body. Her hands were gloved and the gloves were covered in blood; this would have been horrific enough but it was blood in which swam black flecks of carbon.

Human carbon.

SOCO – Scenes of Crime to the public and the press, Free Willy to his colleagues – moved swiftly to do as he was told; a sort of butler with a camera. He proceeded to take a photograph that under other circumstances would have been rightly condemned as 'sick'.

The body had changed. The contractures had gone, literally broken by Stephan, but it was still recognizably tortured and twisted. The torso was almost corkscrewed, the head thrown back, the lower jaw gaping. If ever a human being had died in agony, here it was.

Dr Addison said brightly, 'Well, luckily, I can tell you that we have here a man.'

Sauerwine asked, 'Any indication of age?'

'Not from the face.' This was not exactly a surprise to

anyone as there was nothing but charcoal stuck to bone where once quite possibly Adonis-like features had rested.

She proceeded to slice down the front of the body, helping to share the experience by proclaiming, 'The sensation when you do this is always so horrible. It's a sort of crunchy feeling . . .'

Felty was damned if she was going to succumb to the waves of violent turbulence that were trying to empty her stomach into her mouth. *She's doing it on purpose, for my benefit.*

Dr Addison had a plummy, Roedean-and-Rowing accent that was discordant with her surroundings, and her task, and the presence of gobbets of greasy fat adherent to her gloves. She had long brown hair tied back into a ponytail and large, thin-framed glasses that were forever threatening to drop off the end of her nose and into the corpse.

'It's quite amazing how even a fire intense enough to destroy a car fails to do much damage to the internal organs, except in a few places.'

Nobody felt compelled to comment. She worked diligently on exposing first the abdominal organs, then the ribs. There was an irregular but impressive hole in the left-hand side of the abdomen that exposed the spleen and both the large and small intestines; these were the colour of burgundy.

'Most of the tissue damage is on the left-hand side, as one would expect from a fire in the passenger seat.'

She asked Stephan to cut through the ribs with an electric bone saw and, whilst he was doing this, she conferred with SOCO. When the front of the ribcage had been removed, more pictures were taken before she turned again to the upper abdomen. She delved deeply for a moment before one of her hands emerged to be given a short length of string by Stephan. This then disappeared and from her attitude she seemed to be tying something. Her hands came out and, with a shift in her position so that she faced the feet, she attended to the lower abdomen. This time she seemed to Felty to be nearly up to her elbows and there were definite, and remarkably visceral, squelching noises. Once again, string was produced and something was tied.

What happened then was nothing less than an act of magic.

Dr Addison emerged, took up the knife then plunged back into the body. A purple-red snake began to emerge, led forth by her bloodied hands. That it was there at all was to Felty obscene, that it proved rapidly to be so long and *biological* was beyond belief. She watched in open-mouthed incredulousness as metre after metre appeared, taken from Dr Addison by Stephan and put into a large stainless-steel bowl.

Eventually it was over and Dr Addison looked up at her small but attentive audience. 'I'm going to leave the neck structures in situ for the time being,' she announced. 'That'll allow me to look for signs of strangulation more easily.'

As if we care.

She sliced through the trachea, oesophagus, carotids and jugular veins at the level of the clavicles, then placed a gloved finger into the gaping hole of the trachea. She began to pull it and the oesophagus away from the front of the vertebral column, helped by the blade of her knife.

Another fabulous yet repulsive beast began to rise from the blackened corpse, with Dr Addison, glasses heading dangerously towards the tip of her nose, holding it by the neck. Even Felty had to admit that she did it well and with surprising facility as it emerged. First the heart, nearly smothered by the lungs then, dangling from these, a clutch of organs that Felty recognized only fitfully from the butcher's counter. It was plainly heavy but she showed impressive strength to lift this clear and guide it into yet another bowl provided by Stephan.

Felty allowed herself a long and sincere sigh as their star for the evening stepped back and took a breather. Stephan took the organs away and for a moment she thought that the worst was over but she was wrong.

It was Stephan who took things to a higher level of obscenity. He peered into the gutted, burned carcass and opined, 'No obvious stab wounds. Do you want me to cut down?'

What does that mean?

She soon found out.

Another knife, another unbelievable act as he grasped

the ribs and sliced down, pulling them apart, giving each bony curve a wiggle. When he had finished they projected into the air like the beached remains of an ancient, decayed boat. 'No fractures,' he announced. 'Shall I do the head?'

Felty didn't wait to discover the ominous meaning of this question. Before she was forced into an ignominious and public retreat, she turned and walked towards the door, garnering as much dignity as she could from the cold and clinical atmosphere. She had expected, no matter how restrained she tried to be, to be the object of derision and it was with some surprise that she discovered Sauerwine was following her.

'You all right?'

She nodded and it wasn't with a modicum of truth that she said, 'Sure. Just wanted a breather.'

He smiled. 'The head thing *is* pretty gruesome.'

And she smiled back. 'I was afraid it would be.'

'Let's see if we can make some more tea, shall we?'

The arrival of Malcolm Groshong proved a huge relief for everyone, pricking the uncomfortable atmosphere that had descended on the company and that had been made worse by Eleanor Hickman's unprovoked and surprised enquiry, 'Where's Nell gone?' They continued with their meal but the conversation was desultory to the point of excruciation.

His arrival, heralded by banging doors, was abrupt. When the door opened he appeared flushed and slightly out of breath. 'Sorry.'

'Malcolm!' Helena's impression was that Tristan was positively exploding with joy at this interruption to proceedings. He seemed ready to throw his hands around the newcomer.

Theresa was similarly pleased, not to say relieved. 'You poor man. What happened?'

Groshong was looking round the table with its two empty places. 'Where do I sit?' He sounded flustered.

Theresa pointed him to the place between Eisenmenger and Eleanor. He sat down before saying, 'Problem on the estate.'

'Nothing serious, I hope.'

Groshong looked around the table. For the first time he took in Helena and an expression of recognition took shape. He nodded at her and smiled briefly, but then this glimpse was lost and his face resumed its former troubled look. It was to Tristan that he said, 'There's been a death on the estate.'

Tristan's previously relentless cheeriness met an obstruction that was as unexpected as it was disruptive. 'What?'

Once again Groshong glanced around the table. For the first time he seemed to notice Eisenmenger and his attention lingered on him for a moment before it went back to Tristan. Eisenmenger noticed that he was sweating and wondered just how rushed he had been to get there. Groshong repeated, 'Someone's died.' He paused. 'I'm not sure I should go into details.'

Which was intriguing, especially for Eisenmenger. Eleanor asked, 'Death, Malcolm? Who?'

The maid came in and Tristan said, 'Could you give Mr Groshong a dinner plate?' To Groshong he said, 'You'll forgo the starter?' Evidently this was a rhetorical question for he turned back to the maid and nodded at once.

In answer to Eleanor's question, Groshong said to the company in general, 'Stranger. Not one of the workers.' To Helena's ears it sounded as if this was a small but significant compensation.

Theresa asked, 'How did he die?'

The maid came in with Groshong's plate and while Tristan carved him some meat, he said, 'In a car.'

'A crash?'

Groshong hesitated. 'No.'

Tristan handed him the plate and said, 'Sorry if it's cold.'

Whilst he was helping himself to vegetables Eleanor, displaying a degree of comprehension that surprised Eisenmenger at least, asked, 'So what did he die of?'

And Groshong looked up and said in a low but gentle voice, 'I'm not sure it would be good idea . . .'

Tristan understood at once, Theresa soon after. So did Helena and Eisenmenger, although he was a bit miffed not to be receiving the grisly details. Only Eleanor had mislaid the undercurrent. She demanded, 'Why on earth not? Was he murdered?' She looked around, her attention alighting on, and becoming affixed to, Helena. 'You'd like to know, wouldn't you, dear?'

Helena did the mouth-opening thing. She followed this with the slight-squeak thing, then finished with the look-around thing. Tristan said gently but firmly, 'Not now, Mother.'

She was clearly about to argue, or ignore, or say something even more unacceptable, but this possibility was promptly quashed by Theresa who said, 'But we haven't introduced our guests.' She had assumed a smile that nobody in their right minds would have argued with. 'You must remember Helena.'

Groshong had begun to eat but he put down his knife and fork and said, 'Of course. Nice to see you back, Miss Flemming.'

'Helena, please.'

He nodded acceptance of this concession, then turned to Eisenmenger. Theresa said, 'And this is her partner, Dr Eisenmenger.'

Eisenmenger offered, 'John.'

'Good to meet you.'

Tristan said easily, 'Malcolm's job is twenty-five hours a day, eight days a week. We're lucky to have him here.'

Groshong was continuing with his meal. He gestured with his knife and said, 'So where's Nell? Is she ill?'

Tristan made a face that was almost theatrical. 'She's in a mood.'

Groshong frowned for a moment, then nodded as comprehension blossomed. Eleanor filled in the blanks. 'Poor Nell. Got upset about something. I don't know what it was about . . . nobody ever tells me anything.'

Groshong said at once, 'That's not true, Mrs Hickman.'

'Isn't it? Isn't it?'

Groshong suddenly seemed very protective to Helena's eyes. His face was serious as he assured her, 'You're held in very high regard.'

As Tristan added, 'Absolutely, Mother,' it was noticeable that his tone was considerably different.

Eleanor only had eyes for Groshong. 'Really? Do you think so?'

Groshong nodded gravely. 'Oh, yes.'

His tone was grave, shot through with sincerity.

*   *   *

When Felty returned to the dissection room with Sauerwine, she saw no immediate major changes and this generated a sense of relief that unfortunately soon proved to be false. Dr Addison's back was to her, the posture slightly bent down. It obscured the top end of the corpse and for several minutes the details of what she was up to were hidden. Stephan was in close attendance on the opposite side. Felty glanced around the mortuary. Nigel, the Coroner's Officer, had wandered over to the far corner and was examining an ancient skeleton beside a small bench-top autoclave; Oram was still talking to the Sergeant, although they were in the opposite corner where the telephone was perched on a small shelf, just beside an alcove with a small bench on which some paperwork was laid. On the steel benching along the far wall the bowls of organs had been laid beside large white boards on which were arrayed a variety of scissors, knives, forceps, a long metal probe and a ruler.

Dr Addison straightened up and to Stephan said, 'Thanks.' She glanced around the room, spotted Sauerwine and called, 'No facial injuries.'

Unknown to Felty, this innocuous phrase heralded another scene of hellish repulsiveness for, as the petite doctor moved away from the head and around the top of the body, the results of her labours were revealed. Felty stared in unbelieving horror at the work done, at the near-naked skull from which the blackened eyes stared at the ceiling. The skin of the face and neck lay flapped over the top of the empty, topless skull, hanging down in a curtain, its bloodied undersurface bearing up well to unaccustomed publicity. Similar atrocity had been visited upon the right arm.

Dr Addison continued, 'There is some recent bruising over the right wrist and upper arm, though.'

'Significant?'

She shrugged. 'Possibly. It might indicate a recent fight or something.'

Sauerwine pursed his lips. He glanced at Felty. 'Make a note of that, will you, Felty? Bruising around the right wrist and upper arm.'

She was slow in bringing herself back from the awfulness of what had been done to the corpse. She couldn't stop asking herself, *How will they get it all back together?*

64

'Felty?'

She pulled herself towards her superior, blinked, then said, 'Yes, sir. Bruising, sir.'

She took her PDA from the pocket of her fleece and scribbled this down, but her eyes would not let the corpse rest.

Addison spent the next twenty minutes dissecting the organ block. By now everyone was tired and this, together with the fact that she was working on the benching by the wall and out of the centre of the room, meant that no one, except Stephan, paid her much attention. He was occupied weighing the organs and writing down the results, and generally tending to her demands.

Her last act was to slit open the entire length of serpiginous intestine and thereby release into the already poisoned atmosphere an odour that was so faecal as to be solid. Felty had once had food poisoning and this miasma brought forth unpleasant memories of a time spent with her backside adherent to the toilet seat, her stomach churning, an unpleasant burning sensation around the nether regions.

Addison looked across at Stephan and nodded, at which he picked up one of the bowls of organs and carried it over to the corpse. He did the same with the second, resting them both on the steel of the dissection table. He took a yellow plastic bag off a large roll, opened it out, then put it inside the body cavity; into this he poured the dissected organs, a sickly, sloppy stream of green, red, brown and grey. Dr Addison had turned away, her part of the chore undertaken, and was now stripping off her gloves, mask, hat, gown and apron. She washed her hands at the basin, then turned and produced a smile for Sauerwine that was at once both sweet and poisonous.

'He burned to death,' she announced. Her perfectly enunciated syllables were filled with insouciance; her teddy had lost its ear, the rowing was good at Henley this year, a man had burned to death.

'He wasn't dead before the fire got him?'

'There's soot in the windpipe and lungs. He was still breathing when the fire took hold. Also the surviving tissues show some evidence to suggest carbon monoxide poisoning; he was still breathing as the fire took hold. That and the lack of serious injury suggest that he burned to death. Simple, really.'

'What about the bruising to his arm? Was that significant?'

'I don't think so.'

'You're certain?'

'Of course.' She took this as less than complimentary. Felty decided that she was probably always close to indignant petulance. 'Why wouldn't I be?'

He wanted to say that it was almost unheard of in his experience for a forensic pathologist to come to an immediate conclusion, not without days of consideration, huge numbers of tests and a great deal of cajolery. Instead he asked, 'What about toxicology?'

Stephan said, 'No chance. After what matey's been through, all the blood's turned to black pudding and he most probably pissed himself before he died, so no urine.'

Addison went to the small alcove, gathered up her paperwork and began to walk to the changing room. 'I'll write this up after I've had a shower. Then, perhaps, I can get home at last. It's been a very long – and very fruitless – evening.'

When she had disappeared into the changing room Felty said loudly, 'Bitch.'

Sauerwine smiled at her. '*That* was the word I was looking for.'

They walked from the dissection room, followed by Nigel and the other policemen and leaving Stephan turning his attention to the head, now indecorously filled with cotton wool. Sauerwine said, 'Come on, time to go.'

She followed him out into the night air, now seemingly even colder.

He said, 'How about a drink? There's a good pub not far from here.'

Although the idea appealed as a chance to grasp normality again, she said uncertainly, 'Oh, that would be nice . . .'

Seeing the look on her face, he asked gently, 'But not tonight?'

'I'd really rather not. I've got a splitting headache.'

'Oh, right. Never mind.'

She hoped desperately that he did not think this an excuse.

As they walked to the car she said, 'So nothing suspicious then. Suicide, presumably.' She opened the central locking on the car.

He stopped and stared at her across the roof of the car. 'What makes you say that?'

She was flustered as she said, 'Well, there was no sign of violence.'

'Mmm, maybe. But I don't like fires – too much goes up in smoke whatever Lady Quincy says. For a start, we can't get any tox from the body, so it's possible he was drugged; perhaps that was how he was incapacitated. Anyway, it's not a common way to top yourself, even for the severely depressed. None of which I like.'

He climbed into the passenger seat. As she got in and started the engine he said, 'There was no door handle. He couldn't get out, even if he wanted to.'

'What's happened, Malcolm?'

The meal was over and the atmosphere had gradually become more relaxed, although Nell had not returned. The party was back in the sitting room with the large octagonal coffee table and were taking either tea or coffee, as well as after dinner drinks. It was when Eisenmenger was returning from the bathroom that he become temporarily disorientated and found himself an unwitting eavesdropper.

It was Tristan who had spoken, his voice coming from a doorway just ahead of Eisenmenger on his left. He was aware that it was a dreadful breach of social etiquette but he stopped and stood where he was to listen. The events of the evening – by turn normal, slightly off-kilter and completely bizarre – had left him intrigued.

'A car was found burning on the edge of the estate, by Forester's Row. There was a body in it.' Groshong's low, gruff tone was unmistakable.

'Oh, Lord. What was it, an accident?'

There was a pause before Groshong replied. 'The car was off the road, in a clearing.'

There was a pause and then Eisenmenger heard Tristan's almost frightened tone as he asked, 'Was it . . .?' He didn't hear any audible reply from Groshong. Tristan said then, 'Oh, God.'

Groshong growled, 'Aye. And there's more.'

'What?'

The tone was close to panic and Groshong's next remark was almost contemptuous. 'Don't worry. Nothing catastrophic. The police may call, though.'

'But why? Why should they come here?'

'Because it was on your land. It'll only be a formality. Don't panic, that's all. There's nothing to connect anyone here with the death.'

'You're sure?'

'Yes.' The certainty was a sharp blade to further discussion. This time the pause was the longest yet before Tristan asked in a tone almost awed, 'Is there anything I should know?'

Malcolm Groshong's tone held a noticeable trace of cruel amusement as he said, 'Nothing at all, Tristan. Nothing at all.'

A deep breath. 'Good.' Then, 'Perhaps we had better rejoin the party.'

Eisenmenger moved at once the way he had come as swiftly and quietly as he could.

Neither Eisenmenger nor Helena found it easy to sleep that night and after what seemed like hours of restlessness she finally said into the darkness, 'I wonder what was up with Nell.'

Eisenmenger was on his back, eyes half closed. He said eventually, 'I don't know. Did she know I was a pathologist? That was when she seemed to get upset.'

'I told Theresa, obviously, but I don't know if she passed it on to Nell.'

There was another long pause before he said, 'Not everyone is comfortable with what I do.' The languidness of his reply was forced upon him by the lateness of the hour. Then, 'Tell me what it was like before. When you were young.'

She had been on her side, facing the arched stone window, but now she turned to lie on her back, perhaps staring at exactly the same small piece of ceiling as him. 'It was incredible. I thought it wonderful at the time but now, when I look back, it really does seem to be a fairy tale. We came here regularly – stayed for weeks at a time during the summer – always at Easter and Christmas. Quite often, my mother and father weren't here, but that didn't bother Tristan and Theresa – they had a nanny who did all the hard work in looking after us.'

'I can see that living in a castle would seem magical to a child.'

'But it was a whole lot more than that!' He turned his head to look at her profile against the suffused light from the window beyond. She had lost enough weight for the near-perfect darkness to give her a gaunt look, but the lies told by the gloom also made her impossibly appealing. She explained, 'Tristan and Theresa, and Eleanor, they were all so wonderful then. Then they were so happy, so pleased to be giving. I never felt that our presence was a problem to them; far from it, Jeremy and I always had the reassuring feeling that our being here delighted them.

'And it was the same for my parents. Mummy and Daddy and Tristan and Theresa seemed to be the perfect quartet. I never once saw a cross word between them; there were no rows, no quarrels.'

Eisenmenger felt a qualm of sadness as he recognized his cynicism irresistibly questioning the recalled perfection of all this. Memory he knew was a treacherous companion, forever smoothing over the faults, ceaselessly removing the unwanted from its presence.

'And the castle? The Hickmans have lived here for a long time?'

'Tristan's family have owned it for nearly a hundred years. It was built in the late eighteenth century. Tristan calls it a folly. A country house built as a replica of a castle.'

'Or someone's idea of a castle.'

'If you like.'

Back to fairy tales, he thought.

She said, 'Tristan hasn't changed – he was always so calm and so comforting; never seeming to be upset, never troubled and never angry, at least not for long.'

Eisenmenger could see entirely what she meant. His impression had been similar. Tristan Hickman was charming and able, the perfect man to be the new President of the Royal College of Surgeons.

'But Theresa has aged.'

'It has been eight years,' he pointed out.

'Even so! My recollection is of someone much happier, someone much more coping. Now she looks weighed down; I thought that today she's been playing a part.'

We're all playing parts, he mused. *It's just a question of how well and why we play them.* He suggested, 'What's happened with Nell, that must have been a huge strain.'

Helena said nothing for a while, then, 'Nell's changed.'

'She's beautiful.'

As soon as he said this he wondered if Helena would prove jealous but she seemed to accept that his was a purely objective assessment. 'She always was.'

'How has she changed?'

There was silence for a while. 'She was always small and slim and delicate. She seemed made of something too breakable to last.'

Perhaps she was.

'She was happy, though. Happy and giving. Tonight, though, there were times when she seemed almost afraid.'

'Afraid of me, it seemed.'

Helena laughed. 'Afraid of the big bad pathologist.'

There was silence for a time until he said, 'And Hugo used to tease her?'

'Mercilessly.'

'Tease, or bully?'

'Oh, no. There was no harm in it. Just brotherly baiting.'

'So they got on pretty well?'

'She and Hugo were like two sides to the same person; they were incredibly close even while they were arguing and fighting. In many ways he protected her. That couldn't last, though. When childhood came to an end, so did Nell's happiness. I suppose Hugo was growing up and beginning to live his own life. He had A-levels to sit, then medical school to apply for. Inevitably, I suppose, that meant he had less time for Nell.'

'They were that close?'

There was a pause in the darkness before she answered. 'I didn't realize it at first – none of us did. It was obvious that they were a devoted brother and sister, but I don't think anyone in my family thought that she was dependent on him, at least to that extent.'

'Not even her mother and father, either?'

'Well, Tristan was making a name for himself, don't

forget. He was doing a lot of research – pancreatitis, I think – winning lots of research prizes, that kind of thing.'

Climbing the greasy barber's pole. Another discretionary point on the salary here, another national merit award there. Not enough time to check on the daughter, make sure she's not being impregnated by the local serf's son.

'And Theresa at the time was heavily involved in charitable work. She was chair of some national charity to do with abused wives.'

Thank God it wasn't for underage pregnancy.

'And there was the estate to run, as well. That's always taken a lot of their time, even with Malcolm Groshong. The amount of work Tristan and Theresa put in is quite awesome.'

She's finding excuses for them. But as soon as he had thought this, he felt ashamed. *Who knows? Perhaps she's right. Do I know what's going on under my nose? Did I know that Marie was going to immolate herself in front of me?*

Helena said, 'Eleanor knew, though.'

'What makes you say that?'

'Something she said once. At the time I didn't realize what she meant, but looking back it seems obvious.'

He waited. The stone arch of the window kept giving him the impression that they were sleeping in a church, somehow desecrating it.

'She said that she was afraid for Nell, that she and Hugo were like two people in the same skin; yin and yang, she said. At the time I assumed she meant that they were opposites, which they are. Hugo's confident, Nell's timid; Hugo's strong, Nell's delicate; where he's an optimist, she's always been the pessimist. Now though, I think that she meant something more; I think she meant that Nell couldn't exist without Hugo. When he left for university, she was left unable to cope, as if half her body had been taken away.'

'Yet he, apparently, can exist without her.'

'As I said, Hugo was always the strong one.'

He considered what she had said. 'So having lost Hugo she went looking for support elsewhere . . . is that right?

'Apparently.'

'Did you know this Richard, the father of Tom?'

71

'No. He was a summertime casual – Tristan has to employ a lot of them when he opens the castle and grounds to visitors. Jeremy and I hardly got to know any of them.'

Yet Nell did . . . very well indeed.

'I wonder why she did it . . .' he said after a while.

'What do you mean?'

He couldn't really explain it very coherently. 'It seems odd, that's all. She misses Hugo so she has sex with a part-time worker on the estate. It's hardly a substitute for the emotional support she was presumably craving.'

'You make her sound promiscuous.'

'Many people would say that having sex at the age of fourteen or fifteen is a pretty good definition of "preco-ciousness", if not "promiscuity",' he pointed out.

'I'm sure it wasn't like that at all.' Once again he heard Helena erecting barriers against his implied criticisms. 'Presumably it started out as friendship, but then got out of hand.'

Maybe. 'Still, it's clearly affected her,' he said, in a conciliatory tone. 'She's scarred.'

When Helena's reply came, it was pinned to the ground with sadness. 'The few letters that Theresa sent me never really went into the details; they were always fairly positive, concentrating on the good things. When I first saw her tonight I thought she was fine, but now I'm not sure.'

He said quietly, as if to himself, 'I wonder why.'

'What do you mean?'

'I wonder why Nell's so affected.'

Helena thought he was being obtuse. 'She had a baby at the age of fifteen! It's ruined her life!'

But Eisenmenger couldn't see it. 'Has it? This isn't the nineteenth century, and I don't see Nell condemned to life in the workhouse. She had a baby, but she's got a nanny, she's got her parents and she's got enough money behind her to mean Tom's no more of a burden than a pet would be.'

Even as he said this he was suddenly aware of how apposite the term was. They had only been in the house a few hours but he was already guessing that Nell had little to do with the day-to-day care of her son.

'You didn't know Nell before, John. She was always . . .

72

naive. She had had all the best things in life and I would guess knew nothing of the darker side to living. The pregnancy and all its consequences would have been devastating for her.'

He could see the sense of that.

So why did he suspect something deeper and darker behind it all?

Helena said, 'And Eleanor . . . God, she's grown so old.'

He murmured, 'But only "forgetful", apparently.'

Helena signed. 'And how.' A pause. 'I'm not wrong, am I? She's dementing, isn't she?'

'Fairly advanced dementia, I'm afraid.'

'Is there nothing that can be done?'

'There some drugs that can help arrest or slow it in the early stages, but I'd guess it's a little late for poor Eleanor.'

'They do realize, don't they? They must do.'

'Oh, I think they know.' He sighed. 'Although whether Eleanor does is another matter.'

'God, how awful.'

He could offer her little comfort and even that was flavoured with bitterness. 'In many ways, dementia's worse for those around the sufferer than for the victims themselves.'

Neither of them spoke again that night.

Part Three

'Helena?'

At the sound of her name she turned. Nell was dressed in a simple pale red dress without shoes or jewellery, without make-up. She was standing behind her a little way down the corridor. If anything she looked even more delicately enchanting than the night before. Once again, though, Helena saw sadness in and around her.

She smiled. 'Good morning, Nell.'

Nell came forward slowly. Her eyes seemed so large, so delicate, so aqueous; Helena found them fascinating, almost alien.

'I'm sorry about last night.' She said this penitently, nervously.

'Oh, that doesn't matter.'

'It was a shock, you see. I didn't realize what John did.'

'We should have warned you.'

'No, I was being silly.'

Helena felt huge relief; Nell seemed to have recovered from whatever malaise had affected her. 'Are you coming down to breakfast?'

'I've eaten.'

'Oh. Well, I expect I'll see you later.'

Nell smiled. 'We've got a lot to talk about.'

Tanner sat back in his chair and listened to Sauerwine's report; also in the office was CI Syme. When Sauerwine had finished, Tanner turned to Syme. 'Well, Chief Inspector?'

Both Syme and Tanner were thickset and tall; they looked as if they could make a good account of themselves; indeed, they looked as if they had had to do so on

74

more than one occasion. They might almost have been brothers, in arms if not in blood.

'Fifty-fifty,' Syme decided. 'You can't discount anything at this stage. It's going to depend a lot on what the pathologist says.'

Tanner asked of Sauerwine, 'When do we expect the report?'

'I'll push for it today but realistically not until tomorrow.'

Tanner said, 'Until then, you're to make no assumptions. None at all, understand?'

Sauerwine nodded.

'Do you need any more resources?'

He would have loved some more resources, but he knew better than to ask. 'No, sir. Felty and I can cope for now.'

Tanner nodded. Syme was impassive.

The kitchen was huge, a paradise for the domesticated. It was large and L-shaped, an Aga at one end, a split hob and electric oven at the other. One entire, long wall was smothered in cupboards, an island of worktops with a central sink in the broadest part of the room, two further sinks at either end. Although there was a large refrigerator by one of the sinks, there was also, it appeared, a walk-in cold room just off the kitchen. The table could have seated sixteen.

Helena had collected Eisenmenger and they came into the kitchen together to find Theresa sitting at one end of the table, a half-finished plate of toast and marmalade before her. She was reading *The Times* through delicate, almost spun glasses. Along one side of the table was a small boy, tended by a young, apparently late teenage girl.

At first sight Eisenmenger thought Tom delightful. He had curly brown hair and a thin, solemn face. His eyes were large like his mother's, although his nose was thinner, less snubbed. He was eating an apple that the nanny had cut into segments for him whilst sitting at the kitchen table, kicking his legs in the deliberate fashion that only small children possess. On his face was a frown, a frown that spoke of as much gravity as a bomb-disposal officer ever brought to his trade.

Theresa looked up; the paper, however, did not go down. She peered at them over her glasses, while from under them she sent a smile that was to Eisenmenger's eyes at best tentative. 'Ah, Helena. John. I trust you slept well?'

Helena smiled. 'Wonderfully, thank you.'

Eisenmenger, too, lied. 'Fine.'

Theresa turned to her grandson who had glanced at them but then decided that they were irrelevant to his present needs. 'This is Tom.' To Tom she said in a gentler, more intimate tone, 'Tom. This is Helena and John. Family friends. Do you remember we told you that they were coming?'

Tom looked at her, nodded, then turned again to Helena and Eisenmenger. He stared at them but didn't relinquish the frown, then he returned to his apple and the kicking. Helena felt as if she had been judged and found decidedly wanting.

Apparently satisfied, Theresa turned to the young girl. 'And this is Dominique, who helps Nell look after Tom.'

They both nodded and smiled and Dominique said politely if tepidly, 'Nice to meet you.'

'Dominique is French. From Lyons.'

That she was French wasn't obvious from her accent, only from her demeanour – a mix of self-assurance, disdain and disingenuousness that was as much a signature as an accordion would have been. She was exceedingly tall with very closely cropped hair and cheekbones that had been assembled so high they seemed to Eisenmenger to be almost unassailable, a biological equivalent of the north face of the Eiger.

Dominique, perhaps feeling that it would be appropriate to demonstrate her command of her duties, said, 'Please, Tom. Do not kick.'

Tom looked at her from a face that was petrous, as if he had forgotten how to rearrange it. It was, Eisenmenger noted, something of a fixture. The small boy said, 'I don't want this.'

'Yes, you do.'

This last came from Dominique and Eisenmenger found himself thinking that in classical Aristotelian debating

76

terms it lacked a certain gravitas; nor did it impress her interlocutor, who demonstrated proof of his proposition by throwing the half-eaten apple segment on to the table and shouting, 'I hate it! It stinks!'

'Tom . . .' Dominique's voice was clothed in a warning tone that brought out her accent but perhaps it was her youth, perhaps it was the slight Gallic tremor in the higher register that failed to impress her charge.

'Shut up!' he commanded.

Theresa took a hand, talking in a voice loud enough to drown out the protestation from an increasingly angry Dominique. 'Tom! I will not have you disobeying Dominique like this!'

She began to rise from her place, the menace of this magnified by the decidedly deliberate expression of anger about her eyes. Tom, apparently a wise as well as brave combatant, saw what was coming, made a rapid cost–benefit analysis and retreated into grumpy silence. Dominique saw her chance and came forward to crouch down beside him. 'There, there, my brave little man. Here, let me help you.'

He allowed her to pick up the apple segment and put it in his mouth without further vocal protest, but all the time he was staring at his grandmother from lowered brows. Theresa smiled at him, then turned to her guests. 'Toast? Cereal? We have a selection of cereals – mostly ones that Tom likes, but I think that there's some muesli somewhere . . .'

Helena opted for fresh fruit, Eisenmenger for the muesli, which was a mistake as it was stale. Dominique helped them get settled by finding things. By the time they were sitting at the table, Tom had had enough. He pushed the plate away and pronounced, 'Finished.' From where Eisenmenger was sitting this seemed to be a bit of an exaggeration since a good thirty per cent of the fruit remained unchewed and undigested, but Tom wasn't waiting for external quality assessment.

He pushed the chair back with a loud, raucous and really quite distressing noise, then got down from it. He didn't ask to leave the table and didn't wait for argument. Helena caught a flash of irritation crossing Theresa's face but nothing was said. Dominique called after him, 'Do your teeth, Tom. Then we will go for a walk.'

She cleared his things from the table, throwing the remains of the apple down a large chute in an outside wall, and putting the crockery into the dishwasher. When she had departed, presumably to supervise dental cleansing operations, Theresa said, 'She's not as good as the last nanny.'

'He seems to be quite a handful.'

Theresa looked at Eisenmenger. 'He is no more boisterous than any other boy his age,' she suggested, albeit in the kind of tone normally reserved for admonition.

He had come across a particularly argumentative Brazil nut that would not be overcome and so did not immediately reply. Eventually, 'I'm sure. But it must be difficult for someone so young and presumably inexperienced in childcare.'

This attempt at mitigation carried little weight in the court of Judge Theresa Hickman. 'She does not appreciate that at Tom's age, negotiation and discussion can only go so far. I have told her this, but she has somewhat . . . Continental views.'

Be thankful she hasn't yet introduced him to underage drinking and that distressing French attitude to sex . . .

Helena said, 'I saw Nell in the corridor. She seems fully recovered.'

Theresa consumed toast and marmalade the way a small garden bird consumed stale bread. Her head jerked forward while the food was held completely still. Her teeth closed upon the corner, her lips retracted slightly, and then she jerked her head back. On each occasion, only a small amount of food was actually ingested. Perhaps, Eisenmenger reflected, it was a chewy piece that she had in her mouth when Helena said this, for she was a long time in mastication and subsequent swallowing of the morsel. 'Oh, yes. I suspect she was merely tired.'

Eisenmenger asked, 'Is Tristan at work?'

'In London. Some emergency.'

'The College presumably takes up a lot of his time.'

'He's up there at least two days a week – sometimes three or more. It really is very inconvenient because on those days he's rarely back before ten. Still, after today he should be home until after the New Year.'

It was at this point that Eleanor entered the kitchen. She walked surprisingly well, with an upright, almost haughty demeanour. When she saw Eisenmenger and Helena, though, she halted and her face began to assume first a puzzled, then a near-affronted outward appearance. She opened her mouth but before she could articulate her questions Theresa said quickly, 'It's Helena and her partner, John, Mother. Remember? They arrived last night.'

They were inspected, her eyes darting from one to the other from a face that retained a suspicious camouflage. 'Oh, yes,' she decided at last, although the intonation was false and her face suggested that this was a lie. There was a noticeable lag before she said again, 'Oh, yes,' this time with somewhat more believability. She advanced purposefully towards them and to Helena she said with a smile, 'How are you, my dear? It's been such a long time.'

Theresa interrupted irritably, 'Are you having breakfast this morning?'

Eleanor looked at her. 'Of course!' This was petulant. 'Why wouldn't I?' She moved to the table and sat down in the chair recently vacated by her grandson. 'Where's Tristan?'

'He's working today.'

'And Tom?'

'Doing his teeth.'

These answers – delivered in a tone that was elevated by an octave's worth of impatience – apparently satisfied the old lady. Theresa rose from her place and asked tiredly, 'Your usual, Mother?'

'Of course.'

Eleanor's usual, it turned out, was porridge. Helena had finished her toast and felt impelled by the atmosphere to take her things from the table to the dishwasher. Theresa was throwing oats into a saucepan and slopping milk on to them. Helena said to her quietly, 'Can I help?'

She was met by a fixed, furious look and a terse, 'No.' Things began to melt quite rapidly at this moment and she repeated, 'No.' Then, 'Thank you, Helena.' Next she managed a smile. 'I'm sorry. Not much of a welcome for you.'

Helena returned the smile. 'That's all right.' She hesitated before adding, 'I thought you had a cook.'

'Ha! I wish we did.' She turned back to the porridge that she had put on the Aga and stirred it. 'Mrs Castleman comes in for special occasions only. The maid was her daughter. We can't afford to employ them full time.' She said this as if admitting to reusing the teabags or that her husband had an unhealthy interest in female farm animals. 'Dominique helps, of course, but I do most of the donkey work.'

Eleanor, sitting at the table and staring suspiciously at Eisenmenger said suddenly in a loud voice, 'Where's Malcolm?' He found it rather disconcerting that she continued to pin him with her gaze as the words came forth.

Over her shoulder Theresa called, 'Working, I expect.'

'He didn't come to see me last night,' grumbled Eleanor.

She said this to Eisenmenger as if he would be sympathetic and, ever playful, he responded, 'Does he see you every evening?'

'Oh, yes. Every evening. We discuss the estate. Malcolm always tells me what's happening; asks me for my opinion on what should be done if there's a problem.'

Over the swirling porridge, Theresa smirked. 'Good old Malcolm. He handles her better than any of us.'

'When he comes in, tell him I want to see him.'

Theresa sighed. 'Yes, Mother.' To Helena she said softly, 'To a great extent, Malcolm keeps Mother out of our hair.'

The porridge was beginning to thicken.

Eleanor told Eisenmenger loudly, 'He doesn't do a thing without asking my opinion.'

Theresa smiled. She lifted the porridge off the hotplate and found a bowl in the cupboard, then poured it in. While Helena took the pan and poured cold water into it, Theresa served the porridge to her mother-in-law.

'It's hot,' she warned, before fetching milk and sugar.

Eisenmenger picked up the milk. 'May I?'

Eleanor stared at him for a moment, engendering the impression that she suspected him of deep and deadly nefariousness, before nodding. 'Thank you.'

He began to pour. 'Say when.'

She giggled, then, 'When!'

'Sugar?'

'Just a spoonful.'

At the sink Theresa said to Helena, 'Eleanor has always been a flirt.'

'And John Eisenmenger's no better.'

For the first time that morning Theresa seemed to Helena to gain positivity and lose defensiveness. She laughed and then asked, 'What are you going to do today?' It was clearly a genuine interest.

'We haven't thought about it. What do you suggest?'

Theresa considered while she cleaned the viscous, faintly unsettling residuum of porridge from the inside of the stainless-steel saucepan. 'I'm afraid I can't spend much time with you. I've got a committee meeting this morning and then I must do some food shopping.'

'No problem. Perhaps we could go into Melbury, have some lunch there.'

'Well, if you do, avoid the teashop by the war memorial – they've had the health inspectors in there on three separate occasions.'

'Oh, I see.'

'Rats. They blame the pig farmers – pigs attract rats, you know – but I think that's just an excuse.'

'Thanks for the tip.'

'If Malcolm's got some free time, I could ask him if he'd be willing to show you around the estate. Renew old haunts. I'm sure he wouldn't mind.'

'That would be nice. Perhaps Nell could come with us.'

Theresa betrayed uncertainty. 'I'm not sure what she's doing.' Then, as an afterthought, 'She might be waiting in for Hugo. He'll be arriving this afternoon.'

Helena nodded. 'Of course.'

'Right. The rule is we treat this as murder until it's proved otherwise, okay?'

It was okay with Felty. She followed Sauerwine into his office and shut the door behind her. He sat at his desk but forgot to invite Felty not to stand. 'Only when I find proof positive that there was no one with the motive or the means to murder the poor bastard will I entertain any other assumptions.'

'Yes, sir.'

'What about Leicester? Any news?'

'Nothing good, I'm afraid. The given address was a rented one-bedroom flat. The local boys contacted the landlord but Mr Moynihan had left two weeks ago. No forwarding address.'

'Did they search the place?'

'Nothing.'

Sauerwine had been a detective long enough to accept that this was the norm; perhaps one in twenty leads proved fruitful, the rest a mix of the irritating, boring, bizarre and inexplicable. 'How long had he lived there?'

'Three years, give or take.'

'Did the landlord remember where he came from?'

'No.'

'Plan B, then.'

Felty looked at him uncertainly. 'Sir?'

'Contact all the local dentists to see if Moynihan was a patient.'

Felty nodded, the seriousness of her expression a poor disguise for her confusion. Kindly Sauerwine explained, 'Identification, Constable.'

This didn't help.

'When we finally unearth some relatives, we can hardly show them the deceased and ask them if we've got the right body, can we? Neither diplomatic nor productive. So we're forced to turn to other methods of ID. DNA is possible but problematic unless we find some article of Moynihan's that we can be sure belonged to him and that's got hair or some such attached to it. The alternative is dental records.'

Enlightenment blossomed in Felty. 'Hence the dentists.'

Sauerwine nodded. 'Hence the dentists.'

'But what if he didn't look after his teeth?'

'Then we'll be forced to rely on belongings – never very satisfactory. Too easy to fake.'

Felty, learning all the time, was committing this to memory. Sauerwine then said, 'Have you done the usual checks?'

The look of alarm told its own story.

'Databases, Felty, databases. He's already on one – the NVLA – and chances are he's on a few others. Check with Social Services, Criminal Records and the Passport Office. We've struck gold if he's got a passport or a criminal record. Then we'll at least have a photograph to use.'

She made notes.

Something else occurred to him. 'First, though, I want

you to get over to the hospital. I want the preliminary autopsy report as soon as possible. Preferably today.'

'And if it isn't ready yet?'

'Make Dr Addison's life hell. Think you can manage that?'

She grinned at him.

'Right,' he said. 'While you're doing that, I'm going to ask a few questions in the village. See if anyone might know anything about our Mr Moynihan there.'

He stood up and went to the door where his overcoat was hanging. Following him out Felty asked, 'Is that likely, sir? Maybe he was just passing through.'

Holt was sitting at one of the four desks in the room, typing with surprising speed at the computer, his face a portrait of concentration. His premature baldness might at that moment have been due to cerebral overheating. Sauerwine said, 'We're assuming this is murder, remember? That means the first place we start looking is close to where he died, until we have evidence to indicate we should look elsewhere. That's part of your job.'

They passed down the narrow corridor and the front office where Sergeant Jackson was talking to one of the squad cars, his corpulence well displayed as he bent over the microphone.

Outside in the cold, whiplash wind Sauerwine paused and turned to her. 'You did all right last night. Can't have been easy for you. First one, and everything.'

She had been in the police long enough to be surprised by the compliment. 'Thank you,' she said, genuinely gratified.

He smiled, then reached out to pat her hand. 'Free tonight?' he asked. 'No headaches?'

She shook her head. 'None at all.'

'Excuse me.'

There had been a time when Sauerwine would have called these words diffidently, but life as a policeman had quickly ground such finer feelings out of his mind, at least when dealing with members of the public.

The public.

He was sworn to protect them yet they hated him and, in truth, he hated them. On an individual level, he could

83

live with them – even genuinely liked some of them – but on a general, anonymous level, there was nothing but mutual hostility.

This morning's labours had failed to prove that he was wrong. He had visited every house in the vicinity of the site of the death, exploring an ever expanding circle, and at last he had reached Westerham village itself. Once there he had headed directly for the only pub.

'Yes?'

The man was heaving metal casks out of the back of the Dancing Pig. He had weaselly features and a thin frame off which the striped shirt and dark blue jeans hung like the cast-offs of a scarecrow.

'Are you the landlord here?'

The man was breathing heavily. He had on thick, turquoise gloves and a glistening layer of sweat. Having made a great show of sitting on one of the casks, he looked around the beer garden. It wasn't a bad beer garden – not one of the small, tatty affairs that affronted the Trades Descriptions Act – and it had a decent expanse of grass, several garden tables and a small play area at the end. Turning back to his interlocutor he said, 'Yes. Are you the nosy parker here?'

Holding his warrant card in front of him, Sauerwine advanced from his position at the gate in the fence. He was still a good three metres away when the man said, 'Oh, police.'

Sauerwine smiled. 'That's right. Police.' The word was bandied between them as if it were profanity. 'DI Sauerwine. What's your name?'

The other smiled. 'Sour wine? What kind of name is that?'

'A crap one.'

This brought forth a laugh. 'Amen to that, brother.'

Sauerwine sighed. 'Your name, please.'

The attitude had previously been cagey; now it became positively imprisoned. 'Why?'

There are few things better designed to irritate a policeman than recalcitrance.

'Because I asked.' Sauerwine had stowed the warrant card but continued his advance. 'Do I know you?'

The drop of the head struck Sauerwine as lubricated by guilt but the denial was immediate. 'No, I don't think so.'

'So what's the name then?'

The head returned to its previous position. 'The name's Dowden. Jack Dowden.'

Sauerwine didn't think he was being fed a diet of unadulterated truth but let it ride. 'And you're the landlord here?'

He returned to his barrels, rolling them along the concrete to stand them in a line by the back wall of the pub. 'I said so, didn't I?'

It was cold and there was a vicious wind whipping around the side of the pub; Dowden might have been warm through his manual work but Sauerwine was cold and becoming colder. 'Do you mind if we go inside, Mr Dowden?'

Dowden however did appear to mind, or at least his face gave little sign of joy at the thought. 'Why?'

'I want to talk to you.'

Sauerwine estimated that Dowden was in his late fifties. He had a publican's paunch but he was obviously strong and gave the impression of power. He carried on shifting barrels while Sauerwine looked on and quite deliberately said nothing at all. Eventually Dowden had his casks ship-shape and Bristol-fashion and only then did he grudgingly say, 'Okay.'

He led Sauerwine through a back door into a large square room filled with yet more casks, some of which were connected to clear plastic tubes. From here they went into the area behind the bar. Dowden lifted the bar to let Sauerwine through to the parlour.

'It's very snug.'

Dowden shrugged. 'What of it?'

Sauerwine sat down at one of the tables and indicated that the landlord should do likewise. Dowden asked, 'So what's this about?'

'Can't you guess?'

Dowden appeared to consider. 'Dunno. Underage drinking? Can't be me licence – I only renewed it last month.'

Sauerwine said nothing for a moment. 'You know, I'd swear I've seen you before, Mr Dowden. Are you sure we haven't met?'

Dowden smiled but in a grim, unamused fashion. 'I'm pretty sure I'd remember *your* name.'

But Sauerwine had a memory for faces and names and he had an ear for a lie.

'Last night there was a vehicle fire on the edge of the Westerham estate. A man died in that fire.' He paused, waiting for Dowden to react; it proved to be a wait in vain for Dowden's face remained inscrutable. He was liberally tattooed, not all of them professionally done.

Prison?

He continued, 'The car was an old red Toyota. Have you seen such a car around here?'

'No.'

'Any strangers been in recently? Say in the past two weeks?'

'No.'

The name of Dowden was nagging at him. Not Dowden, but . . . what?

'Has anyone mentioned seeing any strangers, or having seen an unfamiliar red car?'

'No.'

'You're not being very helpful, Mr Dowden.'

Dowden shrugged. 'I haven't seen or heard anything. I can't be more helpful than that.'

Sauerwine tried a different strategy partly at least to gain time while he tried to nail what was bothering him about Dowden. 'You don't like the police, I think.'

Another shrug. 'I don't like 'em, but I don't dislike 'em either.'

'And how long have you been the landlord here?'

'Two, nearly three year.'

'And before that?'

'Look, what is this? I thought you were interested in the car fire.'

Sauerwine smiled. 'I'm interested in people who don't want to co-operate with me, Mr Dowden.'

Dressler.

The name appeared almost as if conjured; something from nothing, breaking the laws of thermodynamics.

Dowden – or Dressler (*Jim Dressler. Part-time bouncer and heavy for whoever would hire him. Got his knuckles burned when he acted as an accessory to armed robbery.*) – said uneasily, 'I am co-operating. I 'aven't seen anything.'

Sauerwine began to relax. He looked around the minute parlour; it was a nice country pub, he thought. He could see himself coming here when off duty. Perhaps he could bring Felty . . .

He returned to the landlord. 'Do you know what I'm going to do now?'

Uneasily the reply came. 'No.'

Sauerwine leaned forward. 'I'm going to go and check your licence to run this place. See what name it's in.'

'What do you mean?'

'Well, I'd be interested to find out whether the name on it is Dowden . . . or Dressler.' He smiled and kept his eyes on the landlord.

'Dressler?'

'Jim Dressler, wasn't it? Four years for accessory to armed robbery. If you kept your hands clean, you'd have been out, what, about three years ago.' He stopped. 'Now there's a coincidence. That's when you took this place over.'

Dressler did not have a face that might be described as handsome, but it now took a turn for the worse and the result would not have disgraced the side of a cathedral. He said quietly, 'Fuck you.'

Sauerwine lost his smile. 'No, I fuck you. Convicted criminals are not allowed to run licensed premises – but then you knew that, didn't you? Hence the false identity.'

Dressler looked as if there was a fifty-fifty chance that he was going to grab hold of Sauerwine and make liver pâté out of his slightly immature features, but after a few moments he leaned back in his chair and took a single but very deep breath. 'There doesn't seem much point in denying it, does there?'

'None whatsoever.'

Dressler stood up. 'Drink? It's on the house.'

'No, thanks.'

Dressler went to the bar and poured himself a large whisky, the optic shaking as he rammed the glass violently up against it. Back at the table he said, 'Okay. What do you want?'

'I've told you. Co-operation. A bit of thought before you answer the questions, for a start.'

The whisky was attacked. 'And if I do?'

Sauerwine didn't seem to follow. 'Well, let's just concentrate on "if you don't", shall we? I think you ought to keep that in mind for the time being.'

87

More whisky met its end.

Sauerwine asked, 'Now. Have you seen an old red Toyota around the village?'

Dresser said simply, 'Yep. Turned up about ten days ago, I reckon.' Sauerwine refrained from saying what he was thinking. 'How many people were in it?'

'I only ever saw the one.'

'Can you describe him?'

He grimaced. 'I never saw him close up.'

'He didn't come in here?'

'Nope.'

There was no other pub in the village. Sauerwine had pinned much hope on this lead.

'Can't you give me any description at all, Mr Dowden? Or should I say Dressler?'

The publican snorted a faint laugh, smeared a sour smile across his face. 'He looked to me to be getting on. Maybe sixty-ish. Short grey hair. A lot of stubble.'

'How tall?'

'I only ever saw him in the car.'

'How was he dressed? Smart? Scruffy?'

'From what I saw, scruffy. Definitely scruffy.'

'And you'd never seen him before?'

'Nope.'

Sauerwine might have looked young and innocent but he had learned enough in his years as a policeman to treat no hostile witness with anything other than sadism. Dressler was a hostile witness and he was hanging over a very deep precipice held only by a cheesewire tied around his scrotum. Accordingly Sauerwine sighed, smiled and leaned forward. In a confidential but superficially amicable tone he said, 'Are you quite absolutely, certainly, confidently sure of that, Mr Dressler?'

Dressler looked into his face, then down at his glass and found it lacking in whisky. When he looked back up at the detective his face bore an expression that Shakespeare (had he been supping a whisky chaser in the bar) might have described as 'much discomforted'.

'Yes.' There followed a pause as if he were giving birth to some sort of deformed monster before, 'But I know he used to live here.'

Sauerwine's attention was suddenly snagged. 'Really? When?'

But Dressler couldn't, or wouldn't, say.

'Yet you know he used to live here. How?'

'I was told.'

Sauerwine had begun to take a very faint liking towards the landlord of the Dancing Pig, but this proved ephemeral. He said, 'Okay. That's the way you want it.' He looked around. 'Must have been a good job, this. I can't understand why you want to give it up.'

Dressler was staring at him. His lips began to shape a sound that might have been, 'Why?' before the penny dropped. 'Oh.' Then, 'One of my regulars. Chap by the name of Michael Bloom.'

Sauerwine noted the name. 'And where can I find Mr Bloom?'

'At the petrol station. He manages it.'

Sauerwine smiled. 'Thank you.' He stood up. 'I'll get along to the petrol station.'

As he was leaving the publican asked from behind him, 'What will you do?'

Sauerwine turned. 'About what?'

'About this. About the licence.'

Sauerwine stared at him; on his face was a perfectly composed expression of puzzlement. He then smiled to indicate that small change had dropped. 'Nothing, Mr *Dowden.*'

Slowly Dressler's face, previously a study in anxiety, relaxed and gratitude – or at least the closest approximation his physiognomy could manage – made a flamboyant entry with all sorts of flourishes. 'Oh! Oh, good. Thank you, thank you . . .'

Sauerwine was outside the door when he suddenly stopped and turned and caused Dressler to pull up suddenly. 'I'll tell you what I *won't* do, though. I won't forget, Dressler. I won't forget.'

He gave forth the smile again, then walked away.

Sauerwine stopped the car about fifty metres from the petrol station. He put in a short call to Jackson, then waited; Jackson came back on the radio about five minutes later and Sauerwine smiled, only then starting the car and driving the last short distance to the forecourt of the petrol station.

It was shabby and run down, two of the pumps out of order, the signs proclaiming this fact being grubby and blowing in the wind because they were poorly secured. There were newspapers, bags of coal, bags of wood kindling and bunches of browned flowers outside the small shop. Sauerwine parked by the air pump, then walked into the shop.

It smelled of hot grease because there was an oven on the counter in which brown and fat-soaked sausage rolls, pasties and pies were displayed in bright lights for his delectation; they looked as far past their sell-by date as the flowers. The man behind the counter was of pensionable age and smartly dressed. When Sauerwine approached him he smiled and said, 'Can I help you, sir?'

Sauerwine didn't bother with official identification. He returned the smile and said in a casual tone, 'I hope so. I'm looking for Michael Bloom. I was told he works here.'

Sauerwine half expected the old man's smile to fade and his attitude to change but it didn't. Instead, 'I think he's in the bungalow, sir. He's not due on until early afternoon.'

Sauerwine looked across at the ugly red-brick bungalow that the old man had indicated. It was situated on the opposite side of the forecourt, square and squat and charmless. 'Lives there, does he?'

The old man nodded, exhibiting a degree of guilelessness that was so unusual Sauerwine was beginning to feel guilt about asking him questions. 'He's my boss.'

'Worked here long, have you?'

'Only a week. It's just a part-time job, to help with the pension.'

As Sauerwine left the shop he said, 'It's been a pleasure. Hope the job goes well.'

And he meant it.

He knocked on the door of the bungalow, noting that the garden was untended, the paintwork around the windows flaking. No response. He knocked again, this time with more force, more authority, but it still took a long five minutes for the door to open.

The face that peered out was looking at him from more than sleep. Fully dressed but clothing rumpled, almost screwed up. Sauerwine's mind was wondering things as he asked, 'Mr Bloom? Michael Bloom?'

There was a slow blink. There was no answer, however. *Drink? Drugs? Drink and drugs?*

'Mr Bloom. Can I have a word, please?'

His hand was reaching for the warrant card in his breast pocket when the other came suddenly alive. His eyes caught something behind Sauerwine and without a word he pushed past, out on to the short path through the weeds, apparently oblivious of his bare feet on the cold, damp ground. Sauerwine turned and saw him striding purposefully on to the forecourt of the petrol station. He began to shout.

'Hey, you! Fuck off!'

His quarry was a shambling figure, poorly dressed and carrying a bright red shopping bag. If it heard him, it made no sign.

'How many times do I have to tell you? Fuck off and don't come back.'

He reached the figure and gave it a push that sent it sprawling on the tarmac. Sauerwine raised eyes to the clouded, grey skies and ran to intervene. When he arrived, Bloom was standing over the sorry bundle, shouting and digging into it viciously with his unshod heel. 'Get up, you old bastard! Get up and piss off!'

Sauerwine put his hand out to restrain him whereupon Bloom spun round as if he had been electrocuted. His face was one of fury, the unfocused dislocation of Sauerwine's first meeting with him entirely gone. 'Get off me, will you?' He looked ready to hit out.

Sauerwine held up his hands. 'Hey. Calm down. Police.'

Bloom's mouth opened, his head retracted slightly and there was noticeable reduction in tension. The figure on the floor groaned.

'Who's that?'

Bloom shrugged as if to suggest that he didn't know, which was neither particularly helpful nor particularly credible. Sauerwine squatted down, put his hand on the top of the back, feeling the dirt of the fabric; the shape shifted, trying to get away. 'It's all right. I'll help you.'

There was a short pause, then the hunched shape became less defensive. There was a distinct odour in the air, and one that was not borne on the wind from lands afar; in fact, Sauerwine began to wish that a wind from lands afar would begin to blow quite strongly. He glanced up at Bloom who was edging away, moving from foot to foot as if regretting his rash decision not to invest in footwear. 'Where do you think you're going?'

Another shrug.

'Well, stay there until I say otherwise.'

Bloom put his arms around himself, and began to shiver but he did as he was told. The shape on the ground was now on hands and knees, more obviously a human and not an oversized hedgehog. The odour hadn't improved, though. Sauerwine put a large amount of air in his lungs, buried his desire to keep his hands in his pockets, and reached out to help what was now demonstrably an old man to his feet. It took a bit of heaving but this was eventually achieved.

He was unkempt, with longish grey hair and a beard covering skin that was veined and rough; his eyes were watery and dark, his hands were nicotined around the red shopping bag as if welded to it.

'Are you okay?'

But he was blessed with no reply. Instead the other began at once to move away, head down and turned away from Bloom.

'Excuse me? Sir?' But he might as well have been addressing the back of the odour that was also departing. Rubbing his hands together, as if to eradicate uncleanliness, he tried once more but without greater success.

He turned to Bloom who was grinning sourly. To the unspoken question, Bloom said, 'Don't bother. He's not worth it.'

'Worth kicking, though.'

'Yeah, well . . .'

'Who is he?'

'Just a tramp. Hangs around here. The customers don't like it.'

Neither do you, apparently.

'Where does he live?'

'Fuck knows.'

Sauerwine looked at Bloom, unsure. The poor sod clearly was a tramp, but the reaction had been so severe . . .

He dismissed the speculation for the time being. 'Okay. Let's get indoors.'

They walked back to the bungalow, Bloom by now so chilled that he was nearly sprinting. The interior of the house was no more appealing than the exterior. Amongst old tabloid newspapers, empty takeaway cartons, beer cans and men's magazines, Sauerwine found a seat in a chair that was clear; not clean but clear.

Bloom remained standing, looking for a cigarette packet in a jacket hung over the back of a chair. On the chair was a toolbox. Sauerwine remarked with heavy sarcasm, 'Nice place.'

The cigarette packet located, Bloom replied through a cloud of blue-grey smoke, 'Thanks.' He made no sign that he had noticed the implied insult. 'What do you want?'

'I'm DI Sauerwine. I'm looking into the death of a man in a car fire near here.'

'Oh, that . . .'

Sauerwine saw him slightly relieved, as if there were other things that the police might come calling about.

'We think you might have known the man.'

Surprise, apparently genuine. 'Me? I doubt it.'

'His name was Moynihan.'

And this elicited a marked reaction. 'Bill? You're joking!'

Sauerwine said that no, he wasn't joking. Bloom found a seat opposite him, smoking thoughtfully, shaking his head. 'I don't believe it,' he said slowly. 'I just don't believe it.'

'We're not yet totally certain, but that's the theory we're working on at the moment.'

'God!' He took another breath of smoke. Then, 'What happened?'

Cautiously Sauerwine said, 'I'm waiting on the autopsy report, but in the mean time I'm trying to find out a little more about him, which is where you come in.'

He didn't allude to the fact that as things stood Bloom was his likeliest suspect, assuming that this was murder.

'What do you need to know?'

'How long have you known William Moynihan?'

'Years.'

Surprised, Sauerwine repeated the word. 'Years? But we understood that he'd only just moved down here from Leicester.'

'But he used to live here, then moved away.'

'How long ago?'

Bloom made a face. 'Dunno. Maybe seven, eight year.'

'And then he pops up here again? All of a sudden?'

'Yeah.'

There was something that Sauerwine thought odd in his behaviour around this answer, something shifty. 'He didn't say why he'd come back?'

'Nope.'

This was too final, too contrived. Sauerwine moved gingerly around to try another direction. 'When he was here before – where did he live?'

'Cottage on the estate.'

Bingo!

'He worked for the estate?'

Bloom nodded.

'What kind of work?'

'All sorts. Forestry, fencing, clearing the covers, helping out with the drives.'

'So Malcolm Groshong would have known him?'

Bloom laughed. 'I reckon he might have done. After all, he was practically his deputy.'

Sauerwine felt a warm glow of interest. Suddenly Mr Groshong struck him as a man worthy of his most ardent attention.

'So why did he leave?'

Bloom had finished his cigarette and now found another before replying. 'Some sort of bust-up. Never told me the details.'

Sauerwine digested this. 'Yet he comes back after all these years.'

'That's right.'

'Did he make contact with Malcolm Groshong? Was he looking for his old job back?'

'Wouldn't say.' This with a shrug.

'So what did he say?'

But Bloom claimed ignorance. 'Something about some unfinished business.'

With Groshong? 'Which cottage did he live in?'

It took him a few moments to recall it. 'The old farrier's place, I think. On the Melbury road. It's gone now, though; Hickman had some scheme to build light industrial units. Arts and crafts, that kind of thing.'

'So when did you last see him?'

Another shrug, this time embellished with a scowl. 'Day or two ago, I reckon.'

'Where?'

'In Melbury. He was staying there.'

'Where and when, precisely?'

A deep sigh followed by a monotone of, 'In the Crown, two evenings ago.'

Sauerwine reserved judgement on whether he believed this or not. He then asked hopefully, 'Did he tell you where he was living?'

He didn't expect to strike lucky, the delight therefore all the greater. 'Lodgings in Wilson Street, off the high street. He pointed them out to me.'

'Number?'

'Fourteen, I think. House with a blue front door. Fucking awful decoration.'

Suddenly Sauerwine was feeling elated; he was still wading through treacle, but it was thinning rapidly with the heat he was supplying.

'Did Moynihan have any family that you know of?'

'He might have had a sister somewhere. I never saw her though.' This was produced uncertainly.

'Might she have lived in Leicester?'

Bloom didn't know.

'Did he wear jewellery? Any earrings, finger rings, body piercing?'

Bloom looked surprised. 'None that I ever noticed.'

The negatives were piling up again. 'What about his car? It was red, wasn't it?'

Bloom smiled. 'Yeah. Nothing but a bloody wreck. Had it for years.'

Sauerwine's interest reared up again. 'Years? You mean he had it when he was last here?'

'Oh, yeah. Standing joke, it was. It was a wreck then, so Christ knows how he managed to keep the thing going for so many years.'

Yet Groshong had failed to recognize it . . .

Sauerwine stood up. 'Thank you, Mr Bloom, you've been most helpful.'

'No problem.'

Sauerwine smiled as he then said, 'But if I see you treating anyone else like you treated that poor sod out there, I'll have your backside in the nick before you can blink. What is it so far? Two counts of assault and one of actual bodily harm, I think.'

Bloom's face darkened, and Sauerwine saw fists form. He advised quietly, 'I wouldn't.'

He waited a moment before walking away into the hall and then out of the door. He didn't look back as he walked across the forecourt but was aware of Bloom watching him, was also aware of the scrutiny of the old man behind the counter of the shop.

Sauerwine decided to buy a paper. As he handed over the money, the old man said, 'Are you police?'

'What of it?'

'I saw you stop him kicking Albert.'

'Is that his name? Yes, I stopped him. He doesn't seem to like poor Albert.'

'He can't stand him. If ever he sees Albert, he goes after him.'

Sauerwine smiled slightly. 'Well, I've marked his card. He might think twice about it in future.'

The old man handed over his change. 'I doubt it,' he said. 'He'd like to see Albert dead. He's said as much a lot of times.'

'Why? What on earth has that poor old sod done to him to make him hate him so much?'

The old man's reply came from nowhere.

'Albert's his dad. Bloom reckons he killed his mother.'

Melbury was small and crowded. It wasn't obviously a tourist trap in the seaside, cockleshells-and-crap-memento way, but it might have been designed for the purpose of enticing human beings; a hint of things that had never existed but that everyone remembered. There were winding lanes, oak beams, an ancient church and ancient hills in the background. There were tearooms and almshouses and even a worryingly unselfconscious town crier. Because of the time of year the winding lanes and shops were fairly empty but it was easy to see that during the spring and summer months there would have been tourist hordes to fight through. Only the estate agents, the building societies and the convenience stores spoiled the ambience, reminding visitors that this was the modern, horrid world and not the Austenian dream that it seemed to be.

Helena and Eisenmenger wandered around, visiting the

things that tourists visit, doing the things that tourists do for an hour or so, then found an unvermined teashop in which to take lunch. It didn't taste too bad either, although Eisenmenger could not keep from his mind the words of a microbiology lecturer at his medical school who had pointed out that it was not in the interests of food-poisoning organisms to impart a bad flavour to food.

Having exhausted the delights of Melbury, they then decided to return to the castle to take up Theresa's offer of a tour around the estate. The drive back took about fifteen minutes; as they pulled into the forecourt, they saw that Malcolm Groshong had just arrived before them. As they got out of the car he called across to them, 'I'm told you want a tour of the estate.'

The tone suggested that he didn't entirely approve of this idea.

'If you're busy . . .'

'I'm not,' he declared, much as a small child might deny having done something naughty behind the bike sheds.

Eisenmenger looked at Helena but she was looking at Groshong. She said, 'It really is very kind of you.'

He made a noise that was half a grunt, half a sigh, then said, 'We'll go in the Land Rover. That thing won't be any use.' He indicated Eisenmenger's Audi, a car of which the pathologist was rather proud, then turned and began walking away, thereby missing Eisenmenger's expression of shocked indignation. Helena, moreover, found this unaccountably amusing.

Helena sat in the front passenger seat, Eisenmenger behind her. Groshong, wearing his shabby waxed jacket and ancient brown cap, started the engine and then put the Land Rover into gear. When he pulled away it was with a jerk that sent gravel spitting backwards and his passengers into the severely distressed upholstery. Their speed as they drove along the path that led to the visitors' car park rapidly reached fifty miles per hour and Helena glanced back at Eisenmenger to see him grinning in a fixed, embalmed manner, proffered him a wink, then turned around again.

To Groshong she said, 'How long have you worked on the estate? Twenty years?'

'Twenty-eight in May.'

She turned once more to Eisenmenger. 'You see, John? There's nobody better to give us a guided tour.'

He smiled and said nothing. Groshong's expression remained fixed but it soon became apparent that his foot was lifted slightly on the accelerator and his whole demeanour loosened slightly, even if he still looked as if he had bitten into a rancid sheep's eye. Eisenmenger was left to wonder at Helena's abilities in savage breast-soothing.

They had passed quickly through the car park, then turned right and were now driving along a road with a high stone wall to their right. On their left they passed scattered cottages, a cricket ground and fields dotted with copses. They passed into Westerham village with its small, triangular pond bounded by tarmacked lanes, a church, the Dancing Pig pub and various picturesque cottages.

About half a mile on the other side of the village, with the road ever-curving to the right, the stone wall was broken by a padlocked metal gate. Groshong pulled in before the gate, then got out, fishing in the pocket of his jacket for a large bunch of keys. It took him a couple of minutes to locate the correct one and then he had a tussle with the lock before it opened. Having pushed the gate back, he got back into the car and drove forward.

'Shall I lock it behind us?' asked Helena.

Groshong seemed surprised as if he had not considered that anyone else would be able, or perhaps willing, to do something for him. 'Thank you.'

When she was back in her seat, Groshong drove forward on to a mud track that ran through thick woodland. It was wet and splashed with half-frozen puddles. Despite its unevenness, Groshong soon had the Land Rover back up to speed; Helena and Eisenmenger were bounced around accompanied by an orchestrated cacophony of a gear-changing engine, springs squeaking and joints rattling. When she glanced back at Eisenmenger, who was prone to seasickness, she saw a pathologist who was clinging to the back of her seat and most decidedly suffering.

The path began to rise. They were in dense forest, so that the mid-afternoon sunlight formed tattered, slanted misty shafts across from their right, and the visibility was soon lost in the gloom of trees around them. The wings of

98

the car were whipped by ferns and creeping shrubs as they passed.

After about twenty minutes, the ground began to level off and the trees to thin. The track curved to the left, then, quite abruptly, Groshong slowed the car, turned sharp right and stopped. They found themselves on the bank of an expanse of water.

'You'll remember this,' said Groshong.

'Westerham lake.'

'Aye.' For the first time that afternoon – indeed, since they had arrived – Groshong seemed to be truly happy, even contented, and Eisenmenger could understand why.

'I can't believe it!'

'I realize that it's a shock . . .'

'I thought he was so nice. I mean, I wouldn't have let him past the front door if I'd known . . .'

Sauerwine closed mental eyes but, with colossal effort, kept the physical ones open while holding a rising irritation well back behind the starting line of the vocal cords. 'No, Mrs Gleason. You don't understand . . .'

Be that as it may have been, Mrs Gleason was not interested in Sauerwine's opinion of her comprehension of the situation. She continued in a voice that was pickled in prurience, 'I wouldn't have had a man like that as a lodger if I'd known. Now I come to think about it, I always thought there was a dark side to him . . .'

She seemed to have ended, certainly she trailed off into contemplation, but before Sauerwine could speak she proclaimed, 'I run a respectable establishment. I won't let it out until I have a month's rent in advance, you know.'

Sauerwine was used to this kind of thing in witnesses, especially those that were of an age and of a sociological grouping. Mrs Gleason was small and nature had done its usual job of amassing lipids around much of her frame, so that her bosom heaved quite visibly with a slightly noisome concoction of shock, excitement and delight. Felty, to judge from her expression, wanted to put Mrs Gleason straight on a few points but Sauerwine, a little more versed in the ways of the strange beast that was the public, felt no such urge. Mrs Gleason would believe what she wanted to believe, and she would propagate those beliefs to her confidantes (in fact to anyone who passed into her orbit) no matter what he or Felty said to her.

Thus, having tried twice to correct her, he now said only, 'Did Mr Moynihan pay by cheque, by any chance?'

'Yes.'

'Have you paid it in?'

Mrs Gleason met this unexpected challenge with a disproportionate amount of fluster before rising from her armchair to make her way to the sideboard. There then followed a large amount of rustling and mumbling in the three drawers before she turned back to her visitors, a look of deep, deep concern on her face.

'I must have done.' She might have been confessing to an inadvertent hit and run. Her face was creased with concerned folds.

'Don't worry, Mrs Gleason. We can always contact the bank.'

'Was it important? I didn't realize . . .'

'Really, no. Come and sit back down.'

Looking at him as if she didn't quite believe that she was free from retribution she did as he bid, so that she faced them nervously as they sat on a sofa that had fallen victim to fashion long ago. They were surrounded by china figurines which might have been cheap and nasty, might have been hideously expensive, neither Felty nor Sauerwine could tell.

'So, you first saw Mr Moynihan on the sixteenth, is that right?'

'Yes, I think it was. It was the day that Mr William went to the vet.'

There followed a silence, one that on Mrs Gleason's part was contented, on the part of her loyal and attentive audience was beyond baffled as they wrestled with strange images. At last Felty enquired, 'Mr William?'

'My Siamese. I've had him twelve years, which is a good age for a Siamese.' She lowered her voice. 'They don't live as long as other cats.' This confidence was followed by a look around the cluttered, over-ornamented room as if afraid that she might have been overheard. Then, 'I named him after my first.'

Felty and Sauerwine exchanged covert glances. What was the woman talking about? Thankfully neither of them had to respond as she then said, 'My departed husband.'

She didn't, however, explain her use of the word 'first', which puzzled them since she had been a widow seemingly for ever; neither the Inspector nor the Constable felt strong enough to request explanation. Shrugging off this frankly frightening glimpse into Mrs Gleason's mental workings, Sauerwine went on, 'Can you describe him?'

She considered deeply, as if trying to dredge through decades of memories, as if she had not laid eyes on Mr Moynihan for half a lifetime. 'He was quite tall.'

'How tall?'

'Taller than me.'

This didn't help. Mrs Gleason would have required a stepladder to change the light bulb in her bedside lamp.

'Over six feet?'

More consideration until, reluctantly, 'Yes. I would have said so.'

Felty duly noted this down as Sauerwine, grasping at what he hoped was the beginning of a thread through Mrs Gleason's meandering thoughts, asked, 'Can you remember if he wore any jewellery? Rings, that kind of stuff?'

The well-worn ritual followed. There was a small cuckoo clock on the wall behind her chair that ticked quietly in the background. Felty began to count the ticks between question and answer. Eventually, 'He had a signet ring, I think.'

'Which finger?'

More ticks were counted. 'His right hand. Little finger, I think. My William used to call it the "pinkie", which I always told him was rude . . .'

She smiled in happy memory and no one dared ask if she had been referring to a conversation with the cat or the husband.

Felty had brought with her a clipboard that she now picked up from the floor by her side. In its plastic pocket was a selection of photographs and from this she brought forth one to show to the witness. 'Could this be the one?'

Mrs Gleason leaned forward and took it to peer at through thick-lensed glasses from red-rimmed, slightly yellowed eyes. 'It could be,' she said, but there was a clear suggestion that equally it could not be. Felty took the photograph back, feeling more disappointment than Sauerwine who had suspected that Mrs Gleason would be true to form.

He asked, 'Did he have any visitors ?'

Surprisingly she was quite definite. 'No. I don't like my lodgers having people in their rooms, so I always ask them to entertain only in the sitting room, and he never did that.'

'Did he spend a lot of time in his room?'

'Oh, no. He was a man of regular habits. He used to come down to breakfast at eight, then leave the house at about a quarter to nine, even at the weekend. I said to Mr William at the time it's almost as if he has a job.'

'Did you ask him? If he had a job, I mean.'

'He said that he was looking for work. He said that he worked on the land.'

'Do you know where he was looking for work?'

She didn't. 'There's lots of places around here where he might have found such work.'

'He didn't mention the Westerham estate?'

Being asked for detail brought back the sudden deceleration in processing power as Mrs Gleason tried to remember. 'He may have done,' she decided at last.

'And he had a car, I take it.'

'Yes. A red one.'

'Can you remember what make it was? Perhaps the year . . .?' Even as she enunciated the syllables Felty was acutely aware that she was asking Mrs Gleason to do something akin to reciting the value of pi to fifty places.

'I'm sorry . . .' Then, 'But it was a bit shabby, I thought. Mr William . . .'

Sauerwine, perhaps unkindly, felt that whether it was the quadrupedal or bipedal Mr William, he didn't need to know. 'Did he mention that he once worked here before? About eight years ago?'

She shook her head. Sauerwine tried. 'Did he mention where he'd come from?'

'He said from the north.' She sounded rather contrite about this, as if she had failed in her duty as nosy old biddy.

Feeling lost in a maze that was constructed entirely of dead-ends Sauerwine tried to establish a feeling of forward momentum. 'So he went out every morning. What time did he return?'

'Six o'clock. I always have tea ready for six. I tell my lodgers that if they want to eat at night, then it's got to be

102

six. I like to be in bed by nine and I get indigestion if I eat too late . . .'

'Every night, he came in at six?'

'Yes.' Then, 'Except, of course, last night . . .'

For an alarming moment Sauerwine thought that she might begin weeping, but she held it in check with great fortitude. He asked, 'Did he usually go out again?'

'More often than not.'

'Do you know where?'

'The pub, I expect. Mr William used to do that, regular. I didn't mind, because it gave him something to do. Better than sitting in front of the television all night.'

Felty was fairly sure they were discussing the husband here but, since it wasn't entirely relevant to the investigation, she didn't press the point. 'Do you know which pub?'

Mrs Gleason didn't and there were at least half a dozen pubs in walking distance of her home in Melbury. Sauerwine continued, 'What time did he get back?'

But she didn't know. 'I'd be asleep. He never woke me, though. He was very good like that.'

'What was his mood like? Did he seem morose at all? Sad? Depressed?'

She considered this but only briefly and apparently not too deeply. 'Oh, no. Nothing like that. If anything, he was quite cheerful, I think.'

And that seemed to be that, except for the room. Sauerwine explained, 'We need to see his room now.'

'Oh! Oh, yes.' She jumped up eagerly. 'Come with me.'

The remainder of the small house was marginally less cluttered. They ascended the staircase and turned left to stand in line on a small landing. Behind them was a bathroom, in front of them was a box room, while to their right were two closed doors.

'That's my room,' announced their hostess from somewhere around Sauerwine's midriff. She indicated the back bedroom, as if warning them against even thinking of looking inside it. 'This is the room I rent out.'

The door opened to reveal a spartan room with a single bed behind the door, a dressing table under the window, a wardrobe and a bedside table. The contrast with the rest of the house was shocking. Mrs Gleason began to enter but Sauerwine said at once, 'I'd rather you didn't.'

She stopped, turned and displayed affrontedness. Before she could verbalize this he explained, 'We really must insist that as few people as possible go in there until we've had a chance to look it over.'

She still looked decidedly unhappy and this was made only worse when he asked, 'You haven't been in there, have you?'

'Of course I haven't! I give my lodgers complete privacy!'

He smiled. 'Of course you do. I knew you would.' He then squeezed past her, followed by Felty who had been donning disposable gloves. Mrs Gleason fell back slightly, as if dazed. Felty smiled reassuringly at her as the door was closed upon her.

For thirty or so seconds she stared at the plain painted-ness of the wood. Then she sighed and made her way back down the stairs, shaking her head and muttering. Mr William had come in through the cat flap and she hurried to greet him, although she was rigorously ignored for her pains.

The cuckoo clock announced that it was three o'clock as only a cuckoo clock can.

Inside the bedroom, and in an unconscious imitation of Mrs Gleason's breathing patterns, Sauerwine sighed deeply. 'I'm having flashbacks. I used to have an aunt like that.'

'I rather like her. She's a survivor.'

Sauerwine didn't trust himself to answer. He turned to look again around the room. 'I don't think that this is going to take long.'

'Hasn't exactly made his mark on the room, has he?'

Felty gave Sauerwine some gloves and they began to pan the sediment of a life for gold.

They found precious little, but they also found a little that was precious.

William Moynihan had been living an ascetic life in Mrs Gleason's front bedroom. No books, no magazines, few personal possessions. They were delighted to discover a comb on the dressing table and this, in a well-practised ceremony, was deposited in a sterile bag that was then sealed and labelled. They pulled back the sheets and blankets on the bed (the bed had been made but in a desultory fashion) and found nothing, as they did when

Felty peered under it. In one of the three drawers of the dressing table were three pairs of dark grey socks, two white vests and three pairs of underpants, also white; in the second was a thick, dark green jumper; the third contained a driving licence, a cheque book and a small and tatty leather wallet that contained a single bank card. All these documents were collected in sterile bags and then sealed. They then turned their attention to the wardrobe where they found two shirts, clean but not ironed, a single pair of trousers, neither cleaned nor ironed, and a suitcase. They took this out, opened it and discovered a single thick envelope. There was no writing on the envelope and it was crumpled and folded and clearly old. Sauerwine took it over to the bed and emptied it.

A bundle of banknotes, bound by an elastic band.

A watch.

A photograph.

While Felty counted the notes, Sauerwine examined first the watch, then the photograph.

'Five hundred and thirty pounds. Some of it's old notes, though; no longer legal tender.'

Sauerwine was barely listening. The watch was a lady's gold watch, clearly expensive. On the back was an inscription: *From Claude to Penelope – a token*. There was something vaguely whispering at the back of his head. He turned his attention to the photograph; old and tatty but still clearly showing a middle-aged couple, seated upon a bench in some gardens somewhere. It had been taken in the summer. The man was thin but with a wide, attractive grin; the woman was holding his hand with a rounded face and deep laughter lines. Something else whispered to him.

'Sir?'

He turned his attention to Felty. 'What is it?'

'Are you all right?'

'Of course. Why?'

'You looked . . . I don't know . . . ill.'

He dismissed this. 'Don't be stupid, Felty. Bag this lot, okay?'

Their search thereafter was short and unrewarding. The final few days of William Moynihan's life had been simple.

When they descended the stairs, stripping off their

gloves and trying not to appear too intrusive in this small house of an old and gentle woman, Mrs Gleason came out of the living room. Behind her there came the sound of afternoon television. Sauerwine smiled at her. 'Thank you very much, Mrs Gleason. I hope we haven't disturbed you unduly.'

Mrs Gleason, though, did not wish quite yet to relinquish her foothold in their romantic, exciting world. Somewhat incredulously she asked, 'Don't you want a statement?'

It wasn't strictly necessary. She had nothing to tell them. Yet, Sauerwine had seen too many policemen leave too many people disillusioned with the police. 'Someone will call around in the next day or two to talk to you, Mrs Gleason.'

They actually reached the front door before her next salvo.

'What about the room? I suppose I shouldn't go in there . . .?'

As he opened the front door, Sauerwine said gravely, 'Absolutely not. It's a crime scene. Nobody must enter it.'

He walked out, followed by both Felty and Mrs Gleason's open-mouthed gaze.

As they reached the car, Felty asked, 'Wasn't that a bit cruel?'

Sauerwine laughed. 'On the contrary, I've made her day.'

Theresa, unpacking the shopping, was taken by complete surprise when Hugo walked into the kitchen and said calmly, 'Mater!'

He had on his face a huge grin that was piercing cheeks ruddied by the cold. His left hand held his gloves while he unzipped his jacket with his right.

'Hugo!' Theresa put down the multipack of tinned tomatoes and went at once to embrace him, her expression mirroring his. Then, pulling slightly away she said, 'You are naughty. You nearly gave me a heart attack.' There was more than a touch of scold in her words.

He laughed then stooped to kiss her gently on the cheek. 'Not you, Mother. You've got the heart of a lion.'

'I'm as tough as old boots, you mean.'

'That too.'

She frowned in mock anger. 'Now, that's enough. You weren't supposed to agree, you know.'

He bowed his head in repentance. To show that he was forgiven she asked, 'How was Christmas? Not too busy, I hope.'

'Fairly bloody. Not exactly relaxing, at any rate.' She made a face of commiseration. He asked, 'What about yours?'

'Fine.' Then, just in case he took offence, 'We missed you.' She hugged him again. 'It's so good to see you.'

He accepted this with something that the disinterested might have interpreted as tolerance. 'So, how are things?'

She opened her mouth but at that moment the back door opened and in came Dominique with Tom.

'Hello, Dominique.' Hugo had a large smile on his face that he now turned to his nephew. 'Hello, Tom my old lad. How are you?'

Tom didn't answer but not because he wasn't clearly delighted to see his uncle. His face broke into a huge smile and he rushed forward to be picked up. 'Good grief, Tom! You've grown huge!' He turned to Theresa. 'What have you been feeding him, mater? Fertilizer?'

Tom giggled. He said excitedly, 'Uncle Hugo! You've come!' Then, with an artlessness that only a child could manage, 'Where's my present?'

Hugo laughed. 'Present? What present? Why should I give you a present?'

'It's Christmas!'

Hugo shook his head. 'No,' he pointed out. 'It *was* Christmas. That's all over now. You missed the boat, old chap.'

Tom's eyes began to grow at once large and round. It might have been that tears were about to appear, except that anger seemed to overtake them and with astonishing speed he began both to howl and to beat his uncle on the chest. Hugo began to laugh but Dominique stepped forward and began admonishing her charge. 'No, no, Tom! You must not do this!'

Hugo, still laughing, said, 'Oh, don't worry.' He put Tom down, then grabbed his arms by the elbows. 'I was only teasing, Tom. Of course I've got a present. I've got you a wonderful present. We'll open it tonight, okay?'

These words of hope broke through the tantrum and Tom's anger subsided. 'Really?'

Hugo laughed. 'Really,' he reassured him.

Theresa said rather sternly, 'You shouldn't tease him, Hugo. He's at a very excitable age.'

Hugo brushed this off. 'Nonsense, mater. It's what uncles are for.' To Tom he said, 'Where's your mummy, old chap?'

Tom shrugged. It was Dominique who said, 'She has gone for a walk. She did not feel well this morning.'

He asked of his mother. 'So how has the lovely Nell been?'

Theresa said as cheerfully as she could, 'Fine . . . fine.' Her eyes were on Dominique who was getting a drink for Tom. Inexplicably, Hugo found this interesting as well. He said absently, 'As I said, how are things?'

'You won't have heard of course, but there's been an unfortunate *incident.*'

The emphasis did at least save this curiously offensive euphemism from complete crassness. Dominique began to rinse out some of the crockery while Tom drank orange juice.

'What does that mean?'

She explained about the body in the car while he watched Dominique from across the kitchen table. He had strikingly dark eyes set in a face that was long and thin, and that bore a noticeable resemblance to his father. A deep frown now scored furrows into his forehead. 'Oh, gosh. How awful. Burned to death in his car. Unlucky sod.' The sentiment was spoiled by callousness. Then, 'But I don't see why everyone's so miserable. It isn't as if he was family, whoever he was.'

'No, but you must see how horrible it's all been.'

He snorted. 'You should do my job. Only this week I had to deal with a chap who'd had a cricket stump stuck up his arse . . .'

This striking image caused even Dominique to glance up from her work. Theresa looked at Tom who rather liked cricket and who was now staring interestedly at his uncle. To Hugo she said, 'Not now, darling.'

He grinned and winked at Tom.

In a clear attempt to change the subject Theresa said,

108

'Nell will be pleased to see you. And of course Helena's here, with her partner.'

He stopped in the act of unlacing his shoes. 'Gosh, yes. I'd forgotten. Helena! After all these years.'

'She's been ill.'

'Yes, I remember. Breast cancer, poor cow.'

'She hasn't fully recovered, so we must all treat her with TLC.'

'Absolutely.' He said this with great earnestness.

It was beautiful. They were facing a sun that had begun its descent towards the twilight of the west and that was thrusting a lance of dancing, broken light towards them. The water stretched away to a dark shoreline that swept back towards them on left and right in a gentle curve. There were numerous waterfowl either on the water, on the bank or in the air. The wind blew complex patterns on the surface of the lake.

Groshong switched off the engine, then got out, with Helena and Eisenmenger following. It was cold but the air was clean and the scene was so perfect that nothing else mattered. A duck quacked, away to their left.

Groshong said, 'We had it dredged about five years ago, then completely restocked with trout. We make a good income in the season from the fishing rights.'

'How big is it?' asked Eisenmenger.

'Two kilometres from east to west, one from north to south.'

'We used to have picnics here. Go swimming, although I remember it was always cold.' Helena shivered, although it wasn't clear whether it was due to the cold she remembered or the cold she now experienced.

Eisenmenger couldn't stop himself asking, 'Did you ever build a pirate ship?' Groshong either didn't hear or didn't choose to react but Helena gave him a glare that would have withered an oak tree.

She turned to Groshong. 'Isn't there a path that leads up here from the castle? We used to use it rather than drive to the lake.'

'Aye. From the north terrace. It comes out over there.' He pointed to the far right. 'It's a long walk and it's pretty overgrown now.'

Eisenmenger saw a sweep of sadness pass across Helena's face, as if the neglect of the path signified the loss of the past, the loss of happiness.

Groshong said suddenly, 'Okay?'

They climbed back into the Land Rover. Groshong reversed it about twenty metres to a point where the track was wide enough to turn. He then accelerated away from the lake and Eisenmenger was once again forced to attach himself to Helena's seat. His discomfort was only increased by Groshong's unexpected swerve to the right, apparently off the track and into the undergrowth. In the front, Helena was faced with ferns and branches no longer just whipping the sides of the car but occasionally lashing the windscreen. The ride became even more violent.

Groshong said calmly, 'This track isn't used very often.'

Helena wasn't certain but she thought that she heard Eisenmenger moan softly.

After about five minutes the way ahead cleared and Helena could at last verify that they were indeed following a path and not acting as pioneers.

'Where are we going?' she asked.

Groshong seemed to ride the rough movements rather as a rodeo rider might ride an untamed steer. 'Old Man's Sorrow.'

Eisenmenger was having a torrid time but he looked up at that. 'Pardon?'

'Old Man's Sorrow.' Slightly louder.

Eisenmenger, no wiser, was too diffident to ask for further elucidation of his darkness but Helena said, 'It's a small heath on the very edge of the estate.'

They were again beginning to ascend but this time it was rapidly steepening. The very first hints of the end of the day reached down to them through the tangles of branches above. The trees began to thin, at first gradually and then more haphazardly, sometimes increasing noticeably in number, sometimes fading to small clearings. Eisenmenger's ears became blocked until he swallowed. He felt the cold that was outside the car.

They emerged on to an open expanse that was steeply inclined and painfully exposed. The path continued across it, eventually fading out towards its centre, and it was here that Groshong eventually slowed and then turned the Land Rover to face down the slope.

'Oh, yes,' whispered Helena in a tone that was awe-struck, happy and sad all at once. 'Of course, I remember now.'

And even Eisenmenger could see why. They were now high on the side of the hills that bounded the estate to the north, looking south with the whole of the estate before them. The lake was a grey mirror near the foot of the hill, surrounded by the browns and greens of the winter woodland. The castle rose from this carpet, struck by the yellowing sun from the right so that long grey tendrils of shadow reached away from it. The colour of the sun perfectly complemented and enhanced every colour before them, forcing a glow from the stone, a life into the dormant woods, a brightness on the surface of the water.

Groshong got out without saying a word, just standing in front of the car. When Helena and Eisenmenger joined him, they formed a line and for a long time no one spoke.

'It was your mother's favourite view.'

Helena glanced sharply at Groshong as he said this. She said, 'I didn't realize. I remember we used to come up here for walks, but I didn't know that . . .'

She suddenly shivered and Eisenmenger, usually impervious to such matters, actually noticed and put his arm around her. Groshong looked down at the ground; he was standing close to a rabbit hole but it didn't seem to be a particularly interesting rabbit hole.

Eisenmenger asked, 'Why's it called Old Man's Sorrow?'

And suddenly Groshong was back to his intemperate-ness and it was with some asperity that he enquired, 'You see that mound?' He was pointing to the left where, in the centre of a large hollow, there was a definite slight protu-berance. 'That's said to be his grave.'

He began to walk towards it and of course they fol-lowed. At the edge of the hollow he stopped and looked down at it. 'His name was Ebenezer Barlow. He lived up here, but it wasn't much of a living in those days. A few sheep, a few vegetables. He married this girl – much too young for him – was bound to end in misery.'

The way he spoke suggested that he was of the opinion that all frivolities ended in misery, and a good thing, too. 'She became pregnant by another man, then left him, taking everything he had. He hanged himself from that tree.' He pointed at the dead remains of a tree that over-looked the hollow with its tomblike, central mound.

All this was sad and depressing enough for his guests but Groshong then went on with a grimly enjoyable air, 'Some say that he used barbed wire.'

'Well . . .'

Groshong shrugged. 'But then that's the kind of thing people would say.' If it was an attempt to lighten the gloom that had settled, it failed; the place was beautiful but now it seemed damned. Helena said, 'Can we go? I'm getting cold.'

'Hello, Nell.'

But Nell didn't answer, at least not with words. Her eyes grew large, her mouth opened and she took in, and held, a deep breath; she looked stunned. Then she squealed, her face seemed to erupt with joyous light and she stood and rushed across the room to her brother. 'Hugo!'

He took her in his arms. 'Surprise!' he whispered. Then, having embraced her, he held her at arm's length. 'How are you, Nell? I've seen Tom. He's become a feisty little chap.'

'Oh, Hugo, it's wonderful to see you. Christmas was such a drag.'

'Well, we'll have to make sure that the New Year's a little better then, won't we?'

'How long are you staying for?'

He smiled. 'Five days.'

'Only five?'

This time he laughed. 'I've got patients to look after, Nell. People are relying on me.'

Her smile was sad. 'What about the people here? What about *me*?'

Another laugh. He was still holding her shoulders but he transferred his right hand to her face; he stroked her cheek with the back of his index finger. '*You've* got Mum and Dad.'

She was nearly crying. 'Perhaps they're not enough.'

'Now, now. Enough of that.'

She buried herself in his chest. Her next words were muffled by tears. 'I've missed you, Hugo.'

He pushed her away but in a gentle way so that he could look at her face, see the wetness. 'And I've missed you, Nell. So let's make the best of the next five days, eh?'

She smiled and then nodded.

Felty, accompanied by Oram, drove the car on to the wide gravelled forecourt in front of the main entrance to the castle. It was just after six thirty and dark and freezing. The castle above them was partially illuminated by floodlights so that the light brown stone glowed and the curves of the turrets and the right angles of the crenellations made weird, non-Euclidean shapes that twisted away, as if passing into unknown dimensions. It would have been impressive in daylight but the frost-filled night and distorted perspectives produced by the lights made it breathtaking.

Oram said, 'I reckon I could get used to living here.'

'You wouldn't like the heating bills.'

When they got out of the car, the gravel felt strange and muted beneath the soles of their feet because it had frozen into an uneven mass. The car dashboard had told them that the outside temperature was six degrees below but even that seemed to be a woeful underestimate of the chill.

Before them was a long stone portico that was as much a cloister as a porch. It was so tall that when they looked up it was as if they were peering into deepest space, a darkness that was relieved by weak, yellow light bulbs hung in a line like lonely suns. Felty noticed a few moths, presumably well dressed in thermal underwear, flying around them.

The double doors were massive and without a letterbox. Oram, keen to leave the uniformed branch, was into observation and it was with a certain degree of exhibitionism that he asked, 'I wonder where the postman sticks his mail?'

'I expect he has to knock and tug his forelock.'

The bell push was copper and covered in verdigris. When Felty pressed it she heard nothing. They waited for what seemed like an age, their perception distorted by the cold and the fact that they couldn't be sure that anyone inside knew they were there. The cold was seeping into Felty's feet and she began to shift her weight.

'I presume it's a long way to walk.'

The wait continued.

The opening of the door was a shock, unheralded by any sign that it was about to occur. A pretty young woman, no more than twenty, stood inside. 'Yes?'

Inevitably the warrant cards were produced. Over hers, Felty said, 'DC Felty and Constable Oram. We'd like to see Tristan Hickman, if possible.'

The cards were examined, in the style that was always used; squinting eyes, slight incomprehension. She looked into Felty's face. 'I do not know. He has only just come in . . .'

'It *is* important.'

The young woman was uncertain but Felty had created a sufficiently compelling aura of authority by her tone, her documentation and the fact that she was edging irresistibly forward that she yielded. 'Please, come in.'

She stood aside and they stepped up and into the castle.

They found themselves in a large entrance hall that was cluttered with all manner of manorial things – suits of armour, ancient but elegant furniture, oil-painted portraits and a baronial fireplace. The woman said, 'Follow me, please.'

She led them through the hall, weaving a path past a grand piano, a host of ornaments and a stuffed bear that looked decidedly pissed off to be forever in aggressive upright pose facing a particularly fine example of Meissen. At the end of the hall they ascended a flight of stairs, turned first right along a gallery, then left into a corridor taking them deep into the castle. They eventually ended up in the room in which Eisenmenger and Helena had enjoyed champagne the night before.

'Please, wait here. I will see if Mr Hickman is available.'

She left them to admire the sumptuousness.

Oram said, 'Bloody hell. Wouldn't mind giving her one.'

Felty sighed. 'Really? You do surprise me.'

'I wonder if she's unattached.'

'I wonder if she finds you as repulsive as I do.'

'She's foreign.'

'Is she?'

'Didn't you hear it? They can never quite get the word "Mister". French, I'd guess.'

'I didn't know you were such an expert.'

He shrugged to suggest that there were many things she didn't know about him. Then, satisfied that he had upstaged his colleague, he began to look around the room. On the table where Tristan had the night before poured champagne he found a Chinese puzzle box made of jade. He might not have been so nonchalant had he been aware of its price – or more accurately its pricelessness.

Felty examined a picture of a grand nineteenth-century gentleman with so much facial hair he seemed consumed by it. 'I wonder who he is.'

Oram looked up. 'An ancestor, I suppose.'

Felty felt it was time to reassert the natural order. 'I *know* that, Oram. I meant, who specifically.'

Oram came and stood beside her and they both looked hard at the portrait, as if intensity of gaze might compensate for ignorance. Eventually he shrugged, 'Dunno.'

She turned away. 'Whoever he is, he probably still stalks the corridors at night, having his way with spectral serving girls.'

The door opened and in came a late middle-aged, distinguished-looking man in a light blue sweater over a shirt and tie. He had on his face a welcoming smile. 'Sorry to keep you.' He advanced into the room. 'Tristan Hickman. You wanted to see me.'

Felty did the thing with the warrant card. 'I'm Detective Constable Felty; this is Constable Oram.'

'Felty? What an interesting name.'

'Only if it's somebody else's.'

Hickman bowed his head. 'I apologize. I didn't mean to be rude. Please, sit down.'

He indicated chairs around the large coffee table. 'What can I do for you?'

'We're here because of the fire.'

'Of course. What a terrible thing! I understand someone died.'

Felty said merely, 'It happened just on the edge of the estate.'

'So Malcolm told me.'

Felty knew that Sauerwine wanted to know about Groshong but she had been charged only with seeing

Hickman. 'Might I ask where you were at about six o'clock last night?'

Seemingly surprised by the question, Hickman said, 'I was driving back from London. Got back here about seven fifteen.'

'And you left London when?'

'At five.'

'Is there anybody who could verify that?'

It was clear that Hickman was experiencing increasing consternation. 'May I ask why that is thought to be necessary?'

'We need to find out where the relevant parties were when the fire occurred.'

If Felty thought that was a reasonable explanation, Hickman was quick to debate the point. 'Relevant? Why am I considered to be "relevant"?'

'The fire did occur on your land –'

'I own a thousand acres, for God's sake! Am I to be considered responsible for everything that occurs within the boundaries of the estate?'

'No –'

'Then I don't see why you are interested in my movements. I have no connection with this death whatsoever.'

'How do you know?'

This simple interrogative tripped up Hickman. He opened his mouth then glanced between the two policemen. 'Well, I'm sure –'

Having wrested the initiative Felty drove forward. 'We believe the deceased was William Moynihan. Does that name mean anything?'

'No.'

'Are you sure? He worked on the estate some years ago.'

Hickman was shaking his head, a smile on his face. 'At times there are over a hundred people working at Westerham, most of them casuals. I'm afraid I rarely get to meet many of them.'

'Moynihan wasn't a casual. He was permanent. Worked as gamekeeper.'

Hickman was again silenced. Felty felt a surge of pleasure. She had watched Sauerwine produce such an effect but had never imagined that she might achieve it. True,

Sauerwine had coached her, but even so she felt that she was handling things well.

Hickman was reduced to a rather feeble, 'Oh . . .'

'So, you see, I was a bit surprised when you were quite so adamant that you'd never heard the name.'

'Yes, but –'

'And hence my interest in your whereabouts last night. I'm not accusing you of anything, but you understand that since the deceased had a connection with the estate, it's standard procedure to find out where people were when the death occurred.'

She looked at Hickman, eyebrows hovering. She had deliberately been preventing him from getting a word in until now. Hickman said slowly, 'Even if this Moynihan man did work for me as gamekeeper, it does not follow that I would know his name now. I'd be hard-pressed to give you the surname of the present gamekeeper.'

'But surely, if you're paying him . . .?'

'I leave the accounts to Malcolm.'

Felty nodded. 'Oh, I see.' She went on, 'Still, you could let me have the name and address of someone who will be able to verify your story about last night.'

Hickman conceded defeat. 'I spent all afternoon at the Royal College of Surgeons in Lincoln's Inn. I was chairing an emergency meeting of the College Council. It didn't finish until five. I can give you the names of twenty people who will vouch for me; amongst them are some of the most distinguished surgeons in the country. I trust that their word will be sufficient?'

'Just two or three will do.'

'Well, there was Professor Robin Fitz, Greville Hugh and Martin Curtis.' She saw that Oram was noting these names down.

'Thank you,' she said graciously. She looked around. 'You live here with your wife and children; is that correct?'

'Child. My son usually lives in Nottingham, although he has today arrived for the New Year.' This was delivered warily, as if Hickman were afraid of conceding too much more.

'Today?'

Hickman nodded. 'Not long ago, I think.'

'Could we have the names of the members of your family, please?'

Hickman complied.

'And who else is in the house? Who answered the door to us?'

'That was Dominique; she's the nanny. There is also my mother, Eleanor, and my eight-year-old grandson, Tom.'

'Anyone else?'

'Malcolm Groshong lives in an annexe on the east side of the house.'

'Does that have a separate exit?'

'Yes. It connects with the main house but it also has its own front door.'

'And, except for yourself and Mr Groshong, was everyone here at six o'clock last night?'

'They were here. We have guests staying.'

'Guests? How many?'

'Two. They've come for the New Year.'

'When did they arrive?'

'Yesterday.'

'At what time?'

Hickman frowned. 'I wasn't here, but I think my wife said that it was a little after six.'

Felty wasn't sure if this was relevant but she knew that she couldn't go wrong by collecting all the information that she was given. She had seen countless junior police officers bollocked for not asking enough questions. 'What are their names? I think that perhaps we may need to talk to them.'

But Hickman had gone back into obstructive mode. 'Is that necessary? I don't really like the idea of my guests being disturbed like this.'

Felty held back her urge to get stroppy. 'A man burned to death last night, Mr Hickman. Maybe it was murder, maybe it wasn't, but at the present moment, I'm operating on the assumption that it was. That means I don't really care whether or not you've got a problem with your guests being disturbed, Mr Hickman.'

Hickman took a deep breath in the course of which he made a decision. As the breath was exhaled he said with a broad smile and half a laugh, 'Of course, of course. I wouldn't want to be accused of obstructing the police.'

There was a pause.

'Their names?'

118

'Oh, yes. Miss Helena Flemming and Dr John Eisenmenger.'

Oram did his duty with notebook and pencil. He then looked up and before Felty could speak, asked, 'When are they leaving?'

Felty swallowed her irritation. Oram's had not been a speaking part as far as she was concerned.

Hickman, innocent of this departure from the plan, said, 'Epiphany, I think."

Which caused Oram some bother. 'I beg your pardon?'

Hickman smiled. Felty didn't but her enjoyment was at least as great as his. Their host said, 'The sixth. The day that the wise men arrived to pay homage to Our Lord.'

Much to Felty's delight, Oram assumed a delicate shade of pink and concentrated on his handwriting. Felty then asked, 'Are they here now? Can we talk to them?'

'I'm afraid not. They'll be in soon, I expect, but they're not here now.'

She decided that it could wait. 'Could I have a word with your wife, then?'

'She's preparing the dinner. Is it really necessary?'

Felty knew enough not to miss a target that was being so politely offered. 'Yes, it is. It will only take ten minutes, and then I'm sure we won't need to bother her again.'

Hickman was unhappy but shrugged. 'Very well.' He left them, rather huffily in Felty's opinion, to return just over five minutes later.

If Tristan Hickman had been somewhat defensive, his wife proved adamantine in her refusal to allow any quarter. She looked at Felty as if she were less a member of Her Majesty's Constabulary, more a contaminant in the air, an unpleasant odour that one can't ever get rid of.

'Could I just ask about your movements yesterday evening?'

'Movements?' The way this word was phrased suggested that Mrs Hickman considered it impertinent.

'Your whereabouts.'

This hardly improved relations. It was with a certain but plain displeasure that Mrs Hickman said, 'I was in all day. Preparing for our guests.'

'You didn't leave the . . . castle . . . at all?'

'No.' The way this was proffered, it was more a warning shot than an answer, a declaration of hostilities.

119

'Does the name William Moynihan mean anything to you?'

'No.'

'You're sure?'

'I told you. No.'

Felty retreated, feeling bruised and somewhat bowed. She said, 'Would it be possible to have a word with your daughter?'

Hickman and his wife exchanged glances. 'Look,' he said to Felty, 'is this all really necessary? None of us knows this man, even if he did once work on the estate. Unless you have some specific reason to link my daughter with him, I must decline your request. She is somewhat delicate and I fear that she would be upset by your questions.'

Felty suddenly felt that she had swum out too far, with the current in danger of taking her even further from safety. Should she insist? Before she could speak, before she could even consider this dilemma, Mrs Hickman weighed in, clearly a seasoned professional in the ring. 'Nor would it be appropriate to talk to my mother-in-law. She is sleeping and I do not wish her to be disturbed.'

Felty – battered by this onslaught and rapidly losing all her previous confidence – was reduced to an open mouth and wordlessness. Her condition was exacerbated by a casual glance at Oram that showed he was enjoying her discomfort. She said eventually, 'We *will* have to talk to them at some stage.'

'If you must, then I would suggest that you ring first and make sure that it is convenient.' Theresa Hickman would have been an effective barrier when the Mongol hordes came a-knocking.

Felty stood. In a desperate attempt to recover some dignity she asked, 'Well, I'm sure that you wouldn't mind if I talked to the nanny before I left.'

Apparently the nanny was slightly less delicate than members of the family. After a little hesitation there was an exchange of shrugs. 'Very well.'

They left and the girl who had let them in returned. She sat and looked at them nervously. Felty noticed that Oram was sitting up a little more, his whole demeanour suggesting that he would quite like to commit a few misdemeanours. She *was* attractive, Felty had to admit.

'Miss . . .?'

'Dominique. Dominique Renvier.'

'You're what? French?'

'Yes.' Felty somehow managed to miss Oram's smirk.

'And you're the nanny here.'

'Yes. I look after Tom. He is Nell's little boy.'

'How long have you done that?'

She considered. She was dressed in a white tee and tight black jeans. She was leaning forward, her face suggesting intense concentration, elbows on knees, frown on forehead. 'I think fifteen months.'

Oram suddenly found voice. 'You live here, do you?'

'Yes. I have a room of my own.'

Felty wondered quite why he wanted to know that. She asked, 'And last night? Were you here? Say, at six o'clock?'

'Oh, yes. I was bathing Tom.'

'What about before that?'

She said simply, 'I fed him.'

Oram asked, 'Where in France do you come from?'

'Nantes.'

Felty turned to her subordinate. 'Is that relevant?'

'It might be.'

She glared at him. To the witness she said, 'Does the name Moynihan mean anything to you?'

More deep consideration. At last, 'No. No, I don't think so.'

'You've never met someone of that name? Never heard it mentioned by anyone?'

'No. I don't think so.' Then a look of wondering horror made itself known. 'Was that . . .? Was that the man who . . .?'

'We think so, yes.'

She closed her eyes, shaking her head, muttering something in French. Felty glanced across at Oram. 'If my colleague has any further questions?' He gave her a grin. To Dominique Renvier she said, 'Thank you for your time.'

'You have finished? Mr Hickman said that I was to show you out . . .'

Oram was standing. 'I bet he did.'

As she was leading them down the stairs to the strange

and cluttered miscellany that was in the castle's entrance hall Felty asked, 'Are they a good family to work for?'

She halted at the bottom. 'Oh, yes. Mr and Mrs Hickman are very good to me. Nell, she is nice as well.'

'And Mr Hickman's mother?'

Dominique smiled. 'She is a very grand lady.' This was her only comment.

They threaded their way through furniture, suits of armour and small tables on which were assorted photographs. Felty noticed a family group and stopped to pick it up. She asked, 'Is that the son?'

Dominique came back to her. It was a group around a wooden table on a wide, stone patio. With Theresa Hickman were an elderly woman, a young girl and a teenage boy. It looked about ten years old to judge from Theresa Hickman.

Dominique looked then nodded. She turned away but Felty was enough of a detective to pick up that something about her had changed, that there was something amiss. 'What's his name?'

Dominique said, 'Hugo.' She hadn't turned back and therefore said this into the dimness in front of her. Beside Felty Oram was staring at the photograph. 'He's a doctor, too, isn't he?'

'*Oui.*'

Felty didn't know what it was, and she didn't know how she knew, but she was certain that here was something. 'How well do you know him?'

Dominique said with curious hesitancy, 'Not very well.'

She had already turned away and was walking to the front door before Felty could ask more. Oram smiled his most oleaginous smile at the nanny as she opened the door for them. '*Merci,*' he said in what he imagined was a perfect accent.

Dominique smiled. 'A pleasure.'

Felty walked out into the cold and the dark and those strangely determined moths.

Eisenmenger and Helena missed Hugo when they arrived back from their trip out with Groshong. They went straight up to their room without seeing anyone, unaware that the police were at that time entertaining their hosts.

They tossed a coin for the first bath, which Eisenmenger won and wasn't quite enough of a gentleman to concede.

'Don't be long,' she commanded.

'Why don't you go and get me a cup of coffee?'

'Cheeky sod.'

He laughed. 'Black with one sugar, please.'

She smiled and went down to the kitchen. It was as she was pouring the water into the coffee mugs that Hugo came into the room.

She looked up, surprise spreading across her face. She smiled, put down the kettle. 'Hello, Hugo.'

'Helena! You're looking wonderful!'

They advanced towards each other then embraced and there was a certain degree of embarrassment as they exchanged kisses. With a big smile he stepped back and said, 'You are absolutely stunning, Helena.'

'Thank you.' She bobbed her head in acknowledgement.

He sat down at the kitchen table and she sat opposite. There was a moment of silence during which he looked at her, almost as if he were making some sort of examination. She began to feel slightly awkward, as if he had surprised her in some nefarious deed or thought. She didn't know what to say. Eight long years of continental drift had separated them so that all she saw now was a vague recollection of what had once been; yet the distance played tricks. The memories were as false as childhood dreams and hopes and there was a heat haze in that separation so that the image of Hugo seemed to shimmer. She saw how easily he moved, how confidently he picked his way along the paths that he moved, and it disquieted her, as if she could not accept that any human being should be so self-assured. She saw in Hugo now the same person she had known as a child, yet she saw an entirely different one too.

An optical illusion.

One figure, when viewed from a different perspective, becoming something entirely different, almost completely opposite. Where as a child she had seen peaks and summits, now she seemed to see shadowed valleys, even crevasses.

'Mother told me about the body.'

'Yes.'

'Cast a bit of pall on the occasion.'

'A bit.'

'Not perhaps the best time to renew an acquaintance.'

'No.' She felt an idiot just chanting words but her brain seemed paralysed by the changed perspective.

'It's been a long time. Not just the eight years, but all those terrible things . . .'

'Hasn't it?' she agreed, nodding. 'Nobody's –'

'I just wanted to say,' he went on, seemingly ignorant of the fact that he was interrupting her, 'that I never got a chance to say how sorry I was . . . it was such an awful thing to have happened.'

'It's all right. You all had troubles of your own.'

'Nothing compared with yours, though. I know that Mum and Dad were really upset . . .'

'They did what they could, I'm sure.'

He paused, looking at her. 'You do know, don't you, that Nell and I would have done more, but Mum and Dad felt it best for us not to . . . get too involved. I was off to med school, and Nell . . . well . . .'

'I understand.'

He seemed to relax at this assurance, but it was a temporary thing. 'I don't really know how we managed to drift apart so completely, though. I hope you don't think . . .'

She found herself intrigued that he should be blaming himself. 'It wasn't your fault. I had troubles of my own. I didn't want to know anyone really.' It was what she always said.

'Troubles?'

She nodded hesitantly. She never talked about this; even Eisenmenger had barely managed to elicit more than tangential references. 'I suppose I had a sort of breakdown.'

She stopped, looked down at the table. He reached across to take her hand in his. She felt his palm to be dry and smooth, almost startlingly so. 'I'm not surprised, Hel. Anyone would have done.'

She shrugged. She wasn't just anyone, she seemed to be implying by this.

'Anyway,' he said, his tone suddenly more cheerful, 'it's in the past now. We can start afresh, as it were. Can't we?'

She had barely begun to nod before he continued, 'Look

how far we've come in life. Who'd have thought it, eh? Me a doctor, you a solicitor.'

'Both of us following in the family tradition.'

'I know. Pater's dead chuffed I've opted for surgery.'

'I can tell.'

'And you've got a medical connection, I understand. This chap, John. Is he a nice chap?'

'He is.'

Hugo shook his head, a sly grin on his face. 'Doesn't it bother you? Knowing where his hands have been? All that dead flesh, the blood and gizzards . . .'

She laughed. 'He doesn't bring the work home.'

A mock shiver. 'I should hope not. Do you check his fingernails?'

Again she laughed, this time feeling genuine happiness.

Suddenly he was serious, though. 'You're very special to me, Helena. I hope he treats you well.'

Surprised, she said nothing for a moment. 'He's been very good for me,' she said finally.

When she looked into his face, she wasn't sure at first what she saw. For a moment, she thought that perhaps it was jealousy, but then the grin returned and he said, 'Good! Where is he? Hiding?'

'He's upstairs. You'll meet him soon.'

'Fine.' There was a pause and simultaneously they both became aware that he was still holding her hand on the table. They looked down together, then up into each other's eyes. He squeezed gently. 'You've grown into a beautiful woman, Helena.'

He released her hand, the smile on his face warm and radiant. Embarrassed she said only out of politeness, 'Thank you, Hugo. And you are a very handsome man.'

His laugh this time was loud and exuberant.

'Lamb Dopiaza, please.'

Felty, who didn't actually like Indian food, was hesitant. She tried desperately to recall which dish she disliked the least but she had completely forgotten and the more she stared at the unfamiliar names, the further she fell from certainty. The waiter was attentive and not impatient, but she was aware that he did not have all night. This flustered her – she did not show it – but this in turn induced paralysis. Time became not only stretched and viscous but hypersensitized. The more she concentrated, the less she thought.

Was it korma or jalfrezi?

Eventually, 'chicken korma, please.'

This pusillanimous suggestion was greeted with haughty disdain by the waiter. He made no sign of this but by some supernatural means she was completely in tune with his thoughts. Sauerwine suggested, 'Mushroom bhagee, sag aloo, okay? What do you want? Rice or bread? I quite like Peshwari naan.'

It was only with a great effort of will that she decided, 'Peshwari naan would be nice.'

'Two Peshwari naan, please.'

The waiter departed, unimpressed.

'I thought we could take this opportunity to discuss the case.'

Do we have to?

'I realize that this is your first big case, so I thought that we might take some time out to talk things through.'

'Oh . . . I wasn't sure.' She had hoped not to concentrate on business, wanted to get away from it, but she saw sense in his suggestion.

'It's just not possible sometimes to consider things in a calm, quiet atmosphere at the station.'

He made it sound as if Newford police station were the centre of a wide and never-sleeping hubbub. This image contrasted bizarrely with the reality of a rural police outpost.

'So, what do you think?'

Exactly. What do I think? She thought lots of things but none of them was relevant. She was tired and she wanted to relax. Try as she might, she couldn't bring herself to concentrate on the death of Mr William Moynihan.

'You see, the most important thing,' he continued easily, 'is to keep taking stock. Every new piece of information we uncover must be tested against what we already know.'

It wasn't usual for a DI to teach a DC, no matter how new to the CID, like this. Policing had yet to adopt the academic approach of tutorials, one-to-one seminars and theoretical discussions on 'The Implications of the New Genetics for the Age of Criminal Responsibility', or

126

'Citizens' Rights – Why the Law has got it wrong'. It was still very much an apprenticeship – see one, do one, teach one – and she knew deep inside that she ought to be grateful for this rare chance to gain from the experience of a senior officer.

Bearing this in mind she said dutifully, 'Like a jigsaw puzzle.'

Sauerwine nodded enthusiastically, clearly delighted that she was proving a good pupil. 'That's right. Like a jigsaw puzzle. Exactly.'

As if the analogy were not trite to the point of crumbling away.

Her transfer to Newford may have been only a few weeks before but it had been quite long enough for her to feel a remarkably strong attraction to Andrew Sauerwine. Not that he was an entirely untarnished knight. Holt was an incurable gossip, and dark winter afternoons spent processing petty thefts and minor drug offences – the tedious white noise of law enforcement – were the perfect place and medium to foster such a habit. From him she had learned that Sauerwine might have a slightly disarming smile and he might give the impression that he was at least partly an innocent, but that there was also something of the shark about him. He had a streak running through him that was, if not cruel, then certainly clinical. She had seen it in the way that he handled witnesses and suspects; there was no reason why it would not surface in his private life. Yet she had discovered that not only did this not matter, it had actually increased his allure.

'So what we have here is a man dying in a fire in a car. It appears for the moment at least suspicious and we are therefore treating it as murder until we can show otherwise.'

Some poppadums arrived and he broke off a piece to dip into one of a selection of pickles and chew while he spoke.

'We believe, although we have as yet no definite proof, that the victim was William Moynihan.' He washed the poppadum down with some lager. 'How are we doing with the identification?'

'The forensic lab has got the comb and has taken five hairs off it. They say that should be enough to get some DNA for comparison with the autopsy samples.'

'What about teeth?'

'The orthodontist has taken impressions of the body. All we need now are some dental records.'

'No luck in Leicester?'

'Not as yet.'

'Any of the other database searches thrown anything up?'

She shook her head. If he was disappointed at this news he hid it easily, continuing through more poppadum, 'Okay. So it seems a reasonable working assumption that he was somehow incapacitated – possibly killed first, possibly not – put in his car and this was then fired.'

'I suppose so,' she said. Her tone of doubt made him look at her.

'Problem?'

'Well,' she said slowly, 'Supposing Moynihan's not the victim but the murderer?'

Eyes fixed upon her, he said, 'Okay, let's suppose it. What follows?'

'He wants us to believe that the body in the car is him. Hence the fire.'

'But then we'll know when we compare the DNA from the hairs and the body and find a discrepancy.'

'Not if the man who was lodging with Mrs Gleason wasn't really Moynihan. Perhaps it was the murderer.'

Sauerwine didn't smile but that was only through a sterling effort on the part of his facial muscles. He pointed out, 'But we have Bloom's testimony that Moynihan was lodging with Mrs Gleason.'

It was only a temporary setback. 'Perhaps he's in it with Moynihan.'

The food arrived then, served in stainless-steel bowls with impressive hauteur and preventing Sauerwine from responding. They were then asked, 'Is there anything else I can get for you?' The waiter sounded as if he would really rather that there wasn't, but did not show much in the way of gratitude when Sauerwine shook his head. They helped themselves to the food for a while before Sauerwine found the right tone to use as he said, 'I don't think I want to start constructing conspiracies just yet. Let's assume for now that Mr Toasty is really William Moynihan, and work on that basis.'

Somewhat deflated, Felty said, 'Yes, sir.'

'Andrew, when we're off duty.'

She looked up at him. 'I didn't realize that we *were* off duty.' She regretted saying it at once.

He looked surprised. 'Of course we are. Relaxed and off duty.' He frowned. 'Are you all right?'

She sighed. 'Just tired.'

He grinned and reached out to touch her hand. 'Not too tired, I hope.' Before she could answer he carried on, 'Anyway, The Star of India doesn't bear much resemblance to the station canteen. Much too plush.'

She smiled gratefully before once more concentrating on her food.

He returned to his theme. 'What interests me is why Moynihan suddenly decided two weeks ago to pack up his belongings in Leicester and come back down here, eight years after he left.'

Felty, slightly inhibited from offering a suggestion by her previous failure, said nothing.

'And then there's Mr Groshong. He interests me. He said that he didn't recognize the car, but other people in the village did.'

'Perhaps he's just got a bad memory.'

'He doesn't strike me as the kind to be forgetful. And then there's the business of why Moynihan left the estate. A row with Groshong.'

'Is that significant?'

He smiled, 'God knows.' He pulled off some of the bread and ate it with gusto. 'That's the point,' he said through semi-masticated Peshwari naan. 'Detection isn't about finding things; it's more about not forgetting things. Never eliminate something unless it's been proven every which way and then one more to be impossible. Sherlock Holmes never mentioned that. He was always deciding things straight off. Not like the real world.'

'But if this is to do with a row with Groshong eight years ago, why does it all blow up now?'

Sauerwine didn't know, but he wasn't about to let that intrude on the occasion. 'That,' he announced grandly, 'is a very interesting question.'

Which answer was no answer at all.

They continued to eat in silence. Felty finished her glass of wine but declined another, opting for water. Their ever-attentive, ever-disdaining waiter supplied this, together with another lager for Sauerwine.

'This is good,' he said. Then, 'Enjoying yours?'

Felty nodded, hoping that his detective skills would not see into the lie. In an effort to keep the thin blue line between them she said, 'Where do the money and the watch and the photograph come in?'

Sauerwine had found a slightly chewy piece of lamb or maybe, Felty thought unkindly, he didn't have an immediate answer. Eventually he said, 'The money doesn't bother me. What's five hundred quid these days? Hardly a fortune and probably just his working capital.' He sighed. 'No. The interesting things are the watch and the photograph. I mean, what's a no-hoper like that doing with a rather classy lady's watch? And why should he have a photograph of a late middle-aged couple?'

'Stolen?'

But Sauerwine knew that it wasn't that simple. 'Either he stole that watch or he bought it, knowing that it was stolen.'

Felty, because she was new and therefore less cynical, said at once, 'He might have bought it legitimately.'

Sauerwine tried hard, but failed, to keep the patronizing tone well down in the mix as he said, 'I don't think so, Sally. His worldly possessions consisted of five hundred pounds in a bundle, a comb and a few clothes. I hardly think that he's going to spend a few hundred pounds on a lady's gold watch.'

'You can't say that. He might have inherited it. The couple in the photograph might be relatives.'

This time he tried less hard with the patronizing tone. 'A photograph of a child I'd accept, but not a couple of people in their fifties, especially as it wasn't old enough to be of his parents. No. I'd wager that the watch was stolen and he had it for a purpose, a purpose linked to the photograph.'

He didn't bother to tell her that there was still something nagging at him from the distance of memory.

'We don't know enough about him to say that,' she persisted, becoming emboldened again by what she saw was his refusal to see anything other than his point of view. 'You said that we shouldn't exclude anything until we know without doubt that it's not true.'

Perhaps it was the lager but this time he tweaked the knob up to ten. 'This is the real world, Sally! It's not some romantic novel where fabulously rich men abandon everything and go to live with people like Mrs Gleason in a room with only their lost love's watch for company in the evening. Believe me, it was stolen.'

She felt flushed, slightly hurt, but ready to defend her viewpoint. 'All I'm saying is that we shouldn't overlook that possibility.'

'He may have been murdered. Never forget that. Two out of every three murders are committed over illegal activity.'

She didn't know if this statistic were true; it was plausible, though.

He saw that she was getting angry, defensive, and he put down his fork. 'Look, to a certain extent, this argument is meaningless. We need to find out where that watch came from. Part of that search will mean a trawl through lists of stolen property.'

Hooray. She knew that it would be her unpleasant task to do this.

He smiled. 'I'm not dismissing what you say, Sally. I'm just more experienced than you are.'

She nodded but didn't return the smile, hurt by his attitude.

He picked up his fork and resumed eating. She had had enough of her meal and merely observed him covertly.

Abruptly he put his fork down and said, 'I'm sorry. I shouldn't have spoken to you like that.'

'No problem. You're a lot more experienced than I am.'

And he was interested in her.

The pool of halfway attractive policewomen was far from boundless which meant that ever since training she had been pursued – sometimes it seemed endlessly pursued – and usually by men (once by a woman) that she wouldn't have shagged for all the tea leaves in Wormwood Scrubs. Usually body language worked, sometimes it had to be supplemented with a bit of a heart-to-heart, only once with a swift kick to the balls. Occasionally she had felt something spark and a relationship had formed.

As had happened with Sauerwine. And he hadn't

pushed it, at least not too hard. All men, she knew, pushed it but she had the kind of personality that automatically pushed back. She did not like to be hurried down paths, manoeuvred, forced to follow other people's agendas.

And he had played it – played her, she supposed – just right. She saw it, but still she didn't mind.

He put in one last forkful, then leaned back in his chair. 'That was good,' he announced. He raised his eyebrows and she said, 'Yes, it was.'

'Anything else?'

'No, thanks.'

The waiter descended and Sauerwine asked for the bill. He turned back to Felty, caught her looking down at the tablecloth. 'Come on,' he said. 'Cheer up. We're making progress.'

There was something about his tone that induced her to smile.

'There,' he declared. 'That's better.'

'I'm sorry. I'm just really tired.'

'Well, I'll take you home now.' There was no hint in his voice that he expected anything more and for that she was grateful. She had enjoyed making love with him, wanted to do it again, but tonight she was exhausted.

Sauerwine, too, had enjoyed that night and was keen to repeat the experience. But, no fool, he knew his prey. He had astutely assessed Felty's character and suppressed his carnal desires for yet another night.

Eisenmenger's first impression of Hugo Hickman was a curious dichotomy. Here, he thought, were good looks, easy-going grace, sociability and an apparently open and pleasant nature; yet there was something about him that he did not quite like. It wasn't a strong emotion and it flickered, sometimes stronger, sometimes weaker, sometimes ceasing completely. The closest he could come to articulation was to regard it as a slight discomfort. Hugo, he decided, was *too* perfect. Hugo, he also decided, was well aware of this fact. Inevitably this realization led him to wonder if the negative aspect of his assessment was born therefore of envy; he was not happy to consider himself envious and strove to fight it.

He did not entirely succeed.

When they were introduced, Hugo offered him a wide grin, a firm, dry handshake and just the right amount of humility; not too much, though.

'A pathologist, I understand. Fascinating subject. Father always taught me to have great respect for the pathologists, didn't you, Pa? What was it you used to say? "Keep the pathologist sweet, because he's the one who has to sweep up your mess. They can save you or break you."'

Tristan proffered Eisenmenger some champagne. With an indulgent smile he murmured, 'Something like that.'

Eisenmenger observed, 'I'm sure neither you nor your father leaves much mess.'

Hugo's smile was somehow all-encompassing and somehow hinting at secrets. 'Absolutely. Nothing we're going to tell a pathologist about, anyway.'

Before Eisenmenger could wonder what that meant Hugo began to laugh, took a drink of champagne and said, 'So, you've snared dear Helena. Lucky man.'

He winked, drank some more and then called to his father, 'Any more of that stuff? It's rather nice.'

Tristan was opening a second bottle. Hugo said, 'She's done well for herself.' It wasn't clear whether by that he meant in her career or her choice of partner. He continued, 'It's been a long time, though. Too long.'

'A lot's happened.'

Hugo gave him a studied look. 'Yes,' he said. 'It has.'

'You were all very close.'

Suddenly Hugo seemed to find his father, topping up the glasses of his mother and wife, really rather fascinating. 'Practically related,' he said absently. Eisenmenger found himself speculating.

He said, 'It's not surprising, though.'

He had never taken much to angling, at least not for fish. Hugo turned to him. 'I beg your pardon?'

'It's not surprising . . . that such close childhood friendships shouldn't last into adulthood.'

Hugo's attitude became interestingly wary. 'But that was circumstance,' he pointed out.

'Was it?'

'Jeremy went to university, I to medical school; that hardly helped. Then all hell broke loose. Nothing to do with us.' He had been working up to certainty as he talked. He shook his head. 'No. If things had been different, we'd still be together, still enjoying quiet times and good company.'

Eisenmenger, naturally cynical, doubted that. 'But circumstances don't just happen; people make them, they change them.'

'The murder of Helena's parents? The suicide of Jeremy?' Hugo smiled but he might have been trying to curdle milk. 'I think I'm a little too insignificant to have a great effect on such momentous events.'

Yet somehow the concept that Hugo Hickman thought of himself as insignificant didn't quite gel.

Helena came in, helping Eleanor, talking to her in a low tone. Eisenmenger noticed Hugo glance across but then saw that his glance lingered and that he watched her closely as she helped the old lady to her seat. Hugo turned to Eisenmenger, must have seen that he had been observed, but didn't obviously react. He said, 'As I said, lucky man.'

Tristan was fetching sherry for his mother when Theresa and Dominique came in carrying trays of hors d'oeuvres. Hugo at once went to them, taking the tray from his mother with exaggerated courtesy. He placed it on the octagonal table in the centre of the room, then turned to Dominique. Eisenmenger saw with great interest that she stiffened slightly as he took the tray; on her face was something that he took at first to be wariness. She kept her eyes on his face, while he kept a wide smile there. Theresa took the tray from him and Eisenmenger was unsure if he saw a slow, sly wink at Dominique before he turned away.

It was only then that Eisenmenger realized that it had not been a look of wariness on Dominique's face, it had been one of hatred.

Part Four

The postman called early on Mrs Gleason because she lived not five minutes from the post office. It was therefore just before nine o'clock that she called the police station in a state of high, not to say stratospheric dudgeon. Oram took the call because neither Sauerwine nor Felty was available and it was therefore he that suffered her indignation.

'It's bounced!' she announced without much in the way of explanatory preamble and, since Oram knew neither who she was nor what it was that might have bounced, his response was not to her liking.

'What has?'

'The cheque! The cheque!'

Oram was tall and thin and had adenoids the size of plums. He spoke through his nose with a nasal twang that after about the seventieth syllable made most listeners wish for some sort of divine ENT surgeon to intervene. Not that Mrs Gleason cared about this.

'Are you saying,' he asked, because he had learned early in his constabulary career to get things straight without delay, 'that someone has paid you a cheque without sufficient funds to clear?'

Mrs Gleason repeated, 'The cheque's bounced! I trusted him, and he's let me down. I'm not doing that again.'

As far as Oram was concerned this was a caller with a minor complaint. 'I'm not sure that I can help you. This isn't necessarily a criminal matter, Mrs Gleason.'

'But he was murdered!'

Using skills that had been honed by three years of policing to a diamond sharpness, Oram divined that perhaps it wasn't a minor complaint. 'Murdered?' he asked. 'Who was murdered?'

'Mr Moynihan.'

At last, the small change fell to earth with an audible clunk. 'Is this to do with the death of William Moynihan?'

And after further explanation, hampered only slightly by Mrs Gleason's tendency to dissemble and her indignation at what had been done to her, Oram at last came into possession of all the facts. He wrote them down, then assured Mrs Gleason that someone would ring her back without delay.

Sauerwine and Felty came in about an hour later. As soon as he heard, Sauerwine couldn't stop himself from celebrating his own brilliance. 'You see, Felty? I told you he was skint.'

'Yes, sir.' She admired his obvious aptitude, even if the tone grated a little. *What do you want – the Queen's Police Medal?*

He sat down at his desk. 'Still, it's interesting.'

She came into the room, closed the door and took a seat without being asked, knowing that it would be all right. She didn't say anything, figuring that he would soon enough dazzle her anew with his deductive abilities.

'He took all his money out of his account to come here,' he said. 'Yet he gave Mrs Gleason a cheque that he knew would bounce. What does that tell you?'

'That he wasn't planning to hang around?'

'Exactly!' To Felty's ear Sauerwine was starting to sound dangerously close to pompous. 'He turned up here with something to do. One very specific thing. He expected it to take a few days, then he would move on.'

'And you think that it had something to do with the watch and the photograph?'

'Of course it did!' He sighed. 'It's all coming together, Felty.'

She said nothing.

'You'd better go and see Mrs Gleason. Get the cheque, then follow it up with the bank. I want Moynihan's financial history.'

'Yes, sir.' She stood up. 'What are you going to do?'

He smiled. 'Think things through.'

When he was alone he leaned back in his chair, the confidence still there but dimmed. He was missing something about the photograph and the watch. It would be a while before forensics were finished with them, but SOCO had provided photographs. He retrieved these and sat and stared at them for a long while. Jackson came in, proffering a cup of tea and a rich-tea biscuit, after about half an hour.

'Problem?' he asked. It sometimes seemed to Sauerwine that Jackson had been there since before Peel had been potty-trained and he had a habit of not exactly treating him as he thought detective inspectors ought to be treated, but he was aware that Jackson was no fool. A slob, perhaps, but not a fool. The tea and the biscuit had become something of a ritual for Sauerwine and Jackson in the three years for which he had been in Newford.

'Yes, and no.'

'Ah,' said Jackson amiably. 'That would be, "No, and yes".'

Sauerwine didn't reply and Jackson wasn't bothered. After about ten minutes of silence, the Inspector threw the photograph on the desk and Jackson, without being asked, leaned across and picked it up. 'What's this?'

'This is the "no".'

'Ah.' He contemplated it while biting his biscuit. Some crumbs of it fell on his uniform. Sauerwine sipped his tea.

Eventually Jackson, his mouth now delicately decorated with moist biscuit crumbs, said, 'Do you want to know what I think?'

Sauerwine normally didn't and, deep in thought, he said only in a distracted way, 'No.'

Jackson was not the sort of man to pay much attention to such a weak rebuttal.

'I think that this bloke's a lawyer.'

Tiredly and without much interest, 'What makes you say that?' He was thinking that Jackson always made the tea too strong but that it was somehow comforting that he did so.

'I know that tie. He's a member of the Law Society.'

He held it out to Sauerwine who, suddenly listening, took it and looked at it again. 'Shit,' he whispered. How had he missed it?

Jackson finished his tea.

Suddenly Sauerwine was thinking again. A single word and he was thinking all sorts of new things. All sorts indeed.

Jackson stood up. 'I'll leave you to finish your tea,' he said, but Sauerwine didn't reply.

'Well done.' Lambert didn't quite manage a smile and his tone was less one of jubilation, more one of grudging admission.

Beverley kept her face correspondingly straight and her tone correspondingly neutral as she replied, 'Thank you, sir.'

He walked away having delivered up a curt nod. She stood in the echoing corridor and watched him leave, a file under his arm. Congratulations from Lambert had been pretty low on her wish list – just above bilateral amputation – and she would normally have gone a couple of hundred kilometres out of her way over broken glass to avoid the humourless bastard, but she was nonetheless suddenly filled with pleasure. Lambert hated her of old and if he thought her success in the recent credit-card case was worthy of comment, then she guessed that maybe the bad old days were at last over. Perhaps this was a surrogate measure of the feelings amongst the senior officers; perhaps she could now begin to move on.

She turned and continued on her way to the restaurant for a mid-morning break, her step suddenly a little lighter.

The restaurant had once been the canteen, but then it had been repainted and carpeted and the menu choice extended to include more than the sausages, mince and fried fish that had once formed the entire repertoire. An area in which low, comfortable sofas had been placed around square coffee tables had heightened the impression of plush modernism but over the years this effect had been tarnished by a variety of strange marks and stains and a light sprinkling of cigarette burns on the seat covers, while the coffee tables were now completely camouflaged by graffiti.

Beverley sat at one of these now, biting into an apple that she had purchased from the semicircular counter and finding that, despite its shiny red and beguiling appearance, it was woolly and tasteless. She sighed, her sense of well-being momentarily polluted by this disappointment.

You're always taken in by appearances when it comes to pleasure. Maybe that's where you go wrong.

She looked down at the apple, which she had put on the table; already the flesh was going brown.

A gilded bastard.

Would Eisenmenger have proved to be another in a long line of sadly deceptive gilded bastards?

Maybe.

But maybe not . . .

Her mobile began to ring and she pulled it quickly from her handbag.

'Yes?'

'Beverley?'

'Who's this?'

'Sauerwine. Andrew Sauerwine. We worked together a few years back.'

She remembered him – how could she not with a name like that? Tall, not unhandsome but callow. Had he had a crush on her? She rather thought that he had. She also thought that he had had the makings of a good detective. 'I remember.' She was deliberately wary, well aware that old colleagues rarely made contact for altruistic reasons; usually such calls meant trouble.

'I'm a DI now. In the West Midlands.'

Oh, great. The last thing she needed to hear was that some spotty, white-socked junior was about to overtake her on the career highway; another greasy wideboy rocketing past in the outside lane while she limped along with a puncture and an overheating engine, her chassis falling to bits.

'Bully for you.'

If he heard the sarcasm he ignored it. 'I've come across something a bit peculiar, something that called to mind an old case we once worked on.'

'Oh, yes?' She dropped the sarcasm but instead picked up uninterest to hide her curiosity. Why was he ringing her? As far as she could recall him at all he had been introspective and serious. She had found this earnestness quite touching, as if in him she could see an earlier, purer version of herself. In fact, now she came to think about it, he had been so quiet that she had not initially recognized his adoration. Only the caustic and sarcastic comments of his colleagues, one drunken night when Sauerwine had probably been tucked up in bed with some cocoa, had alerted her. She had been flattered, she thought; she was always flattered by such attention . . .

Flattered and foolish.

She ignored this unwelcome intrusion with a contemptuous snort that was intended as a coat of reassurance to hide her doubts, except that she could still see a vague outline, even as she was listening to what he was saying.

Then the significance of his words caused a jolt of discomfort that destroyed any equanimity she had been enjoying.

'You remember that double murder we worked on? The Eaton-Lambert case?'

God! How could she forget? The case that had made her but that would never crawl away and die, it seemed.

'What about it?' She tried to maintain insouciance and wasn't sure how well she succeeded.

'The victims had unusual names, didn't they?'

'Claude and Penelope,' she supplied.

'That's what I thought.'

She didn't know where this was heading but she didn't like the look of the scenery. A female detective sergeant with whom Beverley had developed a close working and increasingly social relationship walked past. She was carrying a cup of something and perhaps she was planning to sit down next to her, but decided not to when Beverley looked at her and shook her head. To Sauerwine she said, 'Why do you ask?'

'Well, it's all a bit odd really. We had a chap who burned to death in his car . . .'

'Suspicious?'

'I'm treating it as such for the time being. It's possible he's a suicide – there's a suggestion of previous depression – but there are a few inconsistencies. I'm just checking out a few background details.'

Fair enough. She found herself automatically approving his strategy. He went on, 'He was lodging in a nearby town – Melbury. While I was looking through his belongings, one thing stood out – a gold watch.'

'Stolen?'

'That's what I assumed at first, but then I came across a photograph.' He paused. 'I'm still not sure, but I think it's a picture of the Flemmings.'

'So?' She could feel that she was nearly at her destination and that it was not a place that she wanted to be in.

'There was an engraving on the watch. *From Claude to Penelope – a token.*'

She didn't say anything at first, her thoughts streaming through her head, flying in many directions, landing nowhere. Sauerwine said, 'Now, I suppose it could still have been stolen, but I thought it a bit strange that he should have a picture of the people he stole it from.'

She knew that she had to speak. 'That's assuming that it is a picture of the Flemmings.'

'Oh, of course . . .'

'And it also assumes that the watch belonged to the Flemmings.'

'Well, Claude and Penelope aren't the commonest of names.' He sounded disappointed by her scepticism.

'What do you want me to do about it?'

He was talking diffidently, which gave her an impression that he still looked on her as somehow his superior despite the equality of their ranks. 'I was wondering if you could check through the records on the Eaton-Lambert case to see if the watch was listed as stolen. I can send you a photograph. Also, maybe you could take a look at the picture of the couple; see if you recognize them as the Flemmings. It's a bit tattered and old but quite clear. I'll fax it over now.'

She said as brightly as she could, 'Fine.' Did she sound genuine? 'And I'd be happy to look through the Eaton-Lambert file.'

Sauerwine was pathetically grateful. 'Oh, thank you. Maybe you could talk to the surviving daughter – what was her name? She might recognize the watch, even if it's not listed as stolen.'

She nearly laughed out loud at the thought of going to that toxic little bitch. With a carefully controlled voice she said, 'I don't recall immediately. In any case we may not have an up-to-date address for her.'

'No, I guess not.'

His disappointment was so palpable she was moved to palliate it. 'But we'll have to see. Even if I can't contact her, I can still check the files.'

'It's probably irrelevant; all just a coincidence and nothing at all to do with this man's death, but it needs to be

141

checked out. And who knows? It may throw open the Eaton-Lambert case.'

Oh, my God!

'Well, we'll have to see. Will you send me the photographs straight away?'

'I'm on it now.' A breath's-deep pause. 'I really am very grateful, Beverley.'

She caught in this sentence a hint of the past. Perhaps, she wondered, he was still slightly smitten. She said, 'No problem, Andrew. Happy to help.'

He rang off and she sat staring into her thoughts for a long time.

That morning Eisenmenger, who had been into Melbury to buy a paper, returned via the back road that led to the front of the castle past the adventure playground. During the spring, summer and early autumn the ropes and the swings and the underground tunnel were in constant use, but now this was an empty space, a haunted vacuum.

Except that today it wasn't.

He looked to his left and saw Tom on one of the swings.

He found nothing unusual in this of itself. The aspect that struck him as odd was that it was not Nell, not Tristan, not Dominique that was pushing him again and again, but Malcolm Groshong.

He parked the car on the forecourt and was about to go into the castle when he saw Hugo and Tristan setting off from the northern side of the castle. They each carried a shotgun broken over the crook of the elbow. For some reason, he found the sight intriguing, hinting at a life to which he was an alien. He looked back at Groshong, still pushing the swing. He thought for a long time with the cold seeping in like senescence before he finally picked up the paper from the passenger seat and went into the castle.

Hell!

The fax had done the photographs no favours but Beverley could make out enough detail to match it with the list of property stolen from the home of Claude and Penelope Flemming.

One lady's wristwatch, gold; battery-powered. Make –
Omega. Face – roman numerals. Date only. Inscription on back
reads 'From Claude to Penelope – a token.'

Not much room for doubt there.

Nor, when she examined the image of the tattered
photograph of the late middle-aged couple, had she had
any hesitation, no matter how much she wanted to do
otherwise, in identifying them as the deceased parents
of Helena.

She sat now in her office, a pile of files half a metre high
on her desk, the name *Flemming* clearly stamped across
the cover of the top one.

What does it mean?

This question would not leave her be, a whisper from a
past that was not as dead as she had thought; there was
a hint of menace in its tone, no matter how hard she tried
to quash it, bury it beneath her certainty that here was not
another miscarriage of the justice that society so desperately wanted to believe was infallible.

The day was now mature enough to mean that the
station was becoming soporific; not quiet, just subdued,
the occasional doors that were slammed and the sporadic
cries that were produced in the distance were breaks from
the neon calm. Her office was in darkness, the blinds
pulled down, her world illumined only by a cone of
brightness from her anglepoise lamp into which she
leaned as if lapping up its sustenance. The room was
small and cramped and hot but she knew that wasn't the
only reason that she was damp with perspiration.

Not again. Please, not again.

It had seemed so clear-cut. Claude and Penelope
Flemming had been murdered, beaten to death with a
crowbar, the house ransacked. It had been a shocking,
almost indescribable crime, suggesting a frenzy that
was scarcely human. Beverley had considered herself
to be hardened against the extremes of human behaviour
– the cruelty, the callousness, the violence – but what
had been visited upon a semi-retired solicitor and his wife
had profoundly disturbed her. Even now she revisited
the memory as rarely as possible and only with great
trepidation.

A likely motive had quickly become apparent, with a
small number of expensive items missing from the house,

but robbery with such violence suggested another factor. Drugs had been their first hypothesis – crack cocaine was notorious for producing heightened strength and heightened aggression – but there were problems with the idea that some drug-fuelled psychopath had come a-knocking on the door with crowbar and malignant intent. For a start, no one else in the neighbourhood – leafy suburban Surrey where the gravel drives were long and the golf drives were frequent – had seen or been bothered by this hypothetical perpetrator.

Then there was the inescapable conclusion that the murderer had been curiously knowledgeable with regard to what to burgle and what to leave. Drawers had been emptied and there were numerous signs of searching, but the list of stolen items had been small and quite strikingly exclusive. This had seemed to be at odds with the image of a crazed barbarian bent only on finding valuables to be sold to continue a drug habit. The two hi-fi systems, the three televisions and the newly bought laptop computer had all been left.

Jeremy Eaton-Lambert had been in the frame from the start. The son of Penelope by a former marriage, he had dropped out of university in his second year after discovering the pleasures of cannabis and forgetting the purpose of study. A series of low-achieving, low-paying, low-tenure jobs had followed; Helena, his stepsister, had provided the evidence herself that he had spent the last few months sponging off his parents and this had produced tensions. Neighbours testified that the night before the tragedy there had been a vicious row between Jeremy and his parents; his alibi – a workmate from the packing factory where he had been currently employed – had crumbled with the first slight increment in their interrogation techniques.

All that had been missing was some forensic evidence.

Which she had supplied.

Not *strictly* legal . . .

Not legal at all, she had to admit (albeit in a whisper, in the deep of the night when she was alone) . . .

She wasn't the first to provide that final, little piece of corroboration in a case and she certainly wasn't going to be the last. It wasn't even the first time that she had made use of the tactic to catch someone who might otherwise escape the might of Justice. That honour had fallen to a slimy little bastard by the name of Darier who had taken his pleasure from touching up little girls; the testimony of the victims had looked decidedly shaky and there had been considerable doubt as to the likelihood of conviction until several compact discs had turned up in a locker in Darier's workplace. They had been covered in his finger-prints and contained images that the jury had found abhorrent.

Similarly Jeremy Eaton-Lambert had looked likely to escape his due retribution thanks to the blind gaze of Justice. The evidence had convinced her within twenty-four hours that she was correct in her belief, but it had been circumstantial. The row, the testimony that he was addicted to crack, the traces of cocaine in his blood – all showed her how right she was, but were insufficient alone to send him down.

So she had helped Justice, just as she might help any blind old woman who was unsure which way to go. It had been easy to appropriate one of Eaton-Lambert's shirts when his flat was searched; easier still to acquire some blood that had been taken at the post-mortem examinations and introduce the two. She had been at the time unsure if she had been wise to acquire some of Claude Flemming's cuff links, but the opportunity had been too good to miss; Helena, who had taken the inventory after the crime, had missed them because they had been so small. When Johnson – her doubting colleague – had uncovered them in the boot of Eaton-Lambert's car, her fears that Helena Flemming would recall seeing them in the house after the robbery and had just forgotten to include them in the list had made her almost incapacitated by nausea; in contrast her relief when her ruse had worked had been enough to make her high. She knew that what she was doing was right, that she was merely con-firming the truth, but she was well aware that there were plenty of liberal do-gooders in the establishment who thought otherwise.

Jeremy Eaton-Lambert had been convicted and sent down. That he refused to acknowledge his guilt had not been her worry; that he had slashed his wrists five months later had merely relieved her of that still small voice that suggested wickedly and remorselessly that perhaps, just possibly, she had been wrong.

And now the voice was back.

It was not surprising that one of the stolen items should turn up; they had never been found (except the cuff links!) and the presumption had always been that Eaton-Lambert had handed them on straight away, the need for a fix driving him into immediate action to access cash. Such things often turned up years later, sometimes in the unlikeliest of situations.

No, that wasn't the problem.

The photograph. That was what disquieted her, bringing on that same feeling of nauseous dread that she had experienced those eight years ago as she had waited for Helena Flemming perhaps to denounce her and discover her subterfuge, her tiny white lie. Why did this anonymous dead man have a photograph of the original owners of the watch? It suggested that he had a connection with the case, that not all the dogs were sleeping peacefully.

From the direction of the tall window to her right came the sound of distant sirens.

She felt thirsty and reached into one of the drawers of her desk, bringing from it a plastic bottle of spring water and a glass. Somebody walked past the door, a heavy tread and a moving, distorted shadow cutting across the splay of light on the dirtied carpet of her darkened room.

Is it significant?

Probably not. She had been right, of that she was certain then; of that she remained certain now. Yet she was also well aware that there were others who remained equally convinced of Jeremy Eaton-Lambert's innocence. Johnson, for a start. Once her colleague on the case, then a bleeding heart about it, Johnson had threatened to upset things and she had been forced to take action about the situation; he was out of the force but still around, still a potential problem. Not as large a problem as Helena, though.

Helena.

The stupid frigid bitch had always been in her way, refusing to accept that her precious stepbrother could have been responsible. Even got in the way in the matter of John Eisenmenger, now she came to think of it . . .

She paused, her mind momentarily distracted, but then she barked a harsh staccato laugh. To the warm darkness she asked, 'What is wrong with you, girl? Like a schoolgirl with a wet dream?'

She laughed again, this time at her own joke.

Maybe, she admitted. Once more out loud she said, 'You're getting old, girl. Menopausal. Perhaps you're not just warm and flushed because the window's closed and the heating's on.'

Eisenmenger wasn't that attractive; not a freak but hardly her idea of a stud, and she'd had enough wankers reckoning themselves studs to know the real thing when it walked into pheromone range. So why was she suddenly thinking so much about him? Because he appeared to be decent? Or because he was Helena's and that hurt . . .

She sighed, pulling her thoughts back to the problem. Her rise through the ranks of the police force had been rapid but that wasn't just because she tweaked justice; she was also good. She knew that she couldn't ignore this thing, so she had to make plans and she knew exactly what plans to make.

Sauerwine was just about to leave when Felty returned from her labours in Westerham village.

'Any news?' he asked.

She was excited. 'And then some.'

He indicated that she should sit down, took off his overcoat and scarf, then returned to his desk. 'Tell me.'

'I went to see Bloom first. He wasn't much use – didn't give me anything more than he'd given you – but on the way out, I got talking to Mr Meyerson'

'Who's he?'

'He works for Bloom in the petrol station.'

'Old chap. Nosy?'

'That's him.'

'And what did he tell you?'

'Moynihan was a difficult bastard. Bad-tempered, difficult and ten times as bad when he was drunk, which he was a lot of the time. Rowed with everyone, it seems, at some time or another.'

It hardly helped his cause and Sauerwine showed it, but Felty hadn't finished. 'Meyerson remembers the row with

Groshong because Moynihan went straight to the pub and got very, very drunk.'

Sauerwine sighed. 'The world never changes. They're like hamsters in a wheel.'

Felty said impatiently, 'Meyerson was there. He witnessed Moynihan and what he did.'

It was plain that whatever he did, she thought that it was *significant*. Sauerwine played his part. 'And what did he do?'

'He had a fight with Bloom.'

Sauerwine, until then relaxed and if anything patronizing, was suddenly alert. 'A bad one?'

She grinned. 'Blood everywhere. In fact, Meyerson said that . . .' She looked at her PDA. '. . . Bloom had the shit beaten out of him. His face looked as if it had been run over.'

'Really? Do we know what the fight was about?'

'Bloom called him "stupid", according to Meyerson.'

'Hardly worth starting a world war about.'

'Well, Meyerson did say that he was prone to rows. And Mrs Gleason seemed to think that there was a darker side to him.'

'Does it signify, though?' Sauerwine was asking questions as much of himself as of his constable. 'Does it give Bloom sufficient motive to kill him after eight years?'

'Supposing there was more to it than that? Supposing the row was about something else?'

'Like what?'

She cast around for possibilities. 'Could it have been something to do with the watch?'

Which meant the Eaton-Lambert case. For a moment Sauerwine was silent, staring at Felty but not seeing her. Abruptly he seemed to return from somewhere. He looked at Felty – actually saw her – and said, 'Come on. Time to go home.'

Surprised she asked, 'So what are you going to do?'

He had stood up. 'Go home,' he said disingenuously.

'But what do you think? About the row with Bloom?'

He smiled. 'I think we don't know enough yet. Not nearly enough.'

They walked out into the shared office where Oram had just arrived and was taking off his coat. 'Bloody cold out there,' he remarked gloomily. His desk was beside the

Christmas tree and someone had cut out Oram's face from the local newspaper and stuck it on the front of the fairy's head.

'Have fun, Constable,' was Sauerwine's cheery salutation. Oram smiled and sneered simultaneously; it was an impressive display.

As they passed into the outer office, Jackson was dealing with a young woman who was complaining about her neighbour's dog.

'. . . I'm sure it's killed one of my cats. And a month ago, it had a go at my husband. It tried to bite off his . . .'

The door closed on this potentially disastrous dog-bite.

They stopped and suddenly it was awkward. Sauerwine was smiling but there was something tense around it. Felty said, 'I don't suppose you fancy a quick drink . . .?'

Sauerwine's mouth opened but all that came out was an apologetic glottal-open sound. '. . . Uhh . . . Not tonight, if you don't mind. Things to do.'

She hid her disappointment. 'No problem.' Was her voice too bright, too brittle?

He nodded and they walked to their respective cars in cold and dark silence. As Felty was driving slowly on to the road past the police station she tried not to wonder why Sauerwine had turned her down. She tried, but she failed to stop thinking about Beverley Wharton.

'Sir?'

Chief Superintendent Mott was eating a ham sandwich whilst upon his face there had come to rest an expression of unmistakable distress. It wasn't obvious to Beverley whether it was the taste of the comestible or his presence in the station restaurant that had caused his distress. He was a thin, ascetic man with an enlarging bald spot and a permanent and deepening frown. He had been told by the Assistant Chief Constable to make a greater effort to socialize with the junior ranks and had taken to eating occasional meals in the restaurant as a response, but he had not found it an easy task. No one dared approach him during his time there and he felt conspicuous and stupid, an exhibit in a glass case staring back at the plebeians who came to gawp. He had tried lunchtimes first, then the breakfast shift, and was now reduced to suppertimes, when the numbers were at their minimum.

He looked on Beverley Wharton with eager eyes. It was so rare for someone to approach him in this situation he felt as if a long-lost friend had suddenly appeared before him bearing a key to a cave filled with gold. 'Beverley! Come and sit down. I could do with some company.'

She complied. She had her usual bottle of mineral water and he gestured towards this with the remains of his sandwich. 'Don't you ever eat anything?'

She smiled modestly. Her gustatory habits were well known in the station. 'I've got very little appetite.'

He leaned towards her. 'Not for food, anyway.'

She didn't scream – of course she didn't scream – but she wanted to. She had been aware that he was interested in her – they were all interested in her, it sometimes seemed – but this was the first sign that he wanted more than the odd sneaky peek at her legs. She smiled sweetly, skating over the implication that had now dropped to the floor and was slowly soaking into the carpet to join all the other shit that people had brought in from the street. 'I need some advice. Sir.'

Mott took another bite from the sandwich, leaving a little between his fingers. He looked around the restaurant. He didn't look at Beverley as he said under his breath, 'Nobody's their own master, Inspector. Look at me, I sit here every fucking day and hate every frigging moment of it, but I do it nevertheless. Do you know why?'

She shook her head.

He grimaced. 'Because I was advised to. Note that, Inspector; "advised" to. Not "ordered", "advised". That's even more compelling, that is. Supposed to be good for morale. Ha!'

He threw the last of his sandwich into his mouth and chewed it savagely. 'It's done nothing for theirs, but it's certainly screwed mine up.'

Beverley waited patiently, not sure where this was leading.

He looked at her with a cruel glint in his eyes. 'And now you come to me and you want some advice.' What started as a smile turned rapidly into a leer. 'Be careful with "advice", Inspector. Be very careful, indeed.'

She couldn't see exactly what he meant, but she harboured a suspicion. *Oh, well, if that's the way it's to be . . .*

She said, 'I recently had a phone call – from Andrew Sauerwine. Remember him? He was here about eight or nine years ago.'

'Serious and sober? Got the piss taken out of him?'

'That's him.'

'What of it?'

'He's an inspector now. In Herefordshire.'

Mott's eyebrows rode over the frown, heading towards the bald spot. 'Already? He's done well. Quite the highflyer.' It was, Beverley thought, unnecessary and cruel of him to add, 'A bit like you were, once.'

She skated that one, too.

'He told me of a case he's working on – someone died in a car fire – during the course of which he's come across this in the belongings of the dead man.'

She handed to him the photograph of the watch. Before he could ask, she said, 'It matches one stolen in the Eaton-Lambert case.'

Mott looked at it. 'So? Some of that stuff was bound to turn up eventually.'

'It was with a photograph of the Flemmings – the victims in the Eaton-Lambert case.'

That made him think. He looked at Beverley and she saw something in his eyes that she didn't like. 'What are you telling me?'

'I don't know. I'm just thinking that it's odd . . .'

'Odd? It's more than "odd", Inspector. Who was this dead man?'

'William Moynihan. Nothing to do with the Eaton-Lambert case.'

His look had become a stare. 'He'd better not have been,' he said in a voice that was low in tone, high in menace.

He looked again at the photograph in his hand, considering implications she guessed. It was partly as a result of this that she said, 'The conviction was sound, sir.'

He puckered his lips. 'There were rumours, weren't there? The daughter – the lawyer – she didn't think we had the right man . . .'

'She was always a troublemaker; wanted the publicity. Trendy left-wing police-basher.'

He said nothing more for a while, just stared at the photograph. Then he looked at her again. 'You say it was a good collar. Did you do anything – anything *at all* – to help it along?'

The half-second that elapsed before she answered held so much conjecture and so much significance it seemed to Beverley to be in stasis for a year. *What does he want – the truth or a reassuring lie? If I tell him what really happened, he will be implicated, might cut his losses and end my career right now. If I lie to him, he'll be in the clear, whatever happens.*

'No, sir.'

He nodded slowly as if he understood, and perhaps he did. Perhaps his next question was just cruel teasing. 'So why does this alarm you so much? If the conviction was safe, ignore it. Even if the daughter gets hold of it, there's nothing she can make of it, is there?'

Thanks a lot, you bastard.

'It opens up one possibility that might be difficult . . .'

'Really? What?'

She took a deep breath. 'It's possible that Eaton-Lambert had an accomplice.'

'I don't recall any evidence to suggest that.'

'There wasn't . . . until now.'

'Mmm.'

'It's just the kind of thing the daughter might use to make trouble.'

'Yes, I can see that . . .' His whole demeanour was suffused with hesitation but also, she suspected, something else. His next words confirmed this suspicion. 'If I were a cynic, Inspector, I'd suggest that you're talking bullshit. I'd wonder about you being worried that those cuff links were – how can I put this? – a *red herring*.'

She kept her face straight and put into her voice as much indignation as she dared. 'I don't see that, Superintendent. They were found in Jeremy Eaton-Lambert's possession and were only the last piece in the puzzle. We had the ferocious rows, we had his crack addiction, and he had no alibi.'

Mott had allowed a small smile to creep out and play a few games. 'Oh, absolutely, Beverley. Absolutely.' The switch to the use of her first name was not missed. He continued, 'But there was no evidence to suggest an accomplice. None at all, as I recall. And why would this accomplice wander around with an incriminating piece of evidence in his pocket? And why would he further compound his stupidity by keeping a photograph of the original owners with it?'

She didn't dare to hesitate. 'That's what we need to find out, sir. I have to reopen the investigation, just to tie up this loose end, but we have to do it quietly.'

He stared at the table before them, then abruptly leaned back in the low sofa. His mouth was twisted to one side. To the rounded globe light that hung down directly above his head he said, 'Not officially, we don't, Beverley. It would look remarkably like we were trying to cover things up.'

She wasn't surprised by this, was only glad that he had left a door open. 'But unofficially?'

Another pause for consideration of this peculiarly fascinating light fitting. Then, it lost its allure and he brought his head down to look at her. 'Unofficially . . .' His smile held enough knowingness to fill an encyclopedia.

Here it comes. She could already hear the words; in her mind she could already feel his hands on her breasts, on her buttocks, between her legs. She waited, controlling her breathing. *Is there no other currency I can use?*

'Unofficially,' he repeated, 'I suppose I could look into some form of secondment. I know the ACC in the county. He might welcome a temporary boost to his detective force, especially someone like you who is so experienced . . .'

She was unsure if this were a double entendre.

Mott asked, 'What about Sauerwine? Would he take umbrage?'

She shrugged. 'I don't know.' She thought of the past, of his apparent crush on her. *Does he still have it? Can I use that?* 'Would it matter?'

He didn't reply directly. Instead, 'What are you working on at the moment?'

'Not much now. With the recent arrests, my desk is fairly clear.'

Again there was a certain something in his words. 'Still, we can scarcely afford to lose you . . .' He looked at her. 'It would make a large hole . . .'

Just get it over with, you bastard!

'. . . You're using up a lot of good will, Beverley.'

She smiled; it felt like she was opening a sutured

wound down to bone with her bare hands, but she smiled.

'I'm good at good will, sir.'

He smiled and nodded. 'I had a feeling you were, Beverley.'

'Nell wasn't ready for motherhood. To be honest, I don't think she was really ready for adulthood.' Eisenmenger heard sorrow but little anger in Theresa's words.

'And the father?'

'What about him?'

'Does he never try to contact her? Doesn't he care about Tom?'

It was cold in the kitchen but that didn't explain the frigidity of Theresa's response as she said, 'Tom has no father.'

The simplicity of this statement was in remarkable contrast to the complexity of the situation it attempted to describe. It did not admit of criticism; a decision had been made.

'Does he have a mother?' Quite what made him ask this will almost certainly never be known. The question though, once voiced, was as impertinent as it was unavoidable. Theresa's core temperature took a dive with ice crystals forming where her eyes had been.

'What do you mean?'

Eisenmenger found that the precariousness of his position lent him courage; it might have been false courage, it might have been foolhardy, but it served him in his moment of need. 'She seems . . . distant.'

Perhaps it was the sheer guilelessness with which he pointed this out that caused Theresa first to stare at him, then to relax, almost deflate and say eventually, 'You're right, of course.'

He didn't say anything, didn't even move. She continued slowly, 'For a long time after the birth, Nell effectively rejected Tom.'

It came slowly, drip by drip. 'She had a complete breakdown following the birth. She has never really recovered. At first looking after Tom was impossible for her; then it became intolerable to her. Only recently has Nell come out of it.'

He remarked gently, 'It must have been very difficult.'

He had half expected her to don a brave face and was surprised when Theresa nodded at once and said tiredly, 'She blamed Tom for the loss of her childhood. Tristan said that her refusal to take responsibility for him was a sign of her refusal to enter adulthood.'

'Why blame Tom? Why not blame the father?'

Theresa didn't know. She shrugged and sighed. 'I don't understand much of it. I'm just relieved that she's come out of it.'

Eisenmenger said nothing and Theresa went on, 'Even now she treats Tom more as a younger brother. Tristan and I supply what emotional attention we can; Dominique is an effective practical carer.'

It sounded to him like a childhood from hell, whatever the lavishness of the surroundings, but this time he held his tongue.

Beverley so did not want to be in Newford. Newford was straight out of her nightmares, a place where nothing happened except things that were either unworthy of mention or impolite to discuss in mixed company; things that involved animals or relatives. As she stepped from the car it was just after eight; it ought to have been rush hour, except that the only things she could see were a minibus, a cyclist and, inevitably, a tractor. The high street wound away in both directions lined by shops. She could see a newsagent, a chemist, a small convenience store and an estate agent. She could not see any establishment that she considered *useful* – a gymnasium or a jewellery shop, for instance – merely places where mundanity (and nothing but mundanity) occurred.

She sighed. She had feared that it would be like this but she was a dedicated policewoman.

Especially when her career was on the line.

She had spent the night in a small hotel just on the outskirts of Newford. *God! Hotel!* To Beverley's eye it had been more like a bed and breakfast from an alien land – Manchester, say, from fifty years ago. Most of it had stunk of damp and mothballs, the only exception being the dining room that stunk of cabbage and sweat. The bed – a single bed, of course – might have been specially designed for torture; the sheets had *looked* clean, but then the mattress had *looked* comfortable, and the hotel had *looked* quite charming and hospitable.

So here she was – unbreakfasted and feeling as if she were in a foreign country where the locals were hostile and their customs inexplicable. She felt exposed, vulnerable. She felt, too, nervous. The next hour was going to be crucial in determining whether she could succeed in quashing this particular crisis.

She had dressed with great thought: wary of being too provocative but damned if she were going to dress like a seventeenth-century puritan just to avoid upsetting the God-fearing retards twitching the curtains all around her. Anyway, she was too wise a combatant to lay down her most potent weapon voluntarily, not when she was engaging in a crucial battle. Consequently she now wore tight, black leather trousers that fitted her legs far better than they had graced the cow, combined with a white roll-neck jumper and a black leather jacket. She liked the effect.

It covered everything but was definitely *not* puritan.

She crossed the high street, dodging the traffic that consisted of an ancient bus, three cars and a milk float. Charitably she reminded herself that it was the lull between Christmas and the New Year. 'Probably at least twice the traffic, normally.'

The police station was situated behind the library. It looked to be marginally bigger than a detached house and, she suspected, contained inhabitants at least as dangerous. The entrance was a single door that gave on to a minute lobby no more than two metres square. There were two chairs against the left-hand wall, a door opposite and a closed hatch to her right. A combination lock was on the door, a bell marked *Please Press* was situated by the hatch and from the top right-hand corner a small CCTV camera stared at her. There were several community policing posters dotted around the walls and one or two notices regarding missing persons.

She pressed the bell.

She felt intimidated but was damned if she was going to allow this unpleasant and unaccustomed emotion to show through. She sat on one of the chairs; it was plastic and uncomfortable, presumably deliberately so.

She looked around but her eye was inevitably drawn to the camera.

Time passed.

She cast an eye over the reading material so thoughtfully posted on the grimy walls but found little of interest.

She knew what the game was. She might well have played it herself, in their position. *Teach the bitch a lesson. Keep her waiting.*

She had been fully aware that she was treading on corns, and a policeman's corns are second to none. She was basically muscling in on someone else's investigation. True, she had the excuse that there had been an incidental finding of evidence connected with an old case of hers, but protocol was that she should be kept informed but not invited to take a hand.

Beverley took the view that protocol was just a set of rules and therefore there to be broken.

Inevitably, though, such a liberated view was not shared by all, hence her awareness that the next few hours were going to be vital; handle them badly and she would risk a potentially dangerous proliferation of what was at present a small, containable problem.

She wanted to press the button again but would go to eternal damnation before she did so.

Okay. If that's the way it's going to be.

She fished in the pocket of her jacket, pulled out her mobile phone and scrolled through its memory. Having found the number of Newford police station she pressed the dial button, put the phone to her ear and looked up at the CCTV camera. She gave it a quick, cold smirk.

Three rings and it was answered. 'Newford police.'

'DI Wharton, here.' She paused but there was no response to this. In a light but tight voice she went on, 'I'm in the lobby.'

'Oh.' Another pause. 'I'll be right along.' It sounded as if he were several streets away.

More time passed.

The hatch opened and through the hole created she saw a police sergeant. He was perhaps fifty and the upper part of his body was apparently composed entirely of spheroids. Beverley knew the type at once: Number 37 in the Catalogue of Police Types – *uniformed sergeant, confined*

157

to the station, near retirement, insolent bastard and know-it-all slob.

Sometimes she wondered what number she was in the Catalogue.

'Yes?'

She held up her warrant card. This was examined with something that the uncharitable might describe as woefully inadequate attention and due deference.

She was feeling uncharitable.

'I'm here to see DI Sauerwine.'

'He's not here.'

She could smell cigarette smoke about his uniform but there was another, more unpleasant, sourer smell. Something organic, perhaps. She tried the smile again; it was much as a turkey farmer smiles just before Christmas. 'No? Then I'll wait for him.' Just in case he had any other ideas she added, 'Inside, I think.'

The Sergeant didn't look too happy about that and Beverley's detective skills were up to the task of deducing what was coming next. She therefore pre-empted any possible unpleasantness. 'I said "inside", *Sergeant.*'

The emphasis hit home. His face had not been built for pleasantness but even so his expression now suggested that he was chewing several small stinging insects. He opened his mouth, presumably not to debate the finer aspects of needlepoint or modern dance, but Beverley had had enough. 'Listen,' she advised in a clear, calm and distinctly threatening tone, 'forget the surlier-than-thou attitude. Just let me into the fucking station.'

He went from bad-tempered and uncooperative to bad-tempered and shocked in less than a second. There was a short wait, then with an even unhappier face he grunted, withdrew his head and shut the hatch with a degree of force that Beverley suspected was not actually required.

The door opened and she walked through. When the Sergeant was revealed in all his adipose glory she discovered that the spheroid leitmotif was continued in a southerly direction, his whole body round. He had no neck, presumably because it had been left on the floor of the construction bay along with the charm and the deodorant.

'Thank you,' she offered sweetly. He shut the door behind her and he was about to lead her into the depths of the building when she said, 'Two things. First, your name . . .?'

His answer was dripping with the slothsome offspring of reluctance and dislike. 'Jackson.'

'Second, I'd better have the combination number for the door lock. I may be here for some time and it's going to be inconvenient for both of us if I have to keep disturbing you at your work, Jackson.'

She rather enjoyed the indigestion that registered on his face as he swallowed this jagged little pill. 'Two-four-five-nine.'

She noted this down in her PDA and then nodded. 'Fine. Now, if you'll take me to DI Sauerwine's office, I'll wait for him there.'

He walked – it wasn't a waddle although it ought to have been – ahead of her, which unfortunately put her directly in the slipstream. At the end of the corridor there was a large room in which there were four desks, all empty. Directly ahead of them was another door, now closed, that she guessed led into Sauerwine's office.

Jackson, however, did not take her any further. 'If you'll wait in here . . .'

Here we go again.

It had all been a game, of course. She would have done the same – show her how unimportant she was, how she was unwanted and unneeded. Beverley was good at games, though.

'I think not, Sergeant.'

She carried on walking, overtaking the Sergeant who had come to a halt and needed time to build up momentum for further exertion. She heard him say, 'You can't do that . . .' as she went through the door directly ahead of her, and thereby proved him wrong.

The office was a shock because it was neat. Like an albino witch it had all the right shapes in all the right places, but it was still wrong. Police personnel had a lot of things to do and a lot to do for each and every one of them; keeping the desk tidy tended to rank just below reform of criminal justice on the list of priorities. Active files were generally kept out on a surface – any surface – and that meant that when it was a large investigation, three days in and things generally resembled a complex maze built of paper and cardboard. The introduction of

159

computers had not only not reduced the forest slaughter it had actually tended to worsen it.

Sauerwine was apparently an exception.

She walked around the desk and sat down; Jackson stood at the doorway as if prevented from entry by a hex.

'Could I have some coffee? Black, no sugar.'

The lips parted, there came forth a noise but nothing suggested that her words were being received. Before he could collect what little senses he appeared to possess she said, 'Sergeant? Coffee?'

He seemed to be in a daze and was understandably slow to respond. At last he said, 'I suppose so . . . yes.'

He turned. It was not so much as a nineteenth-century servant might turn to go about his master's bidding, more as a man in a trance might have left.

Her look at his back held no pity whatsoever.

She turned to the office. There were three filing cabinets beside the door; surely he wouldn't lock those when he was out of the office? Surely he couldn't be that anal-retentive?

As it turned out, he was.

Felty was ironing her blouse, aware that she was going to be late. She didn't enjoy ironing and at that moment she didn't enjoy life.

She didn't know why she didn't enjoy ironing but then she didn't need to; it was an instinctual thing – like hating cockroaches or estate agents or BMW drivers. Not enjoying life, though, was a new and slightly disturbing phenomenon. When she had joined the police, most of her contemporaries had considered her to be mad, some had considered her traitorous. A sociological degree course in a middle-ranking university was not conventionally considered to be fertile loam for the seeds of a career in law enforcement, tending, as it did, to engender doubts about the methods and aims of conventional policing, but Sally Felty had always been independent-minded. She had coped with the reactions – her friends had exhibited a range of emotions from shocked disbelief to contempt – with great patience because she had accepted that it would not be easy for everyone. Sociologists had open to them a range of careers but the percentage that opted to

160

mind the thin blue line was small; more of them probably ended up as astronauts.

Yet she had enjoyed it. True, there had been times when she had been beyond despair, when she had been humiliated, in pain, in dread, but these had been in sharp, almost enjoyable contrast to the general atmosphere. She had felt that she was doing something practical to maintain society and every time she had helped in an arrest it had been as if a tiny battle had been won.

She had always known that she was doing *right* and this had been a source of strength for her. This in turn had led her to relatively rapid promotion to plain clothes and her posting in Newford where, she thought, she had settled in fairly well.

She was still healthy, her mother and father were still alive and well, she had a cat.

There was no reason to be unhappy with her life.

She was attacking a blouse. She hated blouses. Designers didn't iron, clearly. Didn't work, didn't launder and didn't iron. They were happy if the bloody things looked good (but only on a stupid skinny tart with tits the same size as her brains), but they didn't have any interest in what happened in the real world.

'Who is this Wharton, anyway?'

She asked the question of the television newsreader who couldn't hear and, even if he could, would almost certainly not have had the foggiest.

The way that Andrew had spoken had suggested that she was a remarkable detective, that she might even serve as a role model for Felty.

I don't need a role model. I need a maid, but not a role model.

She could tell that Sauerwine liked this Wharton. There had been a sense of something – something she had found at the time hard to chase down – as he had told Felty of the Eaton-Lambert case, how Wharton had found the evidence that had brought it all to a close. Only afterwards had she realized what it was.

He fancied her.

Now, as she wrestled her blouse into the semblance of creaselessness and the newsreader winked at her in that falsely friendly way that she hated, she saw things quite clearly. Sauerwine believed that the watch and the photograph had come from the Eaton-Lambert case, which may or may not have been true. It didn't, as far as Felty could see, require Sauerwine to ring up and have a nice long chat with this Wharton.

Now she thought about it, Wharton had been very keen to reciprocate. So what if they had found some artefacts from a double murder eight years before? It didn't require Wharton to rush down and interfere in another case entirely, did it?

Sauerwine hadn't said that he and Wharton had been an item, but then he hadn't said that they weren't.

Why else were they both so keen to renew their acquaintance?

She switched off the iron and put the blouse on.

Time to meet Inspector Wharton.

When Jackson returned with the coffee, she was sitting at the desk brushing her hair. The mug bore the legend *Policemen do it with handcuffs and truncheons* and Beverley found it remarkably easy not to split her sides. Perhaps part of this was because it looked as if the mug had not been cleaned since it left the shop some decades before.

'When is DI Sauerwine expected back?'

Jackson shrugged; the lack of cervical spine meant that much of his upper body was forced to join in. 'Didn't say.'

He stayed where he was in the doorway. Beverley, who had tried every drawer in the office and found them either locked or filled with nothing of any interest, was keen to begin searching the desks in the room beyond. 'There's no need to stay, Sergeant. You should be manning the front desk.'

After all, there might be someone reporting a lost kitten.

He didn't want to go but he knew that she was right. As he turned she breathed a sigh and was already rising from the desk when the door from the corridor opened and Sauerwine came in. He was followed by a young woman with mousy-brown hair and large, dark eyes. She was a good foot shorter than the relatively tall Sauerwine.

Jackson stopped. Beverley could only see his back and his shape made the body language difficult to read but she could guess that he was signalling a mix of warning and apology. She saw Sauerwine's eyes switch from Jackson to

162

her. She was already smiling, coming forward as she saw a wave of anger pass quickly into a diplomatic smile of welcome.

'Beverley.'

'Hello, Andrew. I took the liberty of waiting in your office. I hope you don't mind . . .'

'Of course not.' He turned to indicate the young woman behind him. 'This is DC Sally Felty.'

Felty nodded and so did Beverley but neither smiled and neither moved forward. They both read the message that each was sending; no one felt the need to extend their Christmas card list.

To Sauerwine Beverley said, 'Your Sergeant Jackson was kind enough to make me some coffee. He's really looked after me.'

Jackson, standing behind them, opened his mouth and his eyes in a synchronized exhibition of dumbfoundedness. Sauerwine said, 'Then perhaps he'd like to do the same for us.'

The corpuscular Sergeant nodded glumly and departed.

Beverley had come round the desk and Sauerwine sat down behind it. 'Sit down,' he invited.

As she did so, she was disappointed to see that Felty did likewise. She crossed her legs. 'It's very kind of you to put up with me.'

'To be honest, Beverley, I don't really see why you're here.'

'Don't you? Isn't it obvious?'

Sauerwine smiled. He had a slightly crooked smile that was no less appealing for that. 'The watch and the photograph? It's interesting, I admit, but what of it? The Eaton-Lambert is closed . . . isn't it?'

His face betrayed nothing, but this slightest of pauses was voluble.

So, it's like that, is it?

She had hoped that he would at least understand, if not like, her presence here. It seemed, though, that he had been listening to the rumours about Jeremy Eaton-Lambert's innocence.

'You know as well as I do, Andrew, that you can never be sure that a cold case won't suddenly show signs of life. I think it's worth looking into.'

163

Felty, until then completely wordless, suddenly said, 'We could have done that.'

Beverley turned to her, much as a queen might look at a prostitute. 'I'm sure you could, but you've got your hands full investigating the death of Moynihan. I'm only interested in how he came by the watch and the photograph.'

Sauerwine suggested, 'Unless the two are connected.'

'Is there any evidence to suggest that possibility?'

'Not as yet.'

Felty was still, to Beverley's mind, being a pain. 'Are you suggesting that there's a possibility that Jeremy Eaton-Lambert was innocent?'

Beverley's smile brought winter into the room. 'Not in the least.'

'Then I don't understand . . .'

'Don't you?' The words were so patronizing they nearly curled up as they left her lips. *That doesn't in the least surprise me*, they suggested. 'Well, you see, one thing that we never managed to exclude was an accomplice.' She turned to Sauerwine. 'You remember that we actually started off with the idea of at least two people being involved, don't you, Andrew?'

He nodded and Beverley turned back to Felty. 'Now do you understand?'

They stared at each other for just a moment before Beverley, choosing her timing with practised ease, dismissed the junior officer by turning to Sauerwine and asking, 'So what have you found out about Mr Moynihan? Have you got positive ID yet?'

Felty bridled, a reaction that Beverley noticed at once. *I seem to be treading on toes.* She filed this for potential future use as she paid all her attention to Sauerwine. He was just as fresh-faced as she remembered, just as wide-eyed; she wondered if he had learned to use this yet, to beguile with his charm and hint of safety. Perhaps that was what he was using on Felty.

'Hopefully we've got a DNA match coming today.'

She nodded and he continued, 'Up until two weeks ago, Moynihan was living in a room in Leicester. He suddenly decides to empty his bank account and come to the area, finding lodgings in Melbury, with Mrs Gleason. He'd been staying with her for only a few days when suddenly he turns up severely charred on the edge of the Westerham estate.'

'And before Leicester?'

'Interestingly, eight years before Leicester he was here, working on the Westerham estate as some sort of assistant to the manager, Malcolm Groshong. He left apparently following an argument of some kind with Groshong. He'd been living in Leicester for about nine months, but prior to that, nothing as yet.'

'And you think that that might be significant? An argument eight years before?'

'Groshong was on the scene pretty quickly after the fire.'

She wasn't about to hand out plaudits easily. 'What was the argument about? The one that was so serious he waited years and years to come back to settle it. The one that resulted in his incineration.'

Sauerwine smiled but it was more a defensive posture than a sign that he was finding jollity in the situation. Felty had moved into an upright, alert posture, almost suggesting that she was ready to spring forward to aid him. 'We don't know yet. We were planning to have another word with him today.'

She nodded. To judge by her attitude she might have been his superior, not just an interloper, an air she was projecting quite deliberately; she rather enjoyed the effect it was having on poor Felty.

With what Felty was sure was a perfectly relaxed air of complete control she suggested, 'Well? What are we waiting for? Let's go and see him.'

Sauerwine, though, was hesitant. 'There is one other thing,' he said. There was uncertainty in his voice, but there was also something else, something that she realized quite quickly was enjoyment.

And then Felty joined in. 'It's rather odd, actually.' Her voice carried not enjoyment but quite marked viciousness.

Sauerwine again. 'Felty paid a visit to Westerham Castle last night. She talked with Tristan Hickman, the owner, as well as his wife.'

Where was this heading? That it was heading somewhere was clear; that the somewhere was unpleasant was equally transparent.

Felty, inevitably, had the punchline. 'He's got some

guests staying with him. They came here the same day as Moynihan died.' A pause, just to heighten the drama, then, 'Dr John Eisenmenger and Miss Helena Flemming.'

Oh, shit.

Felty drove well. Not that Beverley was about to tell her that.

Felty was a rival. It was as simple as that; as simple and primordial as that. Beverley was well aware that she was experiencing an unthinking, almost feral emotion, that she was behaving exactly as a billion species of fauna, but that didn't mean that she could ignore it. No matter how illogical the more modern parts of her brain told her it was, the older and more persuasive areas merely had to sigh and smile, knowing that she would dance to their ancient tune. There was not even something to fight over, at least not as far as she was concerned. If Felty had the hots for Sauerwine, Beverley had yet to see why. If she ended up groaning and sighing in his bed, it would be for purely practical reasons; Felty would have no need to be jealous.

Anyway, she had no time for small talk, not with the echoes of the bomb-blast from Felty's news still causing plaster to fall from the ceiling.

What does this mean?

They had to stop for traffic lights at the top of the hill. Sauerwine sat in the back and looked to his right out of the window. He looked bored. Felty just looked sour.

It's not a coincidence. Coincidence is for the lazy, for the stupid, for the optimistic.

The car moved off. They turned to the right and then immediately to the left across the staggered junction. She was panicking, she realized; she must not panic. Nothing had changed, really. She had more information, that was all. More information meant more power; knowledge was power.

So, how to use it?

Moynihan had been trying to contact Helena. He had some sort of business with her, business relating to her parents' murder.

This hypothesis, initially attractive, soon ran out of steam . . .

The road they were on was twisty and hilly. They passed a vineyard and a fruit farm.

. . . After all, Moynihan had arrived in Westerham over a week before Helena. It was unlikely that he could have known she was going to be there, unless it was pre-arranged between them. In which case, why didn't he just visit her in her apartment?

The obverse was equally improbable. She could not believe that Helena could have known about Moynihan's presence in Westerham.

So, Moynihan's business had not been with Helena. Simple . . .

Sauerwine said, 'I see the travellers have gone.'

'They moved on last week, sir.'

. . . Which presented her with a problem, because it led her back to coincidence, and she wasn't lazy, and she wasn't stupid and she didn't have an ounce of optimism left inside her.

If Eisenmenger and Flemming are here, I'm going to have a lot of explaining to do. Even if they know nothing, they'll wonder what I'm doing here. I'd ask questions, so they will, too.

The road became extremely tortuous and Felty had to slow down. A dog ran out about fifty metres ahead, bringing the car almost to a halt whilst they edged past it. Barks followed them as they sped away.

I'm going to have to get Sauerwine on board. Make sure that he has the same script as me.

She glanced sidewards at Felty. *What about her?*

What about her? The police force hierarchy militated against juniors speaking out of turn.

It was still a risk, though.

They reached the outskirts of Melbury. They would have to drive through the town and then on to Westerham.

There were two strategies she could employ and these were not contradictory. She could use the code of *Omerta*, a force every bit as binding for the police as it was for the Mafia, or she could use sex. The problem with the first was that it required him to know rather more than she thought healthy; he would want to know why he was being asked to toe her particular line, perhaps lie for her. The problem with the second was that it was not guaranteed to work. Rare as they were, she had come across the occasional Y-bearing human organism who could resist the call of testosterone, especially if they were already in a relationship. Sauerwine was clearly still interested in her – he always had been (poor bastard) – but if Felty's proprietorial feelings were in any way reciprocated, then she might have difficulties . . .

The traffic in the centre of town was light. They began to ascend away from buildings and into brown, white-scarred fields and greying cold light.

. . . In which case . . .

In which case, I'd better opt for both strategies.

She'd always been a careful and conscientious girl.

They went looking for Groshong at the estate office but his secretary, a middle-aged woman with a sour expression on her face and another hovering behind her lips, informed them curtly that he was out and not expected back in the office until midday.

'Where is he?' asked Sauerwine.

'The West Covers. He's with the gamekeeper, making sure everything's coming along okay for the next shoot.'

'How do we get there?'

She hesitated, as if this information was restricted, or at least ought to have been restricted. 'He won't like being disturbed,' she observed.

Sauerwine glanced across at Beverley who was examining a large map of the estate pinned to the wall. She was tapping it. 'There they are.' She looked at the scale to the side of the map. 'About five kilometres from here. Not surprisingly, in a westerly direction.'

She turned with her eyebrows raised. 'Shall we go?'

She failed to thank Groshong's secretary as she left. Sauerwine said quietly, 'Well, it looks as if we can find him ourselves.'

Felty and the secretary exchanged glances of deep discontent for very different reasons. When she was alone again, the secretary lifted the telephone receiver.

Addison had a lot of other cases to work on and plenty of other things to do; in a few days' time she had a lecture to give at the Royal College; she was supposed to be writing a chapter in a textbook of forensic pathology that was due in a month. The Moynihan case, though, was proving as mesmerizing as it was impossible. Was it even Moynihan? She wouldn't know for sure for another day when the results of the DNA comparison came through. Whoever it was, there was still the not inconsiderable problem of how he had died.

All of the skin unaffected by fire had been clear of significant bruising or laceration; it was impossible to determine whether the charred skin had been contused, but she was fairly sure there were no significant cuts. The internal organs all showed fire damage to a greater or lesser extent; there was some evidence to suggest that he had been suffering from emphysema, his coronary circulation had been quite severely narrowed by atheroma (a cardiac death would have been a kindness that was denied to him), the kidneys had been inflated by thin-walled, urine-filled cysts. All very interesting but nothing to trouble the grim reaper. The head and neck had been too burned to determine whether the victim had been breathing when the fire had taken hold, and there had been no blood to determine the level of carbon monoxide inhaled.

All of which meant that she still didn't know what had happened in this poor man's last few hours and minutes.

She had been a consultant for only seven months and was still therefore under unofficial probation. Her appointment to the department had not been without some controversy. A more experienced candidate had been passed over and at least one of her four colleagues had made it clear that he thought the wrong decision had been made. She couldn't fail so early.

Yet some deaths, she knew, could not be explained by even the best of pathologists using all of the techniques available. Asthma and epilepsy especially were silent in their work, but the cause of any death could be obscured or hidden completely by fire. It was why all burned bodies were treated as suspicious until it had been proven otherwise.

The only saving grace was that a body was surprisingly difficult to burn; easy to char but difficult to destroy. Human bodies had a lot of fat – some more than others – but they were also seventy per cent water; she

169

had been delighted when she had learned this fact at medical school, especially as the lecturer had pointed out that effectively the human body had its own fire control system.

Normally, therefore, bodies deliberately burned to disguise malfeasance still had their tale to tell; another example of wrongdoers failing through stupidity or incompetence or ignorance.

Or all three.

In this case, there appeared to be nothing to suggest that it had been suspicious; in fact all of the available evidence pointed her towards suicide. And there had been many such suicides. As abhorrent as it was to her, she was fully aware that the distortions of deep, psychotic depression were perfectly capable of persuading some to die in the most painful, bizarre or unlikely ways. Suicide by immolation in a car fire was well reported.

I've got to make a decision.

If she bottled it – it was theoretically open to her to decide that the cause of death was 'unascertained' – her position in the department might be fatally damaged. Another pathologist would be called in; it might even be one of her hostile colleagues. No doctor in the world was going to be asked for a second – for which read 'expert' – opinion and then produce the gobsmackingly pusillanimous word, 'unascertained'. It would be either 'natural' (with details given) or 'unnatural' (with implications given). It would also be a verdict on her competence.

Hence she had a decision to make.

And she had to make it soon.

The car did not like the track. By the time they arrived in the shallow valley that according to the map was the West Covers, it was a moving mudcake with the washer bottle empty and windows smeared with brown slime. On three occasions the car had very, very nearly become bogged down. Nerves were not so much frayed as amputated; Felty because she was sure that Beverley, in the front passenger seat, was silently criticizing her driving, Beverley because she *was* silently criticizing Felty's driving, and Sauerwine, in the back, because he suspected that they were not presenting a very dignified picture.

Sauerwine stepped out. His shoes sank into long grass so that his lower trouser legs became almost instantly heavy with cold moisture. Beverley was wearing leather boots that were not waterproof but she made no sign of this; only Felty – wearing thick-soled walking shoes and heavy jeans (Beverley had noticed this with a knowing sneer) – did not immediately regret her sartorial choice of the morning.

Groshong was walking with a small wiry-looking man some hundred metres away. They had seen him glance at them when they arrived and now they saw him not looking at them, sending a message that he wasn't going to hurry himself.

Beverley said mildly, 'I would wager large piles of banknotes that he received a phone call from his secretary about a quarter of an hour ago.'

Needless to say it was a cold day and here the wind blew with especial spite, slicing down the centre of the valley from somewhere that might have been the place where Siberians kept their frozen goods. By the time Groshong had finished his tête-à-tête with what they assumed was the gamekeeper, all three of them were close to hypothermia. The gamekeeper glanced in their direction as he walked past them to one of a pair of Land Rovers, one old and battered, the other new. He got into the battered version and it started first time with a grunt of blue-grey diesel smoke; it then moved off easily over the muddy terrain, which they were all so pleased to see.

Even then Groshong found something to look at in the woodlands that surrounded him before finally turning and walking – slowly – towards them.

He had the kind of stretched grin on his face that suggested he might have warmed himself up with a drop of strychnine.

'Mr Groshong.' Sauerwine sounded almost cheerful.

He was answered with a slight flaring of the nostrils and a deep, frigid breath. At least Groshong stopped moving and didn't just ignore them, which for a moment Felty had actually thought might happen. That was all he did, though.

'Can we have another chat?'

'Why?' It was a reasonable question, except in this particular situation.

Sauerwine kept the cheery attitude; only his mother might have noticed the strain. 'Because a man burned to death in a car and I don't know if he was murdered.'

'So? Nothing to do with me.'

'Isn't it? Do you know someone called Moynihan?'

Groshong stared at him for a moment. 'William Moynihan?'

'That's right.'

He was staring at Sauerwine as he said cautiously, 'Yes. Or, at least, I used to.'

'Tell me more.'

Groshong had come round from 'sneering' to a more amenable 'hostile'. 'Is this relevant?'

'Yes.' By now even his father might well have noticed the strain.

A big sigh, the kind that small children do when they've been told not to take off their shoes with the laces still tied. 'He worked on the estate a few years ago.'

'How many?'

'Don't know. Maybe six, seven.'

'What did he do?'

'General stuff.'

Sauerwine frowned. 'What does that mean?'

Groshong leaned towards him. 'He did whatever I told him to do.'

Sauerwine made a vowelless noise with his lips closed. Then, 'We've been told he was your deputy.'

Groshong laughed, although a comic might not have welcomed him to the audience. 'Oh, really?'

'I take it he wasn't.'

Groshong became animated or, at least, he moved his right arm in a sort of pointing motion. 'He was hired help. He did what he was told. If I told him to chop wood, he chopped it. If I told him to clear a ditch, he cleared it.'

They got the general drift.

Whatever Sauerwine was about to say will never be known. Beverley said suddenly, 'So what did you row about?'

Groshong turned to her. He was imperiousness wearing a waxed jacket. 'I beg your pardon?'

Before she could answer, Sauerwine said quickly in a

loud voice that didn't bury his irritation, 'There was an argument between you and Moynihan; that was why he left the estate. I'd like to know what it was about.' He didn't quite take all the emphasis off this last personal pronoun.

Groshong looked at him. It was difficult to tell if his attitude was one of contempt or contemplation. He twitched his shoulders. 'Something and nothing. Like most rows.'

'I think a little more detail, Mr Groshong . . .'

He sighed. It was a big sigh that might have sucked in a passing fly had it not been the depths of winter. 'I can't remember. It was eight years ago.'

Sauerwine suddenly smiled. 'Eight? I thought that you said it was six or seven.'

Groshong got crosser, a feat that had previously seemed improbable. 'What the fuck does it matter? Six, seven or eight. It was a long time ago.'

Sauerwine obviously thought that the smile suited him because he kept it. 'What was the row about, Mr Groshong? I really would like to know.'

Beverley had the distinct impression that Groshong really would have liked something else. He said after consuming a lot of oxygen, 'Money, I think. It's always about money, isn't it?'

'Can you be more specific?'

Groshong suffered a minor apoplectic explosion. 'He wanted a rise in his wages.' When Sauerwine said nothing, he went on, 'Actually, it was as you said. He fancied himself as my "deputy". Went around telling people that I couldn't cope without him. Because of that he reckoned he was worth more than I was willing to pay.'

'But you thought differently.'

'He was brighter than the average, I'll admit, but he was still just hired help.'

'And he disagreed, so you had a row.'

'Hardly.' Groshong was dismissive. 'He demanded more money, I told him to piss off. He left. End of story.'

'No big argument, then.'

'No.'

Sauerwine looked at Groshong; Groshong returned the

173

compliment. There was a slight whiff of machismo about this stand-off. It was soon interrupted, however.

'Moynihan drove a distinctive red car, remember?'

Groshong switched his attention to Beverley Wharton. 'Do I know you?'

Sauerwine, a flicker of aggravation showing in his eyes, said tightly, 'Inspector Wharton is a colleague of mine. Perhaps you'd answer her question.'

More heavy breathing. 'Vaguely.'

Sauerwine said, 'And the car in which the dead man was found was red.'

Groshong sneered. 'There's a lot of red cars, you know.'

'But he was staying in Melbury. He'd been seen in the village. Are you saying that you weren't aware that he was back, complete with red car?'

'Yes. I am.' He was challenging them to disprove the statement.

Which of course, they couldn't.

Sauerwine said, 'You had no idea he was in the area again?'

'No.'

'So you wouldn't have any idea why he might have come back?'

'No.'

'He didn't come back for a job?'

'No.'

Groshong was now in control of the situation. Sauerwine could see no benefit in prolonging and deepening his hypothermia. 'Well, I think that'll be all for now.' He glanced sideways at Beverley. She was staring at the estate manager as if trying to read him. He continued, 'Thank you for your time, Mr Groshong.'

Groshong turned away without any acknowledgement and walked in huge strides through the long, wet grass to his Land Rover.

Sauerwine took a long, deep breath. Then, 'What do you think?'

Beverley was certain. 'He's lying.'

'What about?'

'About the row with Moynihan. Probably also about not knowing that Moynihan was back in the neighbourhood; if that's the case, then it follows that he at least had a good

174

idea whose car it was that was going up like a Roman candle.'

Sauerwine turned to Felty. 'And you?'

'I agree. He knows more than he's saying.' She wore an expression that suggested she was not enjoying being in agreement with Beverley Wharton. 'But we have no proof of any of this.'

Sauerwine sighed. 'No. I know.'

He walked back to the car, Beverley and Felty doing likewise. The return journey to Newford was in silence. As they drew up outside the station, Sauerwine said to Felty, 'Go back to Westerham. Ask around again. I want to know if anyone saw Groshong and Moynihan together. Also, find out if anyone knows about the precise circumstances of Moynihan's departure last time. Talk to Michael Bloom at the petrol station. He knew Moynihan and he says there was a row. I want every detail he can give us.'

As Beverley and Sauerwine were walking through the station, he said quietly, 'Don't do that again.'

'What?'

Holt was in, sitting at his desk sipping tea from a mug that proclaimed he was the UK's number-one lover; Beverley somehow doubted it. Sauerwine didn't say any more until they were in his office and the door was closed. He sat behind his desk, then said, 'It's still my investigation, Beverley. I'll tolerate you being here, but unless I ask you for your help, keep your questions to yourself.'

She raised an eyebrow. People had regretted saying things like that to Beverley Wharton, but she wasn't in that kind of position at the present.

She smiled, dropped her head. 'Sorry, Andrew.' She kept her voice low; not overtly husky, but just a hint of smokiness. Her eyes came up, still the smile. 'You know how it is. It's hard to keep quiet, especially when you're dealing with someone who you know is lying.'

He suddenly noticed how large her eyes were, how red her lips were, and he was in the past, the years unravelling in the space between them. He remembered how he had been smitten, how she had seemed to him to be carved out of sexual allure.

He couldn't stop himself smiling and slowly he said, 'Yeah. I know.'

She switched it off – whatever it was. 'But you're absolutely right. I promise I'll be good in future.'

Her promise to be good somehow suggested that she could be very, very bad; just as bad as Sauerwine might want her to be.

Supper was a quiet affair. Nell had eaten earlier with Tom and Dominique (or so Theresa assured them) and Eleanor claimed to feel tired and took her meal in her room. 'She often does these days,' remarked Tristan and it was difficult to tell whether he was sorrowful or relieved. Eisenmenger and Helena, Tristan, Theresa and Hugo had eaten pheasant salad in the kitchen, during which Hugo had recounted various surgical anecdotes that ranged from the hilarious to the disgusting to the hilarious and disgusting.

Afterwards Hugo had declined an invitation to join his father and Eisenmenger for a game of snooker, saying that he was going to meet an 'old friend'.

'An old girlfriend, I expect,' Tristan remarked cheerfully as he took Eisenmenger to the snooker room with a bottle of ten-year-old tawny port and a small wager to be settled. Theresa and Helena talked for about an hour and then Helena, feeling tired, excused herself and walked up the back stairs and along the corridor to her landing. She opened the door to the room, at once surprised to see that the lights were on.

Nell was sitting on the bed. She was cross-legged and grinning.

'Nell!' Helena didn't know whether to be pleased or slightly affronted.

'I know I shouldn't have come in without asking, but I wanted to surprise you.'

'You certainly did that.'

'Come here. Sit down.' The tone was not so much commanding as expecting compliance. Helena had the feeling that Nell had a secret to tell. She shut the door behind her and did as she had been bid.

Nell leaned towards her and took her hand. 'Do you remember the games we used to play? In the good times?'

'Very much so.'

'They were wonderful, weren't they? Before it all changed; before we were broken up.'

'Yes. Yes, they were.'

'And wouldn't it be good if they could come round again? If we could recreate them?'

Perplexed Helena said, 'I suppose so . . .'

Suddenly Nell was up and off the bed. 'Come with me!'

At once she was off.

'Nell?'

But Nell was gone, even from the corridor when Helena reached the doorway. *What on earth is wrong with her?*

She called again, 'Nell?'

Nell suddenly reappeared at the end of the corridor, beckoning. It seemed to Helena then that Nell had regressed. She followed, half expecting Nell to run on ahead, as if they were four-year-olds playing tag or hide-and-seek. Yet Nell once again surprised her, this time staying where she was.

'Come on!'

She took Helena by the hand, almost pulling her along. They turned to go up some steep stairs, presumably once backstairs for the servants, then out into a long corridor that was low and narrow. In daylight it would have been lit by rooflights set in the ceiling, but now these were just empty blue-black spaces.

About halfway along, Nell stopped and said in a whisper, 'Be quiet!'

She crept to a door on their left, turning the handle gently and pushing it open a little so that she could peer into the darkness. Then she pulled back and whispered to Helena, 'Be very quiet, now.'

She opened the door a little more and went in with Helena following.

It wasn't entirely black in the room because there was a small nightlight plugged into a wall socket. In the light from this, Helena saw a connecting door to the next bedroom, walls papered with Peter Pans, a ceiling from which hung the crescent moon and stars, a pile of soft toys on the end of a bed cover crawling with Spidermen, and perfectly in the emotional centre of all this, Tom. He was deeply asleep, the cover half thrown back, on his back, at an angle to the bed so that his head had fallen to the side of the pillow. He was, to Helena's eyes, quite simply a

177

vision of perfect childlike beauty, innocence incarnate. Before she was even aware of it, she was longing for the experience of bearing such a fragile piece of perfection, of raising it, worrying over it, doting on it, allowing a part of herself to be stolen by it . . .

'He sleeps an awful lot.'

It wasn't just the words, wasn't just the sentiment behind them, it was the tone that shocked Helena from her unconscious descent into broodiness. She gestured at Tom, now snoring gently, and said in a low, delighted whisper, 'But he looks so beautiful!'

'We play together all the time.'

Helena looked at Nell. She was smiling at the sleeping form but it was *that* smile again – the lost, almost displaced smile that was faintly chilling.

'Of course you do,' said Helena.

'He's very naughty, though. Sometimes he refuses to do as he's told. Not even Dominique can get him to behave.'

Uncertainly, Helena said, 'All small children are like that sometimes.'

Nell sighed. 'I suppose.'

Helena turned back to Tom. He had twisted slightly so that his head was now to one side, his neck extended, his mouth open. There was a hint of the supplicant about the posture, as if he was reaching with his lips for something . . .

I've just had breast cancer . . .

. . . Might still have it. It can suddenly come back, even after years – I've trawled the Internet, filled in the gaps that John left open . . .

. . . If I don't have a child soon, maybe it'll be too late . . .

There was a touch on her arm. 'Come on! I've got something else to show you!'

Nell began almost to pull her again. Helena glanced back at Tom, noticed that he was becoming slightly disturbed, and relented. She allowed herself to be drawn away from that beautiful boy, out of the darkness and into the loud brightness of the outside world. She closed the door as quietly as she could but almost at once the door just along the corridor opened and Dominique, wearing a pale blue silk dressing gown, peered out. When she saw

Nell she said, 'Ah, I wondered who it was. Is everything all right?'

Nell nodded. 'I just brought Helena to see Tom.'

Helena was taken aback by this unexpected appearance. She said uncertainly, 'I didn't realize you were in the next room, Dominique. I assumed . . .' She stopped, unwilling to say what she had assumed.

Dominique smiled. 'I always retire to my room when Tom has gone to bed, just in case he needs me in the night.'

To cover her confusion Helena asked, 'Doesn't that get boring?'

But Dominique disagreed. 'Oh, no. I have my own television and my stereo, and Mr Hickman lets me borrow books from the library.'

Nell was still in a hurry. 'Come on, Helena.' To Dominique she said, 'Sorry to disturb you.'

And Helena was rushed away.

Nell took her to the end of this corridor – at first sight a dead-end – then looked back towards Dominique's room, apparently to check that they were alone. She produced from a pocket in her skirt a tiny key that she inserted into a small door directly in front of them. Helena felt like Alice as Nell opened the door and stepped back to reveal yet another staircase. 'Up here?' she asked, to which Nell's answer was given by a push on the back. This flight of stairs seemed never-ending and began after a short while to curve gently around the left.

'Are we in one of the turrets?'

From behind her Nell's answer was full of excitement. 'Yes! Daddy never used to let us come up here when we were small. Said it was dangerous.' This last was said in a tone of disdain, the small child who refuses to believe that she isn't indestructible. 'I found the key, though. No one knows that I come up here.'

They passed windows both in the outer wall and the inner wall, all dark, the latter interspersed with occasional small wooden doors. The effort of climbing began to take its toll upon Helena.

'What's in these rooms?'

'Don't know. Junk, I think.'

Their climb continued, with Helena now feeling pain in her legs and breathless. She asked, 'Nell?'

'Yes?'

'Where do you sleep?'

'Where I always did. You remember, overlooking the northern terrace.' Before Helena could ask more, Nell said, 'Here! We're here!'

They had reached a ceiling and the stairs continued through it to end partially surrounded by a banister rail. It was an ascent into darkness and she looked back at Nell questioningly.

'There's a light switch to your right.'

It was partially hidden but Helena located it without too much trouble. She found herself emerging and ascending into a large room, perfectly circular. There was a vast amount of junk here but the room was so spacious it didn't appear cluttered; anyway, someone – presumably Nell – had pushed much of it away behind the banisters, leaving a wide area where a brass bedstead covered by a gauzy white canopy stood, surrounded by a miscellany of objects presumably retrieved from the junk. A suit of armour complete with worrying realistic black-handled sword, a rocking horse (one ear gone, mane suffering from alopecia), china dolls and random piles of books made a curious tableau but Helena's eye was caught by the crib. It, too was broken, so that Nell had had to support it at one end with a pile of old Enid Blyton books. It had been placed at the end of the bed. Helena couldn't see what, if anything, was in it.

Helena stood just beyond the top of the staircase, her legs trembling due to the exertion, her breath rasping slightly, and surveyed this room. Nell came around to stand in front of her.

'They don't know about it.' This was delivered in a whisper that had been tweaked into a higher timbre by excitement. She didn't say who didn't know and Helena, making assumptions, didn't ask.

'Your private place.'

'When it all went wrong, I had to find somewhere to hide. Somewhere secret. I came up here. I think Mummy and Daddy have forgotten about it.'

Helena began to walk around the room. The floor was dusty, she noticed. Her footsteps sounded loudly; in a conventional house the people below would have been complaining about having their television disturbed, but here she doubted there was anyone within a hundred metres. By the bed were piles of books and magazines. She bent down to look at them as Nell said, 'I come up here for hours sometimes. Just to sit and think, or maybe read.'

The Lord of the Rings, *The Hobbit*, *Gormenghast*, *The Once and Future King*. It was the reading list of a lonely, lovelorn teenager and it made Helena sad to see it. There were scrapbooks and ring files and single sheets of handwritten paper and photographs, some loose and some in photo albums.

'Do you bring Tom up here?'

Nell's look of astonishment was answer enough. 'Oh, no. He wouldn't like it up here.'

Helena, looking around at the junk, at the shape of the room, at its very hiddenness, doubted that; she doubted that very much indeed.

She moved to the windows. They were slit-like and narrowed as they burrowed into the stone, as windows in turrets should be, but the effect was spoiled by the glass that saved the inhabitants from hypothermia. They gave little scope to the view – a view that was in deep darkness anyway – but she saw the lights of the little forecourt where in the summer the visitors bought their souvenirs, and where the entrance to the restaurant was, and where wooden tables were arrayed on the cobbles.

She turned back to the room. Her eyes fell on the crib. With Nell watching her she walked over to it, peering in. A doll. What else would one find in a crib in a room in a castle turret? She picked it up. It was old and tatty.

Nell's eyes were wide and appealing and upon her. 'You do like this place, don't you, Helena?'

She hesitated before lying. 'It's magical, Nell. Absolutely magical.'

Nell's face relaxed, mutated, became a smile. 'Oh, I knew you would! I knew you would!'

Sauerwine had wanted more information and was soon brought his wish. First the laboratory told them that the DNA taken from Moynihan's belongings matched that taken from the body found in the car. Then last thing, Dr Addison's report was delivered.

'Shit!'

Tanner had wanted to see the report as soon as it arrived and Sauerwine knew that he dared not delay too long. Accordingly he presented it to the Superintendent ten minutes later; Tanner's reaction was much like his.

'"No definite evidence of third-party involvement." What does that mean?'

'She can't prove he was murdered, sir,' he explained.

Tanner was unimpressed. 'I know that,' he pointed out in a tone that was drowned in sarcasm. 'Why can't she?'

Sauerwine didn't particularly want to defend Dr Addison and said only, 'You'll have to ask her.'

Tanner grunted. 'What about forensics on the car? Anything?'

Sauerwine had brought a stack of files, one of which he handed across the desk as he said, 'It was a typical old car. What remained of the carpet showed evidence of mud – several different types – numerous sizes of gravel, sweet wrappers, bits of string, chewing gum and . . .' He paused. 'The window mechanism in the driver's door was jammed. He couldn't open it even if he wanted to.'

Tanner stared at him. 'What about the other windows?'

'They worked all right, but of course he'd have trouble getting to them once the fire took hold.'

'And the door handle?'

'In the back of the car, behind his seat.'

More staring. Then, 'How was the window mechanism jammed?'

'Rusted. The whole car was a bucket of rust.'

Tanner grunted and his expression became more of a frown. 'So nothing conclusive. If he was murdered, the killer merely took advantage of the fact that the car was practically scrap metal. All he had to do then was take off the inside door handle.'

'What about where the handle was? In the back. That might tell us something.'

Another grunt. 'It tells us nothing. It's the kind of place it might have ended up if it had fallen off and he never got around to putting it back on, or maybe the murderer chucked it there when he took it off.'

'Or maybe Moynihan chucked it there when *he* took it off.'

'Why would he do that?'

'He'd decided to burn himself to death in the car. Perhaps he took it off at the last moment so that he couldn't back out when the fire started.'

Tanner's expression was not promising and his voice held a mix of sorrow, amusement and disdain as he said, 'I'm no psychiatrist but I don't think someone who's bonkers enough to decide to die in one of the most agonizing ways they can is going to care whether the door handle's on or off.'

'No, sir.'

'Anyway, there's no evidence that he was bonkers or in any way depressed.'

'People sometimes hide these things very well, sir.'

The Superintendent said nothing but was clearly unimpressed with Sauerwine's amateur psychology.

'And the report of the Fire Investigation Team?'

'I haven't got anything in writing yet, but verbally it was a pile of crisp packets on the front passenger seat. They can't guarantee that there wasn't an accelerant such as petrol, though.'

'Even if there was, he wouldn't be the first poor saddo to douse himself in petrol to make the pleasure even greater.'

'No help, then.'

Tanner snorted. 'No.' He sat and frowned and looked at the report, immersed in contemplation. Eventually, 'So, the pathologist is no use and the forensics are no use. That means we're down to good, old-fashioned walk and talk, Inspector.'

Sauerwine knew that Tanner's use of the plural pronoun was purely figurative. 'At least we have an ID.'

'We do, indeed.' Then, 'Do we have a photograph yet?'

Here Sauerwine was forced to admit to failure. 'Moynihan was claiming Social Security and he claimed to be unmarried. We've found no trace of a criminal record or interest from the Inland Revenue or Customs. He was never in the forces. He's not on the sex offenders' register. He had a shotgun licence but that lapsed six years ago. He had a driving licence issued in 1979.' He stopped the litany. 'But no photograph and no sign of a next of kin.'

'Fantastic.'

Sauerwine took a breath. 'You don't think this is deliberate, do you, sir? I mean, it's almost as if someone's trying to make our task as hard as possible.' He was aware that this was Felty's theory but didn't see the point in cluttering the conversation with needless claims of ownership.

'The criminal mastermind hiding all traces? No, I don't think so, Sauerwine. Cock-up, not conspiracy, is the usual way. The person bright enough to commit the perfect murder has yet to be born.'

'Yes, sir.' He rather wished now that he had given Felty appropriate credit. At the same time he was thinking, *How do we know? By definition we wouldn't have any idea how many perfect murders there are.*

'How's our guest behaving herself?'

Sauerwine shrugged. 'She's not proving to be much of problem at the moment.'

Tanner scowled. 'I didn't want her, you know. I don't suppose you did either.'

Sauerwine didn't comment. He had mixed feelings on the subject; viewpoints both professional and personal.

Tanner explained, 'The ACC leaned on me.' He snorted. 'Owed a favour, I expect, so we get stuck with a cuckoo.'

'Yes, sir.'

'Still, not a bad-looking cuckoo, eh? Could have done worse there, I reckon.'

Sauerwine grinned, the expression very far from an accurate reflection of what he was actually thinking. After a few seconds' thought Tanner announced enigmatically, 'I've got some phone calls to make.'

Sauerwine took his cue and left him.

Later he took a phone call from Tanner in his office.

'We need someone in person in Leicester. I'm not convinced they've put one hundred per cent into their enquiries on this. I've made the necessary arrangements. It would be a good excuse to get Wharton out of our hair for a few days.'

'Yes, sir.'

He put down the receiver and thought deeply for a while. He didn't really see how he could justify sending Beverley on what was likely to prove a relatively minor assignment. He needed her here, he calculated . . .

Then he went out to Felty. 'Right, you're off to Leicester.'

Startled, she asked, 'Why?'

'Because it's been arranged. I want you to go over everything they've got on Moynihan. If necessary talk to the landlord, ask the neighbours, local pubs, shops, bookies.'

'But why?'

'Because it's not their case, and they're human. They don't really know what they're looking for and don't really care if they don't find it.' This impatiently. 'I've told them to expect you tomorrow morning. They'll arrange accommodation.'

And he turned and was back in his office before she could say any more.

She returned to her task, a simple case of tractor theft, but she was no longer unperturbed. She couldn't deny that it was a logical move with a reasonable explanation, but his manner had seemed strange, forced. He had done little less than peremptorily order her to Leicester, almost as if he wanted her out of the way.

But why could he possibly want that?

Eisenmenger had just lost his second frame of snooker. He had already drunk too much port and the last thing he needed was a cigar.

'No, thanks,' he said.

'No? As you wish. I am celebrating. No more work for a week.'

Tristan spent a moment lighting the cigar, then began to collect the balls from the pockets. 'Another game?'

'I'm not in your league.'

Tristan laughed. 'Sign of a misspent youth.'

'Sign of a snooker table in the house.'

Tristan was relaxed to the point of loud laughter. He set up the table then returned to the cigar that he had rested on an ashtray. 'You can break off,' he offered generously, as if that would make a difference.

Eisenmenger leaned over the table. He was actually starting to have trouble focusing and this, in combination with the fact that he didn't really have much idea where precisely he was supposed to be aiming, meant that his shot hit the target only by chance and with no strategic value whatsoever. When Tristan settled down to take his shot, it was as a hustler might have moved in. He pocketed a red then looked up at Eisenmenger.

'Helena's been through it, hasn't she?'

'Just a bit.' Eisenmenger went to the beautiful vintage scoreboard on the wall and advanced the bottom marker by one.

Tristan shook his head, settled down over his next shot, despatched the blue. Eisenmenger put it back on its spot after attending to the scoreboard while Tristan attended to his cigar, then finished his port. He was looking slightly flushed. 'It's funny, you know,' he said, meaning that it wasn't funny at all. 'Breast cancer ought to be one of the easier cancers. Near the surface, and all that; it's usually the ones that arise in deep organs that are the real killers.'

Eisenmenger shrugged. It occurred to him that this was a surgeon's viewpoint. 'There's the biology as well,' he pointed out.

A red disappeared. 'Mmm,' said his host, as if that was the kind of thing a pathologist *would* say, which didn't necessarily mean that it was right. Eisenmenger added, 'And anyway, the survival's improving all the time.'

Tristan was eyeing up the brown and still squatting down as he looked up at Eisenmenger. 'Oh, absolutely. Helena's going to be fine, I'm sure.'

Eisenmenger didn't say anything.

'Still, it's obviously taken it out of her.'

Eisenmenger didn't feel that he particularly wanted to be told how unwell she looked and made a non-committal noise. Seemingly oblivious, Tristan missed the brown, then straightened up. He headed for the port bottle and refilled the glasses while Eisenmenger tried to look as if he knew which was the best red to miss.

'It's good to see her back, though. Reminds me of old times.'

The white ball hit the red but not the red that he had meant it to; balls moved around on the green baize surface but to no great effect and the scoreboard remained unperturbed. As Eisenmenger straightened up, he asked, 'What was Jeremy like?'

He hadn't meant to vocalize the question, wasn't sure quite why he had. Surprised, Tristan was distracted from his consideration of the table. 'Hasn't Helena told you?'

Eisenmenger smiled. 'Helena doesn't talk about him.'

Tristan nodded slowly. 'No, well, Helena was always the quiet one.'

'And?'

Tristan went back to the cigar. 'Jeremy was a lovely boy. Always the joker, always first in line. Not rough, and definitely not stupid, though. Just . . . boisterous.'

It was the kind of statement that danced around the truth.

'I'm not even sure I've seen a photograph.'

'Haven't you?' He considered. 'Well, I remember Jeremy as a tall lad, quite good-looking, with jet black hair and a prominent nose.'

As descriptions went it was as good as most – all but useless. Eisenmenger asked, 'And what was the history? Jeremy was Helena's stepbrother, I understand. How did that come about?'

Tristan laughed. 'You're digging into deep family history, you know.'

'Best left undisturbed?'

More laughter. 'Not at all! What I meant is that the question gets at what links the Flemmings and the Hickmans; why we were such great friends . . .' He suddenly tailed off, as if realizing what he had said, that his use of the past tense had the finality of the grave about it. He said quickly, 'Claude and I were chums at college. We roomed together the whole time. Shared everything.' He grinned, sipped some port and put the glass on the polished wood of the table's edge. 'Even the girls, sometimes.'

'I gather Theresa was also at the college.'

Hickman eyed the table, chose a red but missed it. 'That's right. Claude, poor chap, thought that he had a chance, but he always was hopelessly optimistic.' Hickman was standing in front of the fireplace, above which was the largest mirror Eisenmenger had ever seen out of a telescope. It reflected the chandelier and the painted ceiling. 'I went on to medical school in London, but not before marrying Theresa. Claude was a good sport about it all – acted as my best man.'

Eisenmenger took some port. Hickman had left a red ball tantalizingly close to a pocket . . .

It went in, but only just and it left the white ball hopelessly positioned for the next shot. Hickman moved the pointer on the scoreboard. He said, 'It was madness, of course. Getting married before I qualified, but even then I was a gambler.'

Eisenmenger nodded and smiled, thinking that it must have helped living in a castle with a thousand acres of pocket money to rely on.

'Anyway, Claude did whatever it was that lawyers do – articles, or something – and not long after met a simply delightful girl called Diana. Fell head-over-heels, you know the thing. I reciprocated in the best-man position, and we thought our lives were set.'

Eisenmenger tried a reckless shot towards the yellow, missed it completely. Without a word, Hickman increased his own score by four, then approached the table. They were surrounded by the gold bindings of books that reflected the low light above the green baize of the snooker table. Had they been wearing the full evening regalia they might have been in an ambassador's residence, or back in the early twentieth century.

'And then tragedy. Diana died in childbirth. Amniotic fluid embolism.'

It was rare but catastrophic when it happened.

Hickman put a red into a pocket, then quickly moved on to the black, which he also disposed of with ease. Eisenmenger was kept busy moving the score on and replacing the black on its spot. Hickman went on, 'So Claude was left a widower with a baby daughter to bring up. I think things were pretty sticky for him for a year or two, although he never admitted it. We did what we could, of course, but Claude wasn't one to accept charity.' He put some chalk on the tip of the cue, took another pull of his cigar, then, 'Penny happened to him through us, actually. I had just come into this pile and we had a grand summer ball. Penny was recently widowed herself and had a small son. She was a distant cousin of Theresa's as a matter of fact.'

He bent down over the table, aiming for a lone red near the cushion. He not only hit it but also managed to position the cue ball so that the black looked an easy shot. This he missed, however. Straightening up, he sighed. 'It was always thus.'

Eisenmenger came back from the scoreboard via his port. Hickman continued, 'Within three months they were married – I was more than happy to be best man for a second time – and there then followed nearly twenty years of happiness.' He took the last breaths through the cigar then looked at it before stubbing it out. 'You know, John, I look back on those years and I recognize how lucky we were. It was paradise, really. Both Claude and I were professional men with well-paid jobs; we had beautiful wives, beautiful children. The times that we spent together – both here and elsewhere – were precious beyond wealth.' He laughed softly through his nose, then looked up at Eisenmenger. 'It was bound to end, and there was bound to be a price.'

His voice seemed to carry something close to guilt as he whispered this. Eisenmenger said nothing.

'But what a price, eh? Claude and Penny murdered, Jeremy's suicide. And for me, there was Nell . . .'

There was complete silence in the room. The world around them felt old, and still Eisenmenger said nothing.

'I sometimes think that you have to pay for happiness with sadness. No laughter goes unpaid for; all debts are collected.'

The silence was suddenly uncomfortable; Eisenmenger felt that a cough would have been appropriate but managed without. 'You make it sound biblical.'

It forced a smile from Hickman and relieved the portentous atmosphere but failed to turn things into a laughfest. 'Perhaps. The Bible isn't necessarily wrong, you know, John.'

'It isn't necessarily right either. I haven't got a problem with people who keep an open mind, only those who close them, lock them and then throw away the key.'

It broke the gloom. Hickman said with a smile, 'Fair enough.'

Eisenmenger surveyed the table, much as a newly promoted general might look upon a battlefield for first time. Eventually he selected one of the remaining reds, lined up the cue ball and hit it hopefully in the general direction. The red ball moved but not pocketwards. As he straightened up, he said tentatively, 'Tell me to mind my own business, Tristan, but Nell seems . . . upset.'

Hickman looked at him in surprise. There was a moment when he might have protested, but it passed and he said only with a sigh, 'Yes. Upset is the least of it.' He finished his port, then looked to the bottle. Half of its contents were poured into Eisenmenger's glass, half into his own. 'You might say that it was all a part of the price.'

'The pregnancy hit her hard,' guessed Eisenmenger.

Hickman nodded. 'Hit us all hard, of course, but Nell wasn't ready.' He dropped his head. 'Wasn't ready at all.' Then, looking directly at Eisenmenger, 'She was never strong nor, I see now, particularly mature. She hasn't coped well with Tom, but you've probably guessed that.'

Eisenmenger asked, 'I take it adoption was never an option.'

Hickman hesitated briefly before shaking his head. 'However Tom was conceived, he was still Nell's child. Still a Hickman.'

Eisenmenger thought for a moment that he heard insincerity, then decided not. He asked, 'And marriage to the father . . .?'

Hickman was downing the last of his port, now clearly drunk. He shook his head vigorously. 'Oh, God, no.' Another pause, then, 'Some feckless oaf. Malcolm should never have employed him, but hindsight is a wonderful thing.' He looked at the snooker table, then back to Eisenmenger. 'I think it's time for bed.'

Eleanor was in her living room, reading. There was complete silence in the room, save for the sound of wind outside the window behind her. The only light in the room came from a standard lamp behind her left shoulder. She had dressed for bed and was wearing a thick dressing gown; on the table to her right was a fine china mug filled with hot milk.

The knock on the door was soft and, because she was slightly deaf, not heard by Eleanor. Only its slightly firmer repetition aroused her.

'Come.'

Malcolm Groshong obeyed and closed the door softly behind him. His attitude suggested that he did not want his visit to be public.

'Malcolm!' Eleanor affected surprise, although this was a daily ritual.

'Eleanor.'

'Come in and sit down. Tell me about the estate.'

He did as he was bid, first taking off his shoes by the door. He was dressed in his outdoor clothes and his only concession to the occasion was to undo them so that they hung open.

'You'd like a drink,' she pronounced, much as a doctor might prescribe medication. She indicated the decanter on the shelf to his right and he said, 'Aye,' before pouring himself a large tumblerful.

Michael sat at one end of the bar and drank heavily that night. He did so with seriousness, displaying such dedication that others might bring to constructing models of HMS *Victory* out of matchsticks. He spoke when spoken to, although he paid out his replies with parsimony, as if syllables were precious and not to be wasted. He appeared neither particularly dour nor particularly jocular; he just appeared to be drinking.

Jack Dowden served him when requested, keeping an eye on him, knowing that he was prone to become leery when drunk, but somewhat reassured by Michael's apparent tranquillity. In any case, Dowden had enough to contend with. Trade was considerably up on the last few nights, so that the small bar was crowded and noisy and hot and convivial. At the height of the evening there was little room even to stand. The main topic of conversation was the death on the estate, the main speculation was that it had been William Moynihan, whom some of them remembered from a few years before.

Gradually, towards ten o'clock, the bar began to empty, the heat to dissipate, but Michael made no sign that he noticed or cared. He ordered one more pint, which Dowden thought about refusing, then decided to provide; he did so because it was a tiny bit more profit, because Michael didn't seem that drunk really, and because Michael didn't seem that sober either.

It was nearly closing time when Michael's father came in.

The heat in the bar dissipated completely.

Michael seemed to know; even without turning or raising his head or even looking up from his half-empty beer glass, he knew.

The bar was approached. By this time there were only three other customers present; Rachel Bednar who had a pottery business, her husband, John, who ran a junk and reclamation business, and Mick Potts who was a local builder. They all knew Albert Bloom, all knew the history there was with his son.

The Christmas decorations around them failed signally to prevent the tension from racking up rapidly; even the tree, up until then a reliable source of ribaldry, was suddenly just a sad, decrepit decoration in a small, decrepit pub.

'Pint, please, Jack.'

Most people ignored Albert and steered well clear of him. Jack Dowden didn't much like him either, because he was dishevelled and poor and didn't pass a great deal of money over the bar. But he was a customer.

Everyone in Westerham village knew the story of Michael and his father . . . and Michael's mother and sister. They all had their views on it, and most of them disapproved; none of them wanted to interfere, though. It had been an unhappy thing, the kind of thing that no one would want to experience, but not the kind of thing that warranted nosiness.

He cast a glance at Michael but got no help there. He turned back to Albert, then said softly, 'Got the money?'

The money was produced without any protest. Jack Dowden sighed and then got a glass from the shelf above the bar. He put it under the tap and grasped the wooden pump handle.

'What the fuck are you doing?'

Jack, unsure if this had been addressed to him or his newest customer, looked up suddenly, his right arm frozen in his intention to fill the glass. Michael's eyes were on his father.

'You know this is where I drink. What are you trying to do by coming in here?'

The old man was looking only at the wood of the bar, apparently so intensely that he didn't hear. After a second or two he raised his weary eyes to Jack Dowden's hand around the pump. He said quietly, 'Hurry up, Jack. I'm thirsty.'

Michael stood up. He made it a complete play, a performance, method acting taken to its logical conclusion. In one slow movement he conveyed incandescence, deliberation, exasperation and intent. The noise that his barstool made was as menacing as a tiger's growl, the look on his face as blankly intentful as a crocodile's.

Jack said, 'Look, Michael . . .' The alarm that was clear in every syllable, every facial muscle made his voice quiver slightly. Everyone in the room was watching now, suffused with a heady concoction of apprehension and excitement.

Michael was on his feet.

Albert looked only at the pump handle, then at Jack Dowden's face, but found nobody home.

'Eh? Are you listening to me, old man?' The anger was so huge it might have been sadness. 'Why don't you leave me alone?'

Jack Dowden switched his attention to the old man and noticed for the first time that he was not immune to the tension of the situation, that there was a tremor on his lips, in his hands as he clasped them.

'Because I'm your father.'

This simple sentence might have dripped with truth, might have found echoes in a billion homes, a billion ages past, but here it acted only as a goad.

'Oh, yes? My father, are you? So where's my mother? Where's my sister, eh?' He didn't wait for an answer before, 'Well, OLD MAN? What's the fucking answer to that?'

He moved forward, so that he was standing right beside the figure hunched over the bar. Dowden said with as much force as he could find, as he dared to find, 'Michael . . . don't do anything . . .'

Michael was breathing heavily. The others in the bar saw a man who appeared to be ready to do violence – his demeanour was almost relaxed, but very much in the way a praying mantis is relaxed. Everyone knew what might be about to happen, even the old man. Ignoring Dowden, Michael said, 'How many times do I have to say this? You can fuck off out of my life. You can fuck off, and then you can die. GOT THAT?'

He shouted this last in the old man's ear. A blink was the only sign that it had happened.

Dowden said, 'That's enough now, Michael.'

And it might just have ended then, except that the old

man suddenly turned to his son and put out his hand to grasp a sleeve and said, 'But I love you . . .'

Which was neither a good thing to do, nor a good thing to say.

Michael heard it, digested it and then erupted, all in the space of a moment. With an ease born of the lightness of his quarry, the intensity of his passion and the ethanol in his blood, he grabbed the grubby raincoat and hauled it and its contents off the barstool.

Dowden dropped the glass with a crash and lifted the hinge in the bartop; Mick Potts stood up from his seat by the fire. 'Look, Michael . . .'

Michael wasn't interested. He had on his face now the expression of someone who had an idea; just the one, but a big one. He went past the other paying customers, dragging the old man, ignored Dowden shouting, 'Michael!'

Mick Potts stepped forward. 'Put him down. Whatever he did, it's time to forget it. Move on . . .'

It might have seemed good advice in the head, but out in the room it had an altogether different tenor. Michael dropped his prey, turned to face his adviser and asked, 'Forget it? Forget that my mother's dead? Forget that he drove my sister away? Is that what you think I should do?'

'I just meant –'

Whatever he might or might not have meant was lost to the world as Michael swung a large fist that collided with his mandible.

There followed a commotion caused by Mick Potts staggering backwards and crashing into the table occupied by the Bednars and embellished by Dowden's cry of protest. In the epicentre of the confusion, Michael turned back to his father. 'Come on. I've got business to finish with you.'

He hauled the old man out of the pub, leaving behind him a group of people, none of whom thought it wise to try to debate the proposal.

Beverley returned to her hotel so deeply immersed in her thoughts she totally failed to sneer at the establishment's tweeness; not even at the pathetic collection of leaflets by the small reception desk (she hadn't looked but she knew that they would be advertising places to visit that only the brain-dead or the terminally confused would enjoy), the collection of supposedly witty (but actually witless) golfing prints over the bar, the awful striped wallpaper (surely a job lot from a bankruptcy sale) that screamed raucously of poor taste.

She collected her key, failing to reply to the young girl behind reception who smiled and wished her good evening as she had been told to do, then climbed the stairs to her room almost without realizing it. In her room she slipped off her coat, then lay down on the bed, staring up at the ceiling.

Eisenmenger had slept badly, due mainly to the sea of port that heaved uncertainly but menacingly in his stomach. Helena had already been asleep when he had finally come to bed and he had been forced to tiptoe around the room, pulling the bathroom door closed as quietly as possible, then easing himself beneath the duvet cover with the patience of jewel thief. Thereafter he had lain awake for what seemed to be weeks, feeling twitchy and far from sleep, his mind mulling over what Tristan had said to him.

In the morning, when Helena awoke, he felt as if he had finished a long trek through unfriendly terrain, constantly harassed by things unseen; he felt stiff and sore and pain pressed against the backs of his eyes. He groaned as she sat up.

If he had expected sympathy, he was sharply disabused of this hope.

'I'm not surprised you're hung over. When you came in last night I thought for a moment that someone had let a drunken rhinoceros into the room with me.'

Eisenmenger was surprised and not a little hurt. 'I don't know what you're talking about,' he protested. 'I moved around the room like a wraith. You didn't stir once.'

She leaned across to kiss him, the slightest of smiles stretching her lips. 'I hate to have to tell you, John dearest, but I'm good at faking things.'

He wasn't quick enough to extract his revenge and she jerked back laughing. She hopped from the bed while he

195

leaned on one elbow and glared at her. 'Come here,' he suggested. She was naked.

'You're not that unwell, then,' she inferred.

'I'm recovering. Perhaps you could rub the back of my neck.'

Another smile as she moved a little closer. 'Never heard it called that before.'

'You weren't like this when I met you. I'm shocked at the change in you.'

She moved even closer. 'You've corrupted me, Dr Eisenmenger. I can no longer wear white without feeling overwhelming guilt.'

'I'm more interested in you wearing nothing . . .'

He made a sudden grab, a move that she had seen coming about three years before they had even met; consequently she danced backwards, laughing in a high, genuinely delighted manner. She almost skipped to the bathroom, while he lay back in the bed and sighed.

After a while he got out, put on his dressing gown and went to the bathroom door. He heard the sound of running water and a buzzing noise. 'Can I come in?'

Her voice was muffled and difficult to hear. '*Depends.*'

'Depends on what?'

It took a second before he realized what she was saying. '*Depends on what you want to do.*'

He laughed, then opened the door. She was still naked, standing at the sink, brushing her teeth. He thought about walking across to stand directly behind her delicious-looking backside, decided that he might receive a kick in the matrimonials and opted to stay outside the danger area.

'So we know what I did last night. What did you get up to?'

The toothbrush informed her by means of urgent, staccato buzzings that her teeth were perfectly clean and, if it was to be believed, unlikely to rot in the next twelve hours. She turned to face him having rinsed it and removed the head. 'I had planned an early night. Nell had different ideas, however.'

'Really?' He was interested. He wasn't sure why but anything that involved Nell interested him.

'She's got this secret place – at the top of one of the turrets.'

He smiled. 'Only in a castle.'

She turned because he wasn't taking her seriously. 'But it's weird, John. It's almost like a nursery, except there's no baby. A doll, but no baby.'

He considered. 'The baby grew up,' he suggested, but even he didn't feel that it was quite right.

'She doesn't love Tom. At least not as a mother should love him.'

He sighed. 'I'd sort of got that idea myself.'

'She doesn't even sleep on the same floor as he does, John. Dominique occupies the next-door room, while she sleeps miles away.'

'Sounds like the upper classes to me, Helena. Tom's been sent to boarding school, only it's just in the next wing. Best of both worlds.'

Exasperated at what appeared to be his flippancy she said, 'It's the worst as far as Tom is concerned. He sees his mother all the time, only she doesn't take any interest in him.'

He held up his hand. 'You're right, of course. It can't be healthy for Tom, but don't heap all the blame on Nell. She's obviously had some sort of traumatic breakdown.'

'And then some.'

Almost absent-mindedly he asked, 'But why?'

She shrugged and there was a pause. He moved towards her and they embraced, the sexuality of her nakedness gone. Then she said quietly into his ear, 'I suppose because of the pregnancy.'

They held each other. 'No doubt,' he murmured.

Then, 'What are we going to do today?'

Part Five

Leicester was cold and wet and grey, seeming to make no allowance for Christmas. The wind sliced through Felty as she stepped from her car and climbed the steps outside central headquarters. A man, clearly drunk, shouted at her from across the street; when she turned back he was just standing there, beside an overflowing rubbish bin, shouting and waving his fist. It was clearly meant for her, this diatribe, as she was alone, and therefore inexplicable. She didn't know him, yet he seemed to know her. He was shabby and long-haired; he wore a sort of full-length tunic tied at the waist and must have been unbelievably cold; just looking at him made Felty shiver. A thin, whippet-like dog standing beside him, a string tied to its collar, looked as unhappy as the man was. The man had a tall stick that he was waving around as he cast words into the winter morning.

There was something biblical in the scene, but Old Testament biblical, a prophet of doom. The traffic caused his words to fail to carry to her, but she could imagine they were full of curses and scriptural quotes.

A tall, thin woman came walking along the road, ignoring the performance as if such things were common in Leicester. She began climbing the steps past Felty, but then stopped and followed her gaze back to the man.

'I wouldn't bother about him, love. He's not going to hurt you.'

She then shouted, 'Be quiet, Neil! You're frightening the public.'

Back to Felty. 'Don't let him worry you. He's just mad. Harmless, though. Stands there every so often, ranting about nothing.' She laughed, 'Doesn't even know many quotes from the Bible. After a while he goes on to radio catchphrases from the fifties.'

Then Neil was addressed again, the volume increasing considerably to carry over what appeared to be a convoy of articulated lorries. 'You're not going to get free board and lodging today, Neil. Go and find a bed at the hostel.'

But Neil just continued his performance.

She sighed. 'He's quite sweet, really. They say he lost his wife to a priest but that's probably an urban myth.' She was about to continue on her way when she paused and look interrogatively at Felty. 'Are you Sally Felty?'

Surprised, Felty admitted guilt of this.

'I'm DI Aaron. I was told you were coming. Come on.'

She didn't sound hostile but then she wasn't giving off signals of warmth and joy. She moved off at a rapid pace, the impression being that if Felty didn't keep up, then she wasn't going to break down and cry over it. They went through the entrance lobby where Felty had to be signed in and assigned a numbered badge, then through double doors into a small hallway where there were two lifts on either side and stairs directly ahead. Aaron ignored the lifts and they climbed up inside a cold, soulless ziggurat of concrete steps and metal rails to the third floor. No communication passed between them as they emerged past the lifts and into a busy corridor off which Felty counted ten offices. Aaron took her to the last but one on the right.

'Sit down.'

It was like all other offices in all other police stations – functional and somehow unforgiving, and therefore rather like its occupant. Felty sat as indicated while Aaron found a distressingly anaemic folder and handed it across to her. 'Here's what we've got so far.'

While Felty perused the contents Aaron leaned back in her chair and perused *her*. After a few minutes she said, 'I suppose you'll want an office to work from.'

Felty looked up. 'Please,' she replied as deferentially as possible.

Aaron grunted softly then, begrudgingly, 'There's a spare office on the top floor; you can use that. How long do you think this will take?'

Felty didn't know. 'A day or two?' she hazarded.

Aaron didn't say anything and thereby said much. She

got up abruptly. 'I'll show you,' she said and without waiting she was off.

The trip to Felty's temporary Leicester abode was no less frenetic but this time, just as they passed two uniforms coming out of the lift and were heading for the stairs again, Aaron said, 'We haven't got the resources to have spent much time on your case.'

Which, judging by the meagre sustenance there appeared to be in the folder that Felty was holding, could not be denied.

'We've got a black hole in the budget this year.'

Felty could sympathize. She had only recently seen a memo asking all personnel to reduce their reliance on paperclips and use more staples as the paperclip allocation was three hundred per cent overspent.

'Three murders this week, plus we may have an arsonist operating, so this case – which may not even *be* a murder – has to have a low priority.'

'Sure.'

The room she had been given was small but she could hardly criticize it. She made the right noises and Aaron seemed, if not mollified, then at least not overtly hostile. 'If you need anything, then you know where I am.'

'Thanks.' She was wondering where she could eat, where the toilets were, things like that, but didn't think it wise to place Inspector Aaron in the role of housekeeper. Anyway, Aaron hadn't finished. 'I don't mind you talking to people, snooping around, but I want it made plain – if you uncover anything that smells, anything at all, that occurred on my patch, you tell me first. Okay? You're a guest here, Constable, so I expect you to play by the rules.'

'Of course.'

Aaron held her stare as if deciding whether Felty were being insolent. Then she left.

Felty looked around at her surroundings, suddenly aware that she was alone in a strange city, without friends and without colleagues. That she was now sitting in an empty office, without any personality from which she could take succour, only deepened her sadness.

And even though she had no evidence to justify feelings of jealousy, jealous she undoubtedly felt. Was it paranoia that kept her wondering if her departure to Leicester was being exploited? What was it about Beverley Wharton that she had so quickly and so irrevocably decided that here was an enemy? Why did it matter so much if she left Sauerwine alone with Beverley, as if she were a parent and Sauerwine her innocent child? She knew that Sauerwine had once had crush on Beverley – he had admitted it to her in a joking, self-deprecating way – so was that the cause of her disquiet? Did she fear that left alone this passion would reignite?

Anyway, she told herself sternly, what if it did? In reality, she had no rights of possession on Sauerwine and he was an adult. Their relationship was a new and fragile thing, neonatal, not yet fully formed even. He had not yet, now she came to think about it, actually used the word 'love'. So that was all right then.

Yet she couldn't persuade herself that it was. She may not have known Beverley Wharton personally but she knew the type, knew that she was a shark, that her way of living was to cruise and bed and use. Probably incapable of love, only simulating it, like her orgasms. If she ended up screwing Andrew Sauerwine it wouldn't be for any reason other than it suited her . . .

Which touched upon another aspect of interest. Why was Beverley Wharton so keen to investigate William Moynihan and his curious possessions? Sally wasn't stupid, soon had her strong suspicions that Beverley Wharton's rapid entrance upon the scene had been due to something more than had been admitted. A few phone calls had confirmed her suppositions, told her that Beverley Wharton's insistence that Jeremy Eaton-Lambert was guilty beyond doubt was rather optimistic.

Sally Felty was young, but she wasn't naive. She could guess why Beverley Wharton might want to keep Detective Inspector Andrew Sauerwine sweet.

She emerged from her speculation, finding herself in the same drear, empty office, in the same strange city. She might even have to spend New Year here.

A Happy New Year.

'Was this a good idea?'

'You're only asking that because you think it wasn't.'

Eisenmenger, cold and tired, had had sufficient of the

winter wonderland that was the Westerham estate in deepest Christmastide. He had been walking for what seemed liked weeks and was sure that he would soon see the ocean blue over one of the many hills he had climbed, even though on the map Westerham was ninety kilometres from the nearest coast. On innumerable occasions he had been scratched by brambles that, although dead, retained their vicious appetite for laceration. Twice he had stepped on solid ground that had given way with a light crack into mud deep enough to bury his walking shoes; three times he had tripped and fallen heavily on to his gloved hands.

No wonder he felt battered.

'How much further is it?'

Which at least brought forth laughter from Helena. It rang through the woodland, the wetness lending it a damp, slightly muffled tone. 'You sound like a small child,' she opined.

'Thanks.'

She was about five metres ahead of him. She, too, was breathing heavily, but it was clear from her body language that she was finding it a much more enjoyable experience. She called back, 'We're nearly there . . .'

'Good.'

'Unfortunately, it gets a lot steeper from now on.'

'Bloody marvellous.' As far as Eisenmenger could make out, they'd been climbing for several hours; he fully expected to start requiring oxygen at any time.

Helena stopped and sniffed; her cheeks were flushed, her eyes were bright. Despite his grumblings he was delighted to see it. *She's getting stronger and stronger, at last.*

As he came level with her she explained, 'The surgeon advised walking as the best way to regain my strength.'

He smiled. 'Of course.'

'And anyway, I want to see that view again. It's spectacular, isn't it? I'd forgotten completely about it.'

Eisenmenger nodded. 'And the isolation. That was what struck me. It's not that far from the house, but it's as if it's in a different country, one not yet visited by civilization.'

'Well, then. What are you so miserable about?' She held out her hand, which he took, and they continued their climb together. Occasional birds flew about them in the distance, others scurrying away through fallen, brittle leaves.

Another half-hour brought them to the sloping, open ground of Old Man's Sorrow. The cloud cover was lower so that the sun was indicated only by a bright smudge in the sky just to their right. Up here there was a fine drizzle in the air that was whipped by the constantly varying, never quite ceasing wind.

They covered about half the ground, still climbing, before Helen said, 'Let's stop here for a while.' She was clearly quite exhausted now but not, he thought, unhealthily so. A gigantic, rotting log lay across their path and it was on this that they seated themselves, facing out across the magnificent English woodland.

Helena was so heavily wrapped up that Eisenmenger almost missed the fact that she was shivering. They had been sitting in silence for about forty minutes, lost in the view. He, too, had felt the chill seeping into his body; already his feet were aching with cold. He stood up. 'Come on. Time to go.'

She didn't argue as he held out his hand and helped her up. They began to trudge through the long, wet grass, both silently relieved that it would be downhill for much of the return journey. Crows were wheeling around to their left, above the depression that Groshong had pointed out to them as being the site where the old man had hanged himself.

'Wonder what's got them excited?'

Helena shrugged. 'Dead sheep, I expect.'

They continued walking, while the crows continued their own raucous pursuits.

Eisenmenger's head was down as he said, 'There were no sheep in here yesterday. There are no sheep in here today.'

'So?'

'So where did it come from, this dead sheep?'

Helena, who was just the tiniest bit exasperated, replied, 'I don't know. Perhaps it's a stray.'

'It's strayed a long way, hasn't it? There are no flocks anywhere near here.'

Helena was now exceedingly exasperated. 'Well, perhaps it's not a sheep at all . . .' She was about to say, 'Perhaps it's a rabbit or something.'

Eisenmenger, however, had taken this as an invitation to investigate and he struck out leftwards.

'John?'

He didn't answer, just kept going.

She began to follow, muttering under her breath. He was moving quickly with long strides and she had almost to run, only catching him as stopped at the lip of the depression. He was staring down, a deep frown on his face.

At its centre there was what appeared to be a blotchy grey blanket covering a small mound. Crows hopped around it. 'What is it? A boulder?'

For the second time Eisenmenger didn't reply. He started down the slope, causing the crows to scatter. Helena remained where she was. She saw him reach the mound, then bend down beside it.

'Well? What is it?'

He stood up, staring at it all the time. Only very slowly did he turn round on the spot, as if memorizing the topography. Twice he performed this strange, almost mesmerized ritual, before he made his way back to her. She noticed that he walked very carefully, putting his walking shoes in the footsteps he had created on the way down. Only when he arrived back next to Helena did he look up.

'Are you all right?' she asked.

He smiled. 'I'm fine,' he said. 'But that's more than can be said for the poor sod down there, though.'

Jackson took the call, entered it into the incident log then rang Sauerwine. 'I've got a body,' he announced, as if this were a new concept and unlikely to be noticed by anybody else. His tone was insouciant, no different to the one he would have used had he just learned that someone had been reported pinching underwear from the washing lines behind the almshouses.

Sauerwine, though, reacted in a slightly less sanguine way. 'Human?'

'Yeah. Up on the Sorrow.'

'That's on the estate, isn't it?'

'Right at the edge of it, to the north.'

He was already wondering as he telephoned Tanner, discovered the Superintendent was out, then contacted Syme.

'Right. You, me and Felty had better get up there right away . . .'

'Felty's in Leicester, sir.'

'Is she? I thought Wharton was going.'

Sauerwine hesitated hardly at all before explaining. 'I thought it more logical to send Felty. She needs the experience and it's unlikely to bear much fruit. We may need Wharton's expertise here . . . especially in view of this news.'

Syme made a sound that was the offspring of disgruntlement and agreement then put the phone down.

Beverley Wharton had been given a vacant, but extremely small office at the back of the building. Her irritation at being topographically sidelined was only partially assuaged by the acknowledgement that Sauerwine had at least not expected her to occupy a desk next to Felty, or the other junior personnel. When Sauerwine came in she was going through all the paperwork thus far accumulated on the Moynihan death; a considerably larger pile of files on the floor represented the accumulated paperwork on the Eaton-Lambert case.

'Come on,' he said. 'It might be nothing, but a body's been found on the Sorrow.'

'The Sorrow?'

'Old Man's Sorrow. It's a patch of high open ground near Westerham.'

She caught the significance of that and stood immediately. She took a long black woollen coat off a hook on the wall behind her and followed him out.

They had to transfer to a police Land Rover to get them the last few kilometres to the scene of the death. The journey to Old Man's Sorrow proved far more interesting and far more strenuous than the rather pedestrian drive along tarmac. The forest was interesting enough but even Beverley – for whom only grey, rectangular and dirty were the acceptable contours in a view – was impressed by the vastness, the bleakness, the loftiness of 'the Sorrow'. Once there they joined four other Land Rovers, one of them belonging to the ambulance service, parked about fifty metres from a hollow in which were clustered five uniformed police, two ambulance personnel and two very familiar figures.

Fan-fucking-tastic.

'Sir?'

Syme turned to Beverley. The wind was strong and would not be ignored; it couldn't choose between sudden, sullen silence and impatient roaring. 'What is it?'

'See the woman? In civvies?'

He looked across at Helena, then back to Beverley. 'What about her?'

It was difficult. Beverley had known that this moment would come but not this quickly. After hesitating, she said, 'I'm acquainted with her.'

'Are you? How come?'

Beverley glanced at Sauerwine; his face was neutral, perhaps too neutral. She explained who Helena was, stressing the hostility that Helena felt for her. 'She's obsessed with it; obsessed with me, too. She's spent the last few years making wild accusations, causing me no end of trouble.

'I even saved her life once. Not that she was grateful.'

He raised his eyebrows at that. 'Really?'

She turned the knob marked *Earnestness* up a couple of notches. 'Dragged her out from a house fire. She was unconscious.'

Syme considered this then said slowly, 'A bit of a coincidence, isn't it? Someone so intimately connected with the Eaton-Lambert case turning up here.'

Beverley said at once. 'Exactly. It's just as well I'm here, sir.'

Syme nodded slowly. He glanced at Eisenmenger and Helena. 'Do you think that they might be implicated?'

Beverley shrugged. She wasn't stupid enough to commit to anything. 'I don't know, sir.'

He turned to Sauerwine. 'And you?'

Sauerwine was hesitating and for a long moment she thought he might sabotage her, but then he said, 'I don't see the point in confusing matters at this stage, sir. I think it would be best to keep an open mind for the time being.'

206

Syme nodded. He had a pug-like face that never looked entirely thrilled by anything but she thought she saw agreement.

'Okay, for the time being. But if there's the slightest hint of a direct link between them and either of these deaths, I'm coming down on them hard.'

He strode off.

She turned to Sauerwine. 'Thanks.' A smile, she thought, might help here; not just any smile, but one that rose to the eyes and held questions. Questions and half-promises. 'I owe you.'

He smiled, almost one of embarrassment. 'Yes,' he murmured. 'You do, don't you?'

Eisenmenger saw her first, a glance at the two figures making their way down into the hollow turning rapidly into an intense stare. Helena was looking towards the small marquee that now obscured the body from the elements; no need to hide it from prurient, rubbernecked spectators here. He said softly, 'Well, well.'

She turned as he said this, looked first at him, then at the object of his attention. He couldn't see her face but he could sense the change in her attitude; it would have registered on a seismometer.

Beverley walked past them behind a tall, clean-cut man who looked determined but carried with him an air of unconquerable youth. He ignored them, although she didn't. Her head turned and her eyes took them in but it was much as she might have regarded a couple of rabbits staring uncomprehendingly at the goings-on of a different, higher race. They disappeared into the marquee, leaving Eisenmenger as the sole target of Helena's emotion.

'What the hell . . .?'

He tried blandness. 'A bit of a surprise.'

'What's that bitch doing here?'

'Coincidence?'

She treated this with contempt that would have eaten a hole through hardened steel. 'Don't be stupid. You saw the look on her face. That woman wasn't surprised to see us.'

'No,' he agreed. 'I have to admit that she kept her composure well.'

'So what's going on, John?' Her tone was one of despair.

He sighed. 'I don't know, Helena.'

He was a mess, with blood everywhere. The long grass around him was broken and the winter damp had diluted and spread it, creating a wet, sodden mass both over and under the body. Despite the exposed position of the marquee the air was already warm and fetid within the confined space, due to the lights and number of living bodies clustered around the decidedly dead one on the ground.

The body was on its back, the face coated with blood so that it looked almost as if it had been stripped of its flesh, yet even with all the mess, Sauerwine knew at once who it was. The same hair, long and unkempt, the same shabby grey coat. SOCO had yet to arrive but Dr Addison was there, standing with a Dictaphone in hand, already white-suited for the task to come. She had a thin smile on her face, lipstick that was inexpertly applied making it slightly ridiculous; her hair was tied back tightly and she had on a pretty blue disposable cap but it had been done lopsidedly. The whole affair strongly suggested that she had dressed in a rush. The inevitable cabal of officers, uniformed and others, stood to the sides and either looked and whispered, or looked and were silent. One or two of them were perspiring.

Syme looked ill, as if regretting his last meal. Dr Addison said cheerfully, 'I don't think we're going to have a problem with this one.'

Felty's spirits, hardly those of jubilation, withered when she called at Moynihan's old flat. The landlord had understandably let it as soon as possible and it was therefore now occupied by a tiny, middle-aged man with a bulbous, veined nose and a noticeable tremor; she didn't see any empty bottles behind the sofa but then she didn't search for them. The flat was spartan, which made it all the more obvious that it would bear no edible fruit.

'When you moved in here, did you find anything left behind by the old tenant?'

He was shifty and she wondered if he had a record.

'Nothing.'

'Nothing at all?'

He wore a grubby shirt, open at the collar, and trousers that had a history. He shook his head.

She sighed. One sitting room, one kitchenette, one bathroom and one bedroom; it could all have been quite cosy had the furniture not been second-hand, junk-room tat. It wasn't worth her while doing a thorough search.

'Oh, well. Thanks, anyway.'

She went to the door and he followed her as if herding her away from his secrets. She paused, however, despite his best efforts to eject her. 'Which is the nearest pub?'

He was startled, perhaps fearing a diatribe on abstinence. 'Two streets away. Why?'

'What's it called?'

More suspicion. 'The Bell.'

'What address?'

'It's in Albright Lane. 'Bout two streets away.'

She smiled as she thanked him, then turned to go. She noticed that the table by the door wobbled as her coat touched it. Someone had tried to stop this by folding a piece of cardboard and putting it under one of the legs.

She knelt down and pulled the card out. Unfolding it three times revealed half a postcard – the half with the address on it.

'Did you put this under the table leg?'

Perhaps she had used a rather hungry tone because the little man became even more agitated. 'No,' he said hastily. 'Why?' This last was almost plaintive.

She ignored him; he was the kind of person it was too easy to ignore. It was unlikely that the landlord would have bothered, and it might easily have been the tenant before Moynihan; she imagined that there was a continuous stream of lonely men passing through this place.

It might, though, have been Moynihan.

The address was not this one, although it was in Leicester. Mayo Street. She showed it to her new friend. 'Does this address mean anything to you?'

He read it quickly and shook his head in a similarly rapid manner.

'Where is it?'

'On the other side of the city. Maybe a mile.'

*   *   *

209

Helena stared at the marquee as if able to see through the blustering white fabric. Eisenmenger knew the cold was biting into her – it was biting into him – but the sudden appearance of her Nemesis had taken all her attention. Her face had now been chiselled into intense speculation by incredulous anger. He could see the questions still exploding inside her head.

He said as much to himself as to her, 'No doubt all will be explained shortly.'

She swung around to him and he briefly experienced something akin to vertigo as she hissed, 'I wish! Whatever she says will be a lie, whatever she does will be for herself.'

He was saved from response because the flap of the marquee was pulled aside and Beverley and her companion emerged. In the lead was an older man, burly but looking ill. They paused for some sort of conference, then walked towards them, the burly man in the lead, then a vaguely familiar younger man, lastly Beverley, her face still studiedly neutral.

The burly one spoke. 'Dr John Eisenmenger?' Eisenmenger nodded.

'Miss Helena Flemming?'

'Yes.'

'I'm DCI Syme, this is DI Sauerwine and DI Wharton.'

Beverley stepped forward and smiled. It wasn't over-stuffed with warmth. 'Small world.'

'What are you doing here?' Under other circumstances Eisenmenger would have winced and been surprised at such undecorousness from his companion; under these he merely looked at Beverley, awaiting her reply.

'It's certainly a surprise to see you here,' she conceded. Eisenmenger listened to her voice, hearing easy confidence but wondering if he also detected something else, something less positive. She continued, 'I'm on temporary assignment here.'

'Why?' demanded Helena. 'Have you screwed up again?'

The smile tightened, although the words were drawled. 'Far from it, Helena. I'm gaining more experience. It's important to move around. We're all lifelong learners in the police force.' Eisenmenger looked at Sauerwine and Syme. They showed no sign that she was lying, nor

210

showed any that she was giving them the truth. Beverley said, 'Murders seem to follow you two around. Second one within a few days. Perhaps you're the guilty parties.'

It was a tasteless joke but then it was designed to be so. No one laughed and no one was embarrassed. Syme said, 'I understand that you're a forensic pathologist, Dr Eisenmenger.'

'Was.'

Syme smiled. 'Yet, as Inspector Wharton says, Death has still to lose his interest in you.'

'I think that he takes a personal interest in all of us at least once in our lives.'

The Chief Inspector didn't care for a philosophical debate. 'Be that as it may, Doctor, this is the second violent death in a very short time.'

Eisenmenger was unsure what he was supposed to say and merely nodded. Sauerwine remarked, 'No doubt you peeked at our friend over there.'

'I didn't disturb anything, if that's what you mean.'

But Sauerwine was shocked that his remark should be misinterpreted. 'Oh, no, Dr Eisenmenger. I wasn't implying any such thing.' It occurred to Helena that because he generated an air of naivety he could get away with implying all sorts of things. He said, 'But you must have been a tad curious.'

'Of course I looked, Inspector Sauerwine. I'm just as much a rubbernecker as the rest of human society.'

'And?'

But Eisenmenger had made a career out of being cautious. 'And I'd like to look a little closer before I proffer an opinion.'

Beverley said at once, 'I'm not sure . . .'

But Syme, perhaps inadvertently, perhaps not, cut across her. 'Why not? I'm all in favour of casting the net as widely as possible. It would only be a courtesy to introduce you to a colleague.'

Helena was pleased to see a look of annoyance pass across Beverley's face.

Another four-wheel drive arrived at the lip of the hollow and a second or two later a world-weary man in a bright red anorak and blue rubber boots came down into the hollow, almost slipping as he did so. He carried a metal briefcase that was clearly heavy and he was

211

unmistakably a SOCO. He waved his free hand vaguely at Syme then headed for the marquee.

Beverley took the opportunity to ask, 'So what were you doing up here? It's a long way from everywhere.' The wind played with her hair and she didn't like it.

'It's called going for a walk. They do it in the country.' When Helena was angry, it seemed to Eisenmenger that her eyes almost glowed with intensity.

Beverley nodded. 'One of the less unsavoury rural pursuits.'

Sauerwine cut in. 'I understand you're staying at the castle.'

'That's right.'

'The night you arrived, a man died in a car fire.'

'So we heard.'

'You didn't see anything?'

Eisenmenger hadn't joined in with the jolly badinage until this moment. 'As we came in, I thought I saw a bonfire; then I thought I heard something that might have been an explosion.'

'Time?'

Eisenmenger shrugged. 'It was early night, but beyond that I couldn't say with certainty.'

Syme asked, 'You heard an explosion and you didn't think any more of it?'

Eisenmenger smiled. 'I believe I said that I *thought* I heard an explosion.'

'You weren't sure, then.'

'That would be a reasonable assumption from what I've just said.'

Syme stared hard at him, as did Beverley. Her mouth widened almost imperceptibly into a shade of smile. She kept her gaze fixed very deliberately upon him and away from Helena as she said softly, 'You're too clever for your own good, you know, John.'

Somehow, a moment of intimacy was congealing around him, despite the wind and the cold and haemorrhaged corpse behind them. It was only Helena saying loudly, angrily, 'We didn't murder anyone. What were we supposed to do? Go careering off into the woodlands just because we saw what we thought was a bonfire and heard a distant bang?'

Syme was shaking his head. 'Nobody's suggested anything, Miss Flemming. I just wondered if you could help us with timings, that's all.'

Helena said nothing. From Syme's side Sauerwine asked then, 'So today. You came up here for a walk?'

Eisenmenger nodded. 'That's right.'

Beverley couldn't resist. 'Long way, isn't it? I wouldn't fancy it in this weather.'

Whatever observations Eisenmenger had were forestalled by Helena's intercepting, 'Who the hell cares about what you fancy?'

In a curious synchrony, Beverley's observations on Helena's question were then forestalled by Sauerwine who asked, 'Did you see anyone on your walk?'

They both agreed that they hadn't.

'I realize it's difficult, but did you recognize who the body was?'

Helena said, 'I didn't look closely enough.' Eisenmenger said, 'As far as I could tell, I'd never seen him before.'

Syme nodded, considering these answers. He glanced briefly at Beverley before suggesting, 'Why don't we introduce Dr Eisenmenger to Dr Addison?'

They walked to the marquee. Before going in Beverley said to Helena, 'You don't have to go in if you don't want to . . .'

The tone was considerate, the expression matched; only someone who was paranoid or who knew Beverley Wharton well would have taken offence. 'Don't worry about me. I'm not squeamish.'

And Beverley's shrug was nearly imperceptible, the look in her eye less so. They entered the marquee, a little line ducking into this incongruous tent reminiscent of a fortune-teller's lair.

Helena was at once aware of the smell, a strangely sweet yet infinitely unpleasant smell, far worse than any butcher's shop at end of day. The heat didn't help, nor the damp. The grass was smashed, dark chlorophyll smeared across crushed blades. Eyes were turned to the newcomers, most of them curious, some of them apparently hostile. A bright flash occluded all of them for less than half a second then, too quickly, another.

'And round here, please.' Dr Addison's vowels were perfect; she might have polished them every morning.

213

Scenes of Crime duly obliged. In between the flashes Helena caught her first sight of the corpse. It was only because she was acutely aware of Beverley's attention, if not her direct gaze, upon her that she did not gasp.

'And now here.'

Once again Dr Addison was obliged. Only then did she look up, a questioning look on her bespectacled face.

Syme spoke up. 'Dr Addison, this is Dr Eisenmenger. He discovered the body along with Ms Flemming here.'

She didn't understand the significance. The smile was uncertain and small, not really meant, more one of wariness because she had caught his title. Sauerwine explained, 'Dr Eisenmenger is a forensic pathologist.'

The wariness went for a walk and appeared in her eyes, the smile remaining frozen as if paralysed as she murmured, 'Really?'

Eisenmenger, being what he was, had transferred his attention to the corpse. He saw the bloodied hammer by the left knee, the long-bladed knife in the left hand. It was as if being worked by forces unseen that he crouched down to allow his eyes to begin a long slow survey of the wounds. His attention, rapt and wrapped in this death, did not allow him to see that Dr Addison was now sporting a rather impressive frown.

'What are you doing?' she demanded.

He didn't hear her. His inspection had reached the shoulders and he was leaning over to get a good view of the far side of the neck. She tried Syme and Sauerwine. 'What's he doing?'

Sauerwine's reply was drawn from a deep well of disingenuousness. 'Taking a professional interest, Dr Addison. You don't mind, do you?'

Beverley watched on from the vantage of an interested audience. The dynamic between Sauerwine and Addison intrigued her; clearly he didn't like her, clearly she was young and therefore, presumably, inexperienced. Was he trying to humiliate her?

Helena watched Eisenmenger.

Eventually he stood up with a soft grunt of exertion. 'I assume that you haven't looked at the back yet?'

'Of course not!'

He nodded, ignoring or ignorant of the asperity.

'Do you know who he is yet?'

Sauerwine surprised both Beverley and Syme by saying with some confidence, 'Oh, yes. And I don't think we'll have much trouble identifying who did it.'

Eisenmenger nodded, his eyes back on the corpse. Only Helena was listening as he said under his breath, 'You might just be right.'

She called first at the Bell as it was close. It may have been the nearest pub to the flat but any normal person would have sailed right on by, steering for something a little more attractive in which to drink – like an abattoir. Dried vomit by the entrance door, a small collection of condoms by the cigarette machine and graffiti by the essayful; she didn't want to see what the toilets were like, certain that the reality would be even worse than her imaginings.

The publican was similarly unprepossessing, slimy and giving the impression of deep sexual depravity realized only in his imagination. 'Moynihan? Moynihan? Never heard of him.'

This patently false, shoddily manufactured exhibition of consideration and innocence was done for the benefit of the three individuals who shared the saloon bar with them; they were watching and listening as intently as judges in a singing contest while keeping their eyes elsewhere.

'No? You're sure?'

'Nah.' He turned to his clientele. 'Anyone here heard of someone called Moynihan?'

The response, such as it was, was not helpful. He turned back to her. 'Nah.'

She nodded. Then loudly, 'He died in a car fire a few days ago. Burned alive.' This may or may not have been true, but she had nothing left to lose.

It produced a satisfactory reaction.

There was a horrified gasp and then she heard a breathed *Oh, fuck*, over which there was a shocked, *Poor bastard!* She looked around and saw faces filled not with prurience but with connection. She turned back to the slimy one behind the bar. 'Now. I'll ask you once more. Did you know William Moynihan?'

It was against his better instincts to hold back the lies to

215

a member of the police, but he managed it. 'Yeah.' He followed this up with an immediate, 'Not well, though.'

'But he came in here to drink.'

He nodded. 'He'd only been around a few months, but he came in here regular.'

From along the bar came, 'He was a fucking good laugh.'

Slimy nodded. 'Specially that last night.' This was addressed not to Felty but to her left.

'What happened that last night?'

'He had a leaving party. Free drinks all round. All fucking night.' The tone of wonder suggested that Slimy considered this on a par with water into wine. 'He put five hundred quid behind the bar at seven. By ten we were so happy we could hardly stand.' He was almost lost in the reminiscence, but it didn't help her fall in love with him.

'Leaving? Did he say where he was going?'

'Said he was going to pick up his winnings.'

She frowned. 'Winnings? He used that precise term?'

Slimy hesitated but once more from along the bar came, 'He kept saying that. Kept on about his "winnings". Had a big, knowing smile on his face while he said it, too.'

'He wasn't normally rich?' she hazarded.

'Hardly. Worked as a decorator. Cash only.' The man had a squint. 'Never did to ask where the paint came from.'

'So where did the money behind the bar come from?'

Several shoulders went up and then down.

She said, half to herself, 'He wasn't coming back. He'd sold up his life, thrown a party and then gone off to find his fortune.'

Whatever that was.

She asked, 'Did he gamble?'

'Occasionally. The odd punt on the gee-gees but usually only the big races. He wasn't a regular.' The man with the squint seemed to imply that 'not being a regular' was contemptible.

'And he didn't give you any idea of where he was going?'

She thought that everyone was shaking their head but from behind her came a quiet voice, 'He said that he was going home.'

The speaker was tucked away in the corner, almost in smoky darkness. An old woman, Felty thought, until she moved slightly into a shaft of light from the window beside her, revealing herself to be a prematurely aged fifty-year-old blonde. Felty asked, 'Did he mention a place name? Westerham? Melbury?'

But he hadn't. The blonde hair shook above features that were bloated, almost into a caricature of a face.

Felty took the creased postcard from her pocket. 'What about Mayo Street? Could that be home?'

Maybe it could and maybe it couldn't; they either didn't know or didn't care. It wasn't the kind of place where homes really mattered.

Her audience were losing interest, as if the horror of Moynihan had only a temporary hold, the shock were strictly time-limited, perishable. She could feel little more than boredom there now; they had had the good times with Moynihan, he had gone and now he was dead.

It was the way of their world.

Outside they all realized how horrible had been the atmosphere in the claustrophobia of the tent. Syme appeared to have had enough of the cold, the blood and the perfume of the dead; he spoke briefly to Sauerwine, then walked back to one of the police cars. As he did so another four-wheel drive had already arrived, this one containing three men who bore the unmistakable stigmata of undertakers; even as these trudged towards the marquee, Groshong's Land Rover appeared at the far edge of the small heath, bouncing around over the uneven ground. The track it followed was becoming dark green and clearly delineated on the heath, as if it were the beginnings of a pilgrimage trail, the corpse a beacon for believers.

They waited on the ridge as Groshong got out and approached them. Sauerwine saw confusion on his face but no fear.

'What's going on here?' he demanded, as if he had rights over this scenario.

Perhaps the words were lost in the wind and did not reach Sauerwine's ears for he did not reply, asking instead, 'What brings you here, Mr Groshong?'

He was treated to authoritative contempt for his trouble. 'This is estate land. Why shouldn't I be here?'

Sauerwine looked at Beverley, then at Eisenmenger and Helena. 'I didn't call Mr Groshong. Did any of you?'

No one had.

Groshong snorted. 'You think I don't know what goes on around here? I know everything, Inspector. I know when a poacher takes a bird or a fish; I know when a tree falls.'

Sauerwine considered this briefly. 'Really? Yet there have been one, possibly two murders on the estate, and you know nothing about those.'

Clearly surprised, Groshong asked, 'Two?'

Sauerwine turned to look back down into the hollow. 'Two,' he repeated.

Groshong came forward. 'Who?'

'An old man from the village. Albert Bloom.' He looked directly at Groshong. 'Know him?'

Groshong's expression was convincingly shocked. It took a moment of staring at the marquee before he said, 'Of course I know him. Everyone knows him.'

Sauerwine glanced at Beverley, eyebrows raised. *Genuine?*

She nodded slightly, then asked, 'Did he ever work on the estate?'

He came to, answered slowly. 'Only as a casual. Beating for the shoots, that kind of thing.'

'The last time was . . . when?'

'Six, seven weeks ago, I suppose. I'd have to check with the head keeper.'

'When did you last see him?'

Despite herself, Helena found some admiration for the way that Beverley steered Groshong into the role of inter-rogatee. Eisenmenger kept looking at the marquee, almost mesmerized by it.

'Last week, I think. He was always hanging around the pub. The pub or the petrol station.'

'Why?'

Groshong was about to answer, then something decided him against this course. He closed his mouth and shrugged, not looking at her. Sauerwine asked, 'Michael? His son?'

'Oh. You know.'

218

'I know his son didn't like him.'

Groshong, accepting that he was spilling no secrets, said, 'There was history.'

'What kind?'

But Groshong couldn't, maybe wouldn't, be drawn. 'I don't know all the details. A load of village gossip, but I wouldn't pay too much attention to that. You'll have to ask Michael.'

Which, of course, they were going to do anyway.

Beverley asked, 'Could I have your movements over the past twenty-four hours?'

Groshong seemed to be coming out of his spell, chafing at the harness of suspect. It was with some impatience that he said, 'Working. Here. On the estate. In the morning in the office – my secretary will vouch for that. You know where I was yesterday midday, because you interrupted me. In the afternoon, I was meeting with some reps – my secretary can give you the names. In the evening I was alone in my flat. No witnesses, I'm afraid, except for an hour that I spent with Eleanor; about nine until ten.'

It was Eisenmenger who asked unexpectedly, 'Eleanor?'

Groshong swung round. 'Yes. She likes me to talk to her. Tell her what's going on on the estate.'

He seemed to be daring Eisenmenger to make something of this, but he was disappointed; Eisenmenger nodded and smiled and murmured, 'Very commendable.'

Groshong stared hard at him, interrupted in this when Sauerwine asked, 'How often do you come up here? Presumably not very often.'

A shake of the head. 'There are no drives anywhere near here. We do some occasional forestry work, routine maintenance; and this is used as sheep pasture every so often, but not routinely.'

'Are there any rights-of-way around here?'

'No.'

'So it might have been bloody difficult to get the body up here, but once achieved, there was a high likelihood that it would have been undiscovered for a long time.'

But Groshong disagreed. 'It wasn't difficult at all.'

'What do you mean?'

Groshong gestured to the north. 'Albert's place is no more than a kilometre that way. Just off the estate.'

Felty showed her warrant card to the woman who answered the doorbell. There was a lot to be learned from the way people reacted to a warrant card; already she was beginning to appreciate that those familiar with the police – *familiar with*, as in *known to* – barely glanced at it, as if the gesture itself were a secret sign, Deputy Dawg's greeting. The woman wasn't wearing a Stetson with long, floppy ears, but Felty knew at once that she was facing an old hand. If she noticed that Felty's was a foreign constabulary, she either didn't notice or didn't appreciate.

'What is it?'

'I'm making some enquiries and you might be able to help me.'

Helping the police with their enquiries. There had been a time when that phrase had been innocent but now it was tainted.

'What about?' She sounded tired. Indeed she looked exhausted, as if she'd had a late night. She was dressed in jeans and a T-shirt but her demeanour suggested that she had not been vertical for long.

'Can I come in?' Sauerwine had told her that the relevant questions could always keep, that they were the main course and should always follow a starter of pleasantries.

The house was small but looked tended; the neighbourhood similarly so. Nothing too green but at least the concrete and stone were clean and tidy. She was led into a kitchen-dining room at the rear, the garden little more than a patio on which there were large tubs and plant pots, all awaiting the arrival of distant spring. At the rear there was a small greenhouse, its windows obscured by dust and condensation.

It was very ordinary, very suburban, but Felty sensed something amiss.

She was a large woman, big-boned but kindly-looking. Felty could imagine many men would find her a welcoming, attractive presence.

'I called earlier, but there was no answer.'

It was threatening to rain, a late afternoon cruelty to add to the cold and dark.

'I was sleeping. I didn't hear the phone.'

'Sleeping?'

'I was out late last night.'

Felty heard nothing in the words nor in the tone, but she knew at once the truth. *Prostitute.*

'What do you do?'

'I'm a hostess.'

Their eyes met and they both knew what the other knew. Felty had no need to be overt.

'I'm also a medical secretary at the Infirmary, but only part time.'

'And could I have your full name?'

'Fiona Curshmann. No middle name.'

'And you own this house?'

'Yes. Why?'

Felty said, 'I've called because I think you may have some information concerning someone I'm interested in. Someone by the name of William Moynihan.'

Not what Fiona Curshmann had been expecting. Felty could see at once that the woman knew him, even before she opened her mouth to ask, 'He's all right, isn't he?'

But Felty wasn't about to answer that question immediately. She said, 'I see you know him.'

She smiled and nodded, although still clearly very worried. 'Oh, yes. He's an old friend, although we lost contact for some years.'

'You don't have a photograph, do you?'

This request only made her even more perturbed, but she nodded through this, rose and went out of the room. She returned with a photographic developer's envelope from which she produced a thick pile of pictures. She said nervously, 'I've only just got these back.'

She didn't have to look through them for long before she found one that portrayed William Moynihan. Felty took it, perused it, then asked, 'May I keep this?'

A nod. Felty looked again at it. It could have been their corpse, but then she could have been shown a picture of practically any human being who had ever lived and she would have been hard-pressed to disprove that it had become the charred thing that was their corpse.

She looked up at Fiona Curshmann, saw real fear now, but knew that she couldn't help her. She had to ask the questions that she had to ask, while feeling a bitch, to gain as much information as possible, doing exactly the duty of a police officer, before telling Fiona Curshmann that the man she had clearly cared for was now dead.

They sat in silence in the police Land Rover as it made its undulating, dropping, sliding, slow way back down from the heath. They were accompanied by a driver and by Sauerwine, Beverley having remained to look over Albert Bloom's now empty cottage. In the car silence reigned over them but as they arrived back on the gravel of the forecourt in front of the castle it felt as if a sac of emotion were pulsatingly close to breaking. Sure enough, when Sauerwine went to the main entrance door of the castle and left them alone, Helena turned to Eisenmenger and seemed almost to explode with incredulous anger.

'What's going on, John?' she demanded, as if he were behind some monstrous hoax and hidden around them were other surprises that he had planned for her. 'What's she doing here?'

And, of course, he didn't know. He shrugged, feeling helpless once again in front of her anger.

'That was crap about moving around, gaining experience. She's up to something.' The degree of certainty in Helena's words suggested that she had just dictated a law of the universe by which all would do Her will.

'Undoubtedly,' he agreed, not because he partook of the same degree of conviction but merely because it was a reasonable working hypothesis. 'Unfortunately, it doesn't give us anything positive to go on.'

This didn't deter the brave Helena. 'Not yet, maybe. But I'm going to find out.'

Eisenmenger smiled. 'I've no doubt you will.' He took a deep breath of cold air. 'Still, the situation is undoubtedly intriguing. Two deaths on the estate in less than a week.'

'One of which was definitely a murder, the other less obviously.'

Eisenmenger smiled. There were times when Helena was convinced that someone would murder him because of that smile and she felt a vague desire to hurt him even now, even as she asked, 'What is it?'

'I was just thinking how right you were.'

He refused to say any more, but the smile stubbornly remained. He put his arm around her shoulders and led her into the castle.

'You're joking! Another death?'

Theresa spoke as if the lower orders were really too much trouble, as if this thing never used to happen, back in Edwardian times.

Sauerwine nodded. 'Up on the heath known as Old Man's Sorrow.'

Tristan pointed out at once, 'That's only just on the estate. The very edge.'

This failed to impress Sauerwine. 'So was the first death.'

'Who was it?'

'I've got no formal identification yet, but I have reason to believe that it was a man by the name of Albert Bloom. Do you know him?'

He looked at them, eyebrows raised, caught them looking quickly at each other; the glance appeared to be between two people surprised, not obviously implicated. Tristan said, 'He lived in the village. Has done all his life.'

'May one ask how? How he died?' Eisenmenger heard a slight note of trepidation in the enquiry.

Sauerwine hesitated, then said in a low voice, 'He was quite viciously attacked. I'm not altogether sure you would want to hear all the details.' His eyes flicked to Eisenmenger as if warning him not to wax too lyrical on the ins and outs of forensic pathology.

Tristan put his hands on his head. 'My God! What's happening around here? Is there some sort of mass murderer at large?'

Sauerwine shook his head. 'We've got no actual proof that Mr Moynihan's death was an act of murder, although we're not discounting the possibility.'

This appeared to be scant comfort for either Tristan or Theresa. Sauerwine continued, 'However, I'm sure that you'll appreciate the importance of determining your whereabouts over the past twenty-four hours or so. I'll have to speak to everyone in the house.'

Theresa opened her mouth but it was Tristan who

replied, interrupting his wife's protestation. 'Of course, Inspector. You shall have our full co-operation.'

Sauerwine thanked him gravely. He didn't see any point in telling the world just yet that he already had a very good idea who might have killed the old man.

For once the autopsy did not result in significantly more blood being liberated than was already present at the beginning. Beverley stayed throughout, showing neither interest nor distress, her eyes merely dull beacons of boredom. She sat on a stool, leaning against a wall, sometimes staring at Dr Addison's back, sometimes at the opened, gutted cadaver, sometimes at the ceiling where anonymous dull grey ducts passed between the fluorescent strip lights. Holt accompanied her, as did a representative of the Coroner's Office and the SOCO, but all of these were far more active than she, both passing in and out, sometimes whispering to each other, sometimes changing their vantage point. Beverley ignored them, a higher being on a higher plane, watching another dull play from the theatre of humanity.

Eventually, Dr Addison finished, straightened her back, took a deep breath and stepped away from the bench. She marched to the sink, peeling off first a pair of gloves, then her plastic apron, then a second pair of gloves, then the disposable gown. All of these were deposited one by one into a yellow, soiled clinical waste bag before she washed her hands and turned to face Beverley, who had barely moved her head.

'Nothing much more to report, I'm afraid. As I said at the scene, been dead about twelve hours, give or take two. I've counted seventy-three stab wounds and three hammer blows to the head. The hammer blows were hard enough to cause lacerations in the scalp down to bone and to cause superficial disruption of the outer table of the parietal bones . . .'

Whatever that means.

'. . . The impressions exactly match the hammer found at the scene, and the various stab wounds and cuts are compatible with the knife –'

'Cuts?'

Dr Addison apparently did not like being interrupted

during her discourse, as was intimated by the frown that
formed on her smooth young forehead and the frost-
tinged tone with which she said, 'Yes. Cuts.'

'What's the difference?'

There was an unmistakable smirk as she explained, 'A
stab is a single thrusting motion; a cut involves lateral
movement associated with downwards pressure.' Beverley seemed to have struck some sort of automatic recall
button, because Dr Addison continued, 'A stab involves
primarily the tip of a sharp, pointed object, a cut necessarily requires a long blade –'

'Thanks.' Beverley cut across this flood of didacticism
with drawled sarcasm and Dr Addison coloured noticeably. 'And is it usual? Cuts as well as stabs in a case like
this?'

'In one of such frenzy, yes.' Dr Addison's reply was
superficially assured, but Beverley wondered.

'How many cuts?'

The notes were consulted. 'Eight.' She looked up.
'Why?'

'Any particular distribution?'

Dr Addison was losing her air of confidence. Something
about her voice had changed as she said, 'Most of the stab
wounds were located on the front of the chest and abdomen, although six were on the upper back, seven were
into the front of the right thigh and six into the left. There
were ten into the neck, another four into the left forearm.
There were two long cuts made across the abdomen, one
just deep enough to penetrate the abdominal cavity in its
central portion. Four more cuts were across the neck, two
more across the left wrist.'

When she had completed this catalogue, she looked up
from the paper and stared at Beverley. For a moment there
was quiet in the room before she was asked, 'So what did
he die of?'

'None of the wounds alone was of sufficient severity to
have caused instant death, which means that he died of
blood loss. Of course, this was hastened by exposure.'

A sad, lonely and cold death. Even after all the years, all
the brutality, Beverley still had enough compassion to feel
the awfulness of what must have happened to Albert
Bloom. She got off the stool, was heading for the door
before she turned to ask one last question.

'Any signs of a fight? Bruising, that kind of thing?'

'A collection of small ecchymoses on the right upper arm, consistent with being grabbed there. A few small ones on the shins and a large one on the left buttock. That was all.'

Beverley forgot to thank her as she left.

It began to rain in the late afternoon, casting the gloom of the latest death into deeper shade, emphasizing that they were in the middle of winter with spring far away, last summer long forgotten. Nobody had much to say, except Eleanor who kept on talking about Albert Bloom, how she had known him for years; she kept recalling anecdotes about him, kept repeating them, too, so that as Helena, Eisenmenger and Theresa sat in the small living room with her, their patience became stretched. Eisenmenger was trying to read, Helena to sleep, Theresa to compile a shopping list for the meal on New Year's Eve. Hugo had taken Tom to the pictures, Nell was resting in her room and Tristan was working in his study.

Eleanor, in the habit of those who grow forgetful, would periodically lapse into rumination, only to discover the same topic again after perhaps five or ten minutes, chancing upon it as if new, then beginning the cycle of tiresome exclamation and remark once more.

'I just can't believe it! Poor Albert . . .'

The wind had picked up, making a droning accompaniment to this staccato verbiage, a musical construction from meaningless sounds, something almost beautiful from things individually wretched.

'I remember when he was a young man . . . quite a catch for the village girls, I remember . . . of course my mother forbade me from having anything to do with him, but there was one harvest supper when afterwards, when the band played, he snatched a kiss from me . . .'

On and on it went, never varying in either tone or content, even down to the punctuation and emphases on certain syllables.

'. . . and then, of course, there was that terrible business with his daughter . . . Terrible, that was. Do you remember, Theresa?'

This was new and its novelty seemed to cause some

surprise. Theresa looked startled. 'Remember?' She stared at her mother-in-law. Eisenmenger, glancing up from his book, saw something that he interpreted as annoyance in her eyes. Then, 'No, not really.'

'Oh, yes.' She turned to Eisenmenger, oblivious of his desire merely to read. 'His wife died when she was born . . . what was her name? There was a dreadful fuss at the time. People said that he should have called the doctor earlier but he and his wife were Jehovah's Witnesses . . . Tristan's father had to take a hand, calm things down in the village.

'And then the daughter just disappeared . . . Everyone said that she'd gone off to London, but who knows? Albert had gone funny in the head by then. Sometimes he hit her, I think . . .' She turned back to her daughter-in-law. 'What was her name, Theresa? Frances? Flora?' Another pause, significantly longer, almost deliberately timed to make the listener believe that she had lapsed, that this particular stream of consciousness had run into mud. '. . . Fiona! That was it!'

Distractedly, Theresa asked, 'Really?'

'Oh, yes.' Back to Eisenmenger. 'Michael was no use. Hated his father. Blamed him for his mother's death, though I said that surely he was as much to blame . . .' She swung around to Theresa. 'Don't you think?'

'Yes.' But this was a distracted, almost abstracted response, the items on the shopping list apparently too overladen with fascination to release her attention.

'Oh, yes. Once, I recall, they had a terrible fight. Michael was only young and his father beat him quite badly. Ended up in hospital . . . You must remember that, Theresa, surely?'

Theresa couldn't even manage a monosyllabic response now but she was not pressed upon the issue for at this moment the door opened allowing Tom into the room followed by Nell. Their entrance disturbed Helena who opened her eyes and then rose from Eisenmenger's shoulder where she had been resting her head. Tom ran to his grandmother and snuggled her. Eleanor forgot her ruminations on the Blooms and smiled at him.

Nell sat down beside her mother as Helena stretched and yawned. 'I'm sorry for disturbing you.'

'It's all right. I mustn't sleep too much. Won't sleep tonight.'

'I'm hungry.' This from Tom. It was less an observation, more a suggestion.

Eleanor laughed the laugh of someone who would not have to get up to assuage his appetite. Theresa smiled at him. 'You're hungry, are you?'

He nodded solemnly.

She sighed. 'Well, it is teatime.'

He nodded. She began to rise from her seat. Eisenmenger wondered why Nell was not required to provide the meals on Dominique's days off.

Eleanor said, 'Bless him.'

'Would you like me to help, Mummy?' Nell's question was couched in a tone suggesting that she could summon little enthusiasm for the prospect, that it was a token offered but not meant to be accepted.

Theresa embraced her part in the vignette. 'No, no, dear. You rest.'

Actually, it turned out that Nell did not want to rest. She turned to Helena. 'Helena, I've got something to show you.'

Helena was still tired and Eisenmenger murmured, 'You don't have to go.' Helena smiled at him, then got up from the settee. Nell reached for her hand, took it and immediately began to pull her after her. Once they were out of the room, she whispered excitedly, 'I've been you-know-where! I was searching amongst the junk up there, and I found something. Something that you'll like.'

She continued to urge Helena along, down the corridor, up the stairs, past Tom's room, then to the doorway that led into the turret and on up.

The room struck cold tonight, as if the wind had changed direction and was now finding new cracks through which to thread and to taunt and to caress. At first she thought the room was unchanged, but then she noticed that on the bed was a box. It looked old and dusty. Nell went to it.

'I was looking for the dressing-up box. The one we used to use when we played our games. Remember? When we played at King Arthur?'

Helena nodded and smiled. 'Yes.'

'I couldn't find that, but I did find something else.'

She beckoned Helena forward and dipped through the flaps of the box, unheeding of arachnid squatters. She brought out handfuls of photographs. 'Look!' she commanded, her eyes full of the kind of delight only a child or a damaged adult can manage. 'We're in here! You and me, and Jeremy and Hugo! Just as we used to be.'

Jackson had finished counting paperclips and he had finished sculpting them into unlikely shapes on the flat magnetic paperclip holder; now he was making a chain of them. He had taken the details of a stolen bicycle and he had fielded five calls from a variety of local newspapers and wire services. He had drunk three cups of tea and it was now very dark and he was very bored.

He was not ambitious, hardly ever had been. Aspiration's kiss had long since faded and for many a year he had contented himself with the routine of life, with following an orderly course through the days and years; indeed, through the minutes and hours as well. He did not crave excitement, nor did he desire craving; he might have been bored, but he was surprisingly contented. He was well aware that others thought him slothful, that his uniform sometimes sported unintended decorations of food or other substances organic and inorganic, but that awareness did not perturb him. That someone might have perceived within him many qualities that were, if not actually Buddhist, then a remarkable facsimile thereof, would have left him abnormally speechless.

Yet today he felt out of sorts. He detected within himself a feeling that he had initially thought to be indigestion, subsequently revising the diagnosis to early influenza, only lately deciding it was actually excitement. Two deaths within one week, both violent, both murder, had never before occurred to Sergeant Jackson, just as they had never before occurred to Westerham. Not even the Civil War had seen such infamy. He had not seen either of the corpses but he had glanced at – actually devoured – SOCO's photographs of both corpses and had been impressed with Michael Bloom. The last murderer in the village had been Tom Willebrand, an inept poacher who had clubbed one of the Hickmans' gamekeepers to death in 1957. There was enough residual policeman in Jackson to appreciate that Tom Willebrand was mean and petty in comparison with Michael Bloom's obvious penchant for human despatch; burning one man to death and then turning another into something that resembled a pig that had fallen into a shredding machine showed endeavour indeed.

He found that he was fascinated by Albert Bloom's body. Although there was no doubt that it *was* Albert Bloom, there was also something alien about it now; not just because it was a lifeless body, but because of the obvious violence that had been meted out on it. The earnestness with which death had come upon him had transformed Albert Bloom. Jackson thought that modern art was a load of crap, but he appreciated the work that had gone into that particular installation.

He wished that he had had a chance to read the autopsy report in more depth. When it had arrived an hour before, he had tried to sneak a quick preview but that stuck-up bitch Wharton – what was she doing there, anyway? – had discovered him whilst he examined it with greedy fervour and snatched it from his hands without a word.

Still, he had seen the bottom line. Seventy-three stab wounds, some deep enough to penetrate the anterior abdominal wall, several severing arteries; the three hammer blows to the top of the skull were merely gilding upon a blood-red lily.

Jackson sighed and leaned back in his chair, unable to stop grinning. *Bloody hell, Michael. You got away with it once, but not this time, I reckon.*

The phone rang and slowly he stretched forward to pick it up.

More press.

The photographs took Helena away from her life, away from the present and the immediate past, back into a world that she had tried not to think about for many years. A world that she had enjoyed too much to have tainted by events and, if it was a world that had shaped her, then it was its loss that had hardened her.

The pictures with Jeremy were almost a shock. She had deliberately not retained any images of her stepbrother after his death as part of her attempts to cling to life, to move forward. Suddenly here were so many reminders of him, so many prompts to release suppressed memories.

We were so happy . . . what happened?

The answer was obvious. They had grown up. They hadn't chosen to do it, but that was no comfort.

Everyone grows up, everyone grows apart; only the dead don't grow in some way or another.

Then she thought of the sadness in seeing what had become of Jeremy and Nell and of the death of her parents.

Perhaps the dead are the lucky ones.

But when she saw her mother and father . . .

No. She knew then that whatever fortuitousness the dead possessed, to die was a terrible thing; terrible for the dying and terrible for the living left behind.

They were younger than the portraits she had in her head. Small details of them had been lost, or subverted, or added, so that these people were subtly altered, recognizably her parents yet distorted. She had read, she thought, that someone had described memory as looking at the past through a prism, but it seemed to Helena then that it was more like looking at the past through frosted glass.

She saw also pictures of Hugo and was struck again by how his attractiveness came from a callous air that was evident even from dead photographs; he had always seemed to her to be callous if not downright cruel, yet somehow the fascination she and others saw in him was based on this perception. A kind Hugo would not have been a particularly interesting Hugo.

Nell's image fascinated her. Whilst her face had assumed a more mature configuration, it was clear that her spirit had remained static. The eyes that looked at her now were more injured, perhaps slightly more luminous than those looking into the camera, but they were still the eyes of an adolescent. She was noticeably better nourished in these memories on paper, perhaps also less pale, the attrition of experience, the death of purity.

And her own pictures?

She had taken most of them, it seemed, for she was in relatively few, but there were enough for her to see a young woman with much ahead of her, few scars to bear.

That was the worst of all. Remembrance of her younger self caused an almost physical agony, as if to look on a state of innocence from one of knowledge was a form of masochism.

The wind was unbelievably loud in the turret room. It seemed to circle around, enveloping the room, cutting it off from the world. She could almost imagine that she was Dorothy on her way out of Kansas. Were there draughts or was she just fantasizing them?

She sat on the bed and Nell sat beside her, clearly oblivious to Helena's deep emotions. She was so excited to have discovered these photographs, so pleased to be able to delight Helena with them, that she seemed transformed, reverted to the carefree child that had once enjoyed life. She would exclaim with sounds that were almost squeals of pleasure as Helena slowly went through the pictures, pointing at them and excitedly crying out where they were taken, or when, or on what occasion.

Even if Helena found it all a profoundly moving, if not upsetting experience, the obvious joy it gave to Nell was considerable compensation.

She reached into the box, by now nearly empty. They had looked through their lives, dived again into a deep and reassuring pool of memory, where it was safe because it had happened, where the bad things had yet to occur. She pulled out the last bundle of photographs, discovering that at the bottom there was some sort of album. She assumed that it would contain more photographs and looked first through the bundle but they were relatively boring wedding pictures of a cousin that Nell, possibly genuinely, possible otherwise couldn't remember. She lay back on the bed about halfway through with a loud, theatrical sigh and allowed Helena to finish the pictures alone.

Helena reached into the box and pulled out the photograph album.

Except it wasn't.

When she opened it, there were no images, merely handwritten words. A scrapbook of the letters that Nell had received. Some were from people she didn't know, some were from Tristan, apparently sent from abroad. She saw two from herself, and she only vaguely remembered the words as she read through them; her handwriting was curiously formal and this gave it a sheen of immaturity. She was telling Nell about how Jeremy had been in trouble with the police. He had been stopped late one night when returning from a rock concert, searched and cannabis found.

Helena frowned, unpleasant strands of memory suddenly entangling her. She had quite forgotten that particular incident. Was that the start of his addiction problems?

She hurriedly turned over the pages, uncomfortable to go once again into that piece of the past, then saw it and was paralysed.

Her father's handwriting. She recognized it at once.

She was holding her breath as she read the words.

My Dearest Nell,

It's entirely natural that you should look on Hugo's departure to medical school with sadness. We all know how close you are and this will be the first time that you have been apart for any significant length of time. Helena and Jeremy are similarly close and his trip to Switzerland skiing last year was fraught for her, but it ended and her joy at seeing him when he returned was touching to see. It will be the same for you when Hugo returns in the holidays. Don't forget that it won't be long before you, too, are beginning your first term at university.

We will be seeing you next month and are looking forward to celebrating your birthday. Please let us know what present you want (unless you would like a surprise).

Your loving Godfather,

To see her name in the hand of her dead father, to discover that she had been referred to, that she had once been part of a close group of family and friends made Helena feel light-headed, as if the wild wind outside were sucking oxygen from the room. She felt the greatest happiness, the deepest melancholy as she turned the pages, eager to find more of her father in them.

The door to the interrogation room opened and Sauerwine and Wharton emerged; Oram got up from his desk at once and at Sauerwine's gesture, went inside to stand guard over Bloom. Sauerwine led Wharton into his office, closing the door behind her.

'Well?'

Beverley frowned. She had taken to frowning over the past two hours. 'I don't know. I really don't know.'

Sauerwine was surprised. 'Don't you?'

She sat down. 'You do, I take it.'

'Of course I do.' He couldn't understand her reluctance, found it to be almost a challenge. 'What more do you want? He's a perfect fit.'

She didn't say anything, which prompted him to continue, 'Okay. Play the devil's advocate. I say he's our man, you're not sure. Let's take it from there.' He leaned forward, forearms on the surface of the desk, palms raised and turned towards his chest. 'Albert Bloom was stabbed and slashed with a long-bladed knife in an assault that can only be described as frenzied. The degree of violence is also indicated by the fact that he was attacked with a hammer, being hit three times on the head. You agree so far?'

She nodded.

'The pathologist indicates that the attack took place somewhere in a four-hour slot around midnight; ten until two in the morning. It appears as if the assault took place where we found the corpse, on Old Man's Sorrow. The Sorrow is a desolate place, with few people living anywhere near it.'

All of this was beyond question and Beverley merely waited and thought.

'He wasn't obviously robbed, since he still had his wallet and small change on him, although the wallet had only one five-pound note in it. You've checked the house and, although it was unlocked, the few things of value it did contain were still there.

'So we have a very violent assault without robbery as a motive. The body was found in a desolate location, so it was hardly some passer-by; whoever did this one, did it because he wanted to do it.'

All very true, but Beverley still showed no signs that she was heading the same way he was.

'So, without robbery for a motive, we have to turn elsewhere, which leads us to Michael.'

At last she spoke. 'He doesn't hide his hatred for his father.'

'Exactly! He himself admits that he blames his father for the death of his mother; he also blames him for driving his sister away. You heard him, he's half convinced himself the old man did away with her and buried the body.'

She nodded slowly, then sighed. 'Look, Andrew. Maybe it's different in the country – God knows, most things are – but it doesn't work like that where I come from. Michael admits everything – as you said, he admits the motive, even to the extent of not trying to fabricate sadness that Albert Bloom's dead. He also admits opportunity – he has no alibi for last night and he is quite frank in saying that he had a row with his father in the pub.'

Sauerwine jumped in. 'Yes. A row that became heated, that resulted in him pushing the old man over. A row in which he openly and before witnesses threatened to kill his father.'

She nodded but was still patently worried.

'So what's the problem?'

'You've just said, Andrew. He admits everything, except that he committed murder.'

He couldn't see what she meant. 'It's just a matter of time.'

'No,' she contradicted. 'I don't think it is. I think that he'd have confessed by now if he were going to.'

He shrugged. 'No matter. We've got enough to charge him. I don't think the CPS will have a problem with the case as it stands. Especially if forensics come up with something.'

'Mmm.'

Her tone was doubtful and he took this as a signal that she was still there to be converted. With missionary zeal he said, 'He did it, Beverley. Haven't you ever had that feeling of certainty? You look at the case and you look at the suspect and you just *know*. Instinct, experience, sixth sense – call it what you will, it's as good as fingerprints on the weapon.'

She looked at him but he couldn't see in her eyes what she was thinking, how she was remembering that she had once also sensed a feeling almost of God-given power in the midst of a case, and where that particular 'instinct' had led her.

She was thinking of Jeremy Eaton-Lambert.

Slowly she asked, 'And what if forensics don't come up with anything?'

He shrugged. 'I still think we've got enough to proceed.'

She said slowly, 'He was drinking heavily before he died.'

'So?'

'And he'd overdosed on two occasions.'

Sauerwine asked, 'What's that to do with anything?'

She didn't know, but that didn't mean she was happy and when once again she didn't agree he began to show irritation. 'What on earth is your problem?'

It took her a moment to bring her thoughts together. 'First, he's stopping at the wrong point. He admits everything, everything that incriminates him, but he stops at the point of murder. Most murderers try as hard as possible to make sure that they're never even considered. They remain as inconspicuous as possible, playing the innocent. Michael Bloom seems to have gone out of his way to advertise his hatred for his father.'

That was easily dismissed. 'He's admitting everything because he has to. The relationship with his father was well known and ancient; the final row took place in public. He can hardly claim otherwise.'

'Then there's the forensic evidence –'

'We haven't got the report yet,' he interrupted.

'We shouldn't need a report, Andrew. How many stab wounds was it? Seventy-odd? There should have been enough blood on him to bake half a dozen black puddings. I didn't see any, did you?'

Sauerwine looked uncomfortable at that. He said uncertainly, 'He destroyed the clothes he wore; burned them, probably. We'll find something in the ash in the woodburner. Also there'll be something under his nails.'

She didn't argue with that. Instead, 'And thirdly, there's the case of Bill Moynihan. Where does Bloom fit in with that?'

More assuredly he said, 'That's interesting, I admit, but hardly a problem. Firstly, it's still possible that Moynihan killed himself; if it was murder, the assumption must be that it was Bloom, just on the statistical grounds that there are unlikely to be two murderers operating at the same time in a place as small as Westerham. Bloom knowing Moynihan is the first link.'

'And after that?'

'We know that there had been a violent row in the past,' he said. It sounded lame and Beverley only made matters worse by pointing out, 'Eight years ago.'

He said defensively, 'Maybe Moynihan knew something about Bloom; something about his past.' There was only a slight pause before he said, 'Maybe Bloom had something to do with the Eaton-Lambert case. Moynihan was blackmailing him.'

Her face told the story. *Possible but implausible.* She pointed out, 'Bloom has no significant criminal history that we know of; certainly nothing involving burglary or violence.' His fingerprints and DNA had been taken but they would not have the results of checks on those until the next day.

'Still, it's worth asking him about the murder of the Flemmings.'

She had to admit that it was, although she doubted it. She couldn't help hoping that Bloom wasn't the link to the Eaton-Lambert case; she didn't particularly want a witness to those killings to turn up after eight years and perhaps destroy what was, in her opinion, a beautifully constructed solution to the case.

'It's still not right, Andrew. If you're correct, Bloom murdered one man because he was being blackmailed, another a few days later in some sort of fit of rage. I still don't buy it.'

He sighed, admitting to himself that he wasn't sure if believed it either. Yet he was sure that Bloom was guilty of slaying his father and if the death of Moynihan didn't fit in, then perhaps it was suicide after all.

He stood up. 'Come on. We won't find out anything without questioning him some more.'

'We'll have to charge him sooner or later. If you think we've got enough now, why waste time?'

But Sauerwine was being cautious. Syme and Tanner had gone home, trusting him (at least for the night) to handle matters safely. He wanted to be one hundred and one per cent certain before he committed himself.

My Dearest Nell,

What is there that I can say to comfort you? To say that your Aunt Penelope and I are surprised is no exaggeration. We do not claim to understand how this has happened, but rest assured that both your aunt and I will support you. We fully understand your decision to continue with the pregnancy and hope that out of this terrible thing will come forth some beauty and pleasure and hope.

Please, please do not hesitate to ring or write at any time. We both want to help you in any way that we can in the months and years to come. You will not find it easy to cope, even given your privileged position. Whilst we don't doubt that your mother and father will offer you everything that they can, I know that the chance to speak to a sympathetic and relatively uninvolved ear can make all the difference.

Please do as I suggest.

Your loving Godfather,

Helena felt as if she were trespassing but the chance to read her father's words was beyond resistance. She had not been aware that Nell had turned to her father during the pregnancy. She noted the date – 3 April; Nell would have been four months pregnant. She turned the pages, trying to be as silent as possible, afraid of disturbing Nell for she felt strongly that she was intruding on privacy. She felt like a criminal but told herself that these were the letters of her father and that gave her, she reasoned, some sort of right to be there.

It was unusual for Tristan to visit Groshong and the estate manager was surprised when the knock came on his door.

'Mr Hickman!'

Tristan was soaked through. He looked unhappy and in no mood for pleasantries. He pushed past Groshong, stripping off his jacket before the front door had been closed. He dropped the coat on the floor and went into the sitting room, still wearing his wellington boots, leaving wet footprints on the carpet. Groshong followed him. Before he could speak, Tristan turned and asked, 'What the hell is going on, Malcolm?'

Groshong frowned. 'I don't follow.'

'The body, man! The body on the Sorrow!'

The only change in Groshong's expression was a slight varnish of contempt. He asked slowly, 'What about it?' There was an edge of implacability to his voice, hinting at a perversion of the employer–worker relationship.

Tristan was too far gone into anxiety to worry about the subtleties of the interaction. 'There's something going on, Malcolm.'

'Is there?'

'For God's sake!'

Groshong looked at his employer for a while; he seemed to be scrutinizing him, assessing him, perhaps considering him for a position, perhaps, even, for a confidence. He went to the sideboard, picked up a bottle of whisky. 'Drink?' he asked. Tristan shook his head impatiently. Valiantly overcoming the social stigma of drinking alone, Groshong poured just one glass, then picked it up. 'I haven't the faintest idea what you're talking about,' he pronounced, each word distinct and well formed, each one an emphasis to underscore the central theme. 'There is nothing going on.'

'Nothing? You call what happened to Albert Bloom *nothing*?'

'Not for him, obviously. But nothing for you, for the estate, for the family.'

Tristan took his turn to be lost. He stared at his estate manager. 'But –'

Groshong interrupted him. 'Bloom's murder is nothing to do with us, Mr Hickman. Nothing at all.'

'And Moynihan's death?'

Another drink of whisky, one that finished the glass, before, '*I* didn't kill him, did you?'

'No . . .'

'Well, then.'

Tristan frowned, transferring his gaze from Groshong to the carpet. Groshong added, 'I should imagine that Bloom's son is being entertained by the police even as we speak. Why, I understand that he threatened him only last night.'

Tristan sat slowly down in a chair by the wall, briefly closing his eyes. He took a deep breath, then held it as if it contained an elixir, a hint of ambrosia. After a while he opened them again, now considerably less worried. 'I see. Good.'

Groshong finished his drink, picked up the bottle, then held it up for his visitor. This time Tristan accepted. When they both had drinks in hand, Groshong said reassuringly, 'Nothing for you to worry about, Mr Hickman. Nothing at all.'

'Tell us what happened when you fought with your father last night, Michael.'

The solicitor next to Bloom was making notes, not looking at his client, nor at his client's interrogators. Bloom glanced sideways before saying tiredly, 'I've told you . . .'

Abruptly the solicitor looked up and said, 'Yes. We have been over this ground before, Inspector Sauerwine.' It was almost as if he had been daydreaming, perhaps of more interesting legal work waiting to be done.

Sauerwine had never lost his charming smile. 'Just once more.'

Bloom hesitated, looked at his counsel who shrugged, then began, 'He came into the Dancing Pig. He walked straight up to the bar, even though he knew I was there, knew it would make me mad.'

'Why would it make you mad?'

'Because of what he did. Because of my mother . . . and Fiona.'

'What did he do?'

Tiredly. 'He killed my mother. He refused to get the midwife. Said that he could handle it. He couldn't. She died in agony.'

'How do you know? You were a little young at the time, I understand.'

'The neighbours called the doctor eventually. Couldn't cope with the screaming. They told me.'

Sauerwine leaned back. It was a sign for Beverley to start. 'Seems pretty flimsy to me, Michael. Something that happened thirty-odd years ago, something that you can't even remember.'

'How would you know?'

'I think there's more to it. I think you hated your father because you feel guilty yourself. After all, you were the

240

baby involved. All your father did was to mistake how serious it was . . .'

The solicitor looked up again. 'Is this amateur psychology really relevant?'

Ignoring him, she continued, 'You were blaming him because you couldn't face the truth yourself.'

Bloom affected disdain. 'Whatever.'

'Or perhaps there was more to it. Perhaps he didn't treat you well. Did he? Did he treat you well?'

He shrugged.

'Did you row often?'

'Sometimes.'

'How often?'

Another shrug.

'Did he hit you when you were a child?'

No response at all now.

'He did, I think.'

Bloom sighed. 'Occasionally.'

She waited, just looking. At the corners of her mouth, nowhere else, there was a smile. Then, 'Did he beat you?'

Bloom was becoming nervous.

Receiving no response she asked, 'What did he use? His belt? A hairbrush?'

Bloom dropped his head. The solicitor was now taking an interest of sorts but he might just as well have been sitting in front of a television play. Beverley continued, taking silence as affirmation, 'Is that why you hated him so much? Because when you were small he used to beat you? Was he a bully? Did he get off on it?'

Suddenly Bloom's head came up. 'Yeah. That's right. He used to get off on whacking me. He didn't like being reminded of what he'd done. He was a piece of shit, then. Still was, only difference being that I grew up and he grew old. One day I whacked him back. Paid him back with a few years of interest.' He took a deep breath then slowly a grim smile took hold. 'Then he had his accident. Didn't do too well after that.' He laughed unpleasantly. 'Began to fall to bits. Took to drink, didn't bother any more.'

Sauerwine raised his eyebrows but Beverley was frowning. 'What accident was this?'

Bloom was bathed in completely unconvincing

241

innocence. 'Fell down the stairs. Cracked his head open; did a bit of brain damage.'

'This "accident",' she asked, 'Nothing to do with you.'

'Nothing at all.'

Oh, yeah?

She decided, *There's more. We're not looking at this from the right perspective.*

Bloom had dropped his head again. She cast around for that different angle, found one. 'Tell me about your sister. Fiona, isn't it?'

The nervousness returned. 'What about her?'

'How did your father get on with her?'

No answer.

Interesting. She asked, 'She's three years older than you. Is that right?'

'Yeah.'

She counted five long seconds before, 'Did he beat her?'

The nervousness increased; he was rubbing his hands slightly, as if the sweat were hand lotion. His face remained buried.

'So he did. And badly too, I think.'

She could tell that this was far more important to Bloom than anything that might have been done to him personally. He said nothing, although he shifted in his seat. She said quietly, 'I wonder if he . . . interfered with her.'

Bloom's head came up. 'He fucking better not have done!' he hissed, as if Albert Bloom were not now beyond redemption.

She asked quietly, 'Or you'll what?'

He opened his mouth, closed it, then down went the head again. Into his lap he said, 'I didn't kill him. I hated him for what he did to Mum and Fiona and me, but I didn't kill him.'

Beverley relinquished the role of questioner. Sauerwine said, 'He was a harmless old man, as far as I could see. Not worth beating up.'

Bloom snorted. 'You never saw him fifteen, twenty years ago. Right fucking he-man he was then. Thought it a laugh to beat up on me, beat up on Fi. Bastard.'

'No room for forgiveness?'

'No.' This was said defiantly.

In truth, Sauerwine wasn't sure where to go next at this

point and was just about to return to the previous night when Beverley suddenly asked, 'Where is she now?'

Bloom looked up at her then shrugged. 'Last I heard, Leicester.'

Sauerwine's anger at the break in protocol dissolved. He and Beverley exchanged meaningful looks. He asked Bloom, 'Did she know William Moynihan?'

'Oh, yeah. They were sweet on each other . . .' He suddenly realized where they might be leading him. 'Now hang on a minute! I had nothing to do with Bill's death! I told you . . .'

Sauerwine enquired mildly, 'Are you admitting that you did have something to do with your father's?'

Bloom began to panic. He turned to his solicitor. 'They can't do this! They're just trying to throw everything at me! They're trying to frame me!'

The solicitor, goaded into taking some sort of action, did what all solicitors do and reverted to sarcasm. 'Aren't you getting slightly overambitious in trying to blame my client for every death that's recently occurred around here? I thought you were interested in the unfortunate demise of my client's father.'

'We're interested in how Mr Moynihan met his end as well.'

'I was given to understand there was no proof that it wasn't suicide. You'll have a hard time trying to suggest that my client was responsible for that particular tragedy.'

Which, unfortunately, was true.

Sauerwine, refusing to acknowledge the point openly, turned back to Bloom. 'Your sister left . . . how long ago?'

'Seven, eight years ago.'

It occurred then to Beverley that a lot of things had happened around that time.

'So why? Why did she leave?'

Bloom took a deep breath. 'She got fed up with it.'

'With your father? With the way he was treating her?'

'Reckon so.'

'She was still living at home?'

'Yeah.'

'And he was still abusing her?'

'Yeah.'

'So one day, she just decided that she'd had enough?'

He hesitated before saying, 'It was a bad time.'

'In what way?'

More hesitation. 'The old cunt was hitting her more and more. Really angry with her.'

'Any particular reason?'

He was back with the lap-staring. His reply came very, very slowly.

'She was pregnant,' he announced at last.

Beverley nodded slightly. *Of course.*

'Who was the father?'

He didn't hear; didn't, at any rate, answer.

'Who was the father, Michael?'

Still nothing. Sauerwine glanced at the solicitor who was in turn staring at Bloom.

'We'll find out eventually, Michael. You might as well tell us now.'

Into Beverley's head popped a thought. *Albert Bloom. Albert Bloom was the father.*

But the answer, when it came, was different, if no less significant.

'Groshong. Malcolm.'

They both knew that this was somehow important but instead of clarifying matters it seemed to opaque them. It cemented no links, formed other, tenuous ones. Bloom hadn't finished. 'She was seeing Bill Moynihan at the time. They'd been going out for months; we all thought that they'd be married eventually. Certainly my father did.

'Then she got pregnant, only it wasn't Bill's but Groshong's. That was what the row was about. That was why Bill left, because Groshong sacked him and he lost the tied cottage he was living in. My father went apeshit and chucked her out. She left in the middle of the night. Never told me anything. Don't blame her either.'

'What happened to the baby?'

He shrugged. 'I haven't seen her since.'

'And you haven't tried to contact her?'

'I didn't know where she was. When he came back, Bill said he'd met her in Leicester, but he wouldn't give me the address.'

Beverley wondered if Albert Bloom had been the only one who had been angry with Fiona Bloom at her infidelity. Perhaps Michael was giving them a slightly filtered version of events.

'And last night?'

Bloom had exhausted his patience. 'I told you,' he snapped.

'Tell me again.'

Under his breath he could be heard to say, 'Fucking hell!'

The solicitor put in his twopennyworth. 'We have been over this ground several times before.' He looked at his watch, his attitude stuffed full of meaning.

Sauerwine suggested, 'Just once more, Michael.'

Bloom abruptly leaned forward; it wasn't an aggressive gesture but it was a change from his previous, more passive demeanour. 'I took him round the back of the pub. He's been pestering me more and more recently. Said he wanted to make up with me, said that he realized what a bastard he'd been.' He smiled without humour. 'Said he was sorry.'

'But you didn't want to know?'

'He should have apologized twenty-five years ago.'

'So you roughed him up.'

'Not seriously. He's not worth it any more.'

Sauerwine let it ride. The autopsy report hadn't mentioned serious blunt trauma. He asked, 'What then?'

'I left him out the back of the pub. Went home.'

'And that was it?'

'That was it.'

Sauerwine let it rest there, then slumped back in his seat. Bloom had his story and he was going to stick to it. He looked at Beverley who merely raised rather nicely plucked eyebrows.

The next letter that she read was some months later. She saw the date but not at first the significance.

Dear Nell,

I could not believe what you said in your last letter. Your aunt almost wept to hear your news. Clearly you are ashamed and for that you must be praised, but I must tell you in all truth that you have committed an offence so

'What are you looking at?'

Nell was on her elbows, her head erect as she peered

around Helena to see. Helena, her justification for her actions suddenly dissipating into guilt, closed the book. She twisted around. 'It was at the bottom of the box . . .'

Nell sat up fully, frowning. She saw the book cover, reached for it at once. She opened it, barely glanced at what it contained, then slammed it shut.

The wind slapped against the windows, the vicious lick of a relentless force.

'I . . .' Helena stopped in the middle of guilty explanation.

Nell's face was distorted by a curious concoction; anger, fear, shock. Overlapping yet distinct emotions. 'That's mine!'

It was almost shouted and Helena acquiesced without argument. 'I'm sorry, Nell.'

She received no reply. Nell was clutching the book as if here were Holy Scripture. The look on her face was pure outrage, beyond argument.

After Bloom had been charged with the murder of his father, Albert Bloom, and he had been taken to the cells, and after Tanner had been phoned and informed of Sauerwine's decision, Beverley and Sauerwine sat in his office.

'So, are you the blue-eyed boy? Is Tanner pleased?'

'Pretty much.'

She smiled, then murmured, 'I still think we haven't got it quite right.'

Sauerwine was exasperated but restrained because he was in a good mood. 'It strikes me that his story fits the available facts.' But then he abruptly shook his head.

'No, it doesn't make sense. The witnesses in the pub said that Bloom was in a murderous rage with his father. He expects us to believe that he just told his father off and left him to go home to bed.'

'Witnesses have some very bad habits, Andrew. Sometimes they reinterpret events in the light of what they think they know. A fairly intense argument becomes a homicidal rage once you know that one of them died.'

'If what Bloom said is true, how do we explain how Albert Bloom got up to the heath? It must be eight kilometres. He didn't walk, not at night, not in the depths of winter.'

'Maybe he did. Apparently he often walked to and from the village. Or, alternatively, he got a lift but from someone else.'

'Or maybe Michael took him up there.'

She shook her head. 'That doesn't make much sense to me. If he was in such a rage inside the pub, we have to hypothesize that he bundled the old man into his car, drove him up to the heath, then unleashed some sort of insane attack upon him. It doesn't seem likely. The attack that killed the old man was surely spontaneous.'

But Sauerwine clung stubbornly to his instinct. 'Michael Bloom did it. He hated his father, he had a row with him not two hours before the old man probably died, and he has no alibi.'

Beverley sighed. She was almost convinced.

But only almost.

Jackson knocked on the door. 'He's safely tucked up for the night.'

'Thanks.'

Jackson didn't leave, though. He said from the doorway, 'Poor sod.'

Beverley looked up. 'Who? Michael Bloom?'

'Yep.'

'Are you joking? After what he did to his father?'

Jackson shook his head. '*You* never saw what his father used to do to him . . . and Fiona.'

Sauerwine said, 'I find it difficult to believe that poor old sod did those things. He was pathetic.'

Jackson came into the room. 'Ah, well,' he announced, clearly pleased to be able to add his twopennyworth. 'Albert's fall down the stairs changed all that.'

'The famous "accident".'

Jackson nodded complacently. 'He was in hospital for a long, long time. When he came out, he wasn't the same; wasn't the same at all.'

Beverley asked, 'And this was nothing to do with Michael, I take it.'

'He had an alibi. Six people were able to vouch for him.'

Sauerwine looked at Beverley; they were both thinking the same thing. She pointed out, 'That's not the same thing.'

Jackson grinned. 'No, it's not.'

Rough justice, they call it. But who was she to criticize?

Jackson stood up and wandered out, seemingly proud of himself.

She said to Sauerwine, 'Interesting, but not strictly relevant, I think. It's your case, Andrew. Maybe you're right; maybe the forensic evidence will put things beyond doubt.'

He smiled. 'You'll see.' Then, 'You trained me well, Beverley.'

She accepted the compliment and smiled back. 'I did, didn't I?'

He leaned back in his chair and stretched. 'God, it's been a long day.'

'But you've caught a murderer. Doesn't happen every day.'

'Talking of which, the Superintendent will want to know what's going on.'

He reached for the phone and she stood up. 'When you're finished, how about a drink?' she asked.

Surprised, he hesitated, then grinned widely. 'Why not? Just like old times.'

'We can reminisce. We haven't had a chance to do that yet.'

As she left the room, she saw a familiar light in his eyes and knew that he was still interested.

The phone's sound was an explosive intrusion into their silence. They looked at each other, both aware immediately that whoever it was, for whatever reason it was, this intrusion proclaimed loudly, stridently and irresistibly their guilt. Sauerwine reached across to pick up.

'Hello?'

Beverley lay back in the bed and looked at the ceiling, listening to his side of the conversation.

'Oh, hello, Sally.'

She smiled, the guilt forgotten, the sense of victory too strong to allow any competition from other emotions.

'No, no. Just relaxing.'

Relaxing? Beverley's smile widened. There were very few minutes in the past hour that were capable by any reasonable definition of meriting that particular descriptor.

Then, 'There's been a second killing.'

Understandably this was news.

'Albert Bloom; he lived in Westerham.'

Another pause.

'Multiple stab wounds. Pretty nasty.'

Beverley wondered what Constable Felty had been doing over the past hour; she didn't suppose that it involved much sweat, flesh and erection.

'His son. Hasn't admitted it yet, but he's got motive and opportunity without an alibi.'

Or perhaps it did. Perhaps darling Sally's playing away in Leicester. Perhaps she spent the last hour with a cock in her mouth.

Sauerwine sighed and made the kind of noise a pining lover might make. He was avoiding looking at her and she decided that she didn't wish to be ignored. She moved slightly in bed. Slightly but enough. She came into his peripheral view; or rather, parts of her came into view. More specifically, her left breast came into his view.

Then she moved again, so that nipple of said left breast touched his left forearm; touched and stroked.

She admired his fortitude as he carried on talking. 'That's tenuous at the moment. Obviously he knew Moynihan, but the motive's less clear. It's possible that Moynihan knew something, but it's a bit vague at present.'

She decided to test him further.

He let out an involuntary gasp, which clearly provoked a reaction. 'Sorry. An itch.'

She wondered whether it was her tongue licking his shoulder or her hand grasping his penis that was causing the itch.

'So, what have you found?'

His speech took on a tinge of the staccato, uttered through a breath that was, in distinction to the normal pattern of breathing, going inwards. She moved down his body.

'Really?'

His voice was becoming distinctly higher in pitch. She wondered how it was being received. She had reached his hip.

'Sorry.' He laughed and moved sharply so that her

mouth became detached. Her fingers didn't, though. 'I got stung by some nettles today. It's been bothering me all evening.'

She laughed softly and murmured, 'Liar.'

He moved again. 'It's the radio. I was listening to a play.'

She repositioned herself lower down and was ready to resume teasing when he shifted again. This time, though, he waved his hand. She stopped and looked up at him as he said into the phone, 'That's brilliant, Sally! Absolutely, bloody brilliant!'

Beverley wasn't sure that she liked such fulsome praise for another woman, especially when she was about to apply herself once again to his tumescence but, intrigued, she held fire.

'Tomorrow? Good. And well done!'

Well done? What's Felty done that is so wonderful?

'Yes. And you, darling.'

Reflecting that it was neck and neck between nausea and irritation, Beverley decided that she had had more than sufficient of such schmaltz. She ducked her head over his penis and applied herself to it with some gusto. Sauerwine gasped, breathed out noisily and just managed to switch the phone off before any more questions were asked.

Felty put the phone down in her hotel room, seriously worried.

He was so odd. What was wrong with him?

She lay back on the bed. He had sounded under stress, she decided.

And what was that noise just before the line was cut?

It was almost as if he had been with someone else.

What was that noise?

Her mind raced through possibilities, but all were related, all were equally disturbing. The ceiling above her head was stained brown by nicotine; the whole room stank of cigarettes. Had there been an atomic explosion centred on the room, it would have left a space in the universe that still smelled of cigarette smoke.

She was with him!

There was no other answer. Nothing fitted so perfectly save for that particular odious idea.

Suddenly she knew. The noise had been a gasp.
'Bitch!'

Beverley could have kept on, but Sauerwine was wilting. She climbed off and flopped down beside him. The room quietened, only their breathing, made suddenly loud, breaking the tranquillity.

With her eyes closed she asked, 'Well?'

He didn't understand. 'Fantastic. Absolutely fantastic.'

Which made her laugh, so that he looked at her. 'What about the good Constable? What did she have to say?'

He didn't want to be reminded of a world outwith the bedroom, outwith enjoyment. She understood, she had seen it often before; men led by their pricks, brains in their balls. She felt no guilt that she used such weakness so shamelessly; felt only depression that they never seemed to learn. She said softly, 'What's the problem? Not feeling guilty already, are you? Normally it doesn't hit until the next morning.'

He looked at her. 'It isn't a joke, you know.'

'I'm not laughing.'

He seemed to be having a problem with her attitude. 'Bloody hell, is that all it is to you? A quick shag and nothing more?'

Oh dear. You've got it bad, haven't you, Andrew? She sat up, then slid her legs out from under the cover. Looking back over her shoulder she said, 'Yep. Like it was for you until your squeeze called and you were reminded what a piece of shit you are. That's not my fault, Andrew. You're supposedly an adult; you know – "adult", as in "taking responsibility for your actions".'

She got to her feet, then walked across the room to the en suite shower room. Ten minutes later, showered and refreshed, she came back into the bedroom where he was sitting on the end of the bed, now dressed in a towelling robe. She picked up her clothes and began to dress, ignoring him.

He said slowly, 'Sorry.'

Still she ignored him.

'If you're still interested, Sally said that she found out where Moynihan was staying in Leicester over the past few weeks. She also discovered where he got the watch.'

251

'Where?'

'Fiona Bloom.' He smiled at Beverley's surprise but she ignored him.

There were considerably greater matters to consider. Most importantly, what was the significance of this finding? It can't have been coincidence but that didn't tell her anything. It only gave her cause for alarm. What did Moynihan have to do with the deaths of Helena's parents?

She got up to leave, now depressed. 'I'll leave you to pine.'

He didn't reply and she walked out of the room and out of his house without further communication.

She was used to endings such as this, but that didn't make it any less painful.

'I can't stop thinking about it.'

'No.' Eisenmenger's reply was as much a sigh into the darkness as a vocalized syllable.

As preoccupied as Helena was she heard his despair. 'I'm sorry.'

He reached across to switch on the bedside light, then turned to face her. 'I understand, Helena. It must have been very strange to see those letters and those photographs so unexpectedly, after all those years.'

Her eyes were large. 'It was unsettling. To see Mummy and Daddy again. To see Jeremy again.' She might have been going to cry but no tears came. 'I knew that my parents were aware of the pregnancy, of course – we all were – but I hadn't realized that Nell was writing to my father and confiding in him like that.'

The wind was dying down although it still sounded harsh and demanding.

'He *was* her godfather. Presumably she sought spiritual guidance from him. A logical place to go.'

He heard irritation as she said, 'Of course you're right, John. You always are.'

He decided that silence was the wisest course and merely smiled apologetically. After a moment she sighed and said, 'Sorry.' She said nothing more and Eisenmenger watched her, seeing that she was troubled. He waited.

'It's the last letter that's really peculiar. I don't understand what Daddy was talking about.'

'Tell me again what it said.'

She tried to recall the exact words, then, 'It was a long letter and I only got the chance to read the first paragraph.'

He turned them over in his mind as she continued, 'What could possibly have been worse than the pregnancy?'

It was after three o'clock. Helena had slept fitfully and Eisenmenger, disturbed by this, had fared little better. Perhaps it was because of the lateness of the hour that time seemed to be passing viscously, almost ceasing as they lay and listened to the wind that buffeted the windows. It might have been days later that he asked, 'What was the date on that final letter?'

'October. October 7th.'

More silence, more slowly flowing minutes.

She said suddenly, 'That was three days before.'

He didn't follow. 'Before what?'

'Before they were murdered.' Her voice broke on the last syllable and he saw how deeply, deeply affected she had been by seeing the photographs, reading the letters. He reached over and took her in his arms, hugging as she began to weep anew for the family she had lost so many years ago.

Part Six

At Hugo's request Theresa and Dominique had cooked a traditional English breakfast with grilled bacon, sausages and tomatoes, fried eggs, mushrooms and (for Tom although Hugo also partook) baked beans. It had proved a huge success, even with Eleanor, and had worked to lift the gloom that had pervaded the house on the day before.

Now Eisenmenger was waiting for Helena, their plan to take a walk to try to work off the calories they had just ingested. He only picked up the local newspaper because as usual Helena was taking an inordinate time and he was bored. Normally, he found local newspapers as interesting as credit-card small print, but he had left his book upstairs. Even then, it might have been *Golfing World* or *Shooting Times* that he chose except that the headline had caught his eye.

Son charged with the murder of Albert Bloom.

He read the journalese beneath this banner, a deepening frown worrying his face.

He put the paper down.

He was standing in the kitchen, where Dominique was doing some ironing. He watched her for a long time but saw little of what she did. The radio was on, a phone-in filling the space that it had created, but Eisenmenger heard only noise.

He didn't know how much time passed before she asked, 'Some coffee?'

She had to ask again before he said, 'Eh?'

'Some coffee?' She offered him a smile. She was very pretty.

Distractedly he said, 'Yes. Why not? Yes, please.'

He returned to the paper, or rather to the thoughts that he tried to marshal.

She put the mug of coffee down on the table in front of him and he barely noticed. 'Monsieur?'

He came to, looked at the coffee, looked then at her. The smile came a moment later, as did, 'Thanks.'

He returned to the newspaper and Dominique, slightly put out, went back to her ironing.

Felty returned to the station determined in her course of action. She and Sauerwine were finished. It was quite clear to her now that he had deliberately despatched her to Leicester to get her out of the way; that she had succeeded was an unexpected by-product, one that had not really been the main purpose of her trip.

His infatuation with Wharton was obvious; as obvious as his infidelity.

Well, she knew that she didn't have any claims on him – it wasn't as if they were engaged or anything – but equally she knew that she wasn't interested in someone who was so easily led by the prick. So it was over.

Except that she wasn't sure if she was willing just to let it go at that. She had been made a fool of; perhaps she had a score to settle. Wharton wasn't the only one who could play dirty.

Their walk took them past the courtyard of the tearoom, the wooden benches covered, the umbrellas stored under cover. A few dead leaves rustled and swirled in the corners as the breeze whispered around them. The playground this morning was empty.

'Hugo seems a pleasant chap.' Eisenmenger only said this because he wondered if Helena would share such a view.

Helena was dressed in a thick, dark green skiing jacket, dark blue jeans and black wellington boots. The cold was making her cheeks glow, her breath plume into grey vapour. She didn't respond immediately, not until they had passed the closed, dark gift shop and the playground, and were on the winding path that led through tall fir trees down to the back entrance to the grounds.

255

'Yes,' she said, but it was with a tinge of uncertainty.
'But . . .?'

She shrugged. 'I don't know. Maybe I remember someone different.'

'Age does that.'

The conversation lapsed for a while. Then she said, 'When I first got to know him, I thought he was wonderful. He was always good-looking, obviously bright, and quite breathtakingly charming. Good to be around; a team player.'

He waited for the qualification that he could hear was coming from her words.

'And it was like that, I think, for most of my childhood. I guess it was only towards the end that things seemed to change.'

'What happened?'

She considered. 'We grew up, I suppose.'

Well, he thought, maybe that's all it was; it wouldn't have been the first time that childhood friendships didn't make it through puberty. Helena, though, was dissatisfied with such a simple explanation.

'But it was more than that,' she decided. 'We all grew up, but Hugo grew up more; not more quickly, just more.'

But she didn't like that either. 'Or maybe . . . he didn't grow up as much,' she finished.

Which was an explanation lacking only explicability. Helena hadn't finished. 'The relationships altered, of course. Hugo and Nell grew closer and perhaps away from Jeremy and me . . .' Then, 'There was a fight!' She spoke as if experiencing an epiphany. 'I'd forgotten. Hugo and Jeremy had a fight!'

'A bad one?'

She didn't answer for a while, was lost in this sudden remembrance. 'It was over Nell, I think. Jeremy was teasing her . . . we were fishing in the lake and Nell had caught something – a brown trout, I think. She panicked. I don't really know why, but I suppose that it was bigger than anything she'd caught before. Fishing was just a game for her – it was for me as well – and we were only doing it, I think, because the boys wanted to do it. A hot summer's day, the end of the holidays coming; I seem to remember an air of finality about us, as if it were not just the summer that was fading.'

'Childhood as well, perhaps?'

She nodded. 'Something like that.' She stopped and looked around. They were nearly down at the gate on to the road. She pointed to the left. 'That way.' She marched off between two outhouses along an overgrown path. She explained, 'I used to love walking along this way.'

It was muddy and wet. The storm the night before had wreaked havoc; already they had passed several trees that had been pushed over by the wind, slaughtered by the gale.

Eventually Helena asked, 'Where were we?'

'We were discussing how puberty creates the adult, but in order to do so it must first destroy the child.'

'Very profound.'

'I thought so.'

She laughed briefly. 'We didn't see it like that, of course. There was just a feeling that things weren't quite so good any more. The things that we did weren't as interesting.'

'And so you were fishing . . .?'

'Yes. The argument was stupid, of course, but I think we were bored and it was late and nobody had caught much. Then Nell hooked this fish, only she wasn't able to land it. It got away and Jeremy said something sarcastic.' She thought a while. 'It might have ended there but Jeremy kept on. Eventually Nell became upset.' Once more she paused. 'Jeremy could get like that, if I'm honest.'

It was the most revealing thing that Eisenmenger had ever heard her say about Jeremy Eaton-Lambert; for a moment he became for both of them a solid human being and not a spectre. He said, 'I take it Hugo didn't like it.'

'No. In fact, he suddenly exploded. He didn't even speak, just charged at Jeremy, knocked him over and within ten seconds they were all over each other.'

He was interested but his next question was forestalled by a beech tree that had fallen across their path, forcing them into a detour through waist-high nettles and invisible, treacherous brambles. Only when they had arrived back on the road did he ask, 'How bad was the fight?'

'At the time it certainly seemed bad. It went on, too. I remember Nell and I tried to pull them apart, but we couldn't.'

'Did they draw blood?'

She was struck by the prurience of the question. 'I don't recall.'

'How long did it last?'

'I don't know. Maybe five, ten minutes.'

'And then what?'

She frowned. 'Jeremy stormed off. The three of us packed up and followed him; nobody talked much.'

'And after that? What was the atmosphere like between you?'

She didn't understand why he was asking these questions and this disturbed her, causing her to hesitate. 'Pretty strained.'

He nodded and said nothing. They had been climbing continuously for a long time. Helena, noticeably breathless now asked, 'Why are you so interested?'

'You know me, Helena. I can't resist being nosy.'

She *did* know him, so she knew that it wasn't as simple as he made out. 'Pull the other one, John. What's going through your head?'

He laughed. 'The usual crap.'

She didn't believe him. Her response was half in laughter, half in anger. 'Secrets again? Why's it always secrets? Won't we ever be a team?'

He held up his hands. 'I thought we *were* a team.'

Maybe it was the innocence in his voice, maybe it was her obvious tiredness. 'You have got to be joking! You've got no more idea of teamwork than a shark.'

He had been compared to a fair range of animals in his life, but this was a new one.

I'm not a shark. This thought rang through his head with loud indignation. Somewhat hotly he pointed out, 'Just because I don't talk much, doesn't mean you're not included. Working in a team isn't just about prattling on all the time . . .'

He had been about to say more but the look on her face sent urgent signals to his vocal cords to cease operations forthwith. The vapour that streamed from her nose might have been smoke, a sign of something smouldering. After a pause in which not even the crows had the courage to cry into the cold, she said tersely, 'I don't prattle!'

She turned and walked rapidly away. They were near the crest of a shallow hill and he called out to her, 'Helena! I didn't mean you . . . Not specifically.'

258

She didn't react, just kept on walking and he was forced to hurry after her.

'Helena!'

He caught up with her at the top of the rise where she had paused. It was only when he caught up with her that he saw why. The lake was visible in the distance but that was irrelevant. A beech had been uprooted. Not a particularly old one, and because of this it was surprising that it had become a victim of the storm. It certainly wasn't large enough to have blocked their way.

'Helena! I'm sorry.'

She wasn't listening, was staring into the shallow crater that had been formed by the fall of the tree.

'I didn't mean you, Helena, I was just . . .'

He realized that she was ignoring him.

He, too, looked down at bottom of the hole.

It wasn't immediately obvious, but once his eye had caught the shape half hidden by roots, his brain did the rest.

A small human skull.

'I'm starting to think that this place must be some sort of gateway to hell.'

Tanner's muttered comment was to Syme as they stood inside the marquee – the same marquee so recently used for the death of Albert Bloom – and watched Dr Addison slowly uncover the small bones. Opposite him Beverley caught the remark and her eyes flicked up to his face then back down to the tiny skeleton.

It's only bones.

It was only bones but her imagination did the rest. This had been a baby once. Babies shouldn't die; babies were life. Nothing else signified life as defiantly as a baby.

Am I getting broody?

She felt tired and depressed, almost like weeping. Why was that? It wasn't the first child's body she had seen. This one might not even have been murdered.

Who was she kidding? You don't bury a body under a tree for any reason other than to hide it. But that begged the question – what reason is there to hide it?

Dr Addison straightened up with a groan. 'Three bodies

259

in a week,' she complained. 'I'm not getting any of my other work done.'

Sauerwine, standing next to Beverley, couldn't resist demonstrating cold indifference. 'Shame.'

She ignored this. Having directed SOCO to take more photographs, she said, 'I can tell you now, this baby wasn't very old. Not very old at all.'

Tanner asked, 'What does that mean?'

'No more than a few months, I'd say. The skull bones weren't fused at all.'

Nobody else was particularly interested in her chain of reasoning.

Beverley was looking at the ground around the baby. 'Someone's been digging here,' she decided.

Tanner and Syme came over and crouched down beside her. 'Maybe,' said the Superintendent.

'The digging loosened the roots. That's why it came down.'

She looked at Sauerwine. 'Moynihan had a spade in his car.'

Sauerwine was nodding slowly, trying to fit this into the picture – into any picture at all. To SOCO Syme said, 'Make sure you get pictures of this.'

He asked Addison, 'Any indication of the cause of death yet?'

She was shocked. 'Oh, no. You'll have to wait until I get this lot to the mortuary.'

No one had expected any more.

Beverley turned and walked out of the tent. Sauerwine watched her go, Syme and Tanner ignored her.

Eisenmenger and Helena were talking to Felty. From Beverley's point of view it was difficult to tell if they saw the look that Felty gave her, the one that suggested that she'd quite like her to fall feet first into a meat grinder.

She smiled at Felty. 'Thank you, Constable. I'll take over now.'

If Beverley was hoping to present a front of happiness and unity, the attempt failed. Felty didn't snarl or attack her with claws out, but her attitude as she put away her PDA, turned smartly round and stalked off was neon-lit and flashing red. Eisenmenger looked at the retreating Constable then turned to Beverley. 'Friend of yours?'

Beverley's hearing had never been good. She said to him, 'You're getting good at finding bodies.'

'I'm specially trained.'

'Are you holding back any that we should know about?'

'There are three at the bottom of the lake, including Shergar.'

Beverley nearly smiled. 'And Lord Lucan?'

Helena cut in angrily. 'Sorry to interrupt the double-man comedy act, but there's a dead baby in there.'

Beverley turned upon her a gaze that practically ignited the air between them. 'I'm fully aware of that, Helena. Believe me, I'm *fully* aware of it.' She cut her by turning back to Eisenmenger. 'You were just on a walk?'

'That's right.'

'Why this way?'

'Why not?'

'Nobody suggested that you come this way?'

Before he could answer Helena said, 'I did, actually. We used to walk this way when I was a child.'

'We?'

'My brother and I. Jeremy Eaton-Lambert.'

Beverley didn't even drop her eyes from Helena's face. 'A long time ago, then.'

'His lifetime ago.'

'Have you walked this route more recently? Before today, I mean.'

'No.'

'A coincidence, then.'

'What is?'

'That you should walk this way on this particular morning.'

'Of course it is! What are you suggesting? That we knew it was there? That we brought it with us and then buried it here?'

Beverley treated Helena's sarcasm with contempt that was well towards the regal end of the scale. To Eisenmenger she said, 'It's clearly been in the ground a long time. The storm brought down the tree and thereby brought the remains to the surface. That much is obvious.'

Helena snorted. 'Well done.'

Beverley's eyes flicked across her as they might a

vomit-covered drunk. 'It came down because someone had been digging for something at its base.'

Eisenmenger asked sharply, 'Really?'

Even Helena found some interest. 'Who?'

Beverley looked around. 'How far are we from the place where Moynihan died?'

It was Helena who supplied the information. 'Two, three kilometres.'

Beverley nodded but was thinking too deeply to speak.

Eisenmenger asked tentatively, 'Do you mind if I attend the post-mortem?'

She raised an eyebrow. 'Professional interest?'

'Something like that.'

'I doubt that there'll be a problem . . .' She wasn't about to admit that she would have to check with Sauerwine.

'Also, I'm slightly concerned about the last death. Albert Bloom.'

'What about it?'

He hesitated. 'I'm not entirely sure that Michael Bloom did it.'

Sauerwine emerged from the marquee with Syme and Tanner. Tanner strode off to a car and was driven off, presumably happy to have done some work in the field; Beverley gave Eisenmenger a long, appraising look before she called Syme and Sauerwine over. 'Dr Eisenmenger has an interesting theory.'

'I'm glad someone's got one,' remarked Syme. 'I'm completely out of them. It would take Sherlock Holmes a bloody sight more than three pipes to sort this one out, that's for sure.'

'Perhaps you're linking the wrong deaths for the wrong reasons.' Eisenmenger said this in the elliptical manner that Helena knew so well.

What's he seen?

Sauerwine looked pained, Syme merely lost. 'Meaning?'

'I'm not certain that Michael Bloom killed his father. If that were the case it would save you having to link that death to Moynihan's. Or this one for that matter.'

Sauerwine was caught between profanity and hysteria. 'It would also mean that we'd be back to square one. Three deaths and no explanations.'

Eisenmenger pursed his lips. 'Maybe.'

Beverley found some secret amusement in watching

Syme and Sauerwine coping with Eisenmenger at his most irritatingly professorial. 'Dr Eisenmenger would like to attend the baby's post-mortem.'

There was a lot of hesitation, especially from Syme. He eyed Eisenmenger, then Sauerwine. 'What do you think?'

'I think that Dr Eisenmenger might have interesting theories, but that doesn't mean they're not crackpot ones.'

Syme nodded but then to Sauerwine's dismay said, 'You're probably right, but I'd quite like to hear what he has to say.' He gestured with his head towards the marquee. 'I'm not sure she's up to the job.'

He strode off with Sauerwine following, looking unhappy. Eisenmenger said to Helena, 'What about you?'

'I'll forgo the pleasures of yet another post-mortem examination. I'd better get back to the castle and tell everyone what's going on.'

Beverley, perhaps to be rid of two irritations at once said, 'Felty can go with you. She's going to have take yet more statements, I'm afraid.'

Helena walked back down with Felty, retracing the path she and Eisenmenger had followed a few hours before. She felt tired, almost depressed, and Felty was fighting her own demons, wondering if she were being sidelined again; the result was near unsullied silence between them. Only as they reached the tarmac of the path that led to the castle did Felty say, 'Tell me about the murder of your parents.'

It wasn't the kind of question that she was asked every day and Helena found herself a fair distance from words for a while. 'My parents?'

Felty nodded.

'Why?'

'I read the file.'

'So what's it got to do with . . . all this?'

Felty didn't hesitate but Helena noticed that the rhythm of her reply was slightly wrong. 'Nothing directly. But obviously it's a bit of a coincidence that you and Inspector Sauerwine should meet again at the scene of another murder.'

'And don't forget Inspector Wharton. She's here too.'

'Oh, yes. Inspector Wharton as well.' Helena was not so depressed that she didn't notice the inflection. Felty continued without a pause, 'Do you think it's possible that they're connected?'

Helena didn't know what to say. The concept was too novel for immediate analysis or comment, but it certainly intrigued her. Felty continued, 'I only ask because of all the coincidences.'

'My parents were killed by someone who broke in and burgled the place. It was a spontaneous attack. What could that have to do with these deaths, eight years later?'

They had reached the gravel of the forecourt, their feet crunching into it, an intermittent but intrusive background.

'I'm just working through possibilities, Miss Flemming.'

Once again there was something wrong with the tone but it defied analysis.

'Sounds like a pretty remote one to me.'

They continued trudging. Felty didn't say anything and their lack of speech grew until the gravel's screeching was almost too loud to bear. To Helena's relief they reached the paved area of the portico in front of the entrance door. Into this peace Helena asked tentatively, 'Do you know something I don't?'

Felty had rung the bell. She looked sideways at Helena. The pause was long, her scrutiny intense. 'I don't know, do I?'

'What does that mean?'

But Dominique opened the door at that moment and Felty had an excuse not to reply.

All mortuaries are essentially the same. They have the same constituents – viewing chapel, body store, dissection room, changing rooms and office – and these are cluttered by the same details – such as knives, paper, pens, gloves, aprons, saws, dissection tables, scales, bowls. There is always a predominance of porcelain and steel, and there is no gradation from light to dark, nor softness in the air; air that is always a little colder than one might expect. They are clean places, but it is an unwelcoming cleanliness, a purity that is puritanical.

Eisenmenger sat where Beverley had sat only the day

before and exhibited little greater interest in the proceedings than she had done. He occasionally looked up as Dr Addison worked but it was without real attention. Many people would have kept their eyes averted because the investigation of the body of a baby is an awful, disgusting thing; those more experienced – more inured – might have found the whole process tedious because in truth the examination of long-buried bones *is* tedious, once the emotional responses have been conquered.

Eisenmenger had a different cause for uninterest.

He was reading, devouring, Dr Addison's report on the death of Albert Bloom. He had read it through completely three times and was now beginning again. He might have been learning it for recital, perhaps for an amateur pantomime production.

Sauerwine watched with considerably greater intensity than Eisenmenger, his eyes rarely leaving the pathetic bone fragments. Beverley watched Eisenmenger as much as she watched the autopsy; on her face was a look of curiosity. Stephan busied himself around Dr Addison but was, in truth, as bored as the rest of them.

Eventually Dr Addison put down the instruments she had been using, turned to Sauerwine (ignoring Eisenmenger) and said, 'I've gone as far as I can go for now.'

She began to strip off her gloves. Eisenmenger watched her, aware that he was *persona non grata*. Sauerwine asked, 'What can you give us?'

Dr Addison, centre-stage, began her performance. Eisenmenger listened and watched, feeling like a theatre critic and about as loved.

'The baby was no more than three months old, possibly as young as four weeks.'

'Male or female?'

She was just slightly put out at this unexpected prompt; not a major disruption in the front stalls, more a mobile phone going off. 'At such a young age there is very little difference in the bone structure.' Eisenmenger, like the rest of the audience, heard the tremor in her voice but he, unlike them, knew that she was giving them facts. Sauerwine clearly thought he was being bullshitted. His refusal to say anything was eloquent.

When she continued, she was even more nervous.

'We're going to have to seek an expert forensic anthropological opinion to determine the precise length of time the body's been in the ground.'

This was not the kind of material her listeners demanded.

'No idea at all? Is it weeks or months or years?'

'Oh, it's years. At least twelve months.'

'How about eight years? Is that out of the question?'

Beverley thought at once, *Fiona Bloom's baby.*

'No.' Certainty was not the immediate reaction that popped into anyone's head when they heard that particular sound. 'But I'm not saying that it definitely is.'

'Is there *anything* you can tell us?' Sauerwine might have tried to keep the irritation out of his voice but he didn't have much luck. He sounded like a tired director dismissing someone from the audition and now Dr Addison sounded like an actor who had lost the plot, or the lines, or both.

'Yes,' she proclaimed in a shrill denial of his scepticism. 'Yes, there is. This baby was battered.'

Now that produced a gratifying jerk from cynicism. Even Eisenmenger raised his eyebrows.

Sauerwine asked, 'You're sure?' Not perhaps the most tactful thing he could have said.

'Oh, yes.' She had a new costume on – smugness – and it suited her. 'Four definite rib fractures, a hairline fracture of the left clavicle . . .'

Sauerwine didn't particularly want the shopping list. 'Is that the cause of death?'

'Almost certainly.'

Beverley asked, 'What about identity?'

'Your only hope is going to be DNA. No teeth, obviously.'

'Will there be any DNA?'

'Oh, yes.'

Sauerwine glanced at Eisenmenger as if for confirmation but Eisenmenger kept his features completely immobile. Unfortunately Dr Addison saw the look, deduced things and fed her inferiority complex a big dose of vitamins.

'Am I given to understand that Dr Eisenmenger is here to offer a second opinion?'

This caught Sauerwine by surprise, unused as he was to

the sensitivities of the medical professional. 'No, not at all.' But he reached the end of available words and it was left to Eisenmenger to say soothingly, 'I asked to see the autopsy, Dr Addison. Professional interest, nothing more.' He adopted a small, almost deferential smile. 'In fact I was just thinking what a thorough job you've done.'

Dr Addison's hesitation was a product of her suspicion and uncertainty. She looked for the smallest hint of derision but saw none, was forced to say only, 'Oh.' This was rapidly followed by a terse, 'Thank you.'

He inclined his head and smiled, then dropped the bad news. 'I would quite like to see Albert Bloom's body, though.'

'Why?' This, outraged.

'Because I've got an idea that you might not have considered.'

Dr Addison was rendered temporarily voiceless and, with little more than squeaks replacing thousands of years of speech evolution, she turned to Sauerwine, who asked warily of Eisenmenger, 'What idea?'

'Suicide.'

'Oh, my God!' Theresa looked faint, Tristan slowly closed his eyes as if to shut out the world. Hugo sat with his head in his hands, fingers through his hair; very slowly he was shaking his head from side to side. Helena went to Theresa and put her hand on her arm, guiding her to a chair. They were in the conservatory surrounded by frosted windows and cool echoes amongst cane furniture. She looked ready to cry.

Felty said gently, 'Obviously the baby had been there some time and we won't know much more until the autopsy and various forensic investigations have been completed.'

'Of course, of course.' The look on Tristan's face was distracted; she might have been reciting last night's shipping forecast to a deaf man.

Theresa was shaking her head, tears filling her eyes.

Felty asked with some awkwardness, 'I don't suppose you have any idea how the body might have got there?'

Tristan heard at last. He looked up and said simply, 'No. No idea at all.'

Felty nodded and would have left it at that but Tristan wasn't finished. 'Over the years thousands of people have worked on the estate. Literally thousands. Anyway, we don't – can't – keep the boundaries secure. Anyone determined enough could get on to my land and . . . bury something.'

Felty noted this down. She saw no point in prolonging the interview; it had been little more than a formality anyway, as much to notify them of the discovery as to make meaningful enquiries. She stood up; Tristan, normally the exemplar of a gentleman, stayed attached to the chair, looking across at his wife.

'I won't trouble you any more,' she said gently.

She heard Hugo mutter a single word. 'Shit.'

Then Tristan surfaced. 'Oh, yes. Yes. Thank you.'

He stood up and smiled but there was no enthusiasm in it. As he was walking out with her Theresa said in a lost voice, 'So much death. How horrible it all is.'

They both stopped and looked back at her. Helena said, 'It's all right, Theresa.'

She put her arms around her, squeezing her shoulders gently and was rewarded with a smile. Tristan wore a troubled look but he turned back to Felty. 'I'll show you out, Constable.'

Felty was walking across the forecourt when she saw Groshong coming out of his office. He was talking on the mobile phone, too distant to see his face but his attitude was one of concern and concentration. This study was so deep that she was within five metres of him before he saw her. He snapped the phone shut, his face sour, almost thunderous.

'Mr Groshong, I take it you've heard the news?'

He barely answered, merely nodding curtly. He looked worse than Theresa Hickman.

'We're obviously interested in the identity of the body. I don't suppose you have any idea . . .?'

As he looked at her she found herself uncertain whether he wanted to cry or shout or strike her. 'Gypsies,' he muttered at last out of grey lips.

'Pardon?'

'Gypsies.' This time he practically shouted. 'Those bastards are capable of anything.'

'Do you know for certain that it was gypsies?'

He shrugged. 'Who knows what they get up to? We're always having trouble with them trespassing.'

'So you've never heard any stories about a baby going missing in the neighbourhood?'

'No.' This was so definite it was almost asking to be disbelieved, but she left it at that.

As she walked away she wondered who had been on the other end of the phone.

'No!'

Beverley wasn't surprised at Sauerwine's attitude. Eisenmenger was offering to disprove his pet theory that Michael Bloom was the murderer; she could understand this – there was nothing more infuriating than the wilful destruction of a beautiful hypothesis.

Keep it calm.

'Look, Andrew, it's not the end of the world if Albert Bloom committed suicide. You haven't gone on national TV and announced it all to the world. You've arrested his son and with good reason. If Eisenmenger proves that Addison got it wrong, it won't hurt you.'

They were in the mortuary office, on opposite sides of the room. Syme was in the middle, having just arrived and heard Eisenmenger's suggestion. Thus far he had said nothing.

'What about Moynihan? What about the baby?'

'What about them? There's no proof that Moynihan was anything other than a suicide. The baby died years ago; it was most probably a coincidental find, whether or not it was murder.'

Sauerwine was tempted, she could see. Despite hints that might be no more than phantoms there was still nothing to show positively that Moynihan's incineration had been anything more than a tortured suicide. Obstinately, though, he pointed out, 'There were signs of digging at the base of the tree, and Moynihan had a spade.'

'Which you said he would probably just have had to dig the car out of mud, or something.'

269

Syme pointed out. 'There was no note, no indication that he was depressed or suicidal.'

Which Beverley could counter with ease. 'Only twelve per cent of suicides leave a note; even if we'd found one we'd have questioned its authenticity.'

'But was he depressed? People don't set fire to themselves without a good reason.'

'Who knows? Mrs Gleason isn't likely to have spotted the signs of clinical depression, nor Michael Bloom. Who else is there?'

Syme said thoughtfully, 'Fiona Bloom.'

Beverley saw some progress and said immediately, 'She knew him the best in the last few months.' She watched Sauerwine's face, searching for signs of recapitulation. Then, 'We need to speak to her, Andrew. She might throw some light on why he might have committed suicide. Anyway, there's the question of her baby.'

Syme said, 'Yes. We definitely need to find out a little more about that.'

She sensed that she was winning. 'There's another possibility – maybe the baby wasn't Groshong's at all. Maybe she just told Moynihan that.'

Sauerwine asked, 'Then whose was it?'

'Moynihan's.' His disbelief was unmistakable. She explained, 'They have a row; she spites him by telling him that the baby isn't his. He has a row with Groshong, gets turfed off the estate for his pains. Everything goes quiet until Moynihan bumps into Fiona Bloom in Leicester. Fiona by this time has descended into prostitution. Moynihan gets to know her again, after a while the truth comes out.'

She ran out of logic but she had his attention. Syme said slowly, 'Go on.'

She was speculating now. 'Something happened to the baby just after birth. It was battered so it was either Fiona Bloom or perhaps a partner. They disposed of the body on the estate – end of story, she thought.

'It would be natural for Moynihan to ask about the baby – after all, it's not around and it was the reason they split up. Presumably she lied to him but somewhere along the line, perhaps he found out the truth – about his paternity and about the death of the child.'

She could see that Syme liked this, even if Sauerwine

270

looked thunderous. 'He comes back here to find the baby, perhaps.'

'Or to put right what was done to it.'

This interested Syme even more. 'Meaning?'

'Maybe he came back to avenge the death of his child.'

'And got cremated for his pains?'

'Hence the spade. Fiona told him where to look.'

She watched him work through these possibilities, happy to see it. She didn't care if it was suicide, or murder, or even act of God. She had other things in mind. Then Sauerwine threw in a spoiler. 'It doesn't work.'

'Why not?'

'Because Fiona Bloom left before the birth. Why is it buried on the estate if it was born in Leicester?'

Beverley was only momentarily at a loss. 'We don't know for a fact that she didn't have the baby here. We don't know *where* it was born.'

Syme looked undecided. She said, 'I suggest we talk to Fiona Bloom. If the baby is hers, then she might well be more amenable to telling us exactly what happened.'

He nodded. 'And if you're right, Albert Bloom's death is just coincidental.'

'Exactly.'

He was silent for a moment. 'Is this chap Eisenmenger any good?'

For perhaps the first time since she had arrived, Beverley's reply was totally sincere. 'Oh, yes, sir. He's good. He's very, very good.'

That appeared to decide him. 'Okay, then. I'll contact the Coroner and clear it with him for Eisenmenger to have another look at Bloom's body. You attend the examination. Andrew, I want you to make sure that the lab compares Moynihan's DNA with the baby's. Then somebody's got to go to Leicester to bring back Fiona Bloom for a little chat. That can be done tomorrow.'

'What about Groshong? We don't know for certain that he isn't involved.'

'Let's wait and see if we get a match with Moynihan's DNA. If we don't I think we can pull him in then.'

Syme left them then, and so he didn't see the satisfied smile on her face. She felt a warm glow of pleasure at how things seemed to be going. Lots of trails and lots of

271

potential suspects, and not a mention of a certain watch and photograph.

Sauerwine looked as if he would quite have liked to see another murder in Westerham, but she had the feeling that he was no longer of use to her.

'Sally?'

She was sitting at her desk. The room was otherwise empty. She didn't reply.

'What's wrong?'

'Nothing.' She spoke in such a low tone that he didn't catch it.

'Sorry?'

She turned to him. 'I said, nothing.' Her head returned immediately to its former position, appearing almost to be delicately sprung around a finely engineered pivot.

Had she been a suspect he would have pursued this lie. Instead he changed the subject. 'They're wrong, Sally. I can feel it.'

She made a noise, nothing more.

'Bloom killed his father. The baby was Fiona Bloom's. The question is, who killed Moynihan?'

This time she couldn't even manage a noise.

'Moynihan meets Fiona Bloom in Leicester. He knew that she had been pregnant when she left the village, so naturally he wonders where the child is. At first she refuses to tell him, but eventually he breaks her down. She confesses . . .' He stopped abruptly. 'But confesses what?'

He wrestled with this question silently

Suddenly, Sally asked in a low, controlled tone, 'Have you slept with her?'

He was caught by shock. His head jerked up but then inexplicably he found that he could not look directly at her. 'Who?' His case wasn't helped by querulousness.

Felty might not have been the most experienced police officer to doff a pair of handcuffs but she had sat in on enough interrogations to spot a liar. 'So you did.'

'No!' But this acknowledgement that he knew the subject of her accusation was as good as admission. It didn't take long before he dropped his head. 'Yes.'

She seemed momentarily disconcerted by this admission.

But only momentarily.

'You bastard!' she hissed, her eyes underlined by creases of hate.

'Look, it wasn't like that . . .'

'Like what?'

The question was a good one and it made his cliché painfully obvious. He tried again, not very successfully. 'There was nothing . . .'

'Just forget it!'

She turned away and stared at her computer screen, a self-contained packet, all contacts withdrawn.

There was a goodly stretch of silence before he said, 'I know I shouldn't have done it, Sally. I've been feeling sick, guilty, rotten ever since. I . . . I . . .' He ran out of guilt along that path, tried again. 'I don't love her, Sally. She's . . . quite attractive, but I don't love her.'

This produced no visible reaction. 'I love you, Sally.'

Nothing.

'I can't apologize any more, Sally. I made a mistake . . .'

Still there was no response, a reaction far worse than anger or violence. 'Please, Sally . . .'

More of the same; more of nothing.

'Please, Sally. Talk to me. Say something, for God's sake.'

Nothing.

'Sally.' He walked towards her, reached out to her.

Huge mistake.

'Get off!' She shook him off; it was almost a shudder, as if she had touched some spittle on a wall.

'I'm sorry! I shouldn't have done it, I know that. I was tired . . . you know I had a thing for her once . . .'

At last she looked at him. 'Well, go there now, then. See in the New Year with her. You won't be doing it with me.'

She got up, picked up her bag and stalked out, slamming the door behind her.

'Fuck.'

The next morning Eisenmenger was back at the mortuary in the company of Beverley, Stephan and Dr Addison. Stephan was welcoming, almost amused by the prospect of a battle of forensic pathologists; Dr Addison wore her hostility not just on her sleeve but in a large banner across a frowning brow above blazing eyes. Eisenmenger had seen this before; it was the defence of an uncertain intellect. He couldn't blame her. She was inexperienced and, no matter what the medical education authorities held, there was no substitute for having seen a lot, done a lot, made a lot of mistakes. The secret of becoming good was to accept the errors and use them well.

Beverley, though.

He saw her eyes flick past him as he first entered the mortuary office, saw also the thought in her head – *No Helena*. She smiled at him and he detected relief. 'Here we are again,' she said.

'Indeed.'

'Only this time, we're not on opposite sides.'

He raised his eyebrows, somehow disinclined not to doubt this. 'A team?'

'That's right.'

Stephan came in. 'Cup of tea before you start?'

It seemed like a good idea to an unbreakfasted Eisenmenger. While Stephan busied himself with the kettle he asked, 'Where's Dr Addison?'

'In the dissection room.' He grinned slyly. 'She's having another quick peek at the body. She's muttering a lot.'

Eisenmenger felt like a magician about to perform, with a member of the public inspecting the props before he took to the stage.

'Sugar?'

'No, thanks.'

The tea wasn't bad. Beverley had already had one cup but she accepted another.

'I'd better get back to her. Keep her company.'

When Stephan had left, Eisenmenger said thoughtfully, 'I don't think you should see my part in this as "taking sides".'

She seemed perplexed. 'What do you mean?'

'Well, obviously, I expect Dr Addison to have some hostility to this possibility, but I couldn't help but notice that the good Inspector Sauerwine seemed also to be a little put out.'

'Was he?' Beverley was good at innocence.

'Yes.' Eisenmenger was good at spotting deceit.

She made a face of disbelief. 'I don't know. He might

274

have been a little worried about letting an "unofficial" pathologist loose on the body, but that was purely a procedural thing. Chain of evidence, you see.'

'So the row wasn't about disproving Michael Bloom's innocence?'

'Not at all.'

'It wasn't that proof of murder would suit him, proof of innocence would suit you?'

She put down her tea. Came towards him. He was used to Beverley, knew that this gesture was as ritualized as the courting display of a peacock.

It didn't stop him feeling something close to enjoyment.

She put her hand on his arm and said softly and reproachfully, 'We're just after the truth, John. You know that.'

He knew a lot of things, but he didn't know that.

Her eyes held him for a long time but then the door behind them opened and inexplicably Eisenmenger felt intense and guilty embarrassment, as if the hand on his arm was an overtly sexual gesture, a kiss on the lips, a hand on her breast.

'You'd better hurry up,' advised Stephan. 'She's about ready to combust in there.'

'Good morning, Dr Addison.'

Eisenmenger at least made an attempt at pleasant formality. Debbie Addison contented herself with a glare and a short, low-frequency noise that come from the back of her throat. Eisenmenger kept the smile plastered sweetly on his face and turned to the body.

It was still in the white body bag, purity hiding decay. He indicated to Stephan that he could unzip the bag and remove the corpse of Albert Bloom. As the mortuary technician complied Beverley slipped into the dissection room. Eisenmenger had removed his day clothes and donned greens, over which he now put a large plastic apron. By the time he had put on gloves as well Stephan had removed the bag from around the body. It was no more human than something constructed for a film, except that the congealed blood wasn't resin, the plasticity of the flesh was cold and gruesome, and there was a slight smell in the air around it.

275

Eisenmenger had Dr Addison's report on the desk at the far side of the room. In it on the first two pages she had carefully documented all of the wounds. He now took the report to the body and spent fifty-five minutes comparing the reality with the written word. During this process, he had Stephan turn the body completely round. He also spent a long time probing with a thin metal prod both the three indentations in the head made by the hammer as well as every single stab wound. Then he measured all these marks with a ruler. Every so often he paused and considered the body, his head on one side as if he were creating an object of fine art.

Then he asked of Beverley, 'Did you bring the weapons?'

She produced from her briefcase a hammer and a long knife, each in a thick, clear plastic bag sealed at the top. He looked at them carefully for ten minutes. He even applied the hammer – still encased in plastic – to the wounds on the head, checking the fit. He measured the greatest width of the blade before asking, 'Any forensic evidence from these?'

Beverley said, 'Albert Bloom's fingerprints are on both, together with several smudges, nothing definitely Michael Bloom's, or anyone else's if it comes to that.'

Eisenmenger returned to his contemplation. Eventually he looked across at Addison. 'Do you know, I can't compliment you enough. Your report is perfect. Every wound described completely and without mistake.'

From a stew of resentment, anxiety and pride she fished a relieved smile. 'Oh, well, thank you.'

He positively beamed at her. 'I won't bother to open the body – there's no need.'

Stephan's relief at this announcement was nothing compared with Dr Addison's delight. She came forward at last into the arena. 'I'm glad you're satisfied, Dr Eisenmenger. I won't say you didn't have me worried, but I was always confident that eventually you'd see the truth.'

There was something – quite a lot of something – that was irritating about the supercilious tone with which this was delivered. Accordingly he rather enjoyed turning to Beverley to say, 'I can't prove it, of course, but there is nothing here to exclude suicide.'

'What!' Dr Addison almost exploded forward.

Beverley ignored her. 'You're sure?'

'Pretty much. Enough to sign a statement to that effect.'

Beverley had a great deal of respect for Eisenmenger, but even so she looked at the sliced and diced corpse that was Albert Bloom's with doubt in her eyes. 'I don't see how –'

'And neither do I!' Dr Addison stepped in with both feet shod in hobnailed boots. 'This man has obviously been the victim of a frenzied and vicious attack.'

Eisenmenger could only agree. 'Oh yes. The only thing that I would point out is that the pattern of wounds is more consistent with self-wounding than with the involvement of a second party.'

Beverley saved Addison the task of enquiring, 'In what way?'

Eisenmenger turned back to the body. 'If we look at the overall distribution of the stab wounds, it's curious that there are far more to the front of the body than to the back.'

'So? He faced his attacker.'

'Well, it's possible, of course, but I don't think he's the type to have put up much resistance. I would suggest he might well have tried to run, turn away from his attacker.' Before Dr Addison could argue he proceeded to his second point. 'If we pay more attention to the wounds that are present on the back . . .'

He gestured to Stephan to roll the body so that the back was exposed.

'. . . we see the second curious thing – that all of the wounds here are either on the upper back, or on the buttocks and thighs. There are none in the small of the back.'

Suddenly his antagonist was looking thoughtful. She merely sucked her lower lip as Beverley asked, 'What of it?'

'If you stab a man in the back, you can do it anywhere. If you stab yourself in the back, you can't do it in the small of the back. The arms aren't long enough or flexible enough.'

He gave them a second or two to consider this, then went on to the next point. 'The angle of the stab wounds on the back is quite instructive, too. Those at the top are angled quite steeply downwards, those in the buttocks and legs are predominantly angled horizontally but come from the right-hand side.' He looked up at Beverley. 'Albert Bloom was right-handed, I take it. There are nicotine stains on the fingers of the right hand, so I assumed he was.'

She nodded.

He smiled briefly, then indicated to Stephan that he should return the body to its previous position. 'Lastly, there are the cuts. Take away the rest of the carnage and you have the classic signs of self-inflicted lacerations – especially at the front of the throat. Here.'

He indicated a laceration that stretched beneath the jawline, then turned Albert Bloom's head to expose its left-hand end. 'It's not deep enough to have done any great damage, other than adding to the general blood loss from the external jugular veins, but it is, I believe, telling that here – where a right-handed man would begin the cut – there are actually two trial cuts. See?'

When Dr Addison declined, Beverley approached corpse and peered at spot he was indicating, then stood up. 'Okay, I see.'

'This is preposterous!' Dr Addison's heckle from the back was spoiled by the slight tremor of uncertainty in her voice. When Beverley turned to her she continued, 'You can't possibly believe that anyone would do this to themselves! They'd have to be . . .'

Eisenmenger murmured softly, 'Mad?' He sighed. 'I've seen a man decapitate himself with a rope tied to a car; I've seen another lay his head upon the railway track with a train approaching. Of course they were mad. You've got to be mad to kill yourself in a spectacular or bloody fashion.'

'But this is sustained, not spur of the moment.'

It was Beverley who answered that. 'He'd spent the last twenty years regretting what he'd done to his family. On that night, I think his son had finally made it plain that there was no going back, no redemption. He'd been roughed up by Michael, then he made his way home and, from the look of his house, he'd spent the next hour or two drinking heavily.'

'And the hammer blows to the head? He did those himself?'

Eisenmenger nodded, ignoring the sarcasm.

'Oh, come on . . .'

He observed simply, 'They would have hurt, no doubt about it, but they weren't hard enough to cause immediate unconsciousness, I think.' He looked down at Albert Bloom. 'This was more a sort of self-flagellation,' he murmured, almost as if in sympathy.

Dr Addison ran out of air and patience at exactly the same time. She exhaled noisily, then shook her head; there was a definite resemblance to an irritated horse. 'All I can say is that I fundamentally and totally disagree. It is entirely beyond belief that this man killed himself.'

She exited then, in something that the uncharitable might have described as a flounce. Three pairs of eyes watched her depart; Stephan said brightly, 'I'll pick up the toys later.'

Beverley turned to Eisenmenger, 'Will you write a report for me?'

'Sure.' To Stephan he said, 'Thanks, Steph. You can put him back now.'

He pulled off the gloves and apron. 'If you'll excuse me, Beverley.'

He went into the changing room and the muffled sound of the shower could soon be heard. Beverley looked across at Stephan who was manoeuvring the corpse back into its body bag. She walked out of the dissection room, into the body store and thence into the vestibule. There was a look on her face that the independent observer would have had trouble deciphering; was it amusement, or was it desire?

Dr Addison had departed; there was no one else around.

She walked quietly to the door of the male changing room.

She reached out for the handle. The sound of the shower could clearly be heard in the quiet around her.

She turned it.

It was locked.

She sighed and smiled. 'Next time, John. Next time.'

Jackson sat at his desk and watched the comings and goings. He saw Felty arrive at nine in the morning, her face pale, her gaze interestingly fixed in a forward direction.

'Hello, hello,' he murmured.

Jackson was eating a rather tasty 'dripper'. He was also ostensibly reading last night's duty log, although in reality he was playing solitaire on the computer. It had been a quiet night for New Year's Eve, with only one major fight and three arrests for drunkenness. When Beverley arrived about fifty minutes later, she glanced across at him, her expression the usual one of disinterested contempt.

'No change there, then,' he said softly.

Sauerwine's appearance was less than two minutes further into the day. He, too, looked haggard and grey. Jackson drew from this temporal proximity a conclusion that was correct in substance, even if the details were wrong.

'Well, well. Inspector Sauerwine's been wearing the away strip, I think.'

Beverley had barely enough time to remove her coat and sit at her desk before she was summoned into Sauerwine's room; as she made her way there she completely failed to notice that Felty, who sat at her desk, was attempting to kill her with an intense, almost super-human stare.

'Andrew,' she said, closing the door.

He looked up at her from a wretched face. 'She knows.'

She sat down. 'Who knows what?'

'Sally. She knows that we slept together.'

Beverley sighed. 'So?'

He looked at her incredulously. 'I love her.' Beverley said nothing. She might have asked what he saw in Constable Felty, but she said nothing. He continued, 'She's so angry.'

Amateur. He's just an amateur.

This thought drifted into her head but the corollary was unpalatable.

Does that make me a pro?

Aloud she said, 'She'll get over it, Andrew.'

'And if she doesn't?'

'If she loves you she will.' Even Beverley didn't really believe that one, and he looked now as if she had taken to speaking in tongues. 'Anyway, you're not married to her, are you? You're not even engaged. She has no contractual hold on your wedding tackle.'

He shook his head, unable to look at her. 'I love her.'

Should have thought of that, shouldn't you?

And with this thought she reached the limit of her patience. She stood up. 'I've got to get over to the mortuary. I only came in to collect the knife and hammer from the evidence store.' She walked to the door but before opening it she said to him, 'It's not very clever to think only an hour into the future, Andrew. The brighter you are, the further ahead you look. Perhaps if you'd considered the consequences of your actions, you'd be a little happier today.'

She walked out, looking directly at Felty, suppressing the smile. Sauerwine stared at her back. 'Cow,' he murmured.

Helena had taken one of the beautiful leather-bound books from the shelves and was idly reading it in the library while she waited for Theresa to come down and join her. They were planning to drive to the local church where it was Theresa's turn for flower arranging, the falling rain having dissuaded her from the original plan to take a boat out on to the lake on with Eisenmenger.

Anyway, he had gone into a brown study following his morning's trip to the mortuary and she knew well that he would be minimal company until whatever problem he wrestled with had been broken.

The book was beautiful but dull. A nineteenth-century author who had been long forgotten; the few paragraphs that she had read told her that he was also best forgotten. She put the book on her lap as she heard footsteps outside the library door, which was not fully closed. She assumed at first that it was Eisenmenger and was just about to stand and walk out to him but then she heard other footsteps on the wooden flooring, these unmistakably feminine.

'Please let me pass.' Dominique's voice.

'I'm not stopping you.' Hugo's lazy, ever-amused voice pointed out.

Helena heard Dominique's tentative footstep forward but there came also the sound of another movement. The briefest of pauses followed before Dominique said, 'Let me go!' She was plainly very stressed.

'Come on, now, Dominique. Just a kiss.'

'No!'

'You gave me one once . . . You enjoyed it, I think.'

'You think so?' Dominique's accent was perfectly suited to disdain.

'Yes, I do.'

There was the sound of more shuffling that ended abruptly when the distinctive sound of a healthy smack came to Helena's ears.

'Ow! Shit!'

Dominique's voice was distorted by emotion and deep breathing as she hissed, 'Leave me alone!'

Her footsteps sounded once more, this time retreating the way they had come. Hugo apparently remained still for some time, saying nothing. Then, just as Helena began to fear that he was going to come into the library, she heard a soft laugh and his quiet footsteps walked away.

When Helena returned from the church she announced that she was going to have a nap, and Eisenmenger decided to take the opportunity to go for a walk and think through matters regarding events recent and otherwise. He did not know the estate and had no map, but he would have ignored it anyway. He wanted to think and, when he thought, he followed a single track, with eyes in one direction only. He had that morning phoned an old colleague who worked in the department of pathology at the Queen's Medical Centre in Nottingham; he had asked her to undertake a minor investigative task and just before he had left for the walk she had rung him back. It had given him something very interesting to consider.

It could only have been by total fluke that he found himself back at the site of the baby's grave. It was still protected by a marquee around which yellow plastic taping had been strung; a lonely place, it had now been tainted by an intensity of desolation that Eisenmenger found almost overpowering. The bones might have gone but for Eisenmenger at least there was now a spectre with him; his old friend, old adversary, had come calling.

Death.

Eisenmenger was not a rude man and he did not wish to upset someone who thought of him as a companion. He sat down on a log beside the fluttering tape that told him the police had been there.

Well . . .

There were so many disparate events, none obviously connected . . .

Yet Eisenmenger could see only a single thing although its shape was indistinct and he had a problem with that.

He *knew* that here was something monstrous; he didn't know what, he didn't even know for sure that he could ever know what it was.

He was going to have a fucking good try, though.

Three deaths.

Except that . . .

He had convinced himself that Albert Bloom's death was an irrelevance, at most tangential to the main event, which led him to ponder William Moynihan's unpleasant exit from this mortal realm.

Fire was a very greedy thing; it took without giving and thus was a very useful tool to the murderer.

He couldn't prove anything and could only work on principle: in almost complete reversal of the context that surrounded other deaths, bodies burned to death were suspicious until proved otherwise. Nobody had proved William Moynihan's death was otherwise.

So all he had was one death possibly suspicious, one death probably suicide and one death years old.

They might not even be linked . . .

Except that he saw that indistinct shape.

He was cold, he noticed; cold and damp.

Assuming Moynihan was murdered, then the likeliest explanation of Bloom's suicide was guilt, yet the only obvious link between the old man and Moynihan was Michael, who had known both. Why should Albert Bloom feel remorse at Moynihan's demise? Why should he have killed him?

That link didn't work.

He might have been wrong, of course. Perhaps Albert Bloom had been the victim of an incredibly cunning killer, the same one who had despatched Moynihan.

Except that he didn't like that explanation either. The murderer of Moynihan had not been refined; to have murdered Albert Bloom in a perfect imitation of bloody suicide was refinement to the point of lunacy. This was either murder, or suicide masquerading as murder; it could not be described as murder masquerading as suicide. Anyway, if you were going to fake a suicide, you don't do it with multiple stab wounds and a few hammer blows to the head.

He gave up in disgust, murmuring, 'Shit!' to a robin that was fluttering from tree to tree about five metres away. It ignored him.

He turned his attention to the baby. Almost a fluke that it had been discovered and quite possibly unrelated to anything or anyone connected with the estate in the present day.

But there was still that shape, looming at the edge of vision.

And he formed a modicum of certainty quite abruptly from nothing.

The baby was central to it all; he didn't know how – he didn't even know how he knew it – but that single certainty would not be denied.

He realized what the shape was then.

It was the past, rising to meet the present.

He looked up suddenly as a sound – possibly twigs breaking – pierced the background noises of the wood. He looked around, saw nothing, then returned to his contemplation, assuming that it was just a wild animal.

'Sally?'

'Sir?'

They were alone in the room but Sauerwine couldn't bring himself to beg her forgiveness here, when they were at work. He tried to ride over her frigid contempt. 'I've asked Leicester to pick up Fiona Bloom. I want you to go up there and bring her back here for questioning.'

'Now?' Her voice was resigned, as if he had managed to suppress her completely.

'Straight away. They're planning to have her in custody under caution by noon.'

She stood up. 'Okay.'

She walked past him to get her coat and he might have been a water-cooler around which she had to walk.

He forgot his resolution.

'Sally?'

She turned back, didn't say anything, merely stared at him, her face devoid of emotion.

'I'm sorry. I really am sorry.'

Still she didn't say anything. She didn't even hold the stare. She just turned away and walked out to the car.

Eleanor's fall was in retrospect somehow inevitable, part of the motif. The details were not clear, but it seemed that she fell off the final step of the staircase that led down to the entrance hall; not a huge fall but enough. How long she lay there before Dominique found her – very pale but still conscious and bleeding from a cut to her head – was never made clear. The castle was all but deserted as the Hickmans had gone to a drinks party on the other side of Westerham. Only Helena was around when Dominique began running up the stairs, calling for help.

'What is it?' she called from the bedroom where she had been resting.

'Please! Come and help!'

Helena came into the hallway as Dominique was running towards her. 'It's Madame Hickman. She's fallen.'

They ran back together. Eleanor hadn't moved. Helena, in truth, felt that she probably knew less first aid than Dominique, but thought that it was incumbent upon her to take charge. She knelt down beside her. 'Eleanor?'

The gaze was confused. 'It hurts.'

'What does?'

She tried to move her right hand; it moved vaguely towards the upper half of her body. Helena felt in her pocket and took out a handkerchief which she dabbed at the old woman's face.

The cut appeared superficial but she was no expert; how would she know if there was an underlying skull fracture or even bleed into the brain? She found herself cursing John Eisenmenger who had so cruelly decided to go for a walk.

'Does it hurt anywhere else?'

Eleanor didn't answer so she repeated the question. Eleanor shook her head but it was still vague, almost uncomprehending. It was with something that resembled desperation that Helena felt for a pulse, finding a thin, thready thing that seemed to be chasing after life. Dominique, too, had knelt down beside the old woman and was gently feeling her legs. Helena said, 'The pulse is very fast.'

The only reaction that Dominique provoked in Eleanor was when she pressed lightly on her left hip. She said softly, 'Her hip. It may be broken. I don't know.'

Which gave them a problem. Neither of them felt a keen desire to move an eighty-year-old woman with a broken hip. Helena said at last, 'First we need to make her comfortable.'

Dominique stood up. 'I'll fetch a pillow and some blankets.'

'No, if you tell me where they are, I'll get those. You ring Tristan and get him back here.'

'What about an ambulance?'

Helena shook her head. 'I'll leave that to him.' She stood up. 'Where are the blankets kept?'

'There is an airing cupboard next to your room. There should be pillows and blankets in there.'

When Helena returned, Eleanor had not moved. She lay on her back, her head to one side, the blood refusing to stop and now tracking on to the floor around the side of her face. 'Eleanor?'

Her eyes, although open, were hidden beyond Helena's recall.

'Eleanor?' There was a reaction of sorts and Helena seized this. 'I'm going to put a pillow under your head and put a blanket over you.'

The old woman moved her eyes and her head; a frown of recognition deepened the creases above her head. When Helena lifted the head, it was shockingly light, the hair dry like brittle, tired wire.

'Dominique's calling Tristan to come back. He won't be long.'

The warmth of the blanket seemed to provoke some sort of revival in Eleanor. With Helena sitting on the bottom step beside her she said suddenly, 'It's so good to have dear Hugo back.'

'Oh, yes.' Helena tried to make this sound sincere, even as she was wondering why she had to force herself.

Eleanor had closed her eyes, might have been tucked up

286

in bed after hot cocoa and a digestive biscuit. 'He doesn't mean it, you know.'

Helena didn't know what the old woman could mean. She said, 'Oh, no,' but this was talk of the smallest kind, no more.

'He is weak . . .'

Helena murmured, 'Yes.'

'Headstrong.'

What does all this mean? Does it mean anything at all? She said nothing and waited.

'It's a good thing in a man. Shows strength of character.'

Helena waited, unsure of what to say to this seemingly random list of statements, whether to say it anyway. In any case Eleanor was no longer in a dialogue.

'He'll be good for the estate. I knew that from the first, right from when he was a baby. He had what's made the Hickmans the people they are.'

It was obvious that she was talking about Hugo, but Helena couldn't place the details into context. For long seconds, sounded languidly into oblivion by the ornate antique clock at the far end of the hall, there was silence until, 'I feel so sorry for Nell.'

The voice as she said this was totally unchanged but Helena heard in it significance. *And what does that mean?*

The questions in her head seemed to be asked by someone outside her head.

'They're so close.'

Eleanor moved and as she did so she winced. Helena noticed that she became slightly short of breath and she looked around, wondering where Dominique was. Eleanor settled slightly and another few moments of silence followed.

'Your parents . . .'

Helena's interest suddenly bloomed. *What about them?*

But Eleanor was not to be rushed. She was breathing quite heavily still, and now it was noisy, almost rattling at the back of her throat. She closed her eyes and for a moment Helena thought that she had drifted into unconsciousness but then quite abruptly and with her eyes still closed she said, 'They couldn't accept it.'

Who couldn't? And accept what?

Nothing followed and Helena felt that she could no longer remain silent. 'Accept what, Eleanor?'

Helena might as well have not bothered. Eleanor's next remark followed swiftly and with no regard to what Helena might have had to say. 'Not for the faint-hearted.' A gnomic comment, apropos of little, it seemed.

Helena knelt down beside the old woman. She was intensely pale and her lips were blue. She dabbed at the wound on the temple from which blood was still oozing. Into her ear she said, 'Who couldn't accept what?'

The eyes were open but they weren't looking at Helena or anything in the room. There were no words at all for long moments in which Helena's frustration grew and intertwined itself into every single muscle.

Abruptly and without any change in her eyes Eleanor said, 'There's a bigger picture. I tried to tell them, but they couldn't see . . .'

Helena heard Dominique returning from the kitchen. She leaned closer. 'Who, Eleanor? My parents?'

But Eleanor's agenda was otherwise and her only reply was noisy breathing; when Dominique came into the room she had said no more other than a meaningless moan from the back of her throat.

'They are on their way. They said we had done the right thing.'

'How long will they be?'

'About twenty minutes.'

In the event they were only fifteen. Tristan and Hugo burst in through the front door and went at once to the little group huddled at the bottom of the stairs. Helena and Dominique stood up and made way for them. Theresa following close behind came up to them and said, 'What happened?' Her voice was demanding, sounding angry because of fear.

As Dominique explained as best she could, Nell came in with Tom and hurried him past the stricken old woman. Helena heard him asking what was going on. Theresa interrupted Dominique constantly, her questions suggesting that she was to blame for this catastrophe. Helena saw increasing stress in the French girl and explained, 'No one could have prevented this, Theresa. Eleanor must have just tripped at the bottom of the staircase.'

288

'But why didn't anyone miss her? She might have been there for an hour or more. She looks half dead . . .'

'We didn't miss her because it's a big house.' Helena's tone hinted that she thought Theresa was being unreasonable. Before she could react, however, Tristan stood up. He had a relieved smile on his face.

'We're fairly sure the hip's okay.'

'What about her head?' Theresa still hadn't lost the edge to her voice. 'It looks awful.'

'A superficial cut. They always bleed like buggery.' He turned to Dominique and Helena. 'Did she lose consciousness?'

'Not while I was there. She was a bit vague, though. Almost delirious.'

Dominique, nodding in agreement, said, 'She was awake all the time that I saw her.'

Tristan considered. 'I don't think we need to bother Casualty. Hugo and I will keep a close eye on her for the next day or two – make sure she doesn't "go off".' He smiled reassuringly at his wife. 'She'll be all right. Mother is as tough as old boots. Old boots made of English leather.'

She nodded and relaxed slightly. He turned away, leaving her to take a deep breath. 'I'm sorry if I seemed unreasonable,' she said then. 'You understand, I'm sure.'

Of course Helena did. What she didn't understand was why the apology was directed solely at her.

Hugo, still with his grandmother, called to them. 'Helena? Gran wants a word.'

She walked quickly over to the foot of the stairs, then knelt down. The old lady seemed a slightly better colour, was less breathless. Her eyes were brighter and when she saw Helena her face twitched into a small smile. Her voice, though, was still weak.

'I just wanted to say how sorry I was about your parents. I'm sure you understand, though, why it was necessary.'

Her voice may have been weak but both Hugo and Tristan heard it as well. When Helena looked up at them – her head full of questions again – they were both staring at her intently, their expressions unreadable.

*   *   *

The first part of the return journey with Fiona Bloom was lively because she was drunk and abusive and protested very loudly her complete mystification as to what was going on. Then she vomited in the back of the car. They had bags for that kind of thing but Fiona Bloom didn't care enough to ask for one. By the time Felty had got one to her mouth, the main event was over.

Mostly over Felty's jeans.

'Sorry.' Fiona Bloom's voice gave the lie to that particular sentiment. In the front, the driver's quarter profile bore a smile that Felty didn't much like.

'Bloody great.' As she cleaned herself down with tissues, the acid stench of sick made all the more inescapable because the windows at the back could not be opened, the first germs of persecution began to nestle in Felty's mind. As her prisoner started to snore, her mouth half open in a sort of inane smile, Felty wondered what was going on back in Newford. The feeling that she was again being got out of the way, once it had formed, would not shift and, having arrived, proceeded to taint all other thoughts. As the miles of motorway droned past the car, these idle speculations crystallized into things of brittle but sharp-edged beauty. By the time she had escorted Fiona Bloom to the interrogation room, the paperwork had been done and the driver had departed, she was *looking* for betrayal.

She knocked on Sauerwine's door, went straight in without waiting for an invitation. It was empty.

Jackson wandered in, distributing the daily county crime digest around the various desks. 'Where's the Inspector?'

He didn't even look at her; Jackson had long ago discarded things like eye contact and civility. 'Fuck knows.'

Exasperated, she asked, 'Well, did he go out?'

He was almost out of the door as he tossed over his shoulder, 'No.'

So where was he?

It wasn't a huge building – senior officers on the top floor, this floor and the cells in the basement . . .

Beverley Wharton's office.

Felty walked, almost ran. Again the door was closed and again she knocked and opened it immediately.

They weren't draped around each other; she wasn't on

290

her knees in front of his opened trousers; he hadn't pinned her spread-eagled form on the desk. They weren't touching, weren't even on the same side of the desk.

Yet when she entered, she felt as if she were puncturing an atmosphere of intimacy. They had been laughing at a shared joke and the looks that they gave her were both startled and guilt-ridden. Had they been laughing at her?

'Sally!'

She didn't know what to say. Stupidly, she said only, 'Oh.'

While Beverley retained a smile that never descended below mocking, Sauerwine continued to talk. 'Have you got Fiona Bloom?'

'Yes.'

She saw Beverley's eyes flick down to the stain on her jeans. Did she wrinkle her nose as if the whiff of sick had reached her oh-so-pretty nose?

Sauerwine enquired, 'Where is she?'

'In the interrogation room. I –'

'Good.'

He picked up the phone to call Syme. There was a short conversation before he said to Wharton, 'Felty and I will take the first shift with her. If it proves necessary, Syme and you can come in later.'

'I –'

They weren't listening to her. Beverley nodded and Sauerwine walked towards Felty. His nose most definitely did wrinkle as he came into her proximity. 'Come on, Sally.'

Outside she tried again. 'I'd really rather like to go home and change, if I may.'

'What happened to you?'

'Fiona Bloom was sick over me.'

This made him pause but only for a moment. 'Can't you borrow some trousers?'

From who? Jackson?

'Not really . . .'

He took a breath, then, 'This really is very inconvenient, Sally.'

Oh, really? Try having to sit in somebody else's vomit for a couple of hours. That's what I call inconvenient.

He appeared annoyed and she didn't quite understand.

291

He turned round, went back into Beverley Wharton's room. When he came out, she was with him. 'Okay, you go home and change; Beverley and I will do the interrogation. When you get back, run down the final reports on the forensic evidence on the baby. Then take formal statements from Eisenmenger and Flemming. Then, if you have time, you'd better run through the records on missing babies over the past fifteen years. Get Jackson to help you.'

He turned away without waiting for a reply. Beverley Wharton's eyes, though, lingered, her expression unreadable.

Eisenmenger entered the police station hoping to talk to Beverley Wharton. He had not returned to the castle and was unaware of Eleanor's fall and her strange, mumbled apologies to Helena. His mobile phone was switched off – he wanted peace and quiet while he contemplated the recent events – and he did not think to switch it on to tell Helena of his whereabouts.

He wanted, but did not expect, Beverley to let him see the evidence files on the three deaths so recently discovered. He knew that without them he had no chance of uncovering anything of the truth. He knew also that the situation was delicate; Sauerwine and Beverley clearly had professional differences about the case and there was a danger that if Beverley agreed he would be seriously antagonizing Sauerwine. And it was a very big and cumbersome *if*. He knew Beverley well enough to suspect that her motives were as pure as the driven slush, although what they might actually be was still lost to him.

Beverley, however, was busy.

Jackson was busy, too. Busy and short-tempered. The computer records went back only ten years, which meant that to comply with Sauerwine's orders he had had to pull dusty, musty cardboard files by hand; it gave him a dry throat and a headache. It worsened his indigestion, too.

When Eisenmenger – perfectly politely, he thought – asked how long Beverley would be, he said sourly, 'As long as it takes.'

Eisenmenger considered this. It had the smack of the

truth, even if it lacked the servility a uniformed policeman might once have proffered to a member of the public.

'Can I leave a message for her?'

Jackson was quite possibly capable of expressions more deeply steeped in sourness, but there would have been diminishing returns for the effort. 'I don't know. Can you?'

Eisenmenger had known a lot of policemen in his career; Jackson wasn't the worst, he told himself. 'May I, then?'

Jackson's open mouth and hostile expression were strong indicators that the answer was going to be on the negative side of maybe, but then Felty came in to see how Jackson was doing and when she saw Eisenmenger she was at once strikingly welcoming.

'Ah! Dr Eisenmenger. I was going to come and see you.'

Jackson scowled. Eisenmenger smiled.

'Can you come through? If you've got time, I need to take a statement.'

And strangely he did have time; he even had a cheery grin for Jackson as he passed through.

Helena threw the mobile phone on the bed. Where the hell was he? What was wrong with the man? He was filled with the ability to aggravate; from the first moment she had met him he had irritated her and it had continued ever since, but this was significantly, exponentially, greater. He was forever present when she didn't want him to be or, even worse, absent when required. Like now.

Five hours! Five hours he had been gone. And of course the idiot had switched off his mobile phone. Not for him the consideration of remaining in touch. He had wanted to go off and think through the recent events on the estate – as if it were any of his business, as if it were in any way relevant.

'I need you to ring, John. I really need you to ring. Now.' She stared at the phone trying to will life into it. 'Now, John.'

But it didn't oblige. Her telekinetic powers had always proved inadequate to the task in hand, although in truth she hadn't attempted to use them much since about the age of nine. She sighed in exasperation for about the twentieth time in the past hour, the only difference being that it was the loudest and the longest of the lot.

'For God's sake!'

Why couldn't he behave normally? Why did he have to mutate into this deep-thinking automaton, immersed in the mysteries of whatever particular grisly problem happened to have come blundering into his orbit? When she had been confronted by her cancer, she had had the feeling that it was all just a little bit of a distraction to the main event of people having their throats cut and their organs removed.

This time, though, he was missing the point. These deaths meant nothing to her, an interesting conundrum – he'd even proved that one was a suicide – yet he hadn't spotted that.

The real mystery in the castle lay elsewhere.

The death of her parents.

Yet this insistent idea was so outlandish she found herself fleeing from it.

What could anyone here have to do with the slaughter of her mother and father? These were as close as her family, without the downside of prolonged over-proximity; she had grown up with them. She had already seen her blood-family destroyed – was she really going to implicate the only people who remained from the peace of her past?

Yet that was what she suspected.

Impossible as it seemed, she somehow saw a link between her parents' deaths and these people around her now.

At first she had refused to acknowledge any of this. Better to ignore the sore than pick at it. Better to turn away and live a life separate from worry.

Better? Helena doubted it. She had never been able to endure injustice, especially that against herself or her family.

Consequently the suspicions had returned continually, refusing to die, refusing even to lie down to sleep until Eisenmenger returned.

What had Eleanor meant? Why should she apologize for the death of her parents? Helena was quite certain that it had not been an offer of condolence but contrition that the old woman had given her. It was an expression of culpability, of involvement. It wove connections where none had existed before.

Helena was not about to ignore those.

And, as if that were not enough, there was the tantalizing hint in Nell's book of letters. It had been Eisenmenger (of course!) who had pointed out the near synchronicity of her parents' murder to the date on the letter she had been reading when Nell had interrupted her. Was it the last letter they had written to her? What was this thing that they could not accept?

And what, if anything, did it have to do with their deaths?

The questions could not be ignored.

So where was that irritating idiot?

'I need to talk to Inspector Wharton.'

They had finished his statement and Eisenmenger had just finished signing each and every page of it.

Felty was professional enough not to show her feelings. 'I'm not sure how convenient that's going to be.'

Eisenmenger was aware of something coming, minutes passing. Three deaths had come to light and he knew from somewhere that, without answers, more were likely to follow. Deaths caused disturbances, destroyed the equilibrium, and that led more often than not to further killings. Time's winged chariot was coming and its passenger wanted blood.

'It's important.'

'I'm sure it is, Dr Eisenmenger, but that doesn't change matters. She's interviewing a witness.'

'About the baby?'

But Felty wouldn't say.

'When will she be free?'

'I really couldn't say.'

Eisenmenger's next exasperated question wasn't strictly relevant, but it was just one of the many aspects to the case that troubled him.

'What exactly is her interest in all this?'

Felty's surprise at this question was obvious, as was her hesitation. She said, 'I think you'll have to ask her that.'

Eisenmenger saw something beneath this rebuff but he didn't pursue it directly. He leaned back in his chair. They were in the second interview room, this one considerably cleaner and less abused than the first. He said, 'I know Beverley of old.'

'So I gathered.'

'She's a bloody good copper.'

Felty's face told him that she didn't particularly want to hear compliments like that, thank you very much. 'I'm sure.'

He moved forward in his chair. 'But she's out for number one, and only number one.'

'Look –'

'And sometimes that means number two and three in the food chain get hurt. I've seen it before. Sometimes justice isn't always served by Beverley getting what she wants.'

Felty stood up. 'I think you've said quite enough, Dr Eisenmenger.'

'Beverley's not here through chance, is she?'

Felty's face was fixed into a hostile expression but Eisenmenger saw something around her eyes. He couldn't name it, but he saw that the buttons he was pressing were doing something more than offending her professional loyalties. 'Please, Dr Eisenmenger.'

He stood, picked up his coat and followed her out into the corridor where he tried once more. 'Maybe I can help, Constable. Another point of view sometimes allows one to see patterns that are hidden to others.'

She didn't respond. As they reached the door out into the vestibule, she held it open for him and he walked through. He put on his coat and was surprised to see that she had stopped in the doorway and was looking at him. Then, without a word to him, she stepped back inside, called through the hatchway to Jackson, 'I'm just going out for an hour.'

Turning to Eisenmenger she said, 'Let's find a pub.'

Helena could wait no longer. She felt driven to a move that perhaps in other circumstances she might not have made; she felt as if the rising wind were somehow powering her and John's refusal to return, even to make contact, only added to the restlessness within her. She looked at her watch, almost failed to whisper the word, 'Shit,' then stood up.

It was half-past six and deeply dark. The castle was quiet but then it always was. Tristan and Theresa were out again, this time at some sort of Hunt Ball at a hotel in Newford. Nell, she guessed, would be with Tom, while Dominique had taken on the role of nurse to Eleanor. Hugo had been watching the television in the kitchen, making regular visits to check on his grandmother.

She opened the door, peered out, then walked out of her room, closing the door softly behind her. The chances were that there was no one within a hundred metres of her, but she was extremely cautious. She told herself that she was entitled to take another look through the letters of her father, doubly so now that Eleanor seemed to imply that there was some link between the death of her parents and the Hickmans, yet that didn't stop her from feeling like a sneak thief, that this was a betrayal of the hospitality she had been shown.

She went first to Nell's room. A precautionary knock on the door went unanswered so she tried the handle. It was unlocked – why shouldn't it be? – and she slipped inside.

She looked around, startled at what she saw. Nell's room hadn't changed at all. It was as if it had been turned into a museum commemorating childhood. The wallpaper was the same, the drapes were identical, even the bed-covers, she was sure, were lost in time. The soft toys were still there – the huge Paddington Bear, the large rag doll, the peculiarly creepy clown – still arrayed at the end of the bed, their positions seemingly undisturbed in the eight years that had passed since Helena was last in the room. No concessions to maturity and maternity had been made anywhere.

But there was a positive to this negativity, this refusal to accept inevitability: she knew at once where the treasure was that she was seeking. She went immediately to a low chest of drawers beneath the window on the far wall. In the bottom drawer was, just as she knew it would be, a small wooden box, the hinged lid secured with a tiny brass hook over a pin. It was here that Nell had always kept her most valued possessions. When she looked inside there, amongst the trinkets and mementoes, the rings and the lockets (one, Helena recognized, had been given to Nell by her grandfather, as he had been given it by a great-aunt), was the key to the turret.

She picked it out, closed the box, replaced it in the drawer, pushed that shut and was gone from the room within five minutes.

Her trip through the castle's corridors was similarly uneventful and easy. She unlocked the door, stepped through, then closed and locked it behind her, mindful that by doing this she would prevent interruption.

She then climbed the steps to Nell's secret room.

Eisenmenger was unsure whether to feel elation or shock, surprise or despair. Felty's news altered the lighting, cast shadows of different length and changed shape, made the insignificant consequential, put previously bright areas into darkness. Suddenly he was looking at a different scene with lions and tigers instead of wolves and jackals.

They were sitting in a corner of the Quills, a hotel that was about two hundred metres from the police station. At six thirty in the evening, it was beginning to fill with customers, smoke and noise. People coming in were cold and wet, bringing gusts of wind with them. Felty said, 'So, there you are. She's come down here to cover her back.'

It didn't take immense wisdom to spot the bitterness in Felty's voice.

When Eisenmenger spoke, he felt as if he were broadcasting from somewhere else, a stranger in a strange land. 'Is that fair? It was reasonable to take an interest in the death of Moynihan, given the discovery of the watch and photograph.'

Felty pounced on this, the act of someone who had a mission. 'She hasn't just taken an interest! She's come here to bury her mistake.'

Eisenmenger surprised himself with his reply. 'Maybe she's adding a much-needed perspective.'

Felty, drinking a St Clements, nearly sprayed the environment. 'That's bloody stupid. She's got no interest in finding any of the truth in this whole mess.'

'Maybe, but I've known Beverley a long time. She's got her faults but she's also got a nose for the truth.'

Felty started by looking incredulous then truth, as she

saw it, dawned and her face collapsed into contempt. 'You fancy her,' she declared in a tone that she might have used had she discovered he indulged in coprophagia.

His immediate response – utter denial – did not hold. His whole body assumed a demeanour of outrage, but it lasted a second, if that. The collapse was followed by, 'Of course I fancy her. I'm a man, Constable.'

This was like a man chewing a human eyeball and excusing himself by explaining that he was a cannibal.

'Can't you think with anything other than your dick?'

He swallowed his immediate irritation, overcame the indigestion, and said, 'Actually, yes. Quite often I use my right testicle as well, sometimes the left. Once I used both.'

She didn't laugh. 'You need more than that when you're dealing with that bitch.'

'Look at your boss,' he pointed out. 'A man convinced that he could wrap this whole business up neatly by accusing Michael Bloom of killing his father.'

'Maybe he's right.'

Eisenmenger said gently, 'No, he's not.'

She was defiant and, as so often, he found himself outside the situation and was amazed that he was defending Beverley Wharton, and Sally Felty was defending her adulterous lover. Before she could argue he went on, 'He's not right, Sally. Not about that, and what you've told me this evening only convinces me even more.'

'Oh, please.' When he didn't answer, only taking a drink from his beer glass, she continued, 'What have Wharton's sleazy machinations got to do with anything? They're not going to tell us the truth about this.'

Before he could reply he became aware of a commotion at the back of the pub. A drunk, it appeared, did not like being refused a further drink. 'I think they change the whole picture.'

'How? What do you know?'

Which was a simple question and, as with all such simple questions, was difficult to answer. He knew that it was the thing that unlocked matters, that made the affair soluble, but he had yet to analyse how. He could not yet even say why it mattered to know this thing – he suspected that he might never – but that did not dilute his conviction that with a little thought, a little perspective, the answer could be found.

He said uncertainly, 'I don't "know" much at all. I know that the death of Albert Bloom is peripheral, and that's about it. The rest is logical speculation, nothing more.'

'And where does your "logical speculation" lead you?'

He said with something that might have been temerity but might have been wonder, 'If you accept that Moynihan's death is linked to the baby's death, and that Moynihan's death is linked to the murders of Claude and Penelope Flemming, then you can begin to see links that were previously invisible. You can forget that the Flemmings were murdered on the spur of the moment; perhaps their demise was planned. Therefore, you must ask why.'

She said slowly, 'Because they knew something.'

He nodded, smiling grimly.

She thought again. 'The baby?'

'Presumably.'

'It's Fiona Bloom's, isn't it?'

He smiled. 'Is it?'

'If it isn't, then whose?'

But he didn't answer that. Instead, 'The next logical step is that Moynihan also knew something and was bumped off for his pains.'

'Do you know who the killer is?'

But he said only, 'I'm not sure it's as simple as that.'

'What does that mean?'

He wouldn't say, however, knowing that she would be unimpressed and he was not disappointed.

She looked at her watch. 'I must get back.' She drained her glass.

'Of course.'

She stood up and after a final draught of his beer he did likewise. They walked out together then separated outside the pub. She hesitated before making her way to the station. 'You do know, don't you? Who the killer is, I mean?'

He shook his head but it wasn't to deny his knowledge. 'Not "killer" – "killers".'

'Two?' She was startled but he was to surprise her again.

'I think three.'

*   *   *

300

Hugo slipped into the room occupied by Helena and Eisenmenger. He looked around briefly, found what he wanted on the dressing table, picked them up and then left the room.

Helena's feelings as she sat alone in the turret room on Nell's bed reading the book of letters were identical to those she had briefly experienced so recently before. Identical yet exponentially increased until they were almost a hypnotic, until she felt that she was resting in a state of narcosis. The wind's whining, whipping voice seemed to become more insistent as it was ignored. The lights were gloomy, almost sepia, lending a curiously authentic Victorian aura to the scene.

She had wasted no time, immediately sitting on the bed and picking up the book from the floor where Nell had abandoned it. Then, a deep breath and she started right at the beginning, unwilling to miss a word of what her father or mother might have written. The book contained letters from many people, most of whom Helena had either never known or forgotten.

As she read, she found herself almost trembling, uncertain at first of the reason. She was here, she told herself, as a detective, trying to uncover the unexpected link that seemed to exist between the death of her parents and the Hickmans. It was no different to a legal case; these were just papers to sift through. And this was true, which meant that she could not understand why she was holding her breath as she discovered in the book the first letter from her father. It was dated nine and a half years ago. The words were kindly, the sentiments distinctly avuncular, the content innocuous.

The next was four months later, just after Nell's birthday. This one was from her mother, the writing smaller and less tired by practice, but if the voice of her father had been emotionally shocking – elating and terrifying in equal mixture – then to see this thing that was *of* her mother – and therefore came to *represent* her mother – was almost catatonic in its effect.

Tears came at once to her eyes, not because the subject was moving, but because involuntarily she heard her mother speaking through the ink and paper, a soft, feminine sound that she had not heard for over eight years, that she had refused to listen to, that she had deliberately put in a secured cellar of her mind.

She stopped and looked around the room, the image blurred by moisture, and suddenly she felt lonely, almost scared. It was not a comfortable room. No one lived here, despite the bed and the small island of softness in the middle, no one had disguised the fact that it was an attic storeroom in a remote part of the castle.

Behind her the vast store of junk made shadows of the weak light, cast cold around her. The pictures, the upturned chairs, the boxes of books, the lampshades and the hanging rails melded into strange shapes, composite creatures of the night, part mechanical and part living; gestalt monsters.

She took deep breaths, tried to ignore the voice that told her she should be afraid, that the room was frightening, what with its shadows and recesses, its loneliness and the wind calling outside. Eventually the tears drained away and she returned to the book. She had to hurry, aware that her time was not unlimited.

The eyes that watched her from across the room barely blinked as they took her in.

Sauerwine, tired and frustrated, was having to dig deep into whatever patience he had left. Beverley sat beside him and felt some detachment from the situation. She had been here before, but he would not listen. Too often she had become too close, too tied to a single solution, making facts fit theories rather than bending theories around the fixed points that were the evidence.

Oh, yes. She had been there, all right. Not only did she have the T-shirt, she had a complete wardrobe.

The irony was that this attitude had led to her presence here, in a poky and airless interview room in a Toytown nick staffed by Constable Plod and the Keystone Kops.

Well, she had decided, let him make an idiot of himself, as long as things were steered well away from the Eaton-Lambert case.

Fiona Bloom had opted to dispense with a solicitor; such bravado was usually a sign of either experienced guilt or naive innocence and those latter two words were the last adjective one was likely to apply to their present suspect. She looked for all the world as if she had spent half her life inside police stations, had sat opposite interrogating police officers on every night of the week since she was sixteen. And, for all Beverley knew, she probably had.

'Look, Fiona. Let's try again . . .'

'If you must, dear.' She was probably only a few years older than Sauerwine, but she treated him like a stupid son, a thing of callowness to be taught the ways of the world. It was an effective defence, too.

'You were pregnant when you left Westerham. You say that you had a daughter.'

'That's right.'

'And you called her . . .?'

'Marigold.'

Sauerwine found himself thinking of yellow rubber gloves and decided that nobody called their daughter Marigold any more, not if it were a real child anyway.

'What happened to her?'

'I told you. I gave her away.'

'Who to?'

'Can't remember.'

'Oh, bollocks, Fiona. You don't give away your child and forget where it went.'

'You do if you don't want it. It got in the way of work. My clients were put off when I had to go and change her nappies in midstroke.'

'Did you sell her?'

She smiled slyly. 'Oh, no. That'd be illegal.'

'It's actually illegal to give them away as well.'

She adopted – feigned – a look of surprise. 'Is it?' *So charge me*, was the subtext.

'Was it a couple you gave the child to?'

'Yes. A very nice, middle-class pair. They couldn't have children. Desperate, they were.'

'How old?'

'Middle-aged.'

'What did the husband do?'

She thought a while. 'Something in banking, I think.' A pause. 'Or was it insurance?'

'Did they live in Leicester?'

'Don't recall.'

'And how did you contact them?'

'I didn't. They contacted me.'

They had been round this corner a few times already. Sauerwine adopted his usual expression of disbelief. 'You're asking us to believe that this respectable couple made contact with a prostitute and just offered to take her child off her hands?'

She nodded, her eyes filled with conviction like iced water. 'Yep. That's exactly what happened.' He shook his head, and she said then to Beverley. 'You should take him out more. It's not uncommon for people in my trade to have accidents even in this day and age. There are people who arrange this sort of thing.'

Sauerwine perked up. 'So there was an intermediary?'

'Not directly. I just put the word out, that was all.'

Sauerwine felt as if he were punching ghosts. The story was so flimsy it ought to have been destroyed by a deep sigh and a flick of an eyebrow, but no matter how he tried he couldn't find a way to demonstrate that it was a construction of lies.

Beverley asked in a bored tone, 'Where was your daughter born?'

'Leicester Royal Infirmary.'

'What name did you use?'

Fiona Bloom smiled. 'I forget.'

Beverley nodded as if she understood completely how easy it was to mislay pieces of information like that.

'So the baby who was buried in the grounds of Westerham Castle is nothing to do with you?'

She shook her head. 'No. Not unless that nice couple done him in. That wouldn't be anything to do with me, anyway.'

Beverley smiled. 'Him?'

For the first time Fiona Bloom looked uncomfortable. 'I meant her.'

'It occurs to me that you've forgotten one thing too many, Fiona. The name of the couple who took your child, the name you used to book into the delivery suite – things like that, we can accept. But suddenly you're not too sure about the sex of the baby.'

'It was a long time ago.'

Beverley found this amusing. She said in a stage

304

whisper to Sauerwine, 'I wonder if Fiona can remember the sex of her mother.'

'Look, it was a slip of the tongue, okay? I meant "her". Done "her" in.'

'But you said "him". And that's interesting, because we haven't mentioned the gender of the baby found on the estate. Now, you know the score because we've been sitting here for six hours now and you know that we've unearthed the body of a baby on the estate, and you're here because you were pregnant at about that time and we discover that you've mislaid your child. So why do you assume that the child we've discovered was a boy, when you say that you had a girl?'

'I didn't think . . .'

Sauerwine jumped in. 'You've been lying to us all along, haven't you, Fiona? The whole story is crap. You didn't have a girl, you had a boy, and that boy is buried on the estate.'

'No.'

'We know that the boy was battered. Was it you who did it?'

'No!'

'Who was it, then?'

'It's not my baby.'

Beverley sighed. 'Look, Fiona. This is a small village community, how many babies get born around here? They're hardly dropping out of the trees at the rate of one a week.'

'It's not my baby.'

Sauerwine joined in again. 'Was it your father? Did he batter it?'

'I left before he could get the chance.'

'So you admit that he was violent.'

She laughed. 'Does the Pope wear a silly hat?'

'He beat you, didn't he?'

She was suddenly serious. 'Yes,' she said simply. 'He did. He was a fucker.'

'You're not sorry he's dead, then.'

'Do I look like I am?'

'Your brother killed him.'

She suddenly seemed tired, flopping back in her chair. 'So you said.'

'Doesn't that disturb you? Your brother killed your

305

father, and you don't care at all, it seems. You have a baby and it's vanished, but still you don't care. Doesn't anything bother you?'

She might have been staring at the ceiling, except that her eyes were tight shut. 'No,' she decided after a long moment's deep thought. 'Not a lot.'

Sauerwine joined in the eye-closing thing, adding his own twist by shaking his head. Beverley smiled to herself, then pointed out, 'We'll have the forensic tests back any time now, Fiona.'

'So?'

'So it'll prove that the dead baby is yours.'

For the first time, Fiona Bloom exhibited discomfort. Her head came down as her eyes opened, like the dolls that Beverley remembered from her childhood. 'How? It's been dead too long. It's just bones.'

Sauerwine, too, was alive now. 'And bones are enough, Fiona.'

'No, they're not . . .' She was uncertain, her knowledge of forensic molecular biology somewhat less than her knowledge of the laws regarding prostitution.

They were both nodding and each of them had an expression of grim, amused certainty. She took in each one individually, switching from one face to another, then closed her eyes and, just to make sure, checked them out again. Sauerwine saw the crack, got out his jemmy and stuck it in with a twist.

'They'll show that the baby's yours, because we can compare the DNA from the bones with the DNA we've taken from you. So what then, Fiona?'

She didn't reply, but then he wasn't particularly interested in a response.

'The baby's been battered, Fiona.'

She was thinking. The paradigm shift had occurred.

'Your baby was battered and then buried in an unmarked grave. You'd better have a good explanation about your daughter, Fiona. You'd better start remembering, I think, because unless you can persuade the jury that you had a daughter and that daughter is now alive and well, I think you're going to go to prison for a very, very long time.'

There was complete silence in the room for seconds that stretched into minutes before anyone had noticed. Fiona Bloom stared down at her hands, now clasped upon the plastic top of the table. Sauerwine watched the frown upon her face and listened to the beat of his heart; Beverley sat back in her chair with a slight smile upon her face.

Eventually, Fiona Bloom looked up at Sauerwine.

'Okay,' she said.

'Where's Felty?'

Jackson was making tea; he was always either making it or drinking it, or about to drink it or eyeing the recently emptied mug and thinking about making it. He never washed out this receptacle so that the inside was now a black hole of tannin, a place from which light, once confined to miserable captivity, never made an escape.

'She went out.'

'When?'

'An hour ago, maybe two.'

The annoyance that Sauerwine felt was not assuaged by Jackson's next remark. 'She was with that pathologist, Einstein.'

Surprised, Sauerwine said, 'Eisenmenger?'

'That's the chap.'

'Why on earth would she go out with him?' This question was rhetorical but Jackson was not up on the principles of ancient Greek debate.

'Dunno.'

It wasn't like Felty to be absent when required and he required her now to pick up Groshong who had suddenly become suspect number one. No matter what had happened between them personally, he could not allow her to come and go as she pleased, especially as the investigation was now entering the final, climacteric phase.

He was saved the need to take matters any further, however, because Felty returned at that moment. Before she could speak he said in a voice heavy with sarcasm, 'Nice of you to join us, Constable.'

She was surprised by his anger. 'I'm sorry, sir, I –'

'You were entertaining Dr Eisenmenger. I know. We need to find Malcolm Groshong, however, and we need to find him now.'

'Groshong? Why?'

'Because he's the father of the baby. Because he found Fiona Bloom in Leicester and then took it off her.'

'Why?'

'Because at the moment Christ only knows, and I want to know too.'

Letters from friends, some little more than single-line notes, others paragraph after paragraph of intimate, often irrelevant detail, or letters from relatives close and far. They were all here and as Helena read she found the context for them. This was clearly one of several volumes, an episode in a lifelong habit perhaps of collecting the letters written to Nell. The earliest letter was dated eleven years before, the latest just eight.

Eight. That number again.

She had to stop and cast her thoughts to one side; why was she weeping so easily? Had she healed so little that these peripheral allusions to her past, to her parents, to her childhood, were too painful to bear? Was she doomed to be forever disconnected from the first twenty years of her life, an orphan in more ways than one?

The silence in the room was only deepened and broadened and frozen by the wind outside; she heard occasional slaps of rain against the glass of the windows. Her breathing was artificial and loud in this strange, cold place.

At long last her eyes cleared and she turned again to the letters.

There were gaps of several months, one of over a year, when her parents had not written. Mostly it had been her father, less often her mother, who put down on paper all the trivia that form the bonds of intimate friendship, that signify and strengthen the love between those who know each other beyond the superficial. These lacunae were filled by Nell's parents, Eleanor, people that Helena did not know; she saw not one from Hugo and this made her wonder as she turned the pages over. She kept noting the dates, aware that she was heading for that fateful time when there had been a cataclysmic change in her life – in all their lives – and still she read nothing that suggested any impending doom, saw no clues as to what her father might have been alluding to in his last letters.

I'm only reading half the story. It's like trying to find out whodunit when you can see only every other sentence.

And she wondered why she had thought of a whodunit.

Inexorably the dates on the letters moved towards the

time that interested her they became fewer, and then she reached familiar territory. She read the letter from her father again, wondering if she had misread, if there were some message in the words that she had missed the first time, finding none.

Eisenmenger had walked a long way during the day and was very tired. The appearance of Groshong in a Land Rover was potentially miraculous.

'Lift?'

He was leaning across the passenger seat through the open window. He wasn't smiling, didn't even look particularly welcoming, but for Malcolm Groshong that was the norm. Eisenmenger had no reason not to accept, yet felt uneasy as he climbed in.

You have committed an offence so . . .

This phrase, so portentous, so intriguing, had recurred constantly as she read through the letters. She had tried not to guess what it might have meant, but inevitably there had been a small part of her that had done nothing but guess, a constant, ill-defined background drone of questions, hypotheses and prurience forever playing in her mind.

She reached the relevant letter at last, her eyes briefly scanning the writing until she found that curious phrase again.

> *. . . you have committed an offence so shocking that maybe only God himself can truly forgive you, and move on as if nothing had happened, but that does not mean that we will not remain constant in our love and affection for you . . .*

Her father, ever the lawyer, had always had a courtly hand and a style to go with it; even in this long-past letter to another she heard his clear and precise enunciation, saw his slight stoop and his searching brown eyes.

> *Can one separate the sin from the sinner? We believe so and I have lived my professional life in such hope. In any case, you are young and it would be unfair to place the burden of culpability solely upon your shoulders. This is a shared catastrophe and you, being the younger party, ought to be considered appropriately less guilty . . .*

Helena recognized how he was working this through in his own head, using his professional skills to weather the shock that he so clearly felt. But shock of what?

You have asked us not to speak of this with anyone and of course we'll respect your wishes insofar as spreading this beyond those who already know. Do your parents know that you have told us? Would you like me to speak with your father, offering whatever help and advice we can under these extraordinarily distressing circumstances . . .

But what were they? Helena found herself frustrated into impotent anger that the subject was being danced around, as if it were too hideous to be mentioned, as if it were talismanic of evil.

Her frustration was not to be pricked, however, for the remainder of the letter resorted to the mundane; news of Helena and Jeremy, mainly. Helena was suffering from glandular fever (she remembered how miserable she had felt and, presumably, how miserable she had been with others) and Jeremy . . .

Jeremy had been at university but not doing well. Her father's language could not hide his disappointment and worry. It brought back to her vague recollections of this time – all but obliterated by subsequent events – when there had been talk of excessive drinking, poor academic achievement, unpleasant behaviour. It had been so unlike the Jeremy she had known.

And that was it. The final few letters were irrelevant, the last dated only a couple of weeks later.

She had no clues, only intimations, not of mortality but of deep, dark secrets.

She looked up at the window, black and cold against the lit stone of the surrounding wall.

'What was your sin, Nell?' she asked softly.

And from close behind came Hugo's voice, soft and sad.

'She loved, Helena. She loved too much.'

Helena jumped and twisted around, startled to discover the he was standing behind her on the opposite side of the bed. He was shockingly close.

Close enough to lift the mallet in his hand and bring it down hard on the side of her head.

Part Seven

They were nearing the estate when Groshong's mobile phone rang.

'Groshong.'

He wasn't using a hands-free and hadn't slowed down; his eyes remained concentrated on the darkness ahead.

'Okay.'

And that was it. He terminated the call without looking at the keypad and drove on.

Perhaps two minutes later and barely slowing he turned the steering wheel sharply to the right and drove up a narrow track that led from a partially hidden gap in the wall around the south side of the estate.

'Where are we going?'

'There's something I need to show you.'

Eisenmenger looked at Groshong's profile.

He suddenly felt very nervous.

Hugo looked down at Helena's unconscious form, his hand reaching into his pocket for his mobile phone. His eyes didn't leave Helena as he rang a number.

'Hello, Malcolm. I'm afraid it's as we feared. I have Helena here. I think we need to meet. At the boating house by the lake.'

He cut the connection, continuing to stare. 'But I see no need to rush . . .'

He reached down to touch her face; there was blood trickling down her temple and her face was pale. He touched the blood, pulled back then considered her again. He murmured, 'I always wondered . . .'

He reached down again. She was on her back, skewed slightly to the left with her legs hanging down the side of

311

the bed. He picked her legs up and straightened her body so that she lay on the bed. Then he straightened up again. On his face was a smile.

'*Carpe diem*,' he said then. 'There is a tide . . .'

When he reached down for the third time it was to her knees, to separate them. Her skirt was quite short and had ridden up; his hand moved upwards. His smile broadened and he took a deep breath. He sat there for a few minutes, stroking his hand up and down, moving slowly and languidly.

He sat down beside her, withdrew his hand and began to unbutton her blouse, exposing the navy blue bra beneath. He slipped his fingers under it, running them from side to side. He sighed again.

Abruptly he stood up, and without any ceremony at all spread her legs as wide as they would go. Then he began to undo his trousers.

Eisenmenger was a patient man but after ten minutes of riding along what might, in another life, have been a track through previously undiscovered Papua New Guinea, he decided that he had supped enough from this particular cup.

'Where are we going?'

Groshong was looking ahead intently and Eisenmenger couldn't blame him, given the fact that it was completely lightless and they were travelling through dense forest. He didn't respond for a long while.

'To meet Helena.'

Eisenmenger had not expected that answer. 'Helena?'

Groshong wasn't given to nodding. He said only, 'Aye.'

'That was Helena who called you?'

'Hugo. He's with her.'

Eisenmenger said in a steady voice, 'Perhaps I'd better call Helena.'

Groshong didn't respond straight away. 'If you like.'

Eisenmenger keyed in a number, held the phone up to his ear and waited. Groshong might have had neck spasm so fixed was his gaze upon the road ahead. They were being shaken from side to side but he took no interest in this; he was driving as if he had a mission; Eisenmenger had the feeling that he was being driven into something a good deal darker than the lightless night outside.

Eventually he took the phone away from his ear. 'No answer,' he said. He put it in his breast pocket.

Groshong drove on, his face unchanged.

'No!'

Hugo jumped visibly, swinging round. Nell emerged from the piles of junk, walking unsteadily, as if she were suffering from a palsy. On his face a look of uncertainty gave way to a smile. 'Nell! I didn't realize . . .'

Nell was looking at Helena. 'Why?' she asked, whispered.

Hugo was zipping up his trousers as if nothing had happened, as if nothing had been about to happen. 'She knows, Nell. We can't allow that.'

'But it's Helena.'

He shook his head. 'Doesn't matter. She knows.'

Nell had gone to Helena, sitting down beside her, wiping the blood that had now tracked down to stain the sheets. 'She wouldn't have told.'

Hugo snorted. 'Wouldn't she? What about her parents?'

'They didn't tell.'

He came over to the bed. 'Only because we were lucky, Nell. Who knows what they would have done.'

He squatted down beside her and put his arm around her waist as she buttoned Helena's blouse. 'I didn't want to do this, but for the good of the family, it has to be done. It's not just Helena, is it? What about her boyfriend? He has no allegiance to us; he has no love for you or me.'

But it seemed that she wasn't listening. She asked, 'What were you going to do?'

'Nothing.'

She frowned. 'I'm not stupid, Hugo. I know . . .'

Then why did you ask?

He shrugged and said, 'You'd better go.'

'What are you going to do?'

'I'm going to take her to her boyfriend. Have a chat. See if we can't come to some sort of arrangement.'

She stared at him. 'You won't hurt her, will you?'

He smiled. 'Of course not.'

He bent down over the inert Helena, picking her up

313

easily. At the top of the stairs he looked back at his sister. 'Don't you worry, Nell. I'll sort it all out.'

He smiled again.

She reciprocated, but it was an uncertain, almost forced smile that she offered him.

'There's no answer from Groshong's home phone. We haven't got his mobile number.'

'What about the castle?'

'The nanny answered the phone. She didn't know the whereabouts of Groshong.'

'And the Hickmans?'

'They're out at some social do.'

Sauerwine looked across at Wharton who was standing at the window staring at darkness, perhaps also seeing the spectral reflection of his office. 'What do you think? Has he done a runner?'

She turned round. 'Why should he? He doesn't know that we're on to him.'

Felty said then, 'Sir?'

'What is it, Felty?'

She had a feeling she was going to suffer for what she said next but was more afraid of saying nothing. 'Dr Eisenmenger thinks that there may be more than one killer.'

Sauerwine snorted. 'Does he really? I don't suppose he gave you any names, did he?'

She shook her head and as far as Sauerwine was concerned, that was it. Beverley, however, remained interested. She asked, 'Where is he now?'

'Gone back to the castle, I assume.'

Beverley looked at her watch. 'Hasn't got there yet, I suppose.'

Sauerwine wasn't interested. 'We'd better get over to the castle and look around. That place is like a labyrinth; Groshong might be hiding anywhere.' He got up. 'Come on, there's no point in waiting here.'

Beverley didn't move. 'You go with Felty. I'll wait here.'

'Why?'

She didn't know why but she said, 'Just in case.'

314

Sauerwine looked at her oddly but then shrugged and left followed by Felty, her head down.

Hugo carried Helena down the stairs and then along the corridor, happy that he would not be disturbed; Tom was asleep, Dominique was tending to Eleanor and his parents were out. He was quite cheerful.

Beverley sat down behind Sauerwine's desk and tried to work out why she was staying put. For five minutes she sat there, part of her knowing she had done the right thing, part of her knowing she had not.

Her mobile phone rang.

'Hello?'

She received no answer. There was the sound of a car engine and the sound of creaking and an ill-defined and intermittent, irregular swishing noise.

'Hello?'

She was about to terminate the connection when quite distinctly she heard the words, 'No answer.'

It had been John Eisenmenger's voice, she was quite certain.

'John?'

There was a rustling sound but no human response.

She continued to listen.

'What's going on, Malcolm? Where are they?'

'By the lake. Apparently they've discovered something.'

'What?'

'Didn't say.'

'To do with what? The baby?'

'That's right.'

It began to rain.

Hugo put Helena down on the gravel beside Eisenmenger's car, felt in his pocket and produced a key. He smiled at it. 'Be prepared,' he whispered. He loaded Helena into the back, cold raindrops falling on his back. He looked briefly down at her, considered, then shook his

315

head, a rueful grin on his face. He shut the door as quietly as he could, climbed in behind the steering wheel and drove off to meet Groshong.

What's going on, Malcolm. Where are they?

It was indistinct but recognizably Eisenmenger. Where, however, were who?

By the lake. Apparently they've discovered something.

Westerham lake, then. She knew enough of the estate to know that it was a big lake.

What?

Didn't say.

To do with what? The baby?

That's right.

She listened for more, heard none.

Without switching off the phone she stood up. Covering the receiver she strode out of the office. 'Holt?' He looked up. 'Get a car. Now.'

He saw the urgency and was out of the door without delay.

'Has he scarpered, Sally?'

She noticed the use of her first name but said only, 'Don't know, sir.' It was now raining heavily; a slashing vicious rain that looked cold and was almost certainly colder.

Sauerwine was clearly worried but she couldn't bring any sympathy to bear. She owed him nothing, not any more.

'Eisenmenger doesn't know everything.' He wondered why he had said that as soon as the words were there between them.

'No.'

'Groshong took the child from Fiona Bloom. Even if he didn't kill the baby, he's got a story to tell.'

Felty had turned the car right along the winding drive that took them to the castle forecourt. Whatever reply she might have made was lost because of events.

'Who's that?'

Sauerwine was referring to a figure that ran toward the car. It looked as if it had been pulled from the river, bedraggled and wet. Felty stopped the car and Sauerwine got out. The figure ran up to them.

'Miss Hickman?'

'He's got Helena.' She was already half frozen. Her hair was obscuring her face and she was shivering. She might have been crying but Sauerwine couldn't tell.

'Who has?'

'Hugo.'

'Hugo?' Sauerwine had been certain she would say Groshong. Groshong was the villain.

'We've got to stop him. I don't trust him . . .'

He wasn't sure what was going on and uncertainty was hindering him. Then the radio spoke.

'Andrew?'

It was Beverley's voice. To Nell he said, 'Get in.' He shut the rear door when she was in the car, got in himself and picked up the radio. 'What is it?'

'Groshong's taking John Eisenmenger to the lake. I think he's in danger.'

Another development that he didn't understand; suddenly it seemed that not only was he trying to fit the wrong piece into the wrong place in the puzzle, he was trying to fit it into the wrong puzzle altogether.

'How do you know?'

But Beverley wasn't interested in explaining her miraculous knowledge. 'Just get over to Westerham lake, Andrew. It's a big area to cover. You'll need to rustle up some more cars.'

He looked at Felty, radiating confusion, and found her just staring back. 'Shall I?' she asked.

He turned around to Nell. 'Could your brother be going to the lake?'

He didn't appreciate it at the time, but it was a significant deductive leap. She didn't know. At last he made a decision. 'Okay. Get to the lake.'

'What about Hugo and Helena Flemming?'

'One problem at a time. We came here for Groshong and he's the one we're going to get.'

The waters of the lake were difficult to see in the gloom but Eisenmenger could hear them; the lapping on the narrow shingle beach, the spattering rain on its surface, occasional louder slaps as water hit a flat, hard object. He had been ordered from the Land Rover by Groshong, all pretence at amicability vanishing into the cold. He had thought perhaps to run as soon as they came to a halt but Groshong had put an end to that.

'Don't try to run. Helena's here and I think she's going to need you.'

Shit.

He hoped that the battery in his mobile phone would last.

Helena's here and I think she's going to need you.

Beverley strained to catch the words. Whatever was happening was significant, she knew. Eisenmenger's words – 'more than one murderer' – came back to her. What had he meant?

Where are we?

She listened intently. Eisenmenger was attempting to guide her.

I told you. At the lake.

Groshong's voice was fainter, more distorted, and she had to clamp the phone to her ear.

Where at the lake?

You don't need to bother about that.

Damn!

Groshong produced a broken shotgun from behind Eisenmenger who cursed himself for not thinking that there might have been one in the back of the car. The estate manager climbed out and went around the front to Eisenmenger's side. He opened the door. 'Get out.' He was already soaked, with rain dripping from his chin and nose.

Eisenmenger complied. The rain was freezing. 'Where to?'

Groshong gestured over to the right but said nothing.

Eisenmenger turned and walked in the direction indicated. Before long they reached the side of the lake. Its surface was dancing, a frenzy of chaos that disappeared quickly into dark unknown. Eisenmenger called loudly, 'We're at the water's edge. Where now?'

'To the right.'

Eisenmenger looked desperately for landmarks but he hardly knew the place even in daylight. They trudged along for several minutes before something began to appear from the darkness ahead. Some sort of landing stage stretching out into the water.

He called out, 'Is that where we're going? The landing stage?'

Groshong's voice came back almost lazily. 'Aye.'

Where to?

Try as she might, Beverley could hear no reply. Had she missed it?

A pause, then, *We're at the water's edge. Where now?*

To the right.

So they were right on the lake. Not that this was much help – the shoreline was several kilometres long and in the dark they would have to cover every centimetre of it. All the police in Gloucestershire wouldn't be enough. She had to have something else, a unique landmark of some kind. She said to Holt, 'Get as close to the waterside as you can manage.'

And then the signal cut out.

Sauerwine had called Tanner at home who had promised as much manpower as he could muster. Felty by now had nearly arrived at the lakeside. On the radio he asked, 'Where are you?'

She checked with Holt. 'On the south side.'

'We're on the west.'

'They're somewhere along the shoreline but I don't know where. Apparently they're going to where Helena is.'

Sauerwine looked at Nell and said into the radio, 'In that case Hugo's there as well.'

He thought how best to proceed. 'Okay, you move anticlockwise, I'll go clockwise. Felty can go anticlockwise back round to where you are.'

But Nell said, 'I think I know where they are.'

Sauerwine turned to her. 'Where?'

'The only building around the lake is an old boathouse. It's where we used to go as children. Maybe Hugo's taken Helena there.'

'Where is it?'

She pointed to their left. 'I should think it's about a kilometre in that direction.'

Sauerwine relayed the information to Beverley. 'You'd better do as we originally planned, but I'll go with Felty to this boathouse first. Check it out.'

'How long before we get some back-up?'

'About five minutes.'

Beverley looked at Holt. 'You can die a lot of times in five minutes.'

There was a dilapidated building at the end of the pier; it had presumably once been a boathouse but was now little more than kindling held together by ivy and tradition. Groshong said, 'There. Round the back.'

'The boathouse?' Eisenmenger said this as loudly as he dared.

Groshong said impatiently, 'Where else?'

'Which side of the lake are we on?'

'What the fuck does that matter?'

Eisenmenger had no answer that he wanted Groshong to hear.

They walked around the side of the boathouse. Eisenmenger saw his car, Hugo in the driving seat; he could not see Helena. Hugo got out, looking up briefly at the sky as if pained to be treated thus, then hunched his shoulders as he walked towards him.

'Hello, John.'

'What's going on, Hugo?'

Hugo apparently didn't hear. To Groshong he said, 'Did anyone see you?'

'No.'

Hugo nodded. He said to Eisenmenger, 'If you'd walk over to the car . . .'

'And if I don't?'

Hugo wasn't comfortable in the cold pouring rain but he managed a smile. 'Helena's in the back of this car. She's unconscious. I'll slit her throat.'

'Not much finesse there. Not like Moynihan's death. It was you, wasn't it?'

Hugo didn't seem inclined to elucidate. 'Just do as I ask.'

320

'We're going to die anyway, aren't we?'

'But at the moment, you're hoping for salvation, I would guess. You want time to think of something; the clock runs out as soon as I pick up Helena and dump her in the lake with a few bricks tied to her feet.'

'And how will we die if I do as you ask?'

He looked out past Eisenmenger to Westerham lake. 'It's a big lake; deep, too. At its centre, it's said to be two kilometres down to the bottom. I can't see the police ever finding the bodies.'

Eisenmenger tried disdain. 'So we disappear. And the car?'

'I reckon we've got eighteen hours before you're missed. Time enough to dispose of the car. You left late this evening, wanting to get away.'

'Pretty thin.'

Hugo shrugged. 'Not my best, I'll admit, but no bodies, no murder.'

'Don't bet on it.'

'If everyone tells the same story, there'll be no case to answer. They might have their suspicions but the family will stick together. It always does.'

'Mater and Pater will do the necessary, eh? Like they did when you slaughtered Helena's parents?'

Hugo grinned. 'Poor Claude and Penny? We were as shocked and surprised as anyone.'

'You can tell me, Hugo. I'm going to die, remember?'

Hugo snorted. 'Whatever happens to you, Dr Eisenmenger, I'm not about to confess to a murder or two I didn't commit.'

Eisenmenger didn't want to believe him, yet he almost did. Groshong said, 'Time to go.'

Hugo stood to one side. 'If you wouldn't mind, John, can you pick up Helena for me?' He smiled ingratiatingly but it was the prod in the back with the shotgun that made Eisenmenger move.

'You'd better stay here, Miss Hickman.'

It was the last thing that Sauerwine had said before he had set off to the left and Felty had set off to right.

She had waited two minutes and then got out of the car.

*   *   *

Helena wasn't heavy but the rain had now been joined by a rising wind and the landing stage upon which he was being forced to walk was not only rickety but also slippery.

Where the hell is Beverley?

He called over his shoulder, 'Why don't you just shoot us on land?'

Behind him walked Groshong with the shotgun; behind Groshong walked Hugo with a large torch. It was Hugo who said, 'Why have a dog and bark yourself?'

She can't have got the message.

Eisenmenger said, 'You killed Moynihan, didn't you, Hugo?'

Groshong prodded him hard but Hugo now seemed more amenable. 'That's right.'

Eisenmenger nodded. Obviously he was on his own and all he had left was talk; it was perhaps all he had ever had. 'Why?'

'Because Malcolm needed an alibi.'

'And you were a long way away and without any obvious motive for killing William Moynihan.'

He had reached the end of the landing stage. There was a rowing boat moored there. He turned around, still holding Helena although by now she was becoming heavy and his arms were aching. 'You set fire to that car without killing him first, didn't you? That was cruel beyond belief, Hugo.'

He wasn't visibly bothered by this accusation. 'Couldn't risk hurting him before he died. I know how clever you chaps are. Might have made some fantastic deduction from the remains and the next thing I know, the plod are knocking at my door.'

There was a certain irony that it was at this moment that Sauerwine called from the shore by the boathouse, 'Put the gun down, Mr Groshong.'

Hugo looked around at Sauerwine and Felty but Groshong didn't react other than to put the gun to his shoulder and move right up to Eisenmenger; the barrels now pointed directly at his head. After a moment of uncertainty Hugo saw what Groshong had done and called out, 'Inspector Sauerwine! Not a particularly clement night, is it?'

'There's no point, Dr Hickman. Just tell Mr Groshong to put the gun down and come back to the shore.'

Hugo turned theatrically to survey what was going on at the end of the landing stage. Eisenmenger felt that his arms were about to suffer terminal ischaemia but it was more likely that he would die from third-degree chilblains. Hugo turned back to the shore. 'Why?'

'Don't play silly buggers, Dr Hickman. There's nowhere to go.'

'Isn't there?' He paused. 'How about this, then? How about you let us go or we'll turn Dr Eisenmenger's head into a three-dimensional pizza?'

Sauerwine and Felty were a fair way off and, like the rest of them, very wet. From where Eisenmenger stood the Inspector might have been fully confident, he might have been about to faint. Sauerwine's voice didn't give him much hope. 'Within a couple of minutes there are going to be about fifteen policemen here.'

'Then I suggest you get out of the way straight away. We obviously need to be elsewhere.' He turned to Groshong. 'Malcolm, would you kill one of them, please?'

Groshong moved the gun around to his face at once and for half a second Eisenmenger knew that he was about to die.

'No!'

Hugo looked at Sauerwine.

'All right. You win. We'll back away.'

Sauerwine turned to Felty. 'Get in contact with Jackson,' he whispered. 'We need the entire estate cut off.'

Hugo began to walk back along the landing stage. Groshong gestured with the shotgun for Eisenmenger to follow as he edged backwards.

When they reached the shore, they formed a little group with Eisenmenger and Helena at the front, Hugo and Groshong at the rear. Sauerwine stood to one side. Felty had faded into the woods.

Hugo said, 'Right. We're going to get into Dr Eisenmenger's car and you're going to let us go.'

'Okay.'

Hugo nodded. He whispered something to Groshong who then prodded Eisenmenger in the back. The party began to move along the side of the boathouse.

They had reached about halfway when Nell appeared from the darkness of the trees.

Beverley and Holt were moving as quickly as they could along the far shore when Felty's message came through that Hugo and Groshong were at the boathouse. They immediately turned around and made their way back to the car.

Like the rest of them Nell was completely drenched. She was shivering and looked half dead with cold. 'Don't, Hugo.'

Hugo was undoubtedly surprised but he had a resilient insouciance. 'Nell! You shouldn't be out in weather like this –'

'Let them go, Hugo.'

'Can't, Nell. It's gone too far for that.'

'Let them go.'

'Go home, Nell. We'll be all right.'

'NO!'

That made even Hugo pause. She began to walk forward; her hand was held out. 'Give me the gun, Malcolm.'

Groshong looked uncertain for the first time that evening. Hugo said, 'Please, Nell.'

She continued her march.

'Please, Nell.' Hugo sounded more desperate now. Groshong looked more uncertain. Eisenmenger looked on aware that his arms were now so numb they were like huge fuzzy appendages; Sauerwine called out urgently, 'Don't be silly, Miss Hickman. Come back.'

But she didn't.

'It's over, Hugo.'

Eisenmenger knelt as quietly as he could and put Helena on the ground. Groshong's shotgun was no longer pointing directly at him and his eyes were on Nell. He reckoned he could get to the gun before Groshong would be able to react, helped by the constant sound of rain and the wind in the trees. The trouble was that he would be liable to push the gun towards Nell and, more distantly,

324

Sauerwine, but he hoped to be able to push the gun upward into the sky. Then he would just have to hope that Sauerwine and Felty could get to him before Groshong and Hugo overcame him.

He readied himself, an unverbalized prayer in his head.

And then Helena groaned.

Sauerwine saw Eisenmenger put Helena down and guessed that he might be about to do something.

Don't do it.

Groshong swung around at the sound of the groan, saw Eisenmenger readying himself to spring towards him.

Nell and Sauerwine saw Groshong turning towards Eisenmenger. Simultaneously they began to charge forward.

Groshong became aware of more movement out of the corner of his eye. He hesitated and this allowed Eisenmenger to grab the gun. They tussled for a moment with the gun but Eisenmenger's arms were weak and numb and his grip slipped. Groshong's momentum caused him stagger back and round. His fingers were still on the triggers of the shotgun as the barrels moved in an arc towards Nell, now only two metres or so away.

The gun fired.

Sauerwine was a good ten metres away but he saw it all quite clearly. He saw Eisenmenger grab the gun barrel, he saw his grip slip and he saw Groshong staggering slightly as the shotgun moved back round to Nell. He saw the glare from both barrels as there was a deafening blast.

He saw Nell fly backward, suddenly limp, almost performing a backflip.

A backflip that brought her face, upside down, into his view and a backflip that brought in his view a nightmare for the future.

Her pretty face had gone, replaced with red, ripped

flesh, the rain already mixing with the blood. Both eyes were punctured, the mouth was a ragged maw, the front of her throat gone.

She fell back lifelessly into the flooded mud.

There was a second in which no one moved. A second in which the blast continued in their heads, in which Nell had not died. It was Hugo who reacted first; until then a spectator he now seemed to emerge from stasis but all that he could find was an agonized howl, a scream of protest, an ululation.

He moved forward to his sister, the first to do so. Sauerwine, having paused in shock, then also ran to her. Eisenmenger remained motionless; he knew that Nell was dead even before she splashed on her back to the ground.

He knew also, looking at the remains of her face, that it was a blessing.

Felty, too, stood without moving, her face distorted by horror.

Thus they were all looking down at Nell as Beverley and Holt came crashing through the undergrowth.

They sat around the table in the kitchen. Eisenmenger and Helena sat together at one end, Tristan held Theresa at the other, and Sauerwine and Beverley sat opposite each other between them. Felty sat away from the table on a stool taking notes. Except for Tristan and Theresa all were soaked through but they had not had the luxury of showers and a change of clothes. Eisenmenger had wanted Helena to go to hospital – the paramedics had been incandescent when she had refused – but she had a story to tell. She was groggy and she was paper-white; Eisenmenger knew that she was concussed and had struck a deal with her. He would take her to hospital as soon as they had finished with Sauerwine. Theresa was completely destroyed by the news that had greeted them when they returned from their engagement. Hugo was in custody but had the look of a man who had lost the will to live. Eisenmenger had his eyes on Beverley as he said, 'I think that this all started a long time ago.'

Sauerwine was clearly close to the end of a long and frayed tether; Beverley looked no happier but perhaps for different reasons. Sauerwine said, 'Let me guess – eight or nine years?'

Eisenmenger's smile lasted half a moment, no longer. 'You might say a hundred years; it's difficult to be certain.'

'Oh, great.'

'Let's begin by going back twenty years when the Flemmings and the Hickmans were close and so their children were close. Helena and Jeremy, Nell and Hugo. Helena's talked about the summers and the Christmases, the holidays and picnics; they were wonderful times for her. Idyllic, I would say.'

'Is this relevant?'

He ignored the interruption. 'Unfortunately, all good things must end. Jeremy went to university, people grew up, the foursome was broken up. And with that there was imbalance. Things changed.'

Sauerwine didn't follow him. 'In what way?'

Eisenmenger looked almost embarrassed as he said quietly, 'Incest.'

'What?'

Helena spoke up as if from a dream. 'Incest. He and Nell. My father and mother knew because Nell wrote and told them. She kept my father's letters to her. I read them.'

Sauerwine, shaken and feeling almost in free fall, was throwing glances around the room as if looking for a sniper. Beverley, less animated but also bearing a disconcerted expression, contented herself with staring at Eisenmenger.

Into the silence Tristan said, 'We missed it. That's how good we were at parenting. We completely missed what was going on.' His tone was sadness tinged with self-loathing. Helena heard no self-pity. 'I was the busy surgeon, making sure that I secured the next merit award, dancing the dance that would get me the presidency of the College; Theresa had her charity work. We thought that they had grown up . . .'

They had. Eisenmenger bit down on the words. It was too easy to criticize.

Tristan continued, 'And then Nell fell pregnant.'

Sauerwine's question was almost timorous. 'And was Hugo the father?'

'We didn't know at first. Hugo was on his gap year, travelling in the Far East. When we discovered, Nell at first refused to say who the father was. There had been this lad – Richard – who had been interested in Nell; I suppose we jumped to conclusions that Nell didn't contradict.

'And then Tom was born . . .' His voice broke and tears were clearly visible in his eyes. He looked sideways at his wife as if requesting her to take over but she had her eyes fixed resolutely upon her clasped hands. Eventually he continued, 'He was weak, sickly. We didn't know why . . .'

At last Theresa spoke. 'It was only when Hugo returned that we learned the truth.'

Beverley spoke for the first time. 'How? How did you find out?'

Theresa looked at her. 'You don't know Hugo. He likes to shock, to disconcert. He couldn't resist trying to get a reaction from us.'

Sauerwine looked at Beverley before asking, 'Okay. So we've got yet another crime. I was hoping to have a few of the original ones cleared up.'

Eisenmenger turned to Tristan. 'Your grandson died. How?'

'Hang on a minute!' This from Sauerwine. 'What are you talking about?'

Eisenmenger asked him simply, 'Who else do you think is the baby buried on the estate?'

Sauerwine's temper was not helped by a noise from Beverley that might have been a snort. Having glared at her he turned around to Eisenmenger and asked, 'How can you know that?'

'Well it's not Fiona Bloom's,' he pointed out, although how he knew that wasn't clear. 'So who else's can it be?'

Sauerwine opened his mouth, found nothing to say and shut it again. Eisenmenger asked the Hickmans, 'How did your grandson die?'

Theresa began almost immediately to weep again. Tristan held her and said, 'He was a small and sickly child – you can check with the hospital that he failed to thrive. One night he died in his sleep.'

Sauerwine pointed out, 'There were broken ribs.'

Tristan's voice was tired enough to die. 'Nell loved him. When he died she couldn't accept it. She hugged him, tried to revive him; she was hysterical for days.'

There was silence; nobody disbelieved him.

Eisenmenger, aware that Helena seemed to be looking greyer by the minute, pushed on. 'Which gave you a problem. You could, I suppose, have gone the legal route and informed the authorities of Tom's death, but there was the danger that someone would find out about his parentage. You knew that a paediatric post-mortem involves genetic investigations – that would have been a colossal risk for you.'

Tristan was staring at him but said nothing. Eisenmenger continued, 'So you buried the baby and needed a replacement.'

Sauerwine was at last able to contribute. 'Fiona Bloom.'

'Exactly. Fiona Bloom had left the village a little before and she had been pregnant.'

Sauerwine asked, 'But how would they know where to find her? She was hardly likely to keep in touch with the Hickmans.'

'No, but she had kept in touch with the father.'

Felty saw. 'Groshong.'

Eisenmenger nodded. 'Malcolm Groshong has been this family's support for decades. He looks after not only the estate but also each and every Hickman. He is devoted to this family, would do anything – absolutely anything – to protect it.

'It was Groshong who knew that Fiona Bloom didn't want her bouncing baby boy and he persuaded her to give him a home in a castle, a lifestyle she could never have provided herself.'

Beverley said quietly, 'Lucky it wasn't a girl.'

'It would have been a problem, but not an insurmountable one, I think. Eastern Europe, perhaps.'

Tristan murmured, 'The problem was that Nell couldn't accept him as her son. He was little more than a nephew, I think.'

Eisenmenger had his eyes on Helena when he said, 'You had a greater problem than that, I think.'

Tristan's eyes found his and he saw incomprehension.

329

He looked back at Helena as he said, 'Claude and Penny Flemming.'

Helena looked ready to drop but that brought her back.

Nor was she the only one galvanized by these names. Beverley's face became waxen while Tristan looked round at him and Theresa took her head from his shoulder.

It was Helena who spoke first. 'What do you mean?'

He dropped his eyes to the wood of the table. 'Because they were Nell's godparents and she was close to them. Because she had confided in them. What was the phrase? *An offence so shocking that maybe only God himself can forgive you.* Almost a biblical phrase; certainly one speaking of no ordinary trespass.'

'Nell's incest.' Helena whispered the words, looking across at Theresa and Tristan with eyes that were full of sick realization.

'It was bad enough, I think, that anyone outside the close family circle knew the truth, but I suspect that the final straw was her confession to your parents that the baby was dead; somebody else knew the facts and that couldn't be risked.'

Theresa's eyes were wide, almost unnaturally so. Tristan, too, bore an expression of incredulity. Eisenmenger examined them both clinically. There was an air of decision about him as he turned back to Helena. 'I think a decision was made to remove the risk.'

Tristan spoke at last. 'No . . . You're wrong. It was a horrible coincidence. I was as shocked as everyone else –'

Eisenmenger cut across him. 'Not Malcolm Groshong. I think he was their killer.'

He caught a stare from Beverley, ignored it. Helena was shaking her head slowly. Tristan said, 'Malcolm?'

Eisenmenger addressed Sauerwine. 'I think that neither Tristan nor Theresa knew about the decision that was made to safeguard the Hickman family name. I think that their shock when the Flemmings were killed was genuine.'

Beverley spoke as if she was drugged. 'You said that a decision was made. Who made it?'

Eisenmenger had exploded a few bombs that evening but the one he detonated then was a killer.

'Eleanor.'

*   *   *

No one believed him but that didn't surprise him. Eleanor was old, she was gentle, she was demented. How could she have demanded the execution of two decent, innocent human beings?

'We'll never know now, I think. It may not even have been anything more than a suggestion, reminiscent of the murder of Thomas à Becket. Whatever happened, I think that Malcolm Groshong killed Helena's parents because he understood that that was what Eleanor Hickman desired.'

Tristan was strident. 'This is unbelievable. You're just taking advantage of a helpless old woman.'

'Eleanor has a sense of history and a sense of family; not only does she have them, they have her. She's ruled by them. I think that she saw no other way and in Groshong she had the perfect tool. He's devoted to her; he works for the Hickmans but he lives for Eleanor.'

It was clear that Tristan and Theresa didn't believe him, but it was equally clear that they would never believe him. Eisenmenger said thoughtfully, 'I can't decide if Hugo knew, though.'

He frowned as if the final clue in the crossword was just beyond him.

Sauerwine asked, 'Can we get this absolutely straight? You're claiming that Groshong killed Claude and Penelope Flemming?'

'That's right.'

Beverley shook her head. 'What proof do you have?'

Eisenmenger shrugged. 'None, but it makes sense. It explains the death of William Moynihan.'

'How?'

'Because while all this was going on the feud between Moynihan and Groshong was rumbling on. In order to make the murders look like the unfortunate consequence of a robbery, Groshong had taken certain items from the murder scene, including a watch and, apparently, a photograph.' He frowned. 'I can't work that one out. Why a photograph? It was of no obvious intrinsic value and therefore useless in the attempt to make the crime look like a robbery.' He paused, then asked Helena, 'Was the watch kept in its box?'

She tried to think for a while but was in no proper

state to give the matter deep consideration. Eventually, 'I don't know.'

'That's the only thing I can think of. That Groshong took the watch, box and all, and that the photograph was in the box. He then discarded the box and somehow the photograph fell out.

'My assumption is that then Moynihan found it. I don't know how – he probably borrowed the car in the course of his estate duties; he may even have had the job of cleaning it or something.

'He knew something was going on because he worked on the estate and because he probably had known that Groshong was mysteriously away on the night of the murders. He didn't have enough, though, to pin anything on Groshong, to take his revenge.'

Beverley's sudden intervention surprised Eisenmenger, especially as her tone was almost sepulchral. 'How did he know where to dig? He was the one, wasn't he? The one who dug at the base of the tree.'

To everyone's surprise it was Tristan who answered. 'He worked on the estate, doing forestry and general maintenance. I wonder if he noticed the disturbed ground. He must have suspected something was going on; it was only shortly after that they had the row that resulted in Moynihan getting his marching orders.'

There was silence for a while until Eisenmenger said, 'And so there it lay for eight years, until Moynihan happened to meet his old sweetheart, and to ask her awkward questions. Like where the child was, and why did she have a watch which he had a shrewd idea had been stolen when the Flemmings were murdered.'

Felty suddenly asked, 'But why did Groshong give her the watch in the first place?'

Eisenmenger smiled. 'He loved her.'

Sauerwine nodded as if it were obvious.

Eisenmenger continued, 'Moynihan wanted revenge in the form of blackmail. He turned up here and made it known to Groshong that he could prove a few unpleasant facts. I would guess he demanded money.

'Groshong needed him removed but couldn't easily do it himself. Hugo, though, was in Nottingham. A long way away and not obviously connected with William Moynihan in any way.'

Theresa found defiance. 'No. I won't have it. I won't . . .'

Eisenmenger said to the room in general. 'I checked. On the night of Moynihan's death, he was due to be on call but swapped at short notice.' To Sauerwine he said, 'I would suspect that further enquiries will be unable to locate him anywhere in Nottingham at the relevant time; you may even manage to place him quite close to the scene.' He saved the best for last. 'And he confessed to me, out there, tonight.'

And there it was.

No one felt good.

Part Eight

After a night and a day in hospital, Helena was dis-
charged. Eisenmenger had already moved out of the
castle, taking a room in the Crown in Melbury, and she
joined him there. That night they talked far into the night,
trying to assuage Helena's anger and confusion, largely
failing.

She asked, 'Did Tristan and Theresa really not know?'

He shrugged. 'I honestly believe that they weren't there
at the planning stage; I think that the decision was made
by Eleanor and carried out principally by Groshong . . .'

'There's a "but" in there.'

He smiled. 'But they're not stupid – far from it. They
believed what they wanted to believe. They asked no
questions and they looked under no stones.'

'No.' She considered this, then picked up on something
he had said earlier. 'You said "principally". "Carried out
principally by Groshong". What did you mean?'

He said tentatively, 'I wonder how far Hugo was
involved, if at all.'

'But there's no evidence.'

He was frowning and had become lost in thought.
'There's a streak of cruelty in Hugo a mile wide. The way
your parents were killed . . . I just wonder.'

Her eyes were wide. 'How can we prove – or disprove
– it?'

He shrugged, then took her hand. They were sitting in
bed, drinking champagne, an indulgence Eisenmenger had
insisted on. 'I don't know.' He sighed, looking troubled.

'What's wrong?'

'I don't think,' he said slowly, 'that what's happened
will affect your brother's case.'

He had expected her to react as if he had professed a

desire to drink a virgin's blood but she said only sadly, 'No.'

He was stunned. 'You're not angry?'

She put down her glass with studied deliberation, concentrating carefully on making sure that not a drop was spilled, then she turned back to him. She had a warm, welcoming, almost sensual smile as she said, 'You really think I'm a fucking dipstick, don't you, John?'

This surprising use of profanity was uttered in such a sweet, endearing tone, too. He was sure that he had a million things to say, but none of them surfaced apart from a rather uninformative, 'What?'

'I'm the lawyer, John Eisenmenger, not you. Everything that we heard tonight was hearsay. Malcolm never confessed anything to anyone, remember? Eleanor's not fit to stand trial – probably can't clearly remember what did or didn't happen. We've got no proof that Hugo was involved in the original murder.

'And even the watch and photograph aren't conclusive. I was the one who compiled the inventory of what was missing. I'd have to say that I couldn't be a hundred per cent sure that the watch was in the house at the time of the murders. If I were Groshong, I'd claim that I found it somewhere in the castle, didn't realize its significance.'

'Pretty thin.'

She shrugged, a gesture he found delectable. 'Without forensic evidence to link Groshong directly, it'll take a lot more than we've got to overturn Jeremy's conviction, I think.'

He pointed out, 'You could lie. Say that you were certain the watch was there at the time of the murder.'

She laughed. 'And scupper Beverley once and for all? It's tempting, isn't it?'

'But . . .?'

She turned on her side to face him. 'But there have been enough lies told in this case. I'll prove Jeremy innocent, but not by perjuring myself.'

'So Beverley escapes again?'

'So Beverley escapes again. The bitch lives to fight another day.'

He pulled her towards him and kissed her, then held her. After a moment's silence he said, 'You remember how you remarked that I was a sort of in-house opinion?'

She nodded. 'Were you offended? I didn't mean –'

He interrupted her. 'This might be completely barking, but maybe we should set up a consultancy. You for the legal side, me for the pathology.'

'Doing what?'

'Defence work. Appeals, that kind of thing.'

She smiled. 'Righting wrongs? Fighting injustice? Going where no man has gone before?'

'It was just an idea.'

He seemed slightly hurt by her flippancy. Gently she pointed out, 'Murders aren't that common. How would it pay?'

'Perhaps it wouldn't have to; your other work would still be there, and I can carry on with the locum work – they're always there to be done. And then, in time, who knows?'

She considered the idea. It was with a sideways bob of her head and small smile that she said, 'Why not?'

They kissed again and after a moment's silence she said, 'I think I'd like to go away.'

'Really? Where?'

She considered. Then, 'I don't know, but somewhere a long way away, and for a very long time.'

It sounded like a good idea to him.

He turned off the light.